Connecting FLIGHTS
– Short Stories

Connecting FLIGHTS
– Short Stories

Andy Langdon

HOLBORN OWL
PUBLISHING

Copyright © Andy Langdon 2012

All rights reserved. No part of this publication may be reproduced or transmitted in any form or by any means, electronic or mechanical including photocopying, recording or any information storage or retrieval system, without prior permission in writing from the publishers.

All characters in this publication are fictitious and any resemblance to real people, alive or dead, is purely coincidental.

First published in the United Kingdom in 2012 by
Holborn Owl Publishing
www.owlbooks.org

ISBN 978-0-9572235-0-9

Produced by
The Choir Press, Gloucester
Front cover by
www.jdv-design.net

For
Jukka and Arto.
My darkest hour was their finest.

Hana,

I hope my writing has some of your warmth and charm.

Keep on talking to strangers and enjoy the adventures!

Andy. L.

oct '13.

Contents

Prologue	ix
Cup Final Day	1
The Flipside of Dermot Young	7
Water and Glass	33
Tunnel	52
Glass and Water	59
Chisgo	66
Wheel of Fortune	94
End of the World	117
The Forgotten Present	131
Millionaires	155
To Catch a Thief	167
The Neighbour	183
The Verdict	196
The Lonely Spy	222
Abandon Ship!	251
Playing for the Queen	270
Black Christ	294
The Battle for San Vincente del Cerrito	301
Epilogue	331
Acknowledgements	337

Prologue

'Then will he strip his sleeve 'n' show show his scars ... 'n' say these wounds I had on Crispian's day.'

'What was that, Trevor?' asked the younger of the two women, the pilot, firing the gas burner at regular intervals.

'Delirious, his condition is deteriorating,' said a middle-aged man. He had the look of a doctor and had just finished examining the wounded figure sitting in a corner of the basket. The patient's hand on his stomach couldn't hide a patch of dark red spreading across the white linen. The mumbling continued.

'He needs a hospital, doesn't he?'

They looked out across the canopy of trees which since mid-morning had stretched as far as the eye could see.

'I've still got my bag. But if I try to extract the arrow here he could bleed to death. He's already lost a lot of blood. I don't want to delay much longer.' He sounded anxious. 'We need to land.'

'Well, we've got out of worse scrapes than this.' The next speaker was tanned, maybe Latin American, showing a row of even white teeth. 'But land ... *where*?'

There were six of them in the balloon including the wounded man. They had been airborne for nearly a day and the optimism they had all felt on leaving the barren wastes of the Altiplano was still evident.

'I can't quite believe we've escaped. I thought I was going to grow old there,' said the pilot. 'I guess the others will.'

'They had their chance,' said the older woman. She was East-European looking and had the well-toned muscles of an athlete.

'This story shall the good man will—' As the babbling from the injured man caught her attention she dropped to one knee, gently holding a water bottle to his lips. But he went on: '—will tell his ... his son comes safe home.'

'Over there!' The lookout thrust out his arm and pointed. 'A river and a valley – where the trees are less dense, some sort of clearing.' His lined hand covered bushy white eyebrows to shield the sun as, straight chin jutting out, he scanned the horizon. In his other hand he held a compass. 'Just beyond that massive egg-shaped rock.'

The others followed his direction and saw the river, a turquoise ribbon, flowing through a gash visible in the trees. Some distance after the landmark rock the river broadened out by an area of bare earth dotted with what appeared to be huts or buildings. In the valley behind, the jungle looked partly cleared: solitary trees and bushes, signs of cultivation.

'How do we know we're not flying straight out of the frying pan into the fire?' asked the man with the Hollywood smile.

'Good point. A certain irony to survive what we've been through and then be eaten alive by cannibals,' said the pilot. 'But there's one thing that would put the fear of God into even the toughest indigenous inhabitant.' She paused. 'How about a bit of music to herald our arrival?' She had already stopped firing the burner.

'Are you thinking what I'm thinking?' said the one who could have been a doctor.

They turned towards the lookout. A trickle of laughter ran through the group for the first time since the early light of dawn when they had escaped in the basket under a bombardment of arrows.

'You're the skipper,' the lookout said to the pilot. 'They won't have heard anything like me before. I can promise you that.'

'All we have to do is work out how to get this balloon down.' The pilot smiled at the others. 'Did anyone remember to pick up a set of instructions at check-in?'

'We few, we happy few ... we band of brothers.' The murmuring from the wounded man continued, already quieter than before.

The balloon was starting to lose height, beginning its gradual descent towards the valley in the jungle below.

Cup Final Day

07.54 am
After hanging up his shirt on the on the peg, he flexed his fingers and exhaled sharply. The next time he put that on he would know the result. He surveyed the empty changing room. Big days had their own special atmosphere. He'd seen a small group of diehard supporters waiting at the entrance when he arrived. One of them had raised a hand in salute. For some of them this was the biggest day of their lives – you could see it on their faces. And they were relying on him to put in a performance – work a miracle even. The thought scared and motivated him. This was what he had trained for. He looked at the clock. Five minutes to the hour. He recognised a discarded shirt thrown down on the bench. Typical, Luke, he thought and picked it up. Luke was always ahead of him – now he'd be with the rest of the team busy on his last minute rituals. This was it. Time to go.

Cam pushed open the swing doors, and feeling like a gladiator marching into the Colosseum, set off down the corridor towards the operating theatre.

09.32 am
'Oxygen levels good. Blood pressure one hundred and twenty over eighty. Heart rate steady,' said Luke, the anaesthetist. 'It's your call.'

Cam knew what they were thinking: *Are we in or are we out?*

He had told the patient the day before: 'A large malignant neoplasm on the pancreas. After ninety minutes we'll know – do we de-baulk, then get out and sew up, or do we stay?' The difference for Cam was four or five hours in the operating theatre. For the patient it was life and death; not today, maybe a year or two from now. But then he remembered the biopsy work; grade four, growing fast. Second thought, make that Christmas.

He was still undecided, looking at the options, but the team didn't know that. The spleen would have to go – a splenectomy was relatively easy – he could do that in his sleep. 'Possible adrenalectomy. Distal panreatectomy for sure.' Getting quickly more demanding. 'Good news: duodenum looks safe and the bile duct is preserved. Good news: we've got access past the main thrombatic artery. Very good news: no metastases we didn't already know about.'

He looked again at the white mass covering the mid-section of the pancreas. 'Bad news, these capillaries. The splenic vein has to be tied off. It's border line re-sectable. The celiac artery could be compromised. It's massive.' They could all see that.

Good news. Bad news.

The problem was the network of capillaries. The tumour had grown over and closed off the large vein from the spleen. As a result countless tiny blood vessels had spread out across the cancer, like cargo lines supporting an invading army. He'd never seen anything like it.

'What a mess,' said Luke. 'Nothing for it but to sew up.'

Cam looked up. Did Luke just say 'penalties'? He was hearing commentary on one of the greatest cup matches of all time: Man Utd versus Liverpool, Wembley.

'Greenhoff down the wing ... beats his first tackle and then skips the second.'

He could picture the player now: red shirt, number four on the back, socks around his ankles. And he'd get the cross in. He always did and no one knew that better than big Joe Jordan in the middle.

'Greenhoff makes the cross and the ball flies over. It's a downward header to the far post. Jordan. One-nil. It's a brave header.'

'It really is a bit of a mess,' said Luke peering over. 'The tumour has grown in front of the artery. Even if we succeed in removing the front of the tumour here,' the anaesthetist pointed, 'we don't know what lies behind—'

Good news. Bad news.

'Scalpel,' said Cam. They were following big Joe, going in where angels feared to tread.

11.23 am

With the omentum, the unnecessary flap draping over the intestine, and the spleen both gone they saw the full size of the tumour and the task in front of them.

'Jesus!' exclaimed Luke. 'You didn't expect anything like this, did you?'

Bad news.

This wasn't the first time Cam had done the operation, maybe the third. First, two days ago driving home after a tough game of squash, and the second in the early hours of this morning. His first coach had told him: 'Don't just train your muscles, son. Train your mind.' He always did the operation in his mind first, every cut, every turn, and every surprise, even in his sleep.

'It's amazing he walked around with it for so long,' Luke murmured. 'It's like a football.'

Football again. His anaesthetist was football mad.

'Can you turn up the radio?' said Cam turning to the surprised-looking nurse. 'I need to concentrate.' Cam listened intently as he started to move his fingers behind the back of the tumour, white, large and alien. He wanted to get a feel for his enemy.

'And now they're chasing the game. It's like both teams are playing twist or bust. Here comes Lou Macari. He's turned Fenoughty like a kipper. Still Macari, weaving his magic, shades of George Best in his heyday. He must be running on empty but still he comes past another tackle—'

The theatre staff were looking at him, waiting for his sign.

What was it the patient had said to him yesterday? 'If you're not sure, if it's fifty-fifty ... I want you to go for it.'

'Macari has bedazzled the centre-back. He's floating into the box. It's full of defenders but he's squeezing through, past one tackle and another. He's left the last defender for dead, like a magician carving up the enemy. Just the keeper to beat. It's a truly mesmerising run. This for the Cup—'

Cam's fingers felt a narrow space at the back of the tumour. Room to manoeuvre.

Good news. 'Everyone set? Tell back office we'll need more coffee. Luke, we're going to extra time. Vital signs are good. Check?'

'Check,' said Luke.

'Okay, we've got the problem with the adrenal glands. Partial adrenalectomy. And then the capillaries.'

'Can you do it?'

'One capillary at a time. This cancer chose the wrong surgeon to pick a fight with. We'll do it. Watch me.'

'On the other hand,' Luke remarked, 'maybe it's more like a giant onion, embedded.'

'Right. And we know what happens to onions.' Ever so gently Cam pulled his hand out. 'Especially in *my* kitchen.'

17.04 pm

'Okay, nurse, I think we're ready to sew up. Ready to go home?'

'Well this is my second shift, remember.' She looked at Luke. 'I had a three-hour rest at half-time.'

'He'll sleep a good few hours yet,' said Luke, inspecting his drips. One thing's for sure. He's lost weight.'

'What's that? Can hardly hear you.' Cam took off the last of the clamps. 'And why *is* the radio on so loud?'

'It was your idea to turn it up,' said the nurse, passing over the threaded needle.

He knew other surgeons peeled off their gloves at this point or instructed a junior doctor with the staple gun but Cam saw himself as a man of tradition. He liked old-fashioned needle and thread as well as the banter at this stage of the operation. 'That's better,' he said as the nurse went over to turn down the sound of pop music from the radio. 'Huh! If it was up to Luke we'd have football commentary in theatre.'

'Oh really? And what's wrong with that?' asked the anaesthetist.

'Just not when it's me under the anaesthetic.'

'You don't trust me?'

'I wouldn't trust your concentration, not if it's a big game.'

Luke admired Cam's handiwork. 'He's going to have a fine scar. A walking Mercedes advert.'

They started a familiar discussion about wounds they had stitched up together.

'Sixty-five. One more and we're done.' Cam was almost done stitching the roof-top-shaped wound. 'Clickety-click, sixty-six.'

'Sixty-six,' said Luke, 'a lucky number.'

'How come?' asked Cam.

'You can tell he's not the football one,' said the nurse. 'I wasn't even born then. And I know.'

17.28 pm

The two men, surgeon and anaesthetist, were in the changing room, showered and changing back to the clothes they had arrived at work in.

'Nine straight hours' surgery.' Luke looked at his watch. 'How do you do it?'

'What, take a sharp object and start rooting around in somebody's body?' Cam raised his arms and stared at his hands as he spoke.

'No. I mean concentrate like that.'

He was silent for a moment as if pondering the question for the first time. 'Do you know, I don't know. Being there helps.'

'Sorry. Come again?'

'A tutor once told me if you feel comfortable in three-dimensional imagery, chances are you'll be comfortable in the operating theatre.'

'You make it look so instinctive and natural, that confidence—'

'But not arrogance, I hope?'

'What's the difference?'

'Maybe it's thinking of the people you could be letting down.' Cam paused, buttoning up his lucky shirt. 'You know, reminding yourself of the possibility of failure.'

'Cam. What you did today. It was *incredible*. I know four other surgeons who wouldn't have gone through with that. At times out there you were playing by different rules; just dazzling.' Luke glanced across to his colleague. 'So where do you get it from – your inspiration?'

'What was that?'

'You heard. Come on, let me buy you a pint. You deserve it.'

'All right. You set 'em up. Fifteen minutes. There's a few people I've got to chat with first.'

The Flipside of Dermot Young

'I've got something you must see,' said Dermot, pulling my arm. 'Come with me.'

It was May and the evening breeze had dropped to scarcely a whisper, no longer an issue on the par four that lay next to our respective houses. When the Hayling Island estate agent had listed proximity to the golf course as a selling point, Dermot had pretended not to be interested. 'No, I don't really play.' Like hell he didn't! Dermot didn't just play golf, he dreamed golf. It occupied every cell of his forty-nine-year-old body. He was infected with golf the way some people are infected with cynicism.

Invariably, after the last of the day's golfers had drifted away, back to their responsibilities and loved ones with tales of defeat or glory, Dermot, as if out of the ether, would materialise around the fourth green. One of my favourite parts of the course had been landscaped into the headland with a view of liners steaming into Portsmouth and even France on a clear day. I would see him there most evenings, feet spliced apart, shoulders slightly hunched in studied concentration, practising: 'Just a few balls to keep my eye in.' Putting and putting. Putting and missing.

His problems started on the green. He would drive straight and long off the tee, then often a magnificent approach shot, usually in regulation onto the green, before calamity struck. Dermot's demons set in. 'This year will be different,' he would tell me. Like the arrival of swallows to herald summer, late spring wouldn't be the same without his boyish optimism. But year after year, poor putting ensured he never bettered his handicap of plus two. For Dermot the pro-circuit remained an unreachable dream.

And now I had confirmation it must be late spring for I heard that familiar refrain again. 'I've been working on my putting,'

Dermot nodded his head in the direction of the headland. 'Come on, old man.'

I felt no excitement on hearing this, just dread at the inevitable disappointment that was sure to follow. 'Let me guess,' I tried not to sound how I felt, 'a new breathing technique?'

'I'm not for myself until the Hick-Boo gets out of the cupboard,' he declared standing silhouetted against the dipping sun, orange over the sea. 'Things have changed in time and space. Come and see.'

Even after nearly thirty years I sometimes didn't have a clue what Dermot was talking about. What arcane matter was he referring to now? He strode in front of me towards the green, a big bear of a man in a light brown corduroy jacket with blond hair almost down to his shoulders.

'A new swing?' Then for the first time I noticed a long aluminium box under Dermot's arm. New putters were the worst.

Since the initial shock of meeting this oddball physicist on the Himalayas, a putting green, back at St Andrews University, I had in time become used to his manner. Dermot liked to lead the way as if his was the only force or voice in the universe. I guess nobody knew Dermot like he did, like I did. People didn't get to know Dermot. They experienced him, tried to keep up; like me, already a dozen paces behind on our way to the fourth green.

After St Andrews we had drifted apart, with some occasional rounds of golf and vows for more regular contact, until the next long separation. Then, five years ago, my neighbours put their house up for sale, and on the off-chance I'd mentioned it in passing to Dermot. Right by the golf course, it had been too good an opportunity for him to miss. Our friendship was soon back to the intensity of student days. He made everything seem larger than life although, as before, Dermot retained his mysterious ways. He would disappear for days, even weeks sometimes, and there would be no ring of the phone or doorbell to signal his return. Instead, I'd just see him out on the headland, putting, like he'd never been away. Dermot had never married and if he confided in anybody – which I somehow doubted – it wasn't me. Golf was the bond that held our friendship together, always had and always would.

At the apron of the green Dermot laid the box down. He opened the lid announcing, triumphantly: 'Voilà!' before carefully taking out the latest new putter. Except that this was dimensioned like no putter I had ever seen before. The shaft didn't seem to be a uniform thickness. I didn't know where to start. 'The shaft's in the middle of the putting face,' I said. 'It looks weird.'

'Uuh-huh. Thought you might say that. I've been through the *Rules of Golf* and you'll find that there's a lot of leeway for putters.' Dermot was keen to begin practising, wielding the putter in front of him admiringly in the last rays of evening sunlight. 'For example, as you just pointed out, the shaft or neck or socket of a putter may be fixed at any point in the head.' Dermot really was prepared. 'And before you ask, the putter is allowed two grips. Don't worry, old man. This baby passes muster.' Dermot was throwing down a handful of balls from his bag. 'Now I want you to walk over and be ready to lift the flag.'

I knew not to question him when he was in this mood and I walked towards the flag as instructed. The fourth green is one of the trickiest on our course. For a start it's enormous, the size of a tennis court. On top of that it has a downward slope away from the apron which will pounce on any ball that isn't dead true. Finally, if the size and borrow doesn't do for you, the contours will. On a frosty morning the green looks like a mountain range in miniature: valleys, gullies and inclines all over its surface. A nightmare. And the truth is any club golfer would be pleased to get down in three. Now, with the ridiculous-looking putter, Dermot was eyeing up the putt, raising his putter to the flag pole and carefully selecting his line. It was a long one, over thirty feet.

'Get this and drinks are on me!' I shouted out in an effort to ease the tension.

'Damn it man, will you be quiet!' Dermot barked back. 'I need to concentrate ... ready on the flag?' I held the pole but there was no chance that he would sink this. The putt went on its way and straight away I saw he'd sent it way too far left – there was never that much borrow. The weight was good but as every golfer knows, line is the key. There was no need for me to even lift the flag. I started to wonder how long this was likely to take – would we make last orders?

'Flag!'

Slowly but surely the ball was turning towards me. That line was like the lane to Havant station – bends all over it – and the ball, as if following its own manifest destiny, made for the hole and dropped. I had never seen a putt like it, not even on TV. It was bewitching, a stupendous monster extravaganza showboat of a putt. Dermot had pulled the rabbit out of the hat.

'Nothing to say?'

I was speechless.

An hour later we were in the snug at The Jigger Inn. Dermot was waxing eloquent after his virtuoso putting performance. And it had been impressive; ten- and fifteen-footers, and then more; whoppers of over thirty feet. It was like he had been reborn as his hero Jack Nicklaus. He looked well: a day in the sun gave his face a tanned and healthy colour and he was on a roll. Sometimes Dermot was like this; his enthusiasm a tidal wave imperiously sweeping everything before it. At other times he would be quiet, as if feuding with fiends in his head.

I was still in shock. 'You looked so certain,' I said placing a pint on the bar. 'I've never seen you that confident.'

'Rather, confidence is the key. It's what I have been missing all these years, old man.' Dermot was leaning towards me, his eyes alight. 'I've studied all the stats. Take Tiger Woods. Now, in his best year 2000, he won three successive majors. And what's the best thing about his game?'

'Everything?'

'Sure. But especially his putting. Putts win matches. Tiger took only twenty-seven putts per round. Nicklaus in his pomp was only one less.' Dermot was in full flow, I was just a bystander to the main event. He launched into more analysis: who was good off the tee, best short-iron men, but most of all, analysis of the putts taken. And he knew it all from memory. It was actually quite impressive the way he recalled these statistics. But statisticians don't win matches, golfers do. After two pints Dermot was just getting warmed up. I knew the signs and decided to make my excuses.

As I reached the door I turned to wave goodbye. I searched for Dermot's shock of unkempt hair amongst a sea of heads at the bar, but he had already vanished like a reflection of someone you once knew, passing by in a shop window.

I didn't see Dermot for six weeks after that. Mary, my wife, was going through a bad phase in her treatment for depression and I knew my place should be in the house, not on the golf course. Dermot would be too much for Mary in our quiet home, so I never picked up the phone. I was doing my best to play the supporting husband but I don't mind admitting that I looked for opportunities to nip out – papers or shopping.

The next time I bumped into Dermot he was crossing the road from the electrician's in the High Street. He was in a hurry, looking at his watch and clearly in one of his 'up' moods, taking big strides. For a large man he had surprising agility.

'Jooohn, old fellow,' he hollered. Arms outstretched and pointing to the heavens. 'How's it going?' In spite of myself I smiled. People who didn't know Dermot were likely to (literally) stop and stare. In this mood he reminded me of an extravagantly over-the-top fifties' film star. 'The Harbourmaster's Cup.' Dermot was starting this conversation while still standing in the middle of the road. 'Have you registered?'

'Well the truth is I've had other things on my mind recently. You see, Mary—'

'I know, it's not easy,' said Dermot, waving the traffic through as he reached the pavement. 'But maybe to help, you could be my caddy.'

'Caddy?' I enquired bleakly. For a moment I was wondering how my being a caddy would help Mary to beat her depression.

'Truth is, I'm a bit nervous. Harbourmaster's Cup – it's the big one, the start of the season. And I really *need* a caddy whom I can trust.'

'But you're always nervous, that's half of your prob—'

'Behind every great golfer is a great caddy.' Perhaps it was just as well he interrupted me. 'Come on, old man, nobody knows the course like you do.'

'Okay, I'll think about it. But I'll need to check with Mary.'

The Hayling Island clubhouse was stylish, art deco. It would make a perfect setting for a 1920s Hercule Poirot mystery. Fifteen minutes earlier Dermot had holed out on the second morning of the Harbourmaster's Cup with a characteristically mesmerising putt to post a closing seventy-two – that would take some beating by anybody's standards. We now sat in leather armchairs in the clubhouse bar, waiting to see just how good Dermot's round had been. The man himself was in no doubt.

'Great Scott! My putts were amazing. I am a Rembrandt!'

'Will you take Cradbrook up on the offer of a pint at The Jigger?' Our playing partner Dan Cradbrook, crushed by Dermot on the course, had offered him a drink, 'any evening that suits you'.

'Forget the pint. Forget Cradbrook. I told you: *If I'm not for myself who'll be for me?*' Dermot cracked his knuckles. 'I know the way and I know how.'

'Shouldn't we discuss a game plan, if it comes to a play-off?' His certainty disturbed me – we hadn't won anything yet. He must have heard what I was saying but it hardly looked like it. He was staring out of the window, no doubt imagining a definitive drive to a distant green. Sometimes down at the pub, I'd ask him a question and get the same sort of response. Then, like now, I wondered what drew me to friends like Dermot. Come to that, what drew friends like Dermot to me?

'But we will.' Finishing his whisky, he stood up. 'Come on, let's see if any of these suckers and mugs are ready to give me a real test.'

Dermot had at times been full of himself – his first-class degree and the job with British Aerospace were two examples which sprung to mind – but now he believed himself invincible and in spite of myself I was fast becoming one of his disciples.

We just had to wait for the returning pairs of players – had anyone else played out of their skin that hot summer afternoon? In came the players and long faces told their own story. And then just as we started to think we'd done it we heard rumours that Kearney was playing the round of his life – that knocked a little wind out of Dermot's sails. Kearney birdied the last to equal Dermot's score.

'It's a play-off,' the scorer announced. 'Three holes starting at the sixteenth.'

'May the best man win,' said Kearney, shaking hands with us at the sixteenth tee. It was as much as Dermot could do to shake hands – he was already looking through his clubs, leaving me to cover up for his aloofness. I prided myself in always seeing the best in people and I knew that if ever I really needed him, Dermot would be there for me.

'Nice to see you, Angela,' I said. Kearney's caddy was his wife Angela, not a bad player herself, and someone I had always got along well with. 'It seems we're better caddies than players.'

'Yes we are, aren't we ... how's Mary? I saw her last week in town. She looked tired.'

'Ups and downs. The doctor says it's only to be expected.'

'I could drop in, that's if she wants.'

'Of course, Angela. Mary has always liked—'

'John, don't you realise we've got a club selection to make?'

'I'll call you soon, John,' said Angela, backing away from Dermot. 'And good luck.'

'Sorry, Dermot. Angela wanted to know—'

'What are you doing talking to Kearney's caddy?' Dermot's voice had taken on a new hardness. 'This may not be important to you, but it is to me.' Here was a man on a mission.

I pulled the three wood from the bag. 'Remember, the bunkers are all on the left.' I wasn't going to argue with him, not now anyway. The three wood was the right choice for Dermot, he just had to hit it straight. He didn't, and although Dermot putted well, so did Kearney. We were one hole down with two to play. Kearney went into the lake on the seventeenth so it was all square going to the last. Dermot had eyes only for his approach shot to the green. 'What do you think? Lay up in front of the bunker or go for the green?'

'Let's see what Kearney does.'

Kearney did well. He made the green with a superlative short-iron.

'Damn the man!' cursed Dermot. 'If the wind hadn't dropped just then, he was in the bunker for sure. What confounded luck.'

'Come on, Dermot.' I tried to sound supportive. 'Let's just think about our own shot. Maybe we should go for the green as well?'

'You bet.'

Watching him address the shot I could see that he still wasn't as relaxed as he needed to be. Sure enough, we landed in the bunker. 'Tough luck, Dermot!' shouted Kearney from the green where he had a shortish putt for the hole and the match. He really sounded like he meant it.

Angela smiled at me, one caddy to another. I laughed – for some reason the famous James Bond golf scene came to mind; Goldfinger's midget caddy with the deadly bowler hat, very different from Angela.

'Laughing at me now,' spluttered Dermot. 'Fine friend you turned out to be.'

'Calm down, man. I'll explain later. And anyway it's your bunker shot.' It looked like the Harbourmaster's Cup was slipping away from us and I was sorry. I'd forgotten how much fun it was to be out on the golf course.

Dermot's bunker shot landed a long way from the hole and he looked like thunder. I felt it best not to offer any advice. He was focused on the line; my job was to keep quiet and raise the flag. Dermot settled down over the putt. Forty feet, I thought. That's as long as a bus. The eighteenth green is a tricky one to read, very similar to the fourth where we had practised for the first time with the new putter. It seemed ages ago. So it was with some déjà vu that I watched the ball on the way to the cup. Too fast, too much left, I thought. And once again Dermot had read it better than I had. It was in.

'Take that!' said Dermot, clenching his fist. 'A real humdinger!'

Kearney prepared for his four-footer. Get this and he was champion. It slid an agonising (for him) foot or so past. Dermot had an opportunity to concede the putt but he was absorbed with his scorecard.

So for the moment Kearney's ball stayed where it was, about fourteen inches from the cup, a tiny putt. Sudden death hole coming up. Kearney waited. Conceded putts should only be offered, they should never be requested. That's why in match play you'll notice a golfer lingering over a very short putt – hoping his opponent will tell him to just pick it up. Conceded putts almost always come, of course, on short putts. And this was a very short putt. No wonder Kearney was deliberating.

I looked at Dermot, who was looking anyway to avoid Kearney's gaze. He knew what was going on. I wondered, did Angela? I was just about to say something to Dermot but too late; Kearney, tired of waiting, went for the putt. I wondered later whether Dermot's reticence had an impact. Was Dermot hoping it might? Kearney missed the putt just around the edge of the cup.

Dermot was the surprise winner. I heard the sound of a high-speed camera shutter and noticed a press photographer, something we'd soon get used to.

After the Harbourmaster's Cup win Dermot never looked back – but I did. I see the constant blue skies, dry fast fairways, but most of all it is the moment on the eighteenth with Kearney and his putt which stands out. Was this the first sign that things weren't quite the way they should be?

The day I got my big idea I went off to find Dermot. In the couple of months after the Harbourmaster's Cup triumph he had been playing tournaments further and further afield, with me as his caddy. Now we had a rare Saturday at home. As I could have guessed, he wasn't in the house but instead in the converted stables round the back. He seemed different in here, more reflective somehow. The stables were intended as a workshop but I suspected Dermot spent more time there than the house. He had all the creature comforts he wanted: comfortable chairs, music, his prized whisky collection and a bed.

Usually Dermot had at least one or two projects on the go. He didn't like being called an inventor; 'people get the wrong idea'. He once told me, 'Instigator is more me, old boy, the pioneer spirit.'

In any case, the big breakthrough had never come, but Dermot lived in eternal hope. There had been some spectacular near-misses along the way: the voice-commanded TV and the automatic key finder are two you'll never have heard of. He sometimes reminded me of Toad from *Wind in the Willows*; indefatigable. 'Wait till you see my next project!' was his battlecry.

When I arrived Dermot was working at something on the enormous workbench that dominated the large room. 'Did you design the putter in here?' I asked. All through that long, dry and hot summer, as the greens got faster and faster, more and more tricky to read, Dermot's putting had just gone from strength to strength. And the more he kept winning the more people kept talking – but mostly about the putter. It was a case of tall poppy syndrome, I figured. He was standing on top of the local golf world and their instincts were to cut him down to size. 'Dermot?'

He looked up from the workbench where he was soldering something. 'You said on the phone you had something important to tell me.'

'I have.'

'Dermot, so far you've surprised a few people. We've even got the reporter on the local paper ringing me up to find out where your next tournament is.'

'Southampton. I've checked.'

'Dermot, listen to me.' This was something I had prepared earlier. 'This year the British Open is at Royal St George's.'

'The Open.' He looked up at me, with big blue eyes humble for a moment. 'I'd never qualify.'

'The *Senior* British Open.'

'The Senior Open, you have to be over fifty, old chap. I'm only forty-nine.'

'Today is August twentieth, which means next week,' I remembered his birthday, a week after my sister's, 'you'll be fifty and eligible to qualify. I've checked.' I gave him a minute to let it sink in. 'The way you're playing, we'd have more than a real chance.'

'I don't know.' Uncertainty in his voice. 'It's too early ... isn't it?' He went back to his soldering but I could see he wasn't concentrating.

I didn't get it. I was so excited but he seemed strangely reluctant. I'd noticed this before. It was as if he wanted to succeed only so far; when the pressure rose, the press arriving on the scene, it seemed that something inside him froze. But only off the golf course. Once he had a club in his hand the pressure seemed to melt away. Maybe that was the problem; press and publicity. I chose a fresh tack. 'Anyway, it's not as if it's the *real* Open. I'd be surprised if there's any more journalists than for the previous tournaments.' Dermot paused in his soldering for a minute and I continued. 'Of course you could just try the qualifying and then see how you felt about if afterwards ... that's if we even qualify.'

He put the soldering torch down.

'Only qualifying,' he said. 'We'd be lucky to have one man and his dog watching.' He looked at me. 'We've come this far without any trouble.' The familiar glint had returned to his eyes. 'Okay, old man, you're on, let's see how far we can go with this.'

We drove to Royal St George's the evening before the qualifying competition for the Senior Open. The sun was throwing long shadows over the hedgerows as we sped along in Dermot's two-seater across the South Downs.

The MG was Dermot's pride and joy. He loved things old. He preferred Orson Welles to George Clooney. Even his manner of speaking, 'old man', was dated, but I liked him for it. You always got the feeling that he didn't quite fit into the world of today. Sometimes he appeared lost, hankering after a distant age — typified behind the wheel of this British racing green Mark II 1967 MGB GT. Girlfriends came and went but he and the car awere inseparable. He had made a few modifications over the years: the manual sun-roof had been converted to automatic, a device that was controlled by the press of a button on his keyring; the headlights had been rebuilt as if he needed to throw shadows on the moon; and above the cigarette lighter was now what looked like a radar screen alerting him to the presence of speed traps up to five miles away, which was just as well since what he had done under the bonnet he wouldn't even talk about: 'Better if you didn't know, old man.' Suffice it to say, the MG went like the wind. And Dermot was born a racing driver. It suited his big, hair-in-the-wind personality. He didn't grow up, instead the world grew up around him.

I was amazed how tiny Sandwich was. Like St Andrews it was only the golf course that put it on the map. Everywhere you went was golf. The pub we were staying in had walls covered with autographed photographs of champions past and present.

Encouraged by pints of the best real ale we recalled some of the famous victories of that summer.

'And the look on Kearney's face when I holed that putt. It was beautiful.' I remembered the missed opportunity to concede the putt but the way Dermot was playing that day there was nobody who could have beaten him fair and square anyway.

'Just think if twenty years ago I'd been killing them softly like this summer,' sighed Dermot wistfully. 'If I'd had the putter then. Fancy another?'

'Last one then.'

Watching Dermot at the bar, flirting loudly with the waitress, I felt a wave of affection for the man. I was never so lonely in my life until Dermot showed up. He was the best friend I ever had.

'Roll on tomorrow!' I said raising my glass.

Dermot smiled and put a hand on my shoulder. 'I wouldn't want to have anyone else but you at my side, old fellow. Cheers.'

And now like a secret love affair the dream was stealthily starting to creep over us. We were only eighteen holes from a start in the British Senior Open, live on Sky Sports TV.

It was quite a different feeling at six-thirty the next morning. A gaggle of golfers surrounded the notice board. Out of one hundred and twenty starters only the top twenty-four qualified, and these players had all won tournaments. To one side stood a small group of local caddies, well wrapped up and looking knowledgeable, for hire at sixty pounds a round. Dermot and I had never talked about money and I wondered if we ever would.

'They all look like professionals,' I whispered to Dermot.

'I know. And this is only the qualifying.'

'I was talking about the caddies.' Dermot smiled. We were both smiling a lot more after a birdie at the first and then two successive pars. At this rate we were in with a real chance. On the fourth the tee shot went through the back of the green. Dermot scowled. After twenty years it had little impact. 'Dermot, you're off the green but you can still take the putter.'

'It won't work,' said Dermot glumly.

'Sorry?'

'Grass is too long, I'll take the wedge.' He got within twelve feet but now he was in striking distance with the putter.

'Flag!'

Once again Dermot was putting out of his skin, reading these new greens like he'd played them all his life. 'That'll do me!' said Dermot, triumphant at the turn. Four under par with nine holes to go.

'Just keep your game together, Dermot. We're doing nicely.' And not looking where I was going I tripped over a tree-root sending the bag and the clubs flying one way and me the other. Trust Dermot to get his priorities right, I thought, picking myself up, as Dermot was more intent on rescuing his beloved clubs than me.

I was smiling again after Dermot's next shot, a glorious drive three hundred yards to the middle of the fairway. We were going to the Open on this form. Was I tempting fate? Dermot missed a relatively straightforward four-foot putt – unlike Dermot to misread the lie so completely. He looked aghast at his putter. 'Wind getting up,' I said as we made our way to the tenth. 'Good we're out early.' Dermot trudged behind, head down. Not good. Throughout the next seven holes he said no more than a handful of words. And the less he spoke, the worse he played. What surprised me was that the sublime putting of the summer had vanished like swallows in autumn.

The confidence was gone. A competitive score in the high sixties now looked a forlorn hope. We were finished and we both knew it. At the scorer's hut we carded a dismal score of seventy-six, the back nine twelve strokes worse than the front nine. We departed like commuters from a plane, just keen to leave. The dark clouds that loomed overhead matched our moods – the bravura of yesterday now seemed childlike.

'That's golf.' I patted him on the arm as we made our way to the MG. 'There'll be others.'

'I blame you.'

I was stunned. For the life of me I couldn't see what I'd done wrong. 'I'm sorry. What?'

Dermot drove in silence. I looked at the sodden countryside; the only chattering was the windscreen wipers battling with the torrential rain. I would have to think seriously about this whole venture. Mary was depressed at home and now Dermot was down in the doldrums. I needed this grief like a hole in the head. When Dermot dropped me at the end of the drive two hours later, there was no talk of when we would next meet. He left in a spin of gravel. The rain started to fall in stair-rods.

The next morning I woke early and went for a long walk. Nothing beats the fresh sea air to clear the mind of its worries. This Sunday morning the beach was deserted except for the complaining seagulls overhead. Stride for stride I felt my positive spirits returning. Yesterday we had lost a golf match. Nothing more and nothing less. I knew in my heart there really were more important things in life. After making the headland, opposite the fifteenth, I set course for home, determined to spend more time with Mary and less time on the fairways and greens.

Emboldened by this new resolve I was soon making breakfast and fresh-ground coffee. The croissants were in the oven when the phone rang. Usually it was for Mary but I answered anyway. It was Kearney. I couldn't believe it.

It took me a minute to register what he was going on about. He must have checked the qualifying scores from yesterday. Surely Kearney hadn't rung up to gloat? I was prepared to be shocked as I stammered out a reply. 'We should have done much better than seventy-six. We were on for a good score ... and then Dermot's putting after the turn—'

'But John, why are you sounding so defensive?' His voice had an infectious excitement. 'I rang to congratulate you. The man qualified. It's a first for the club. Wait till I tell the others!' And with that he hung up.

Was this some sort of practical joke? For the first time in my life I understood what was meant by the term 'reeling from shock'. In a minute I was online and there was Dermot Young with a score of seventy-six. Not good; so much I already knew. But glancing further down the list I saw much worse scores, in the high seventies and eighties, even the nineties. Nearly everybody who had come after us had done very poorly and I began to recall the storm and the wind attacking the soft top of the MG as we had left St George's. An early tee-off time had saved us. The rest of the field had had to contend with high winds, wet club faces, the ball running slow on the sodden fairways. And there it was in black and white: the qualifying list with Dermot Young at the bottom. By one stroke we had secured the last qualifying place.

I let out a shriek of delight. 'YES!!' Then I grabbed my jacket. I was in Dermot's drive in less than a minute. The house looked deserted, the stables locked. Then I saw the empty space where the MG belonged. I had my phone. 'Hey Dermot, it's me. I'm in your drive. Where are you?'

'I'm out getting the paper. Home in five. What's up, old boy? You're not in the stables?'

'Locked.'

'Course ... I locked up ... uhm.' He sounded down, worried even. Clearly he hadn't heard the news. 'But wait, why don't I come over to you?'

Outside the stables I was standing impatient. With Dermot, the eternal optimist, 'home in five' could mean anything. Then I had a vague recollection of a spare key hidden under a half-broken brick. I wondered was it still there? It was. Triumphant, I let myself into the stables. Music was playing: Berlioz I think. He must have been in here already this morning.

I saw on the large workbench in the middle of the room that

Dermot was working on something. Wires and rods lying in complex disarray like some giant stick insect caught in a spider's web. Moving closer it somehow seemed strangely familiar, the peculiar-shaped foot. Then I realised that I wasn't looking at a radio antenna and it wasn't a foot at all. It was a club head. Covered in wires and connections, this gadget was none other than Dermot's new putter. I was still staring in bewildered fascination at this monstrous contraption, oblivious to time, when Dermot burst in.

'John, I said I'd pop round.' He saw me standing beside the workbench. 'Ahh ... so you've been poking about ... couldn't resist it, eh? You remembered the spare key ... I overlooked that. You've caught me in a dashed awkward spot. Happy now?'

'What does it mean?' I felt out of my depth. 'And what does it do?'

'Well I guess now's as good a time as any. It was bound to come out one day. I'll explain.' Dermot walked over to the workbench. 'Here I was just doing some adjustments, but let me show you.'

'Dermot, this looks like cheating to me.' He didn't reply, but proceeded to thread the wires back inside the tubing. No speaking between us, just the last brooding bars of Berlioz's symphony.

Within a few minutes the putter was looking normal again; well, its familiar abnormal look at any rate. Except now I knew that it was filled with wires and sensors and God knows what else. 'Dermot, you said this putter was legal!' I didn't even want to touch it. 'So how about we run it down to the clubhouse and let the club secretary have a look at it?'

'Our own Major Calloway? The devil we will. Do you want me to give myself up?' Dermot snorted. 'John, that putter stays here and you stay with it.' Now he spoke quietly and emphatically like Harry Lime himself. I half expected him to smoothly pull a Colt 45 from his jacket as he menaced me. If I wasn't so concerned I would have laughed.

He put down the assembled putter deliberately. 'Don't look so gloomy, old chap. It's not that awful. We despise the Americans, they've had thirty years of swing coaches, sports science, video analysis and they produced Watson, Nicklaus, Lee Trevino and Tiger Woods. Over here we invented the game, played like gentlemen and what did that produce? Nick Faldo.'

'But it's against the rules. It's not fair play.'

'Rules? Fair play? Have you ever thought of who wrote the *rules* for this fine country of ours? Here, men are born to be king, the old boys' network goes strong to this day. Tell me, is that *fair*? Keep your precious honesty.' The usual glint in his eye had turned into a zealous ardour I had not seen before. 'And the difference? The difference between these men of privilege and the rest of us is that I have worked for my small advantage. Really worked. I happen to have developed the world's first intelligent golf club. And as the inventor of this astoundingly clever contraption should I not be allowed to be the first and main beneficiary? Other people get fame and fortune from far less ingenious discoveries. So why not I, old boy? Why not I?' His voice cracked with emotion.

I had to turn away. When I looked back he was staring at the floor. 'And anyway, what's the damned point? You saw me yesterday – it doesn't always work.' Once again I was reeling; this was Dermot, the sportsman I had admired for so long. But here was the cue for me to drop in my own bombshell. Dermot didn't know we had qualified so I told him now. In a detached way I saw that the effect on him was electric.

'But John, don't you see – this changes everything! We can have another crack at it, the title. The Senior British Open. When I get the putter working again. How much is the prize money?'

'I don't know, but it's plenty,' I replied in a weary voice. 'Three hundred thousand, give or take.' Whereas for me the feat of qualification signalled the game was up, the stakes were now so high, it seemed to be those same stakes that spurred Dermot on.

'Just think, old man, I'll cut you in, a fifty-fifty split. Over one hundred thousand for you and Mary – imagine what a good holiday would do for her spirits.' It was true. It would do Mary, us, no end of good. I hated myself for even entertaining the thought. 'Just one tournament with the putter, one tournament and after that I promise, I put it away and we never use it again, until it's all legal.' He was beseeching me now, hands spread out in front of him, looking me straight in the eye. 'If not for me John,' he pleaded, 'for Mary's sake.'

'Leave Mary out of this,' I said in a voice that I hoped sounded more solid than I felt. 'You might as well pack it in now. You're certain to be caught.'

'Not a chance, old boy.' The old Dermot, self-assured and invincible. 'It's foolproof. I'll show you.' Curiosity made me follow him to the putting lawn behind the stables where he went through the familiar routine, this time with a commentary: 'When I raise the putter above ninety degrees a sensor activates the infrared camera. Infrared, don't forget, is light – electromagnetic energy, and that's what we're using as source code.'

'Hold it. I'm not one of your scientist cronies, explain it to me like I'm a ten-year-old ... and slower.'

'Okay, missile systems are divided into two broad categories, active and passive homing systems. The second is a lot simpler. What makes this technology work for us is that we have a fixed target so we can use a simple GOLIS guidance system.'

'Sounds like a teddy bear.'

'Go-onto-location-in-space.' I looked none the wiser and Dermot saw he still had to dumb down further. 'Look, the very first smart missiles that the Germans used in World War Two, the V2s, they were also operating on passive homing; locking on direction is simple. For years the problem was *terrain*; golf greens are not flat. Then I had a stroke of luck. I was assigned to the TERCOM project at work.'

'Ter-what?'

'Terrain contour matching. At work it means a missile

following the contours of the landscape. For us it meant following the contours of the green.'

'That's why you were keen to practise on the fourth?'

'Not just the fourth. I've lost count of the holes over the years, John. Don't you get it?' He took a stride closer. 'This is my life's work. Other men make their mark with family or careers, symphonies or paintings. For me it's this. I call it the *Hick-Boo*.' He held up the putter in both hands, like the proud father of a newborn baby, 'This is my achievement. It'll change the face of golf. One day every golfer will want a Hick-Boo. Let's face it, for every golfer the putting is the part of the game they dread. Even the best golfers never look happy making putts, do they? Come on, have you ever met a golfer who told you he enjoyed putting?'

And here I had to admit that Dermot did have a point. I loathed putting just like every other golfer I know. Getting onto the green is where you succeed but once there, it is all about avoiding the ignominy of failing, three-putting or worse. I noticed my hostility was on the wane.

'So how does it, the Hick-Boo, actually work?'

'Originally I worked with radar, which was fine until someone had a mobile phone nearby and then I got interference. I would have been found out in a jiffy. That's when I hit on the caddy idea. And that's where you come in. It doesn't work without you.'

'Me! But I don't know anything about this.'

'No, that's the beauty of it. But we need your input, or, to be more specific, your hand. When you put your hand on the flag pole it conducts just enough heat for the infrared fingerprint that the Hick-Boo's camera locks onto. And the beauty of infrared is that it doesn't interfere with any other systems. When you use the remote to flick the channel on your TV there's no interference with any other signals. It's invisible. It's why we can't be caught. This putter has the invisibility of a stealth bomber – electronically I mean.' Dermot paused. It was a fine effort but I was still in the dark.

'But how does it actually work when you're taking a putt?'

'When you put a hand on the flag that's when we achieve

ground zero. Tercom then takes over; that's the brains of the operation, guidance and control system if you like. Tercom talks to me and I make the putt. I'm the missile operator, you might say. So I'm still the critical stage of the operation. Sure, technology helps, but at the end of the day if I screw up we miss the putt.'

'Tercom talks to you?'

'Yep, a miniature wireless speaker in my ear.' Dermot produced from his pocket a small ball, with tiny grills on one side. 'I made it myself,' he said proudly, 'Nano tech.' He went on to explain the details.

So finally I got it; there was a speaker inside Dermot's ear. Once I had triggered the Tercom, or whatever it was, the putter signalled Dermot; a high-pitched note was too far right, a low-pitched note was too far left, a warble was swing too hard (putter raised too high), a flat buzz was swing too soft (putter raised too low). It almost literally spoke to him.

'What do you say, old man? One last big hurrah. This tournament, we check it works and then we go to the authorities, do it all properly. Come on. What's the harm?'

So that was it. The buck stopped with me because I knew that Dermot was incapable of choosing his path anymore. He was obsessed. I told him: 'You're like an addict. You'll do whatever it takes for you to win.'

'Okay, I'll toss you for it,' said Dermot. 'Heads we play and tails we pull out of the tournament.'

In some strange way, this could be a way out of my moral dilemma. I nodded and Dermot tossed his silver crown coin high into the air. I watched it spinning in the morning sunlight and Dermot caught it smartly, bringing it to the back of his hand. We both peered forward to look. I must admit when I saw the result I realised that deep down inside it was what I had wished for. 'And you're sure we won't get caught?' With those words I sealed my destiny. We both knew it.

So finished what was perhaps the most surreal conversation I'd had with anyone, even Dermot. Later on, a lot of stuff became clearer to me. Like for example the collapse in the qualifying, when I had stumbled and dropped the golf bag. I had knocked the sensitive electronics in the putter, hence its state of disrepair when I found it on the workshop bench. Also the fact that it didn't work from off the green as long grass interfered with the technology. And Dermot's fiddling with the putter, which I'd put down to nerves, was actually calibration adjustments.

Now I only had to get on with the rest of my life, bearing in mind that we were playing in the Senior British Open on Thursday. The next two days at home I wasn't myself. Mary noticed it. I had decided not to tell her anything. No doubt she put my demeanour down to nerves. In any case Dermot had sworn me to secrecy, but it was a new experience to wander around my home with such a secret heavy in the air. I resolved to tell Mary just as soon as the Open was done with.

Those forty-eight hours crawled eerily past, and so it was a big relief when we were back in the MG speeding to Sandwich. Dermot was still Dermot, if anything even perkier than normal. Maybe now he had an acolyte to share his achievement with, everything was easier. I was just getting used to carrying around a guilty secret. When I was apart from from him, I thought what we were doing was wrong but together, well, Dermot had such a persuasive manner.

The first thing we noticed was the TV crews at the course. That made us nervous, and not just about playing golf; more importantly, would we be found out?

Within minutes I had spotted the previous year's winner, Bernhard Langer. There was Tom Watson and Cory Pavin. We were walking with legends. The excitement inside me was immense. In our foursome we were joined by a golfing colossus, Greg Norman, one of Dermot's heroes. The Great White Shark, two times Open Champion, teeing off with *us*!

It was only after we had made the first green in regulation and Dermot commanded: 'Flag!' that I had the sensation of my feet returning to the ground. I remembered why, or rather how, we were here, and it felt just plain wrong. How did I get myself talked into this, I wondered? When Dermot dropped the first of many fine putts that day, 'Just call me Greg', the legend himself, applauded: 'Great shot, sport!'

I felt like a fraud. I did something I hadn't done in twenty years: I blushed. My legs felt heavy. I wasn't sure I could continue carrying Dermot's bag for another hole, let alone three more days. So from the next green I started willing Dermot to fail, and the feeling never left me. But it was a faint hope; he was driving well off the tee, his short game was good and the putts kept rolling in. With every hole completed it seemed to me that Dermot's raised fist acknowledgement to the galleries became higher and more confident.

If this was a story about how my good friend came from nowhere to win the Senior British Open, then this bit would be the section I would lavish most time on. I would take you through the victory hole by hole, the birdies, the eagles, all those prodigious putts. But that is a tale which has to be told by someone else, somewhere else. My story has already run its course.

Dermot completed the third round with a breathtaking putt. After three rounds he was leading the competition by one shot. Players and caddies shook hands as we walked from the green.

'I'll leave you to hand in the score card,' I said, walking off.

Dermot watched me go. 'See you at breakfast, old man.' This was typical of our conversation now. Something was broken between us. We didn't have much to say to each other and when we did it was usually to exchange words, to snap at each other on the course.

I wasn't sleeping well. That evening before the final round I left the hotel in the early hours to walk down to the famous clubhouse overlooking the eighteenth. And there in the shadows I spied the unmissable hunched shoulders of Dermot crouched by the green. Was his conscience troubling him also? I slipped silently away.

*

The next morning we had an early breakfast together, punctuated by occasional conversation, alone in the hotel restaurant. Like the last days of a marriage it was clear to me that the sands of time had drained from this hour glass.

'It's not working, is it?' I told him.

'The Hick-Boo?' Dermot looked up from a large plate of egg, bacon and mushrooms. 'Never worked better. Fifty-six holes of competition golf without a glitch, perfectly calibrated. It's a legitimate breakthrough. Relax, old man.'

'I mean you and me ... one day you'll be found out.' But he was in his not-listening, switch-off mode. 'Someone's bound to denounce you.'

'But not you.'

'How come you can be so confident?'

'Because if you breathe a word about the Hick-Boo, I'll be sure to drag you down with me.' His tone was menacing, spitting out the words. 'You could say goodbye to your chance to get some real help for Mary. She could take it very badly, I mean—'

'Shut it, will you? I'll caddy for you today.' I was ready to leave the room. 'One last round and then I quit.' I knew exactly what Dermot was getting at. 'What you're doing with Dermot is just brilliant,' Mary had said on the phone. 'I'm so proud of you. The whole village is.' Exposure would finish her. I was trapped.

I stood up to go.

'Eleven o'clock tee-off,' Dermot spoke in a normal tone again, as if we were still the best of friends and nothing untoward had happened. 'I'll be at the driving range earlier if you fancy joining me.'

I left the dining room thinking I still didn't know what was fuelling Dermot's sudden anger: losing his chance of greatness, me not supporting him, or a genuine desire to help Mary?

Dermot did go on to win the Open by two strokes from Tom Watson, sealing it with what one Sky TV commentator labelled 'the putt of the century'. He pocketed the winner's cheque with a two hundred and forty thousand-pound smile. For me, the whir of shutters from the press corps cameras sounded like the drum roll accompanying the condemned man to the scaffold. I had the sensation of time standing still, the slow descent of early autumn leaves drifting in the sun. The man I had known for thirty years, or at least the man I thought I knew, walked straight past me to meet the press. Now, making my own way to the taxi rank, I realised I had to start getting to know myself.

A couple of days later Dermot's cheque for one hundred thousand pounds arrived, with a short note. *Some deductions for expenses, old man!* I guess that meant sophisticated electronics equipment. I left the cheque in the envelope for a couple of weeks. If I had Dermot's current address I would have gained some satisfaction from using *Return to sender*. But since his Open triumph Dermot was already off on the American circuit.

Some weeks later when I was feeling a desperate need to help Mary, who was very down, I cashed the cheque and booked us the holiday of a lifetime. Three glorious months on a Caribbean cruise; lazing on-board deck with gin and tonics, unremitting blue skies, paradise beaches, making new friends, reading books – and I didn't pick up a golf club.

Now, late in the evening, we'd returned home to a cold Hayling Island in the middle of a wet winter. I could be sure of one thing as I gazed through a rain-soaked landscape: the course would be deserted the next morning. Even though it was dark I felt my eyes drawn in the direction of the fourth green, Dermot's inveterate haunt.

'You got an interesting looking packet in the post!' Mary shouted from the kitchen. 'Could be a present. I've put it in on the side-table.'

I felt so relieved she was back to her normal self. The holiday really had been a case of just what the doctor ordered. And I was fifty today. Just a few months behind Dermot, whom I had already seen last week on Fox Sports channel leading the Senior Masters at Augusta. On TV we saw him with some unfamiliar caddy, sinking a typical amazing putt with the Hick-Boo. I watched the caddy hold the flag until the last moment. Dermot had him well trained. I wondered if he was in on the secret.

'Good – the cleaner remembered milk.' I heard kitchen cupboard doors. 'Cup of tea?'

'In a minute.' I was already twisting the cork on the malt whisky bottle I had bought at the airport. I wondered whether I would be able to get the haunting images of Dermot out of my head when I went onto the golf course for the first time since Sandwich. And in my hand I held a small airmail packet from America. I recognised the handwriting.

I decided not to wait for Mary, put down my whisky tumbler and opened the package. It was small and heavy and wrapped in bubble wrap. A coin.

I looked at the telephone on the desk next to me. All it needed from me was a phone call to any Sunday newspaper. I flipped Dermot's lucky silver crown into the air and down it came heads. Then I tried again, still heads. It gave me an idea. I turned the coin over: heads. So Dermot wasn't gambling back on that August morning. But he was gambling now. I wondered why? My inimitable friend, unfathomable from first to last, or my nemesis? I looked at the phone and started to chuckle.

Water and Glass

Collioure, South of France – 1970

Jennifer had made the same walk six mornings in a row, down the cobbled street between prettily painted French houses to the beach with the vast shimmering apron of sea, and she dreaded every step.

'Come on, hurry up, Jen,' commanded Michelle, who was walking briskly in front of her carrying an assortment of creature comforts, including a large transistor radio. Turning around she explained urgently: 'I'm sure those boys will be back today so we've got to bag the same spot, right?' Not waiting for an answer she pressed ahead, adding over her shoulder – unnecessarily, thought Jennifer – 'And remember – you've got the other one.'

'Wearing the face that she keeps in a jar by the door,' Jennifer said to herself.

'What's that?'

'*Eleanor Rigby*.' But Michelle was already ten feet ahead and out of earshot. Jennifer had realised a day in the sun was a serious business. She was eighteen years old and this was her first holiday with Michelle. Her first beach holiday. Jennifer vowed to do neither ever again.

'Isn't this just heaven?' exclaimed Michelle when at last they had found a spot, ten feet from where they had lain all day yesterday. Holding the Ambre Solaire in an outstretched hand she said: 'Time to catch up on some UVs – can you do my back?' Jennifer studied her friend's ample torso. She didn't know where to begin. 'Jen, you should work on your tan, you know. White alabaster might be cool in museums but on the beach it's ridic.'

Jennifer made another vow; never again to agree important things, like who to holiday with, whilst under the influence of alcohol. 'Your trouble, Jen,' said Michelle, lying on her front and counting out how many cigarettes she had remaining, 'is that boys don't know where they stand with you. Half the time you're living in a dream.' Rummaging for her lighter, she said, 'Come on, slap it on. I can't wait all bleeding day, you know.'

Jennifer was about to squeeze out some oil when she suddenly remembered. 'Oh!' she half gasped. 'I've forgotten my book. I'll have to go back.'

'Well hurry up Jen, I don't know why you even need a book. I mean, this is meant to be a *holiday*.' Michelle turned around and scowled. 'Like, we may as well put up a sign: BORING SWOTS, LEAVE IN PEACE.'

Not a bad idea, thought Jennifer. 'Buried alone with her name,' she muttered. Beatles lyrics always seemed to be turning around in her head. Sometimes they slipped out in conversation.

'Come again?'

'Nothing. I'll be back. Soon.'

'And get some ciggies!' Michelle shouted after Jennifer's retreating figure. 'And what about my back?'

On her way towards the apartment Jennifer spotted a small group of holidaymakers gathered in the market, where twenty minutes earlier there had been no one. She walked over to see what the commotion was about. They turned out to be clustered around a sign advertising excursions to the Salvadore Dali Museum in Figueres, just across the border in Spain.

At the edge of the crowd a guy, about her age with long and disarranged black hair and glasses, lurked like an Italian gigolo. She was surprised when he answered her request for information; 'Ten minutes,' in perfect English, 'but you'll need your passport.'

Jennifer made the bus in seconds flat, managed a thank you to her dark-haired acquaintance one seat in front and as she sat down breathed out a sigh of relief. This was the escape she had been dreaming of in double chemistry; the allure of the unknown. So far this holiday she'd been happy for others to take the initiative, but where had that got her? Six solid days on the beach under a sweltering sky.

Eagerly she consulted her Henderson's guidebook for Figueres which recommended the hot chocolate in a café called Roberto's next to the museum where, if you were lucky, you might even see the great man himself. There were still twenty-two pictures remaining on her camera film.

The Italian guy, who was really English, had a t-shirt with Pink Floyd emblazoned across the front. She wondered if she could ask him something about it – who knows where that conversation might lead – but he was engrossed in his own guidebook. Maybe they would meet in the museum.

The museum was different from any she had ever visited before. Her classmates from school would have declared the place 'far out'. With some effort she restricted herself to six photographs. The place was swarming with people and after a couple of hours admiring exhibits she was starting to feel light-headed. She regretted missing breakfast. A couple of times she saw the guy with all the hair again, entering another gallery, but by the time she had subtly followed him the room would be empty. She cursed herself for not bringing a bottle of water. Her mind drifted back to the boy, the bus, to Henderson's and then ... of course ... the café next door!

'Excuse me, is this chair taken?' she asked. Roberto's wasn't busy but she would prefer a seat with a view. 'I could always take another if you'd rather.'

A thirty-something Spanish-looking lady shook her head and flashed a wide smile at her – probably doesn't understand a word, mused Jennifer. She sat down with a glass of water and a hot chocolate – not her normal selection on such a hot day but in deference to Mr Henderson she felt she had to try it. The hot chocolate was delicious.

Suddenly, there he was once again, Pink Floyd, striding out

from the exit door, just a few minutes behind her. 'Now *he* is your type,' said the woman opposite.

Jennifer continued reading her guidebook for a moment before looking up and asking, 'Sorry, were you talking to me?'

'That is man for you, someone who knows what is he wants.'

The woman had a nerve. 'You mean I don't?'

'Like your glass of water, lady. Water needs glass and glass needs water. One of these without the other is no good.'

'Isn't that rather old-fashioned? Not all women want to be told what to do.'

'The man, he can also be water if the woman is glass. Just the two together is no working. For you it is water that is no working.'

Jennifer felt like saying 'Why don't you let me finish my hot chocolate in peace?' But instead she asked: 'So what happens if I choose water?'

'Then you try again, just like me, but my problem is glass. Always I find the glass, when I should be looking water, and we crash to bits—'

'Smash to pieces.'

'Yes, always glass crash to glass. But water is so … so … how you say?'

'Wet?'

'Yes … wet, for me water is very wet.' She held out her hand. It was covered with rings. 'Three times I crash to bits.' She gazed at Jennifer and then out of the window. 'Ah! My taxi.' She stood up. 'Remember, lady, glass not water,' and was gone like the white rabbit.

Newspaper taxis appear on the shore … was that Salvadore Dali or Lennon, she wondered. In the heat she couldn't be sure. Before she had a chance to continue this *Alice in Wonderland*-type conversation she was alone again.

Back on the bus she slumped exhausted into her seat and started wondering if perhaps she had imagined the whole strange conversation. Then, somebody spoke about the amazing

Dali and she nodded off. She dreamt she was a pair of giant lips stalking plasticine porters on station platforms and only woke up as the bus pulled into the market place at Collioure. Looking up at the town clock, she noticed she was late.

'Where in hell have you been?'

At the door of the apartment she bumped into Michelle, suitcase in hand. 'Sorry, there was no time to tell you—'

'Jesus creepers jelly brain, tell me about it, second thoughts don't bother. I'm already late. Jean-Pierre is picking me up – he's the spit of Alain Delon.' In urgent rapid-fire phrases her friend explained to Jennifer how the French guys had indeed returned to the beach and that now Michelle had an offer she simply couldn't refuse. 'I feel so fricking guilty leaving you, Jen. You're going to be bored rigid without me, right? Where did I leave my passport?' Jean-Pierre (presumably this was not *the other one*) was picking her up from the town square. 'Everything's so sudden; I mean like, this was meant to be *our* bitchen holiday, right? Gotta split. Toodle pip.'

'Goodbye. Très bien ensemble.' But Michelle was already gone into the Mediterranean night. Jennifer felt strangely intoxicated and alive to be on her own.

The only problem, Jennifer figured the next morning, was cash. Money had been tight anyway but now if she was looking for more of a culture holiday and less of a beach holiday, it was going to cost more. She decided to take a leaf out of her grandfather's book: 'When you're short of funds, treat yourself. Plan from a position of strength.' She found the most exclusive restaurant in town, *Le Clocher*, where she picked out a corner table with a view to the square as well as the Mediterranean and ordered a coffee. Next she took out her sketchbook, in which earlier that morning she had made a drawing of the monastery on the top of the hill. She drew a line down the next blank page. She wrote a large plus at the top of one column and a large minus in the other. Pluses and minuses, she mused; her grandfather would approve. In the plus column she wrote *cello concert?* (she had seen the flier last week), *Beatles cassette-tapes, pad paid for, traveller's cheques – £50*, and after a moment's hesitation *boy with the hair – name?* On the minus side of the page: *money short, French nowhere near fluent, home on the 20th.*

She couldn't decide if *on my own* should go in the plus or minus column. In the end she added *No Michelle* to the plus side and *No friends* to the minus. She was starting to wonder if the minus column was getting too long.

Alan knew his finances would stretch each day to two coffees and four beers, and he would still have five francs left for lunch. He had nearly a month before university started. Even though it was early he would celebrate with a beer, à la *Ice Cold in Alex*, his new favourite film. He could enjoy one of his ten-a-day cigarette ration. Alan reminded himself he must send another postcard to the folks to let them know he was doing fine. If only the guys in the sixth form could see him now. His daydreams were interrupted by the sight of a girl sitting at the smartest restaurant in town – no ordinary girl, but the one from the Dali trip. He recognised the pale oval face and her curly brown hair, even half-obscured under a large white hat. She must be loaded, he thought.

Nothing ventured, nothing gained. It would be easy enough to start a conversation – why, if it wasn't for him she might not even have found the Dali museum. He would go over and say hello.

Alan employed his familiar routine; to calculate the exact number of paces to his destination, sixty-seven should do it he figured. He adjusted the guitar on his back and set off, thinking that in a minute from now he might come face to face with embarrassing rejection or meet the girl of his destiny. He took large steps, counting as he went: 'Seventeen ... eighteen—'

'Alan ... Alan Drage!' someone shouted.

He stopped in his tracks.

'Alan Drage!' the voice shouted again.

This was a different embarrassing situation to the one he had been anticipating. Everyone in the square was looking at him; including, he noticed, the girl from under the white hat. Then he saw someone he recognised running towards him. 'Crikey! This is a surprise,' said Alan. 'What are you doing here?'

'Looking for you.'

'Me? Why?'

The older man spoke gently: 'Alan, I'm afraid I have bad news ... it's your dad,' he placed a hand on the boy's shoulder, 'his heart.'

'But he is okay, isn't he?'

'Well the doctors say his condition is stable but your mother is ... she needs you, Alan. We put an SOS message out on Radio 4 eight days ago. Then your postcard arrived and I decided I had to set off on the trail. And now I've found you,' his Uncle James added proudly.

Jennifer watched the two of them walk away. She was disappointed. Still, she was a free spirit. And she could remove the question mark from his name on the list. She wrote in the plus column: *Alan Drage in town* and then on instinct picked up her Kodak to take a photograph. She had reason to be optimistic; more had happened in the last twenty-four hours than the previous week.

Apollo theatre, Shaftesbury Avenue, London – 1986

Alan took one large exaggerated step – *one hundred and twenty-eight* – and smiled. YES! He'd done it again. His next step took him through the main entrance door of the Apollo. He was early for once and besides the girl in the box office, the theatre was deserted. The make-up girls wouldn't even have arrived yet. He planned a nice relaxed coffee and a read of the sports pages, which he hoped to pick up from the main lobby area.

Jennifer was quizzical, studying the logic of Tim's argument. The last line of his letter which she had just read irritated her: 'I know it isn't the first time I've messed it up, but really it was just a *fling*. For Paul's sake couldn't we give it another go?' Her husband and the father of their son Paul was thirty-five, a year older than her, and still he only seemed to be playing at being a parent. He didn't appear committed to her or their son. She crumpled the letter into her pocket.

She needed coffee, not excuses. Privately she considered that if optimism was an Olympic sport she would have the gold medal, and while the chances of a coffee currently appeared unlikely, she still had a couple of hours to kill before the show. So spying a man in a white dinner jacket coming from the direction of the bar she decided to take her chances.

'Ah ... excuse me, waiter.'

The man stopped abruptly as if surprised. Perhaps it was too early after all. But the way he remained standing, looking at her, gave her encouragement.

'Is there any chance of a cup of coffee?' Then, on second thoughts, 'Or something stronger?' She removed her Walkman headphones and flashed her best smile. A mother, at thirty something, and she knew she could still turn heads in the street.

'Sure, why not?' the waiter replied.

Following him through the theatre she was confronted by empty chairs. She saw her mistake; she'd never drunk in a deserted bar before. She couldn't start now, especially not in the afternoon.

As if reading her thoughts the waiter volunteered, 'Look, would you mind if I joined you? I've had one hell of a night actually ... and there's plenty of time before curtain up.'

She liked his voice: he spoke slowly, savouring each word. 'You don't need to be working?'

'Working?' He seemed surprised. 'Oh no, don't worry – I'll be busy later.'

He was fairly busy now behind the bar and after some clanking of bottles eventually returned with two gin and tonics, which he placed with a flourish in front of her on the bar.

Emboldened by the thought of a drink with a stranger, correction, a rather good-looking waiter, she threw her normal caution to the wind. 'Here's looking at you, kid.'

He stared at her for a moment, and she wondered if she was going to blush. 'Are my eyes really brown?'

She thought his voice was a more than passable Bogart imitation. 'One of my favourite films.'

'Mine too.'

They stared awkwardly down at their glasses. She remembered a Stanley Kubrick film she'd recently rented on video. 'Let me guess, you've been chased by an axe murderer?'

'Closer than you realise.' He took a packet of cigarettes from his dinner jacket. 'Sarah – that's my soon to be ex-wife, is like a Red Indian on the war path. Cigarette?'

'No thanks.'

She felt more comfortable with the next silence. There was a ping of the lighter and the flame shot unnecessarily high into the air. He leaned forward and whispered conspiratorially: 'Keep a weather-eye open for a seafaring woman with one leg, matey.'

Jennifer laughed. *Treasure Island*, she planned to read to her son, and his West Country accent sounded remarkably convincing. 'You want me to say I've never met you before?'

'Haven't we?' He continued with mock gravity: 'Say, you know you were great back there.' He was now sounding like Gregory Peck. 'Trouble? You're not what I'd call trouble.'

She was laughing. 'What was it you had, a hard day's night? Sorry, I can't keep up ... uhm.'

'I can't call you Jim boy, me laddie. What's your you name?' Then he switched from pirate's brogue back to suave Gregory Peck. 'Or should I just call you *trouble*?'

'Was it a car accident?'

'No, a marriage.'

'I mean the one leg.'

They both laughed, falling against each other. In the company of this funny man Jennifer didn't notice the time passing as he continued with a witty, sometimes hilarious, résumé of his two marriages. At times her jaw ached from the laughter. At last he concluded: 'So you can see, both my wives had very clear views of what I should be doing with my life and so have I. Sarah and I were like two tectonic plates grinding away and seeing who will break first.'

'Two glasses.'

'Both empty, yes. I'm sorry.'

'She sounds like Miss Pablo-Fanques.'

'You've lost me, I'm afraid.'

'One of Salvadore Dali's mistresses. I met her once,' Jennifer added vaguely. 'At least I think I did.'

'Dali, why doesn't that surprise me? Yes, Dali, you know I once ... maybe I should give my ex-wife a more dramatic name, something more appropriate.' He inspected his empty glass. 'But I'm forgetting my part. Yo-ho-ho, we need more rum.'

'You seem well educated for a waiter. Sorry that didn't come out—' she went on. 'I mean I wasn't thinking—'

'Not a bad university, mine. I mean, at least they didn't overlook the basics like reading. Grammar on the other hand—'

She followed him to the bar where he was searching for a bottle.

'Sorry, I mean ... where did you—?'

'It's not where I come from that counts. It's where we're going. There's something I want to show you, if you've got time?'

'Plenty, I'm meeting a friend later for the play I mean ... shouldn't I pay for that?'

The waiter was steering her through a door across the bar. 'Don't worry, I'll sort that out later.'

He was leading her up some spiral stairs.

'What a view!' She could see the glimmer of buses crawling down Piccadilly Circus towards Leicester Square. 'It's like the Beatles in the *Let it Be* concert. I wish I had my sketch book with me.' She took time to wander around the rooftop.

The waiter was removing the cork from their bottle of wine. 'Thought you'd like it,' he said.

Leaning over the rail looking down at the traffic Jennifer felt her thoughts running as free as her hair in the summer breeze. 'Up here my independence seems to vanish in the haze.'

'Say that again.'

'Up here, my independ—' She turned to face her waiter. 'Did you remember glasses?'

The roof was baking hot. They found a corner with some shade and sat down with their glasses to talk about books and films. Jennifer couldn't remember when she had last felt so free, so young. They could have talked for hours.

'It's been great, hasn't it? What a fantastic afternoon,' said the waiter, standing up. 'But I fear duty calls.'

He leant forward to give her a kiss, which she just didn't want to end. Tasting his lips on hers she realised she had been waiting for this uplifting feeling not just today but for a long time.

At the foot of the stairs they stopped for a moment in front of a crowd of smartly dressed people. These was a buzz of conversation. A bell was ringing which made Jennifer think of Cinderella. She checked her watch. 'Crikey! Is that the time?' and rested her hand on the lapel of his white jacket. 'I hope you're not going to lose your job because of me.'

'I feel like I've known you all my life.'

Jennifer thought his voice had a wistful tone and felt he was staring right through her. 'Glass and water,' was all she could utter.

'Okay, but then I'm going to have to run.'

The waiter raced over to the bar and was just placing a glass of water in her hand when he noticed a woman watching him from across the room, her lips in a thin line. 'Oh dear, I'm really for it. They're sending out a search party.'

'With an axe.'

'Must dash. Enjoy the show.' Walking away from her but loud enough for her to hear: 'Of all the gin joints in all the world, she walks into mine ...'

His words touched a chord. Some strange feeling of destiny

stirred inside her. As she passed the Box Office she stopped to ask, 'Excuse me, the waiter, the tall chap; you know, slightly Italian looking? I just wanted to find out his name.'

'Sorry, deary, the bar staff don't come on till seven. You'll have to wait five minutes.'

On the way out to meet her friend she stopped at the poster advertising that evening's *whodunnit*. There was no mistaking the arched smile, the jet black eyebrows, the tanned face. Alan Drage, the lead actor, and she had treated him like a waiter. But that wasn't what disturbed her. There was something about that name. She felt she had heard it before, but where? Must have been in the review.

Stepping into the Oxford Circus air after the show Jennifer's feet had a lightness of touch she associated more with foreign pavements and the promise of adventure. Before they departed her friend remarked: 'Tim should have more affairs, you seem to thrive on them.'

The remark brought her feet back to the London street. It had been a long day. She felt tired, and something else too – the last time she had felt like this was when she was pregnant with Paul. Perhaps that was all the more reason to patch things up with Tim.

A couple of days later, following a hunch, she finally found her pre-university sketchbook that was stuck at the back of her LP collection. She saw what she was looking for on the page after the monastery sketch from Collioure: a photograph, more hair but unmistakably the same strong, good-looking features. She had written all those years ago *Alan Drage still in town*. Well, she thought, he still is.

Alexandria, Eygpt – 2004

Alan Drage stood by a stone pillar in the car park of the Serapeum, Alexandria. He was waiting for the villains to make the drop. Alan was wearing civilian clothes as this was an undercover operation. In his job, he reflected, there was a lot of waiting and hanging around but he had the feeling it would soon be time for action. Slowly a bead of sweat crept down the side of his face. It was the hottest part of the day. Out of the blank heat and silence a white sedan suddenly careered into the car park. Its tyres screeched to a halt and three gangster-looking men got out, slamming doors.

'Police!' Alan shouted, emerging from behind the stone pillar. 'Drop your weapons!'

They hesitated for a second, then the nearest, maybe the leader, nodded to his colleagues and went for his tool, following the script this time. Alan saw the flash of steel-grey gun barrel and ducked before letting off two quick shots. He leapt sideways, somersaulted and thumped into the side of the pillar before finishing neatly in a sitting position to take aim at the third villain, now running from the scene.

He held the gun up, aimed for a long second and then relented. British police didn't shoot villains in the back. The first two lay prone, bleeding slowly into the desert sand.

Good work he thought – aged forty-nine and he could still move like a young man. Daytrippers returning from their tour of the temple had stopped to watch and now applauded. He smiled in appreciation, touching the brim of his Panama hat which looked like it had miraculously stayed in place throughout the fracas, but was actually held in place with double-sided tape.

'Cut. That's it for today,' shouted the director. 'Same time tomorrow, folks.'

'Nice shooting, guv,' said one of the villains to Alan as the two actors stood up and started to brush sand from their clothes.

'At last,' said the other. 'How many takes was that?' He was free to go. A couple of the tourists wanted autographs – even here Alan was recognised – the price he paid for being Britain's top TV detective, and much as he complained to friends and colleagues, secretly he loved it. *Inspector Drake Investigates*, into its fifteenth season, regularly topping ten million viewers and now going on location.

Alexandria was Alan's idea: the closing take would show him enjoying a cool and well-deserved lager. The city offered him the advantage of being able to have his pride and joy, the luxury motor yacht *Inspector*, parked right here in the harbour.

'Message from Lynn.' Carla, his assistant, had emerged from the phalanx of lights and cameras. She had been with him from the start: a strong, handsome woman and more than a match for any one of his five ex-wives, who were themselves no pushovers. 'Can you phone? It's urgent.'

His other ex's had nick-names: Boadicea, Cleopatra, Artemis and Lysistrata (who went on a sex strike). He still had to find a name for Lynn – Circe perhaps? To start with they had all seemed different to him, but after all these years he could see a pattern to his wives – polished, beautiful and hard, like diamonds – which they pretty much all did, mused Alan.

'Oh and your son called,' remembered Carla, 'from the harbour.'

'No doubt working through my whisky collection with some new flame.' His son from Boadicea was twenty years old and keen to follow in his famous father's footsteps, something he hadn't encouraged. So far with a couple of walk-on parts, Drage minor had managed to avoid rave reviews, which hadn't surprised him. But Alex was still his son. 'Anything for him on set?'

'I'll ask around.'

It was amusing, thought Alan, that in truth there was a lot less Drage acting in Drake than many people realised. As the years had rolled by the bank balance had swollen and the line between Drake and Drage had become increasingly blurred. Drage acting Drake, Drake acting Drage – who could tell the difference? Could he? In hotels he was sometimes Drage and other times Drake. Sure, he was typecast. As he pointed out to friends, he could afford to be.

'Okay, that's cool, Carla. I'll see you back at the hotel. I think I might explore a little – we still need to find a location for the last scene.'

'Don't forget your phone,' said Carla, 'I've charged it for you.' He was in two minds about taking the bulky phone with him but the studio liked it and paid for it. He hailed a taxi, feeling like an adventurer heading into the unknown heart of Alexandria.

Jennifer took some money from the cashpoint. She was still surprised by these holes in the wall where money came out, even in foreign countries. On the other side of the wall she imagined a little gnome-like creature with a home-made white handkerchief cap and John Lennon glasses, counting out her money.

She was on her way to meet Sofie. The two had planned to meet in the street that sold woven rugs. Buying presents for her husband had always been difficult but a couple of days earlier he had said: 'I've always wanted a hand-made Turkish rug' – news to her. She took out of her bag the map and detailed instructions Sofie had given her earlier. She still had half an hour.

Tim, who hated shopping, would be at the hotel looking for football on the TV. How long had they been together? Was it really twenty years? Tim took charge of everything except holidays. That was her thing, the one time the family would be sure to be together – except this time their son Paul was busy building a nuclear power station somewhere. Last year's holiday had been France.

She was deep in her thoughts and must have missed a landmark. What was certain was that she was lost. The streets were starting to look less and less reassuring. This was hopeless. She decided to ask directions from the next European-looking person she saw. A man in a Panama hat walking about twenty yards behind looked promising.

Possibly it was instinct that told her to turn around just before her assailant leapt out of a concealed doorway in the alley. Her first reaction was to push him away as he reached for her handbag. From the corner of her eye she saw the Panama-hat man getting closer. There was something familiar about him.

'Help! Somebody please! Help!' she shouted.

The Panama hat kept walking, not running. She felt a hand grab her jacket; she pushed again and heard her jacket tearing. What was she doing resisting? And then as the Panama hat came back into her vision, realisation dawned; her Sir Lancelot was none other than Inspector Drake – no mistaking his long dark hair and Roman nose – what luck! She felt another pull at her coat. Where was the inspector? She looked up. Drake seemed undecided, helpless, hopeless even. Her attacker, not much more than a boy, now appeared nervous. Almost reluctantly, she thought, he pulled a knife.

'Give him your wallet!' shouted Drake.

Jennifer was thinking '*Why?* There's two of us and I've got Inspector Drake on my side.' She swung her bag at the assailant. She missed and the bag whistled harmlessly by.

But her assailant took a step back, with Drake just a yard behind. The boy could see the odds had changed. He was less sure of himself, looking over his shoulder. Jennifer reckoned one decisive move from them and the boy would run. She gestured to Drake to come closer but he hung back, rooted to the spot, his arms hanging uselessly by his side. On screen he seemed taller. The man with the foolish grin is keeping perfectly still, thought Jennifer who was thinking clear and straight. She would have to act. She screamed as loud as she possibly could: 'Help! Help!'

The boy turned around to see who could hear and as he did so she kicked at his knife hand. The boy yelped – more in surprise than pain, she guessed – and dropped the knife. Instinctively she picked it up and her assailant, mistaking her action for confidence, started to back away. Shortly, he was running away from them. Jennifer was left alone with Inspector Drake in the alleyway.

'Are you all right ... you're okay?' Drake was functioning now. 'Here, you'd better give that to me.' He reached his hand out for the knife. 'Sorry, I wasn't sure what to do back there. I was about to ... are you all right ... you're not hurt?'

She noticed that just as on TV he had the same way of speaking slowly. Now she thought maybe he was just ... well, slow. She passed the knife to his open palm. 'No thanks to you.' She noticed the tremble in her voice and regretted the words immediately. 'I mean, I'm sorry, the shock.'

She watched Alan Drage – she remembered his proper name – take his mobile from his bag. He seemed to have found a faster gear. She assumed he was going to call the police. 'Hello, Carla, it's me. Look, I've just been involved in a mugging. We beat him off. Get the press down here, this is great PR. I've got the attacker's knife in my hand. Of course I'm holding it by the blade, yes, fingerprints. I'm fine, few scratches ... yes, a real mugging ... hold on a minute.'

Jennifer didn't want to hear any more. She was already walking back down the alley.

'Hey, come back. I don't even know your name.'

Jennifer quickened her stride. She still had her wallet. She could get a taxi and be on time to meet Sofie.

Back at the hotel there was a knock on Jennifer's door. It was Sofie, carrying a portable computer. 'Hi, Mum, you're not going to believe this. Inspector Drake is here in Alexandria, he's having a press conference; something about saving a mystery lady from an attacker.' She went over to turn on the TV.

'What's that?' asked Tim coming out of the bathroom.

The screen showed Drake's familiar face. He was offering a candle-lit dinner on his luxury yacht for the lady he had saved, cutting a noble figure as he described how she had fled in panic.

'Mum's favourite copper!' exclaimed Tim.

'It's true. I know I once said I could watch Drake eight days a week, but that was before we came to Alexandria.'

'What's Alexandria got to do with it?'

'I think your father has just been missing a tan all these years.

He's a lot more handsome.' Jennifer turned to face her husband. 'It was my good luck meeting a man from the motor trade.'

Tim reacted in surprise, dropping the towel he had been drying his hair with. She gave him a kiss, full on the mouth.

'Ugh! Gross, do you have to, Mum?'

'And I do appreciate you being round as well, Sofie. Let's go.'

Jennifer was pleased to leave the hotel and the TV pictures of Inspector Drake behind her. To think all these years she had secretly harboured ...

'Mum, why is it that Dad assumes he's always got to be the guide?' Sofie interrupted her reflections. 'Does he think women can't read maps?'

'Well I'm hoping your father has found us something special,' she said linking her arm through his and her daughter's. 'He's had enough time after all.'

'That's right,' said Sofie. 'When some of us were busy shopping—'

'I was recommended this place. A bit different, a surprise you might say,' said Tim. 'A little bit off the tourist track but it should be safe enough.'

'Dad, you should have let me print a route from the computer.'

'Sofie, what you see here is a dying art ... reading a real map.' Tim appeared lost but happy, thought Jennifer, a good man. Roll up, roll up for the mystery tour. She was grateful to have her daughter and Tim to follow, whichever direction they agreed upon.

'Mum, you never finished that explanation of how you tore your blouse—'

'I was just thinking, Sofie,' said Jennifer effortlessly, 'you're old enough to be drinking wine when we go out.'

'Mum, I have been for years.'

'And Sofie, you know there's nothing to worry about. We girls have got our very own Inspector Drake in town to look after us.

Better still, this one is the genuine article – aren't you darling?' She squeezed Tim's arm.

'I had a lucky escape,' said Sofie.

'What on earth do you mean?' asked Jennifer.

'Weren't you planning on Ringo for a boy's name? Imagine school!' They walked three abreast in the shade of a high wall before they stopped as they approached the corner, and Tim once again consulted his map.

'Don't say it, Mum.'

'What?'

'Here comes the sun.'

Tunnel

'Good morning.' He greeted the prisoner, who sat at the small wooden table, Bible in hand, glasses glinting in the light of the single forty-watt electric light bulb. No word in reply. Six weeks he'd been visiting this cell and so far the prisoner had refused to answer a single question. The silence was starting to get to Ronald. Last night he'd even dreamt of the sullen and shaven-headed apparition. He felt like striking that resentful face to illicit a response. The prisoner was only twenty-five or so, lightly built and, he suspected, not the type to fight back.

Ronald heard the sound of the guard outside in the passageway drawing home the bolt. He was alone one again with the nihilist. The interrogator smiled grimly and resolved to keep his cool; the survival of the Owslafa depended on his getting the prisoner to talk; becoming violent would solve nothing. Today the prisoner would talk, Ronald was confident. He placed both mugs down on the table before sitting down.

'Coffee?'

He heard the drone of the generator; the limited electricity they had went on light, not heating. Ronald regretted not bringing his poncho with him – it was cold. Steam rose from the mugs and disappeared into the gloomy recesses of the cell.

A scrape of the stool. Something.

'It's real, not instant, from the Beschermer's own personal supply.' The aroma of coffee beans was overpowering. 'Naturally, he makes you this gift with his blessing.' He pushed the mug across the table.

The nostrils of the prisoner's strong nose were twitching. He couldn't have smelt coffee for at least a year; that's how long the visitors had been living inside their walls. Ronald and his compatriots had descended on the monastery by hot air balloon eight years before and had met with very little resistance. Since then, there had been no visitors as such, only the travelling merchants who intermittently appeared to sell their wares – until the group of thirteen. No-one, not least the Beschermer, had believed their story as to how they'd happened here; one didn't just *pass by* this sector of the Altiplano.

'Go on. There's no catch. See ...' He changed the mugs in their position on the table and took the nearest one, tasting the coffee for himself.

'Cain brought of the fruit of the ground,' his eyes downcast, the prisoner spoke as he picked up the coffee, 'an offering.'

Ronald tried not to betray his pleasure or surprise on hearing these words. He didn't mind the innuendo to Cain; he'd been called a lot worse.

'Let me know if you want any sugar.' He attempted a lightness of voice, the natural tone you might use chatting to a friend at a café in Amsterdam. 'Do you take sugar?'

Silence.

'So if I'm to be Cain, does my offering make you Abel, the first martyr?' Ronald noticed a flicker of interest behind the prisoner's glasses. 'What *do* you believe in, Michael?' He dragged his wooden stool over the stone slabs, closer to the table. 'Tell me, do you believe in *anything*?'

The Beschermer had picked out this prisoner as the one least likely to resist. 'Put him in the cell, find out why they came here. And how they plan to escape. I've seen them writing notes to each other. They're planning something.' The prisoner had spoken at last. Ronald knew it was a good sign, it meant some trust had been established. Without it ...

'I believe ... I believe in Sofie.'

'Sofie?'

'And Kalugina and Cam and Kerridge and every one of them and I don't believe in any of you warped abductors or your way of life, if you can call it living.' The prisoner took a large mouthful of coffee as if afraid the mug would be removed after this outburst.

No flicker of emotion showed on Ronald's face. 'And this coffee, it's just a start.' He paused. 'Don't worry, I'm not going to take it away from you.' He noticed a relaxing in the prisoner's shoulders. 'For certain we know there's an escape planned and you are involved. All the Owslafa knows that. There's going to be punishments across the board. But I can make things better for you all.' Ronald knew the key was to avoid at all costs the you-don't-owe-your-friends-a-thing tone, although he personally knew it to be true. Ronald leant forward.

'We're all quite happy here,' said the prisoner. 'Why should we want to escape?'

'Yes, your friends are so busy playing games, the cricket and whatever, all so very *English*. I wonder, do they care about what happens to you?'

'Maybe, maybe not.'

'I think maybe they do, in which case the most important thing is we prevent this ridiculous escape gambit. They're almost certain to die in the attempt so we must stop this foolishness, keeping your name out of it of course. We have to work out the best way – maybe we keep you here for a few weeks after we've foiled the plan. They will never know and you'll have done everyone a favour, saved the lives of your friends as well as your own. Later, we can even introduce a regular morning coffee. I can provide you with a code name and we can develop a system for you and me to communicate. We have to work out how we can pull it all off but I can't do a damn thing until your current predicament is resolved. So come on, Michael, why don't you tell me, what's the plan?' Ronald leant backwards and opened his arms in the manner his local priest had used to welcome supplicants to communion. Outside, he saw the first light of dawn through the small window.

He waited.

'A tunnel,' said the prisoner in a flat and resigned voice, no vestige of defiance remaining. 'It's a tunnel.'

'When?'

'I don't know when.'

'You owe it to your friends, you have to protect them from themselves. I'm willing to work with you as long as it takes to get this whole thing sorted out.' In spite of the cold Ronald pulled up his sleeves to his elbows. 'When is the breakout?'

'I wasn't personally involved.'

'It's very important we get the whole truth, don't you think?'

Silence.

He could alert the guards. The risk would be that they could make arrests but they might never find the tunnel – the monastery covered a vast area. It would remain a constant itch. He must take his time. First, find the entrance, then, the arrests. 'Okay, where does it start, east or the west side? It probably makes sense to start on the west side, doesn't it?'

'I told you, I wasn't personally involved.' The prisoner had the same flat tone, his chin down in the feeble light, his spirit broken.

'Actually the investigation is going on at full speed, the Owslafa suspected a tunnel all along. My worry is that they're going to throw caution to the wind and your friends could get hurt. You have a chance to cut your friends some slack. I'm not making any promises but if we act now we can make a difference. So where is the tunnel?'

'I've already said too much.'

'Look, I'm not going to put you down as one of the ringleaders but you can just tell me who they were, then we don't have to punish the wrong people. And we can leave your name out of it altogether. Perhaps we've been too harsh on you all. For example, the Beschermer has been considering that the vow of silence should only be for ascetics, not for our ... guests. See, already you being here is making conditions easier for you and your friends. Why don't you tell me about the tunnel? Has is been difficult to dig, hard work I mean?'

'I really don't know so much about it.'

'But you were there.' Ronald raised his voice a fraction. 'Quit acting dumb, you were involved, weren't you, Michael? Tell what you know and we can smooth out a path that keeps everybody happy. Much better that we do it this way than bring you out and humiliate you in front of all the others. You wouldn't want that. I don't want it to come to that.'

'Okay, it's at the east entrance.'

'Go on.'

'It starts at the washrooms just beyond the watchtower.'

Roland pictured in his mind the place and saw straight away the shrewdness behind this choice; the visitors went in and out of the washrooms all day, often carrying bedding and sheets to be washed, under which they could hide all manner of implements and equipment that would be required for digging. And it was only thirty metres from the east perimeter wall, the perfect place to start and hide a tunnel operation. 'And when is the breakout? Is it soon?'

The prisoner nodded, defeated.

'How far have they got?'

'Close.' The prisoner was speaking in barely a whisper, his face in shadow. 'Any day now.'

Ronald Van Wijk felt elation – years of police interrogation experience hadn't failed him. Now he knew where and he knew when, with luck the Owslafa would catch the culprits red-handed digging the last few metres. He couldn't wait to announce his breakthrough to the Beschermer.

His thoughts of how that meeting would go were interrupted by shouts from the guards on the other side of the door. Over the commotion just one word rang out. He leaned his head in the direction of the door, and listened more carefully, to check he'd heard it right. There was no mistake. 'Escape!' echoed down the long stone passageway outside the cell and he heard barking; the dogs had been let out.

Ronald leapt to his feet and cast one look back at the prisoner before he banged on the door. 'Hey, guard, let me out.' He banged the door again. 'Guard, what's going on?' He had to wait for what seemed an age but was in fact only a minute, before the bolt was drawn back on the other side of the cell door.

A short while later Ronald was back in the cell. The prisoner hadn't changed position, still the Bible in his hand. The difference was in the eyes; they looked straight at him, direct and challenging.

'You and your *tunnel*.' They were not adequate words to describe the rage Ronald was experiencing. His hands were each clenched into fists. 'You were just wasting my time, weren't you? Just at the critical point. Very well planned, wasn't it, to make me look ridiculous? I could have been out there helping, preventing the escape even. Instead I was just wasting my time with you. That was the idea, wasn't it?' He was almost shouting at the prisoner. 'I'll make you pay for this. You'll see.'

He aimed a kick at the stool and sent it flying across the cell. 'Well don't think your friends can get far in that balloon. The heavy precipitation on the Altiplano means a risk of vertical wind sheer at a speed of fifty metres per second. Believe me, I know. Even if they are lucky enough to survive the hundreds of miles of high plateau, they've got thousands of miles of jungle. They're as good as dead already, another thing they have in common with you.'

'I told you what I believe in.' The prisoner spoke in a new confident voice, quite different from the broken tone of earlier.

'This means you'll be shot of course. You won't be the first.' Ronald, with an effort, was managing to get his voice sounding more normal. 'It's out of my hands now.'

'I thought the Owslafa had renounced guns?'

'Who said anything about guns?' Ronald walked to the open door that he hadn't bothered to shut. 'Guards, take him to the place of atonement and sound the bell.' Two guards walked into the room and stood each side of the prisoner. They hoisted him to his feet and started to walk towards the door.

'Hold it! Bring him back,' commanded Ronald. 'We're going to search him.' He ripped off the single white cassock but it was clear that the naked man underneath was hiding nothing. 'Put your cassock back on and pass me that Bible.' Ronald picked up the Bible, and turning it upside down, shook it – nothing. 'Keep it, you'll need it.' He handed back the Bible. 'Okay, get him out of my sight.' The prisoner left between the two guards, without a backward glance.

Standing alone in the empty cell Ronald went to the desk and pulled out the only drawer. A cheap exercise book, untouched, a pencil sharpener and an inch of sharpened pencil stub. Besides the two stools, the toilet bucket in the corner, two mugs, the bed sheet and a few armfuls of straw, the cell was bare. Ronald froze. Something was amiss.

He remembered bringing the pencil and notebook at the prisoner's request six weeks ago. That pencil had been new, unused. Where had it gone? What had it been used for? He checked the pages of the exercise book again more thoroughly; no cut pages, all clean.

He didn't have to really search the cell, just lift the sheet under which the prisoner slept. Apart from straw on the bare floor, nothing. There was nowhere to hide any writings.

What had he written with the pencil? The cell offered nothing, not a clue.

Nothing.

He slammed his fist on the table. From the courtyard he heard the melancholic tolling of the bell.

Glass and Water

Sofie snapped the laptop shut and out of habit checked her watch. One hour and twenty-six minutes until the rendezvous at the monastery. Collioure was almost deserted, just a boulangerie boy setting off on his rounds, two minutes later than yesterday. She wanted to get up and down from the mountain before the midday sun and calculated that, with her chosen combination of short tartan kilt, small light backpack and training shoes she would be able to cover the ground at a good pace. She knew that her light-reactive sunglasses and hair in plaits meant she had the appearance of a vicar's daughter but today that was the look she wanted. The Abbess, who had already received a donation to the monastery funds, was expecting them.

Sofie was determined to enjoy their last walk together. She set off up the mountain with the sun still to make its appearance. She selected Coldplay on her MP3 player: *Tigers Waiting to be Tamed*.

Alex was awoken by the sound of argument from below and then, thank God, a slammed door. For a further ten minutes he lay in the bed listening to the noise of seagulls but no waves. Having resolved to get up, he checked his wallet and was dismayed to see it was empty. Dimly he remembered two girls, Swedish. What were their names? He went to the kitchen, put the kettle on and checked the fridge for milk. Didn't one rhyme with boot?

Sitting down with his black tea he looked around the floor of the apartment – not many clues as to what had happened the night before. But his tried and tested ruse, the casting director stunt – 'Chance of a walk-on part, no Equity card required' – had seemingly worked. He saw a matchbox on the table that hadn't been there before, empty.

But no extra guest or guests for breakfast this morning. More was the pity. In some ways he didn't blame the girls; this place didn't have much of a view. A better apartment with direct access to the beach would have made more sense and it wasn't like his dad couldn't afford it. But for now he needed a solution to the more pressing problem of cashflow. Was it time to pull the lost wallet scam? He tested with his finger a dried croissant that was probably two days old and considered whether he was hungry enough to eat it.

Without Mum to slow her down Sofie had made faster progress on the descent than she expected. She had a booking for *La Clocher*, a corner table that moved into shadow at one o'clock and afforded one of her favourite views over the Mediterranean.

On the quay stood a young man, a few years older than her, late twenties perhaps, strumming a classical guitar. It sounded like Vivaldi and she stopped to listen. 'Bravo!' she politely applauded when he finished.

Only then did he seem to notice her, and smiled as if surprised someone would stop to listen. She felt sorry for him; she was the only audience and she knew what that felt like. But his response caught her unawares.

'Here, you have these coins,' he said, picking up his cap from the ground. 'I play for appreciation, not money.' He proffered it. 'Take it, you deserve it. Get lunch.'

Sofie stared straight back. She didn't know how to reply. She saw in an instant that there were seven euros sixty. So possibly a nice glass of Chablis, but not lunch. It seemed churlish to point it out. She replied, 'Well how lovely. How about we have a glass of wine together? I'm Sofie by the way.'

'Super idea! How do you do. I'm Drage, Alex Drage.' He held out his hand and Sofie wasn't surprised to feel the soft skin of his fingers. Clearly, he hadn't been practising much recently.

Alex struck a course for the smarter side of town with the comment; 'Second thought. How about we have lunch together and I'm paying?'

They set off and she had a chance to study her companion. He was striking looking with lovely skin and long luxuriant hair – she liked that, and his laugh.

They meandered past a few restaurants before stopping at *Le Clocher*, where on recognising her, the waiter took them five minutes ahead of her original booking to her corner table.

'It's too sunny here. That waiter has given us this table just because we're tourists. Would you prefer to move to the shade?'

'Let's see. The view here is spectacular, isn't it?' said Sofie, who had her back to the sea over which Alex was gazing.

'Isn't it just?' said Alex. 'So what do you do?'

'Do? All sorts of things. I spend a lot of time working in libraries and I also like to play the cello.' She wasn't going to boast that she had been offered an exhibition to study at the Juilliard School; anyway she hadn't decided herself whether to take it yet.

'So you're some sort of librarian?'

The libraries she spent most time in were found in the Deepnet which at 91,000 terabytes was about 500 times more data than what most people called the internet. Still, she liked his company and it was after all thirty-seven days since she had last kissed a man. 'Yes, you could say that.' She smiled.

The waiter hovered into view. 'Better leave this to me,' said Alex. 'French is pretty much my second language. '*Je vouloir manger la poison puis le crabe avec bonne vin.*' He spoke confidently with pronunciation that was more Shepherd's Bush than Montmartre. Then added for Sofie's benefit, 'The lobster in Collioure is usually very good at this time of year.'

The waiter was speechless for a moment. '*Je suis désolé, mais je ne comprends pas.*' He turned to Sofie for help.

Sofie leaned forward: '*Mon ami essayait de vous dire qu'il souhaiterait des crevettes en entrée puis du homard en plat principal.*' She returned the menu. '*Quel vin pouvez vous nous recommander?*'

The waiter was happy to recommend a Sancerre blanc to go with their lobster. Alex was complimentary about her French, explaining that his own always took a few weeks to brush up. 'You should hear me at the end of season,' he joked.

'Well, I can't take any credit,' said Sofie. 'Something good to be said for family holidays any—'

'I don't believe it,' said Alex feeling one jacket pocket after another. 'I must have left my wallet in the apartment.' He looked at her wide-eyed with disbelief. 'I can see it now, on the table by the door. Oh dear, you'd better call that waiter back and cancel our order. I'm sorry. What an idiot I am.'

Sofie remembered from the guitar playing that he was left-handed and now his eyes went up to her right as he spoke. 'Do they know you here?' she asked. 'Have you visited this restaurant before?'

'Bit out of my league I'm afraid,' said Alex. 'To tell you the truth I'm not exactly in the habit of inviting out every attractive woman I bump into.' He added shyly: 'In fact I can't remember the last time I did.'

Sofie recalled the menu page from memory. I was only budgeting for one, she thought, and did some quick mental arithmetic. She didn't like to use credit cards at random but she knew that with the extra seven euros sixty she could pay for the lobster and wine and one coffee each, but no desert. 'Tell you what. You were very generous earlier. I can just stretch to lunch.' She lent down to pick up her laptop. 'And you can always pay me back this afternoon, when you find your wallet.'

'Oh that's great.' Alex sounded relieved. 'What a nice treat,' he said and grinned widely.

The wine arrived.

'I must send one email if you'll excuse me.' It took twenty seconds to bypass *Le Clocher*'s encrypted security. She found that Dormouse was online. She typed: *Quick favour required.*

As her request raced around the world to wherever Dormouse's nest was, Sofie settled back. She enjoyed life stories and felt sure that Alex had the imagination to tell a good one. A few glasses of wine later he had not disappointed her and was now waxing lyrical about his acting career. If Sofie had understood it correctly, Alex, for the life of him, couldn't see what was wrong with the idea of *Drake & Son Investigate*: 'All my friends agree it would be something fresh for IDI—'

'Sorry, IDI?'

'*Inspector Drake Investigates* ... a win-win for both Dad and me.'

'It certainly sounds different.' Now that Alex had mentioned his father, she could clearly see the family resemblance. She guessed that Alex must be about thirty years younger than his dad. 'So you've already been in the series?'

'Naturally. I know just about everybody: writers, producers, you name it.'

'We often watch Drake at home, my mum was a fan. But I can't remember your episode. Remind me.'

'Oh. They've not been such big parts ... yet,' he replied sounding bashful. 'But I've talked too much. So you play the cello, nice instrument but a bit tricky to take backpacking.'

They would soon be at the point where they had to make a decision as to whether to order a second bottle; judging by the speed at which Alex emptied his last glass, she guessed he already had. 'Yes, my mum loved music. In fact she heard du Pré playing in Collioure when she was a student, they were the same generation.'

'Du Pré?'

'She's dead now. Another thing she has in common with my mum.'

'I'm sorry, I thought earlier you said you were with your mum this morning?'

'Yes I did, didn't I?' For a minute Sofie pictured the urn holding her mum's ashes which she had carried up the mountain to the monastery, before leaving it on a ledge overlooking the valley. She decided to leave the memory undisturbed for the moment, waiting for the right occasion, like a newly bought dress hanging in the wardrobe. 'Sorry, I meant to say I was thinking of my mum walking up the mountain. We went all over but this was her favourite place.'

'Family holidays, that sounds idyllic. I've got more stepmothers than Snow White.'

'My mum had this idea that in a successful relationship one was defining and the other adjusting. She was the adjusting one. You could say like ... glass and water.'

'Good idea,' said Alex. 'How about we order another bottle of wine while we're at it?'

Another bottle would take them exactly thirteen euros over her cash reserves. 'Let me just check my mail.' She sometimes worried about Dormouse, a hacker who hankered after anything military. She read: *Balls-to-the-walls job. Alex Drage, 2 CCxx transactions at Le Clocher in the last 3 mos. Gd tip to check CCTV DB's. 5 sightings in last 3 mos. FTA. D.* Dormouse had surpassed him or herself. There was a JPEG file attachment: a photo of a clearly recognisable Alex leaving the restaurant with a young girl on his left arm, cigarette in the right hand, dated last week. Sofie quickly typed a reply: *That helps. Time to hit the silk* – Dormouse would appreciate some paratrooper slang.

As she suspected, his eyes signalling right betrayed him like lipstick in the wrong place. Alex had been lying through his teeth. 'I tell you what, how about we get some champagne,' she said checking the time before snapping her laptop shut for the third time that day. 'And the chocolate mousse here looks great, it's a special day after all.'

'You surprise me.'

'Oh why's that?'

'I thought the trend these days was for high-powered android smart phones? In fact,' announced Alex, 'I'm thinking of getting one myself.'

Sofie's own smart phone was in her back pocket. She needed the laptop for its multiple windows, special coding characters and heavy graphic programs. 'Yes, maybe I should look into that too.'

'But chocolate mousse – a girl after my own heart. Leave it to me,' said Alex. 'If you're sure you can afford it?'

'I'm sure we'll manage one way or another.' Alex summoned the waiter as Sofie went off to find the ladies.

With a champagne glass in her hand, Sofie, for the next twenty minutes or so, for once turned off her body clock and recounted some of her own life history, savouring the excellent Moet & Chandon.

'What you need is a little bit of excitement.' Alex didn't seem to have been listening but now his knee was touching hers under the table. 'And then a relaxing afternoon. I've got something lined up.'

'What I need is water, not glass.'

'Fine, we can get some bottled water on the way to the film set. Oh damn, there, I've blown my surprise. We're filming *Drake Investigates* in the next town. We could just drop in and I could show you round, meet a few people or—' He took the opportunity to gaze at her directly for extra emphasis, 'or we could just go straight to my apartment. It's overlooking the ocean and I've got some great gear.'

'That sounds heavenly.' Sofie tried to sound like she meant it. She knew what she needed. 'Let me just freshen up first.'

'Sure. We've got all day.' With a goodbye glance in his direction, Sofie stood up. She had already checked the grate over the window in the ladies' toilet. It would be off in a jiffy, even without a Swiss army knife. She'd be in Vienna by nightfall.

Alex returned her smile. 'Don't be long.'

As her mother would have said, 'If Olympic medals were awarded for gigolos, it looked like Alex was already hearing the national anthem.'

Chisgo

From the kitchen Chaz watched the clouds banked up like battleships in a blockade, sending down wave upon wave of rain in an unremitting attack on the walls and windows of the house.

The news was on CNN. Jodie said they were now an international family. The announcer was reporting a missing flight presumed lost over the Andes, mainly British passengers. The plane was out of Laz Paz in Bolivia on the way to Rio, a small two-engined job. They'd flown in many similar.

'Is that a Colombia story?' Jodie shouted from the hallway. He turned the TV off as she came into the kitchen.

'Nothing interesting. Small plane crash, all goners. Some piano player.'

'Omigod!' Jodie breathed in sharply and pulled up her hand to cover her mouth. 'I've always hated those little planes. Anyone we know?'

'Chill, baby, he was a classical virtuoso, Quintell or something, never heard of 'im. Poor bugger. What time are you back from your dancing?'

'Honey, it's *salsa* not dancing. This is Guadalupe's heritage.' Jodie was now checking the contents of her handbag. Almost as if the previous minute had never happened, thought Chaz.

'You should see the ways her limbs move. I swear to God she's not joined together like the rest of us.' She glanced at the large modern clock in the shape of a heart on the wall. 'Is that the time?' She picked up her bag, shouting up the stairs: 'Guadalupe, we'll be late. Time to go.'

Chaz stood by the window as the land-cruiser left the gravelled drive that looked like a river bed run dry with pools of standing water dotted about. A high brick wall enclosed the large lawn which was scattered with detritus from the storm. It was time to get the gardening company in. They lived in a village for security, but didn't know the neighbours and he didn't know what beer they served in the local pub, all of which suited him fine. When they went out they preferred the anonymity of the city. Jodie and Guadalupe were driving to Guildford.

It was his habit to watch the large electronic gates swing shut behind the departing car. Check complete, Chaz wandered down the long parqueted corridor leading to his study and went over to his antique desk. He took the key from its hiding place and unlocked the second drawer on the left. A pile of thin enveloped airmail letters, neatly stacked. Always the same handwriting and the same, just discernible postmark: Bogota, Colombia. The most recent had arrived a week ago. Two or three every year, even after they had moved twice. Last week's had the familiar threats and demands. Each time he did nothing. The last three letters he had managed to intercept without Jodie noticing; another secret between them.

He sat down in his favourite red Chesterfield leather armchair and poured himself a generous measure of J & B whisky. It was too early in the day but seeing the letters brought it all back. His thoughts returned to Esteban and Guadalupe, the sticky streets with their hint of excitement and threat of violence in the sultry heat.

Seven years earlier

'Guadalupe,' murmured a boy. 'Guadalupe—' He was about ten years old, with jet black hair falling down to his Brazil nut-coloured shoulders.

A nun sitting reading in the corner of the room marked her page and came over to the side of the bed. She quickly felt the boy's pulse, then went to the door, her shoes clacking on the sanatorium's stone-flagged floor and called out: 'Guadalupe, come back. Your brother has woken up.'

There was the sound of light footsteps in the corridor before a slender girl, maybe three years older than the boy, came quickly into the room. She moved lightly and effortlessly as a butterfly and settled on the chair next to the old wrought-iron bed. She put her hand on her brother's arm.

'The worst of the fever has passed,' said the nun.

The boy opened his eyes. 'Guadalupe. Can we go to the observatorio tomorrow? Can we?'

'Of course we can, Esteban. It's a promise.'

'Beware the Chisgo,' said Esteban. He closed his eyes. 'Promise?' already sounding asleep.

'I promise,' said Guadalupe tenderly. She placed a hand on his leg.

The nun waited a few moments then said, 'Come on, darling. We'll let him sleep.'

The girl nodded but seemed reluctant to leave the side of the bed. 'He'll be okay, won't he? Will he be okay tomorrow?'

'He can stay here tonight, a good night's sleep is all he needs. It's only summer flu. He'll be a new boy in the morning. You'll see. Who's Chisgo?' The nun ran her hand through the girl's long shining hair as she spoke. 'He's called that name out before. Is that someone in your family?'

'We don't have any family, just each other. I don't know any Chisgo.'

'Remember, Guadalupe, you'll always have the Sisters of Mercy, we are your family. Now get along, the other children will be thinking I have favourites.'

'Everything will be all right, will it?'

'Put your trust in the Lord. Miracles are possible, especially at the orphanage of Forrmando Vidas.'

The chameleon, *enyalioides cofanorum*, was almost fully grown, about ten centimetres in length. Its natural habitat was the upper Amazon basin but it had hitched a nine hundred and twenty-eight kilometre ride on the baggage of some Dutch botanists who had celebrated their return to civilisation with a night at a five-star hotel. Now it was into its third full month on the inside of the Superior Hotel in Bogota. The environment seemed safe but it was cold, an alien world. Pale cream like the wall, it darted in tentative spurts, stereoscopic eyes alert for the presence of danger. Reassured, it moved again and was soon lost in the shadow of the high ceiling above the revolving door.

Chaz, relaxed in a sumptuous white leather armchair in the lobby, admired the skills of the lizard that effortlessly remained unnoticed in a hostile environment.

'We could be waiting all day for Adrian and I ordered tea thirty minutes back,' complained Jodie. 'It's like the Third World.'

Chaz smiled at Jodie, sitting opposite. He liked touring and without the publicity that came with it, Jodie's albums would never sell. He and Jodie's agent Adrian knew that was never truer than today. On *Heart*, Jodie's latest album, her voice had definitely lost whatever youthful bloom it may once have had. The publicity tour, although exhausting, was already boosting record sales. Jodie still believed it was her singing that made the difference. 'Hey come on, Chaz knows best. They love you here, baby.' He stroked her cheek. ' And anyway Colombia *is* the Third World. Just think where we'd be if we hadn't come by this city—'

'I know. I know. I'm just nervous,' she said biting a fingernail. 'We're so close, this time. And we're like prisoners in this hotel.'

'Bogota is no different really than any other place.' Chaz used his just-another-day-at-the-office tone to placate his wife. Over her shoulder he saw the hotel manager talking with someone in uniform. Hotel porters guarding against unlicensed taxi drivers and hookers were a familiar sight but here the enemy was kidnappers and the porters carried Colt pistols. He savoured the unreal atmosphere of the place.

'I'm sorry, honey. It's just this whole situation, it's so ... so stressing. Has Adrian rung?'

'Yep, finally and he's on his way.'

'Whatever that means,' tutted Jodie.

'He says the orphanage is expecting us – so we'll go as soon as he gets here. And the press conference is set for the day after tomorrow.'

'Remember we promised them a trip to the observatory thingy.'

'We still have to make things kosher with the Mother Superior,' said Chaz. 'The trip can wait.' He noticed that the hotel manager was leading the guy in uniform over to some guests on the other side of the lobby.

'I don't know why we even need a press conference. We're doing this from the heart,' said Jodie. 'I mean for Guadalupe, not for the publicity.'

'Sure. But whilst you've got a TV camera trained on you, you may as well mention *Heart*. We could even pay the orphanage some royalties.'

'Someone else after my money.'

'I don't need tea. I need a real fucking drink!' Chaz was starting to regret wearing a long-sleeved shirt. The hotel was air-conditioned but he felt the sweat, damp under his arms. That was the trouble being the manager of a rock-star, you couldn't dress down. The t-shirt said *I need a manager* so where did that leave him? In a smart shirt and safari suit, he thought glumly. He put on his sunglasses and wondered where in Christ's sake Adrian was – his job was here but he was always disappearing somewhere. 'Do you know, I think this might be Adrian's last trip.'

'Why?' Jodie sounded surprised. 'I thought he liked the job?'

'I think he's stealing from the expense account. He's been behaving oddly recently.'

'Maybe he resents us starting a family.'

'And the way *Heart* is selling we won't necessarily need another album.'

'Or an agent—'

'Exactly.'

'And take those sunglasses off,' said Jodie. 'They make you look like a gangster.'

Comments like that reminded him of the unspoken balance of power between them. After twenty years of marriage she was still A-list and he the hired help. 'Excuse me, sir.' The hotel manager and his guest had arrived.

Chaz stood up and decided to remove his sunglasses. 'How can I help?'

'Sir, I'm extremely sorry to interrupt, but the captain from the National Gendarmerie—' The manager sounded apologetic and was already backing away, 'he has some routine questions for you.'

For a moment Chaz was perplexed. Where was the mandatory sub-machine gun that policemen in Colombia draped around their neck? But looking closer he saw the pistol.

The policeman showed him an ID badge: Captain Barraquer. 'Could I have a look at your passport please?' asked the policeman, stepping forward. So that's why managers had jackets, thought Chaz – pockets. He obliged.

'Have you seen this girl?' He passed a photograph for Chaz to study. No pleasantries, softening up the suspect. This policeman got straight to the point. The captain was skinny and looked more like a runner than a detective. He was young, maybe thirty-five, with a serious air and the most amazing white teeth. For a minute Chaz felt as if he was guest starring in a Hollywood movie. The policeman's eyes flicked across Chaz's face, scanning for any sign of something out of the normal.

Chaz was looking at the picture of a pretty girl aged about eighteen with brown eyes, a wide smile and flashing white teeth. A feeling of *déjà vu*. 'Why do you ask? Who is she? What's happened?'

'If you could just answer the question.'

Chaz, already feeling uncomfortable, detected some absence of respect as the officer spoke. 'No, I haven't seen that face before. Well, I could have but there were hundreds of girls looking just like her at the concert. Right, Jodie?' He passed over the photograph.

Jodie studied it carefully. 'Do you want us to keep an eye out for her?' she asked. 'Could she be a friend of Guadalupe's?'

'Why should she be?' said Chaz. 'There's about six million people living in this city.'

'Keep your hair on, I was only asking.' Chaz had a flashback to hot summer days receiving punishment in the headmaster's study at the exclusive boarding school his parents had found. With each swish of the cane he had never flinched a muscle or uttered a sound, in complete control.

'No one will be seeing this girl anymore,' said the policeman. He really sounded sorry, thought Chaz, like it was one of his own family. 'We have a witness linking this girl to a guest from this hotel.'

'Did you get his description of the man?' asked Chaz, quietly but quickly. Too quickly he realised and cursed himself – at this rate he would soon be a suspect.

The policeman took his time before replying: 'We did as a matter of fact; European ... *male*, fair-skin and *tall*.' Suddenly, Chaz felt like sitting down. The policeman continued: 'It's the summer season, there are plenty of Europeans around, but why would you be interested?'

'After a while you get to know everybody in a place like this,' said Chaz, 'even the wildlife.'

The policeman's eyes followed Chaz's to the space of wall where the lizard had been. 'What was that?' But the wall was empty. Chaz shook his head but the policeman was already pursuing a fresh line of enquiry. 'Guadalupe. Who is this Guadalupe?'

Chaz was happy to explain how at a recent concert Jodie had asked for a volunteer from the audience to join her in a duet. Guadalupe, a thirteen-year-old girl, had been pushed up by her friends at the orphanage onto the stage. Within seconds it was apparent she could 'sing like an angel'. The girl had formed an immediate bond with Jodie, who had been excited to learn that the girl was an orphan and available for adoption.

'So your band is adopting a thirteen-year-old singer?'

'No, it's not like that at all. Anyway, we're adopting her brother Esteban as well,' said Jodie. 'It's not like it would be a spur of the moment thing—'

'Give me a call if you plan to leave the city.' The policeman returned the passport to Chaz and added a business card. He took a hard stare at Chaz's face before abruptly turning his back on them.

'Bastard,' said Jodie when the policeman was out of earshot. 'He treated us like criminals.'

'Relax. He's only doing his job.'

'Look what the cat's brought in.'

Adrian flopped down into the chair beside them. 'What was that all about?' He was tall and lanky and his ankles stuck out a long way from the ends of his jeans. Adrian was nervously scratching at the back of his neck which Chaz recognised as a sign that he was worried about something. 'Sorry I'm late by the way,' he added. 'Complications at the orphanage—'

'What do you mean, complications?' Jodie spoke so loudly that others in the hotel lobby turned around to stare. 'What complications?'

'Nothing we can't handle,' said Adrian.

'Thank God for that,' said Chaz. Jodie was ready to kick off at the slightest provocation. He knew the signs.

'Mr Adrian.' The hotel manager had returned. 'I'm sorry about that uhm ... intrusion. It's just they found a girl. Strangled and well, sorry, that's all—'

'Yeah,' said Chaz. 'Barraquer, the policeman told us.'

'Strangled?' exclaimed Jodie. 'But he didn't say anything about strangled. Ugh. What a place.'

'They think she may have been to the hotel. But you see so many girls.' The manager looked to his men guarding the door and raised both hands in the air. 'This is Bogota after all. Your escort for the orphanage is here. I can vouch for the driver. He is a good man. And we agreed thirty dollars. Don't pay any more.' He stared up at the wall and frowned.

'Well, good timing – a minute earlier you'd have been interrogated by the police. Wouldn't he, Chaz?'

Chaz had also noticed the lizard was back.

'I said, "Wouldn't he, Chaz?"'

'Oh that. Just routine,' Chaz said. 'You've got nothing to hide, have you, Adrian?

'Me? 'Course not,' said Adrian, scratching his neck and shaking his head.

'And the window in my room doesn't open,' said Jodie to the manager. 'Can you get it fixed?'

They were starting to walk out of the hotel lobby. The manager explained that repairs to the windows had been interrupted because the portable crane rented for the job had been kidnapped en route three months previously. They were still waiting for the ransom request. 'So, Miss Jodie, in Bogota a crane is kidnapped for ransom, so what price for a famous music star?'

'Why don't you just rent another crane?'

'Miss Jodie, this was already the second crane,' replied the manager. 'Have a good trip.'

They emerged from the hotel to the glare of the afternoon sun. Chaz saw the posse of policeman, dressed in army fatigues, two-up on enduro motorbikes, and the pillion rider carrying the sub-machine gun. He counted three bikes – one more than this morning.

The hotel manager opened the door to their limousine; bullet-proof (they'd been told last time) and windows blacked out.

'I can't wait to leave this place.' Jodie fell into the limousine's reclining seat. 'It makes Warsaw feel like a picnic.'

There was a roar of bikes revving up; sun-glassed and tooled up, the cavalcade prepared to roll off. 'Won't be long now, babe. Just formalities to get through. Right, Adrian?'

'Walk in the park. That's what you pay me for.'

Chaz stole a glance at his wife before looking out of the window at the now familiar Sunset Street sliding past. Palm trees lined the road and the streets were busy in daytime. The limo stopped at the lights opposite a run-down looking night club; in flaking red paint a large lizard was spread across a tired yellow wall.

'Mine was closer.'

'You fibber, mine was.'

'If yours was, it was because you cheated.'

'Didn't!'

'Did!'

'On the life of the Virgin of Copacabana—'

'Guadalupe?'

'Yes, Esteban.'

'Are the taps in England really made of gold?'

The two children were sitting on the wall of the ornamental fountain at the front of the Forrmando Vidas orphanage. They had their shoes off and were throwing small pebbles at the statue that stood in the middle of the fountain.

'You must remember to speak English to them. It is due to the gift of the lady who appeared at the orphanage that we have learnt English. Last time you were speaking too much Spanish.'

'I accidentally forgot.'

'This time you must try harder *not* to accidentally forget with Jodie, and especially Chaz.'

'Chisgo.'

'Chisgo. What is that Chisgo thing?'

Esteban had a book, *Legends of Colombia*, on his lap and opened it to show a page to his sister: 'Look, Chisgo.' The picture was of a creature, half-man, half-beast, emerging from the jungle with straight, straw-like hair and large blue eyes with hooded eyelids.

'Put that book away.' She looked at the young boy and shook him by the shoulders. 'Lots of Europeans look like that and it doesn't make him evil.'

'Beware the Chisgo—'

Don't you forget Esteban, that this is a chance of a lifetime for us. And I told you, Jodie says they have gold taps in the bathrooms.'

'Does the water taste better?'

'Remember, if it wasn't for me you wouldn't even get this chance.'

'But you wouldn't go to England without me?'

'Niño loco! I'm your big sister. I'd do anything for you.'

'Even a trip to the observatorio?'

'Promise.'

'Cross your heart and hope to die?'

'Before our Lady of Guadalupe.'

They spat on their palms and shook hands just as the cavalcade of motorbikes and black limousine approached down the track to the orphanage, with a cloud of dust billowing behind them. Out from the limousine stepped the three Europeans.

Jodie hurried over towards the fountain. 'My dear children,' she exclaimed. Chaz, walking next to Adrian, felt slightly embarrassed; seeing his wife approaching the children with her arms outstretched reminded him of Julie Andrews in *The Sound of Music*.

The Mother Superior, flanked by a nun on either side, came out of the door under a stone arch.

Adrian stopped to read to the others an inscription over the door: *Providing hope and future for little children through Christ.* He added, sotto voce, to Chaz: 'Place feels more like a monastery than an orphanage.'

Before Chaz had a chance to reply the Mother Superior was inviting them to follow her. They all trooped inside, shoes resonating on stone floor. A crowd of barefooted children followed behind.

In his office at the Estación de Policía, Antanas Pombo, the assistant chief of Sumapas Paramo District, was inspecting two different-sized cigars in his hands when there was a knock on the door. He could see through the glass window who it was and sighed, leaving his brown leather boots on the table. His left boot barely concealed a Walther PPK and more conventionally holstered on his waist was a .38 Colt Detective Special. 'El Capitán, entrar!' He motioned to Barraquer to step in but didn't offer him a seat. 'What is it? I've got a meeting of the assistant chiefs to get to.'

'The Hotel Superior case. The young girl, strangled.'

'Isn't that the hotel with the kidnapped crane?'

'Chief, we've got some new leads, I mean for the girl. I'd like to do some DNA.'

'Barraquer, you've saying this business requires a certain amount of finesse?' He finally decided on the shorter cigar. 'I don't have the budget for that. For the virgin's sake, she was an orphan, wasn't she? I mean, who cares?'

'But that's it, Chief, don't you see? The killer will think we won't really follow it up.' The young captain took a step closer. 'He'll have left clues. You know me, I always get my man. With a DNA test—'

'Captain, if all butterflies were guarding Jade, I'd already be retired. Do you know how much it would cost if we did DNA for every case? One thousand, six hundred and thirty-four murders last year, that's three hundred and forty-three in our district, about one a day ... it's impossible, we both know it.' He struck the match on the side of the desk. 'You've got to stop behaving like John Wayne in an old western. Welcome to Bogota, the real world.' He paused and lit his cigar. 'So what was the clue?'

'One of the hotel residents swore that he saw the girl getting into a rental sports car with a European.'

'Sex tourists are scum.'

'And the English singer Jodie Jones is staying at the hotel. Found out that they are planning on adopting some kids from the same orphanage; you know, the old monastery. Maybe coincidence, maybe not.'

The chief nodded and reflected for a minute. 'Okay. Forty-eight hours. That's all I give you and then you're going liaison with narcotics. That's the high-profile stuff. But I'm going to be late for my meeting. Keep me posted.' When Barraquer left the room the police chief stood up to shut the door and returned to his desk. He picked up the phone.

The Mother Superior showed them into her office at the end of the corridor and Chaz noticed mahogany chairs and to his surprise, a brushed aluminium-style laptop on the polished table. He now vaguely remembered Adrian saying something about the orphanage having an internet site.

'Shall I be mother?' suggested their hostess.

'I could call you Mum if you like,' said Chaz. 'Your English is very good.'

'Mother Superior will do just nicely,' she replied with no hint of a smile.

Chaz looked to Adrian for help.

'So we've got all the documents and the passport applications are being fast-tracked,' said Adrian. 'Do we have the guardian for the signatures of release?'

'Esteban,' said the Mother Superior quietly, 'would you please stop banging your feet on the chair and show me what book it is you're reading?'

Esteban looked reluctant to show his book, but Chaz was able to make out *Legends of Colombia* superimposed on a picture of green jungle.

Jodie was leaning towards the boy: 'Do tell me, what's the story about?' Chaz saw Jodie was really interested in them both – the boy as well as the girl.

The boy looked up at Jodie wide-eyed and spoke slowly: 'Es una historia de la selva—'

'English!' commanded Guadalupe.

'The bad man is sleeps in the forest when the day and when the night comes to find the girls ... for to kill!' At this point the boy opened the book straight at a page which showed a picture of a yellow-haired monster, recognisably human, coming out of the jungle brandishing a knife.

What sort of bedtime reading was this? Chaz was now intrigued.

'Ah, the Chisgo, a long time since I've seen him. I remember my own mother warning me about him,' said the Mother Superior. 'A scary creature, but only after dark.'

'My mother used to read me *Peter Pan*,' said Jodie. 'Maybe we'll leave the violence behind.'

'I'm afraid it's not quite as simple as that, Mrs Jones. You see this is part of his cultural heritage. Maybe after all, it would be easier for all concerned if you were to adopt someone from your own country.'

Silence. Nothing escaped the children thought Chaz; was that Esteban smiling?

'And Guadalupe, I believe I heard you singing along to the radio this morning? We all love your singing at the Christmas concert.' Now Jodie looked to Chaz, worried. It was only May. The inference hung heavy in the air like incense. 'Dolcis. I believe you have prepared an estimate of expenses for the prospective adoptive parents.'

The nun who had hitherto stood as still as a statue behind her boss produced a leaf of foolscap paper from a folder and handed it to Chaz. 'Signor.'

Chaz welcomed not having to talk. The first time he read *one hundred and twenty thousand dollars* he thought it must be a mistake. A couple of weeks ago when he had spoken with the adoption expert she had advised him to budget for around five thousand dollars per child. He handed the page to Adrian, pointing out the numbers.

Adrian raised his eyebrows. 'The amounts here, Mother Superior, aren't they rather on the high side?'

'Make a tree good and its fruit will be good.' The Mother Superior clasped the wooden cross that hung around her neck. 'Your contribution to the orphanage could be a very positive message for the TV and newspapers.'

So that was it, thought Chaz, she had found out about the press conference. She had them over a barrel. At least he didn't have to write the cheque. He stood up. 'Adrian, write the cheque.'

Jodie had eyes only for the children. Chaz wondered what sort of impact they would have on his freedom. He had a sudden desire to be alone and without a further word left the room and followed the corridor into the courtyard, dry and dusty in the Colombian sun, where he put on his sunglasses.

The chameleon was starting to feel restless in the hotel; the glare from the modern halogen lights was increasing its activity and desire for social behaviour. With one eye it noticed a large spider but it swayed on the wall only slightly. It had already eaten that morning. With its other eye it spied the hotel manager pointing in its direction and gesticulating to some hotel porters. Vaguely the chameleon remembered times in the forest and wondered if it was a safer place to be.

Adrian told himself there was nothing to fear walking down Sunset Street towards Night of the Iguana. He tried to look nonchalant as he had to pass the car guards sitting with machetes on their laps spaced at twenty metre intervals down the street. He knew that as a foreigner on foot he stood out. People watched him, he supposed, with a mixture of envy and curiosity in equal measure. He was reassured by the sight of the police, two astride the obligatory enduro motor-bike, on just about every corner. Emboldened by his smooth progress he recalled his previous visits to the nightclub. It was a place where hot chicks shimmied up to unsuspecting guests like lizards up a storm pipe. Adrian quickened his step.

Once inside he was immediately disappointed. Except for a solitary dancer with hardly anything on, who moved rhythmically to a Latin-American beat, the place looked strangely quiet. He looked around but all he saw were a few sad-looking punters at the small circular tables with empty champagne buckets. There was no sign of the girl he'd met the previous night. She had hinted to him that next time he could expect more than a kiss. Adrian suspected that money might be involved and tonight he had a fold of American dollars a centimetre thick in his money clip. That was the only good thing working for Jodie and Chaz, neither of them had a clue about money. The kiss from the night before he still remembered, like a roller-coaster ride on coke.

At the bar he ordered a large whisky and remembered with satisfaction the meeting with the Mother Superior. Afterwards, he had feigned disgust with Chaz at the price hike but inside a small voice was cheering. Making arrangements earlier he had hinted to the Mother Superior that she would actually be doing Chaz and Jodie a favour by inflating the price.

The trouble with Jodie and Chaz, he reflected, watching the ice cubes melt in his glass, was that they didn't live in the real world. Any problems and the answer was simple; write a cheque, or better still, get Adrian to do it. The only thing they couldn't buy was a family – until now. They certainly felt they could buy *him*.

But he enjoyed his self-appointed secret mission to rock the boat and they had no idea about the extent of troubles 'good old Adrian' created for them. Colombia had been his idea, inspired thinking. He relished watching the two of them slowly crack up under the heat and pressure of this whole adoption business. They paid the ferryman but he was the puppet master. He wasn't finished yet.

'Mr Adrian, hello. ...' He felt long fingernails running up the front of his trouser leg and warm breath in his ear. He knew she wouldn't forget him. Goose pimples raced up his legs and arms.

He bought her a cocktail and himself another large whisky. She offered him a hand-rolled cigarette that had a distinctive aroma. After some very promising kisses and a few drinks they got down to discussing business. She was good to go and for a modest fee a partner could be recruited. But first security had to be arranged and money paid up front. For two such angels of the night Adrian had no hesitation in lightening his money clip by two hundred dollars.

An hour later, his head was buzzing and felt thick. Dimly, he realised it was a scam. The girl wasn't coming back. He stumbled out into the warm tropical night. Sunset Street was quiet, strangely deserted and dimly lit, like an accidental photograph. This was a new side of the city. He saw the group of youths walking up the street carrying what looked like bamboo poles; not gardening implements, surely? He could always go back to the club and call for a taxi. Why didn't he think of that earlier? It was difficult to judge in this light but the poles were starting to look more and more like baseball bats. He tried to remember whether Colombia had a baseball series. Was it possible that they were going to a practice?

He was just thinking that maybe after all it would be wise to break into a gentle jog when he heard the disgruntled roar of a revving motorbike. A headlight lit up the red-painted lizard behind him and in seconds the enduro had mounted the pavement alongside him.

'Jump!'

Adrian recognised the captain from the hotel and grabbed hold of the dark blue jacket.

They sped off down Sunset Street. In just a matter of minutes they were back at the hotel. 'Thank you, Captain, you ... I don't know what would have happened—'

'After midnight the police go home and we hand over the streets until morning. Lucky I was looking out for you.' The policeman was taking off his gloves. Adrian noticed he had amazing white teeth. 'There were a few questions I wanted to ask.'

'Anything. Sure. Go ahead.' For once, Adrian didn't feel like a drink.

'First the hire car.' The policeman took out a notebook. 'It's a white Mercedes coupé, isn't it?'

*

Over breakfast Jodie was already outlining some plans for an album she and Guadalupe could record together. Chaz was looking around the hotel dining room for any sign of the lizard.

'It's amazing how she can just pick up a tune. Like me she's never had a singing lesson in her life. She's a natural. What do you think?'

Yesterday afternoon Jodie and Guadalupe had been singing duets at the orphanage. Chaz kept quiet on the ridiculous idea. When the reality-check came he would have someone else deliver the message to Jodie. 'Remember, in the press conference tomorrow the key thing is that we talk about what is good for the children, not for us.'

'What would I do without you?' she said. 'Yes we should emphasise that this is not a spur of the moment thing. I mean we've wanted to be parents for years, haven't we?' She put her arm over Chaz's. 'I mean, we've really tried, haven't we?'

'That's it, baby. Chaz will make sure things work out.' He smiled at his wife and wondered when her last facelift was. 'I'm looking forward to the observatory trip this afternoon. Esteban can hardly wait.'

'That book of his gives me the creeps. When we get home we'll do away with all that superstitious mumbo-jumbo. The Mother Superior can go hang, I'm not rearing any jungle savage. What did she call it, *cultural heritage* – where does that get you? Drugs, violence, and the rest. You'd think she'd be pleased to find the chance of a better life for those urchins.'

Chaz was listening with half an ear. 'Isn't that the police captain?'

Indeed, the policeman was walking towards them.

'And that's another one with his priorities all wrong. Why isn't he tracking down criminals instead of persecuting innocent Europeans?' Jodie sounded irritated.

Chaz was quiet. He pulled down the sleeves of his jacket and waited for the captain to approach. Something moved just above the door – the lizard. Chaz caught its eye.

*

Chaz and Esteban were queuing for the giant telescope. They were at the observatory and it was hot and crowded. Jodie and Guadalupe had gone for an ice cream but the telescope had been the one thing that Chaz was keen to see.

'Can I have an ice cream too?' It was a minute before Chaz remembered that the boy was with him. Since they had picked up the children from the orphanage that afternoon the boy had studiously avoided talking to him.

'Sorry, Esteban, we'll lose our place in the queue.'

'Guadalupe is getting one.'

Chaz explained that Esteban had been offered an ice cream along with his sister but had instead chosen the telescope. 'We'll get you an ice cream later.'

'I'm not going any further until I get an ice cream *now*.' Esteban sat down on the floor. 'And anyway the telescope isn't my choice, it's yours.'

Chaz looked down at the boy. The Latin-American looks and features – no one would ever mistake him for his son. The heat of the observatory, the police captain with his questions and insinuations, Jodie and her pretensions, Esteban and his superstitions. His load was full. Something inside him snapped. There was a father behind him in the queue so Chaz bent down to whisper quietly in the boy's ear: 'You stand up now or I'll pull your tongue out so you never taste ice cream again.' He pinched the boy's arm to show he was serious.

With wide terrified eyes the boy stared back, mesmerised. 'The Chisgo!' he screamed. 'It's the Chisgo!'

People stopped to stare. Chaz, embarrassed, loosened his grip and the boy ran into the crowd of people.

'Tell me exactly what happened,' demanded Jodie. 'What do you mean you lost him?'

'One minute we were just chatting and the next he had run-off ... maybe he thought he saw you,' explained Chaz. He would have to find a way to make Esteban pay for this.

'I can't believe it,' said Guadalupe. 'Esteban is not the sort of boy to run away.'

'I'm sure he'll turn up when he gets hungry,' said Chaz.

Chaz discreetly checked his watch without Jodie noticing; two hours since Esteban had pulled his stunt. No doubt soon they would get an update from the manager of the observatory who had all his staff out searching.

'And if they offer us another lift to the hotel,' sniffed Jodie, 'they can forget it. I'm not leaving him.' She sat, eyes downcast, holding Guadalupe's hand.

Welcome to family life, thought Chaz. Still, now cleared of visitors and screaming children, he could appreciate the architecture and style of the observatory. The moment the manager accompanied by a police officer returned, Chaz saw straight away from their faces that there was no good news to report.

'He must be here somewhere,' said Jodie, who had been crying.

'Nada, vacías. I'm sorry, Miss,' said the manager. 'Nothing, it's empty. We searched every room, every exhibit, I'm truly sorry. But one thing we found.' He held out in his hand a small book that was familiar to all of them. Chaz didn't need to read the title to know it was the *Legends of Colombia.*

Guadalupe put her hand up to her face: 'I know that book. It's Esteban's book of legends.' Chaz saw her bottom jaw starting to crumple, waterworks imminent he guessed. Her voice was starting to wobble: 'Something evil has happened.' She burst into tears.

Jodie put her arm around her shaking shoulders and gave an accusing look in Chaz's direction.

'I'm going to give that police captain a call,' he said and held up the card he still carried in his top pocket. He went outside. If possible it was even hotter than midday. He had a sudden desire for a cigarette and found a kiosk. He bought a packet, Marlboro – his first in years – but still the soft packet was familiar and reassuring in his hand. He took the sunglasses from his pocket.

'FIVE MILLION DOLLARS USD. NO POLIS NO NEGOTIATON TWO DAYS ELSE ESTEBAN GETS IT – WE CONTACT YOU.' Adrian read out the note for the third or fourth time at Jodie's request.

The envelope with Jodie's name scrawled across the front had been left at the hotel reception some time the previous night. 'We don't know when or by who,' they had been helpfully informed.

'I still think we should contact the police,' she said. It's been two days since they took him and this is the only lead we've got.'

They were in Jodie's hotel suite which had a connecting door to Chaz's own bedroom. 'For all we know the police are in on the racket,' said Chaz. 'Don't you think it suspicious they are so high profile in the hotel?'

'What's the problem?' said Jodie. 'We've got the money; we can pay, can't we, honey?' She turned to her agent. 'Adrian, we've got enough in the account, right?'

'Well technically yes,' Adrian answered. 'I'd need to make a few phone calls.'

'Great idea. Let's just give them what they want.'

'I knew you'd support me, honey,' said Jodie.

Chaz sighed. 'Listen, if only it was that simple. First, if we pay up there is no guarantee that we get the boy alive. Second they can just ask for a larger payment. These negotiations can drag on for years and years you know.'

'You mean we do nothing? Is that what you want me to tell Guadalupe?'

'Okay, sure ... good idea.'

'You do your own dirty work.'

Jodie looked ready to storm off any moment but Chaz felt in control. He was good in a crisis and he still had the Cuba card up his sleeve. He was the story's beginning and the story's end.

'Listen, Jodie. I've thought it all through. So sit down and I'll tell you how we are going to do this.'

He told them the plan: they would leave the country because then the negotiators would think they didn't care; not an unreasonable supposition – they hardly knew the boy. Meanwhile they would leave Adrian behind to conclude the negotiating. 'It stands to reason that we're much more likely to get a result with you out of the way, Jodie. People see you as a licence to print money. You know they do.' He figured that Jodie, who frequently complained of little else, could do nothing but agree.

She nodded.

Chaz waited until he also got a nod from Adrian before continuing. 'Okay, that's settled. And we keep the police out of this. Adrian, let's meet later at the Night of the Iguana. I'll ring you.' Right now he was finding the hotel oppressive. 'Adrian, car keys?'

'Where are you going?' Jodie asked. 'you know we're not meant to drive anywhere alone.'

'Small problem. Nothing for you to worry about. Chaz will sort it, baby. Back in a jiffy.'

Chaz managed to avoid the Mother Superior and found Guadalupe alone at the orphanage. Looking at the girl he marvelled that he had written a cheque only a few days before for hundreds of thousands of dollars. The heat and the jungle atmosphere was messing with his head. He went straight to the point. He told her of the ransom note and his plan.

'So you're just going to leave town and hope it works out all right?'

'Guadalupe, you've got to come with us. It's the only way.'

'And leave Esteban? My brother?'

'Listen, Guadalupe I've watched you and Jodie. You know that coming back with us to England is the best lucky break you're ever going to get. Do you think I care if you come or not? There are a hundred Guadalupes out there who would jump at this opportunity. Forget your brother, come with us. It's your chance, take it or leave it.' Chaz really didn't care what she decided.

Barraquer was in discussion with a white-coated technician at the forensics laboratory. A file marked *Hotel Superior* lay on the table. The technician picked it up saying: 'Bueno, bueno, when the official del Estación de Policía shows an interest in our methods, El Capitán—?'

'So what did you find out?' asked Barraquer.

'As you know, strangulation without sex is an uncommon crime but I would say you are looking for some kind of wire.' The technician was leafing through papers as he spoke. 'I was able to find a lot of clean DNA evidence samples; tissue under the fingernails – the victim put up a fight. She struggled and one ... real beauty.' He held up a sealed plastic bag containing a strand of hair for Barraquer's inspection. 'I've tested it for artificial colouring, negative. So I would say not a Latino, more likely American or European. It matches the DNA from underneath the fingernails.' He produced some charts of shaded columns but Barraquer didn't look at them.

'So I'm looking for a European with blond hair—'

'Or Americano.'

'And if we had a matching sample from the suspect, statistically what are the chances we could get a conviction?'

'Sí, sí, a reference sample that matches the evidence sample. It could be saliva or a hair, but on its own, I'm not sure would it be enough. If the law was up to mathematicians that's all you would need, but—'

'But a murder weapon would help us a lot. And you're saying a wire, like a guitar string?'

'Very possibly, but the metal kind not nylon, I would think. Have you got any leads, El Capitán?'

'Leads I have. It's time I'm short of.'

'Que teniente?' The technician looked up at the policeman who was already walking from the laboratory.

'If you were a murderer from out of town, police on your tail,' Barraquer turned as he pushed on the door, 'and you had a perfectly good passport, tell me, would you hang around?'

Adrian, with a cold beer in front of him, was back in the Night of the Iguana waiting for Chaz. It was still early and the bar was empty. He contemplated sitting but felt more comfortable standing near the door – he'd see when Chaz walked in. He didn't have to wait long. 'Hello, Chaz. What'ya having?'

'Whatever you've got.'

Adrian nodded to the barman who placed a bottled beer on the bar in front of Chaz. 'Nice bar but what's wrong with the hotel?' said Adrian. 'Why the mystery?'

'Some things Jodie is better off not knowing.' Chaz's hair hung lankly to the shoulders, like it needed a wash and a cut. He looked tired, thought Adrian, who wondered how well Chaz had been sleeping.

'So what errands do you want me to run now?' Adrian asked. 'Something unspeakable?'

'No lip, Adrian. Remember who you're talking to.' Chaz went on to explain his big idea. There would be no negotiating with the kidnappers but Jodie must never find out.

'So I wait a couple of weeks and then get the plane home. I don't make any contact with kidnappers or police.' Adrian took a swig from his bottle. 'I don't even try and make a deal?'

'That's right. You just sit by the pool. Take it easy.'

'And what about Guadalupe?' Adrian had learnt to expect the unexpected with Chaz but even by his standards events were moving off kilter.

'Come on, Jodie is like a girl buying a puppy. She loves this one but next week there'll be another. Leave Guadalupe and Jodie to me.'

'Come again?'

'Don't worry. That's my department.'

This is what Adrian hated most about Chaz – he made sure people like him knew just enough, never on the inside, always just out of the loop. No matter, he thought, just smile and play ball. There was close on a cool million in the current account. He could take that and disappear. He knew places to go. 'You're the boss.' He turned to the bartender. 'You sell whisky here?' The barman, who seemed to know when to remember guests and when to polish glasses, just nodded. 'By the way, the captain, what was his name, Barraquer?'

'What about him?' Chaz was on full alert now, Adrian noticed.

'Yeah. He was snooping around. He was interested in Peru. You remember the time we were there a young girl was—'

'Adrian. Just remember who you're dealing with.' Chaz glared at him. 'Oh and another thing, first thing in the morning get on to the bank and cancel the cheque to the Mother Superior. That whore's been asking for it.'

Adrian remembered the captain's request. 'Is that the captain now?'

Chaz turned to look at the door as a new punter arrived and as his back was turned Adrian plucked a long blond hair from the shoulders of his employer's jacket.

The chameleon had survived the recreational 'lizard hunt' conducted by the afternoon shift of hotel porters. They were close to capturing him but a football goal on the hotel reception's TV had distracted his pursuers and he had scrambled to safety. His survival instinct, honed over millions of years, was telling him that even with camouflage he was starting to push his luck on the pale white hotel walls. Like a politician clinging to power with the mob on the streets, it was time to beat a retreat.

Twenty-four hours after his rendezvous with Adrian, Chaz tipped the bodyguards as they performed their last duty, wheeling the mountain of matching monogrammed travel luggage to the oversized bags drop-off point at El Dorado International Airport. Jodie was crying and they were checked in.

'So Guadalupe is coming along to say goodbye? I don't see her. Is Adrian with her?' Chaz had told her that Guadalupe would be joining them with Adrian and Esteban just as soon as the hostage release had been finalised. Still, he had one ace up his sleeve.

'Listen, babe, I've had good news from Cuba.'

'Cuba. You mean the adoption agency. I thought we'd given up with them—'

'I heard just today. They've got us a darling Cuban girl, only a year old, and we can pick her up this week.'

Jodie stopped in her tracks. 'Healthy ... I mean, no AIDS?'

Chaz nodded. 'Yeah, I checked. She's perfect. Ticks all the boxes. But we have to be quick – I mean there's other families that are interested.'

'But we've put down a deposit?'

'You bet. And the best thing is that this will really be like our own baby girl.'

'Does she have a name already?' Jodie had stopped crying and for the first time in days looked happy, thought Chaz.

'So what the fuck if she does? She's only one year old. You can call her anything. Call her Guadalupe if you like.' Nice touch, he thought. 'It's really like it's our own baby. Chaz has sorted it, like I said I would.'

'Our own little family in a little English country cottage. You know it's what I've always dreamed of; roses growing around the door and neighbours dropping in for a cup of tea and a natter, a little village with a nice quaint pub where we can be just Mr and Mrs Jones and—'

'You know, babe, I'm always thinking of what's best for you and as soon as we get out of this place, the better.'

'But it doesn't mean we give up with Guadalupe and Esteban. I mean we don't forget them?'

'Of course we don't. What sort of people are we? Come on, we'd better get to Departures.' Chaz remembered that Guadalupe would be turning up about now at the hotel with her bag packed, ready to sacrifice her brother and make the trip to the UK. Too bad she was going to be just a couple of hours too late. But he added for good measure, 'Let's just hope she turns up to say goodbye before they call the flight.'

Walking towards passport control Chaz checked his pockets for his passport and tickets. In the left pocket of his jacket he felt the guitar E-string. He'd been waiting to find a safe place to dispose of the evidence. And he laughed to himself; imagine explaining that one at the security check-in! He dropped a couple of steps and checked there were no police in the immediate vicinity before reluctantly dropping the keepsake into a waste bin.

'Come on. I bet we'll find Guadalupe waiting for us at the departure gates.' Jodie turned to him as she spoke, the face that launched a million record sales, blonde and cheeky.

Beauty and the Beast, he thought; he smiled, pleased that he had kept *Legends of Colombia*. Chisgo, he liked that. Virgins look out – Chisgo was on the prowl! He thought for a moment about putting his sunglasses on but then decided not to. In the bathroom mirror earlier he had noticed that the scratch next to his eye was almost completely healed. He caught up with Jodie. 'Everything's going to be okay. Trust Chaz.' He linked his arm through that of his famous wife's.

At the same time a thin brown hand on the end of a Brazil nut-coloured arm slipped into the waste bin and extracted the guitar string smeared with microscopic traces of dried blood.

Back at the hotel, the porter's attention was distracted by a large group of Spanish schoolgirls arriving. The chameleon saw its opportunity and darted through the revolving door. It felt vulnerable on the ground but quickly it was out the other side, out into the Colombian heat and soon up a palm tree welcoming the sound of Amazon Basin crickets which reinforced the feeling of freedom at last.

I was cold and lonely in the cell. Sometimes I woke up in the middle of the night in the uncomfortable bed and wondered for a minute if I was still on the island. I think more and more about Amorgos these days. It was too late to tell my own story. Then I polished my glasses and looked at the Bible; it gave me an idea. It would take an age to write but time was the one commodity I had plenty of. I picked up the pencil and started at Genesis.

Wheel of Fortune

'Hello, you look like an Englishman.'

I heard a voice from behind my back as I was leaning against the rail. I turned around and saw a tanned girl with golden hair and the most amazing smile that made dimples appear in each cheek.

'I am Alison,' she said offering her hand. I was so taken by surprise at her approaching an ordinary guy like me, that I could not help blushing. I shook her hand, mumbling my name: 'Michael Taylor.'

'Hi, Michael!'

'So you're going to Amorgos?'

'I didn't know the ferry was going anywhere else.'

Alison had this effect on me; getting me either tongue-tied or making the most inane comments. After this unpromising start I was pleased to find we seemed to have a lot in common although, unlike her, I was going to the island to work. I had a three-month contract to teach English to a couple of kids, whose mother was British and father Greek. Alison was here to 'chill out' after finishing her history studies in Oxford, with a first class degree, of course. She was going to stay with her Greek godmother, her mother's student friend from uni. I suspected Alison's parents were footing the bill.

As two 'Englishmen abroad' it was in our mutual interest to get to know each other and we exchanged phone numbers so that we could meet up. She was way out of my league and I felt like some poor relative gratefully collecting every smile Alison donated. I could see she was accustomed to that and she used it, flirting with me like a siren.

Little did I know then where it would all end up. Looking back now I think Greek gods and fate were involved from the very beginning. The ferry arrived at Amorgos in the early hours. The few passengers who alighted with us were soon swallowed up into the inky blackness.

'Is anyone picking you up?' Alison asked, pulling her suitcase along the jetty. 'I think Maria – that's my godmother – is sending a driver. Maybe he could drop you?'

I admitted my plan was to hang around until dawn and then find the way to my employer's house.

'So, that's decided then,' she said, 'leave it to me!'

At the end of the jetty we saw a cigarette glowing like the sinister red eye of a Cyclops.

'Kaliméra,' said a coarse voice. 'Miss Alison?'

'Yes, I am. And I have a friend with me, Michael. What is your name?'

'Stelios.' He shook our hands. 'I not speak English much.'

Alison was trying to make herself understood with much gesticulating and very slow English. She took the address I had given her and gave it to Stelios, pointing at me. 'Okay? Can we drive Michael to this address, please?' She was using her charm and sounded very appealing.

Stelios had no choice. He shrugged and said 'Páme!' then grabbed her suitcase, lugging it to the car, a battered Opel – just one of the incidents I was to witness of people putting down their weapons in front of Alison. She just had that power.

On Thursday evening, two days later, she phoned me. I had been busy settling down to my duties and the new environment. Of course, I had been thinking of Alison. I was wondering what she was up to, but I felt I could not make the first approach – maybe she didn't want to have anything to do with me.

'Michael, can we meet?' Her voice was music to my ears.

'Yes, of course. I'm free in the evenings. When would you suggest?'

Our rendezvous was at the harbour, Katapula, which had a very different ambience now from when we arrived in the middle of the night. It was a cosy place with a few tavernas and a boulevard that stretched by the sea. Another hot day was transmuting into a balmy evening. Alison was already waiting and she skipped towards me like a little girl, her dress radiating white in the fading light. 'Kaliméra,' she said, giving me a kiss on the cheek.

'Alison, how's it going?' I felt hot all over. 'You look great.'

'I have so much to tell you.' She grasped my hand and started to pull me to the nearest taverna. 'Let's go and have a drink!'

I'd hardly touched my chilled retsina before she was telling me about her beautiful location the other side of the island. 'And this rich old woman, my godmother's friend who owns the villa, well the whole headland actually, she's having a party.' Alison's words were tumbling out as she bubbled away. 'And guess what?' she said, sounding like an impatient child waiting to give you a present. 'You are invited too!'

'Me? But how come? She doesn't know anything about me.'

'You'd be surprised. On this island the inhabitants know everything.'

'Will there be other people coming?'

'Of course, it's a *party!* From all over the island, as far away as Athens.'

'Sounds great,' I said, cursing my awkwardness.

'She's a recluse but highly respected and her parties are famous.'

Maybe because she was loaded, I thought. Rich people always had lots of 'friends'.

*

Alison was excited about the people we were going to meet and what she was going to wear, while I wasn't sure whether I was going at all. I voiced my doubts but she insisted I come. No doubt I was to be her crutch until she found someone more interesting. Alison's headlong willingness pushed her onwards and upwards. And she was clever and had charisma – no wonder she always got what she wanted. But can any human be perfect?

'Promise you'll come because I wangled the invitation. It would be rude to refuse.'

'Okay.' I had no other option.

'Stelios will pick you up on Saturday, eight sharp.'

On Saturday afternoon I got another phone call from Alison. 'Michael, do you have anything smart to wear?'

'Well, depends on what you mean by smart?' I stood on the other end of the phone in two minds whether to call the whole thing off or not.

'You need at least a white shirt and smart trousers, not jeans and definitely not shorts!'

'Got the message,' I said, already regretting my decision.

Stelios arrived before eight but I was ready. The father of the family had lent me some decent trousers and a bow tie, which I had finally mastered. It was still hot and I was already sweating. Alison was sitting alone in the back of the Opel, looking glamorous.

'You look handsome, Michael!'

I was blushing and sweating even more.

'You should dress up more often, and white suits your blue eyes and dark hair. And do you know, Michael, your nose is really quite noble.' She touched my hand. 'My godmother is sick – so we have no chaperone.'

I was so taken by her attention, I gave her a kiss on the cheek.

I was used to mediocrity in every way: me, a thin-faced guy with glasses, a man who nobody stopped to look at twice. I understood that for Alison it was important how things looked.

'Look, what a sight. Wow!' exclaimed Alison when we were still in the car. Arriving at the large villa I was struck by the pillars and antiquity of the place but it was the magic of the garden that took my breath away. What had got Alison so excited was the sight of hundreds of lanterns swaying in the dusk. Shadows seemed to play a mysterious game of hide-and-seek around the statues, which were everywhere. The garden looked beautiful and macabre at the same time. We heard sounds of laughter and music against a backdrop of waves crashing on the shore below.

'Over there,' she whispered, reaching for my arm and pointing to the entrance. My skin crawled; everywhere I looked I saw people wearing white masks like actors in a Greek tragedy. On a small stage a string quartet was playing an overture, by Mozart I think. As we got closer we saw a servant who was presenting a mask to each guest.

'Your hostess would like you to wear these, if you don't mind,' he said to everyone both in Greek and perfect English.

Alison and I took our masks. At least mine was big enough for me to keep my glasses on – even so, we couldn't recognise each other any more. The masks were evidently of high quality. They were detailed and elaborate and, even immobile, held your attention. Alison had a lop-sided smile, almost a grimace, and I had a stern and cross look. What a pair we suddenly looked.

'You didn't say it was a masquerade,' I said, feeling hot and uncomfortable.

'Coz I didn't know. But come on, let's have fun. Follow me. We'll get something to drink and say hi to the wicked old witch.'

Our hostess was standing by a young man and holding his arm. She was the only person we saw without a mask. Although she must have been at least seventy, she was slim and elegant with a beautiful olive complexion. Her steel-coloured hair was thick and wavy. 'Kaliméra. Welcome, both of you.' She spoke perfect English and addressed us as if we were old friends.

'Thank you, Madame, for inviting us,' I managed to say. 'I'm Michael Taylor. Pleased to meet you.'

'I know who you are, Michael. I hope you enjoy Amorgos. It is a magical island. You will see.' Her voice resonated confidence and authority. Dark piercing eyes seemed to look straight into my soul.

Did I imagine extra emphasis on the word magical? The whole set-up was affecting me. 'It's a wonderful setting—'

'Alison, sorry to hear about your godmother,' our hostess interrupted. 'Do send her my regards. Now, go and make the most of your time here tonight.' She turned on her stiletto high heels. It appeared that we were dismissed.

'Could she really recognise us behind these masks?' I asked.

'There are some odd stories about her. You know people here are quite superstitious. They really believe she has magic powers and can read the future. To me she sounds nutty as a fruitcake.'

Alison stopped and turned and we looked behind to our hostess who was greeting the new arrivals. Silhouetted against the headland the old woman had an aura of invincibility around her like an ancient Greek goddess, mysterious, inexplicable and ageless.

'She gives me the creeps,' said Alison.

'I need a drink. Want one?'

'Sure. I'll wait.'

I headed off to where the bar was. When I came back Alison was next to a dark-haired stranger wearing a wide smiling face but when I got closer I realised I was looking at the back of his head.

'Champagne?' I asked.

'Lovely, thanks,' said Alison.

The stranger turned to reveal the most sinister mask I had

ever seen. The evil grimace caused me to start and spill champagne on my shirt.

'This is Janus,' she said brushing her hand over his shoulder before taking her glass. Alison was flirting at a hundred miles per hour, pulling at a strand of her long fair hair. 'Janus, meet Michael, a friend of mine.'

'Are you living on the island or just here for the party?'

'My home is here for half the year, from the spring till autumn.' His voice was vibrant and his English very good with only the slightest accent.

I was annoyed he had taken my place as soon as my back was turned. Now I was thankful for the protection of my mask. He couldn't see my real emotions; neither could Alison.

'*Tourist* season, you know,' he added with a trace of mockery.

'Janus is dealing with Constantine's business,' Alison added. 'He was just telling me how much travel is involved.'

'Constantine's?'

'Our hostess – she is a very wealthy woman.'

Now I could see he looked like the young guy holding Constantine's arm when we were introduced, but I wasn't sure. I looked to the headland. Our hostess stood there alone and for some reason I was slightly disconcerted to see she seemed to be looking in our direction.

'Cheers!' I said, raising my glass.

Alison was looking around and straightened her mask. In the girly voice she saved for the right men, she asked: 'So, could you tell us, Janus, why are we all wearing masks?'

'Constantine wants her guests to get to know each other without the hindrances of age, looks or clothes. Behind the masks we are equals and it is easier to speak honestly with strangers. All that matters are the words we use and the ideas we convey.' Janus sounded matter-of-fact, almost bored and didn't seem bothered to hide it.

'That's the strangest thing I've ever heard! What do you think, Michael?'

I was still thinking of what to reply when Janus continued: 'Let's take you, for example. I don't know if you are ugly or beautiful. I chat with you and after a while I'll make my conclusions ... maybe you are a complete product of your class: a perfect bourgeois girl who has never considered any other way of life or reality, who has ambitions to become somebody and get rich and who thinks this way she can master her life and its uncertainty.'

I noticed Alison's body language tensing; straightening up like a bull in front of the matador. Touché, I thought. Was that a lucky guess from Janus? Or was he playing some mind game? Alison's face kept its same lop-sided grin – I couldn't see her real expression. Now the mask was protecting her. I started to see the brilliance of the idea; guests could quite literally save face in conversations which were meant to be brutally personal and honest. This was no place for pleasant chit-chat.

'And that gives you the right to play God and say who is good and who is evil? Worthy or unworthy?' Alison took a big gulp from her glass.

'No, I only can help you to see your blind spots. We do all have them, you know.'

'Do you? Do you know yours already?' Alison sounded scornful. It was a new side of her to me.

'I know what Constantine has shown me. We should be mirrors to one another and reflect honesty. Of course, many people cannot face this picture and they choose to deny it.' His eyes flickered behind the fixed grimace. 'Are you familiar with Jung's ideas about the life circle?'

'What do you mean?'

Janus continued his speech and now I was all ears.

'When you are young and vulnerable you need to wear masks to protect your weak ego but at some point in your life you have to grow up, leave you masks and face the world as an authentic person. Be your real self. The masks or the different roles give you time to practise and get stronger.'

'Of course! Don't we all grow up when we get older? That's the way life goes.' Alison tried to sound mature and experienced.

'Wrong. That's what people think. But in reality, most people live in *mauvaise foi*, bad faith, conforming to the rules of society even though it would be against their inner self. They become the prisoners of their roles.'

'So, if I get a nice job and get rich, I'm not a good person? Because that's what most people do in a society. They pay taxes, they buy things and support the system.' Alison was defensive but I was intrigued.

'All I can do is hold up the mirror, what you see reflected there is up to you. Ask yourself, what is success in life? But now if you excuse me, I have to meet other guests. Enjoy your evening and we might see each other later.'

'Not if I see you first,' retorted Alison. 'I'm with Michael this evening.' As she spoke Alison slipped her arm through mine.

'Such confidence in such youth. I like it. Perhaps later.' He bowed smoothly and moved away with the smiling mask looking back at us, as if in appeasement of what had passed between us.

We watched the retreating figure. I think we were both a bit shaken. 'Well, what did you think of that?' I said after a moment.

'He was an arrogant, patronising and self-righteous idiot. What a nerve to attack me like that! I'm not such a bad person, am I?'

'He didn't say exactly that. I guess he tried to make us think about our values—'

'It didn't sound like that to me. And you didn't say anything to back me up!' She was angry with me too, like a spoilt child, used to getting her own way. 'This whole set-up is ridiculous and phoney. Anyway I meant what I said. Let's stick together tonight – this is not my kind of scene.'

But now I understood the name of the game and realised it was mine. I could shamelessly stare at anyone and everyone. I felt a strange excitement at the prospect of the evening in front of me and judging by the steady stream of boats arriving at a long jetty, the party was just beginning.

For the next two or three hours we circulated, drinking more and more champagne. To begin with I was following Alison around like a sheepdog, and she was looking great even though I couldn't see her face. Or maybe because I knew what was behind the mask. But as time went on I felt brave enough to be alone. At some point, it must have been getting toward midnight – the party was in full swing and the boats were still moored at the jetty – I went to fetch another drink, then I felt someone pulling at my arm. She wore a half-mask of an enormous butterfly that covered the top half of her face but allowed me a view of full red lips.

'Try an olive,' she said leaning forward so that I was enveloped by a strong fragrance and smooth skin.

I went to pick one from the small silver tray she was carrying.

'Not with your fingers,' she whispered, 'the Greek way – with tongues.'

Before I knew it her lips were on mine. Our mouths twisted and she was kissing me long and sensually, her warm breasts pressed against my chest. She pulled my hand up to her neck. Her hair was up, displaying small and delicately pretty ears. My head was spinning. And then as soon as she arrived she had gone.

Only the salty taste of olive in my mouth confirmed I hadn't imagined the whole thing. But of Alison there was no sign. I tried to pick out her mask from amongst the crowd of figures in animated discussions milling around the lanterns, drinks in hand, the mountains behind, but I couldn't. I suddenly felt dizzy, drunk with the day's sun or too much champagne, and all those masked faces around me ... I wasn't thinking straight any more. I needed to get out of there, quickly. I didn't say goodbye to anyone. I just left and started to walk home to clear my head.

*

The following week I had to spend with my employer. We made sailing trips with the children. The kids were well behaved, so the work was hot during the day but not too hard. I just played and talked with them. I couldn't call Alison and I was a tiny bit concerned about her. I also thought about the kiss from the party. On my return from one afternoon sail, I got a phone call. 'Hi, Alison, how are you? Sorry I lost you at the party, I just had to leave, too much to drink. Is everything fine with you? You know ... I'm sorry—'

'Stop fretting, Michael, I'm fine. Can you meet me tonight?'

We agreed to meet at our usual place at Katapula, at eight.

She was there before me. The dimpled smile was so Alison; enterprising and fun. But I sensed that she was not quite herself. 'You're looking great,' I said. 'How about your hangover after the party?'

She took a sip of her drink and didn't say anything for a while, which was unusual. 'You know I saw you coming away from the bar with two glasses. You beckoned for me to follow you and I did, or rather I followed your mask – because when I caught up with you, it was him – Janus.'

'The one with the double-faced mask?'

'Yes, Janus the two-faced god. At some point he must have swapped masks, to fool me.'

'Go on.'

'Well then he pointed you out to me at the bar, you with the girl.'

'That! It was over as soon as it started.' I said something about my encounter with the Greek girl bearing olives.

'I suspected something like that, a beautiful girl like that—'

'Thanks very much.'

'They were playing with us,' she said simply. 'It was all staged. At the time I was so cross with you, I allowed Janus to escort me to Constantine's table. I got the feeling she was expecting me.'

I remembered the girl's exquisite ears and lips. Why hadn't I been more alert? 'So what happened next?'

'Constantine asked me if I wanted any advice for the future.'

'What did you say?'

'What do you think I said? Of course, I said "Yes". She told me to pick up a couple of tarot cards from the pack. I couldn't really refuse even if I wanted to ... so I picked my first card.' She paused. 'It was the Wheel of Fortune. Do you know anything about tarot?'

'No. Well, isn't it black magic, something superstitious?'

'That's what I thought, at first.' Alison started to speak faster. 'Originally, it was an ancient card game but in the hands of a master it can also be used to help you understand the future—'

'So what does this Wheel of Fortune mean?' I knew I sounded sceptical.

'She said it means *change* and I should always be ready for that. Changes are always good for us even though at first they might look like bad news. She said the most important thing is your own attitude. You decide your own wheel of fortune.'

'What did you say to that?'

'Nothing really.'

'What happened then?'

'I picked up the other card.'

'What was that?'

'Lovers.'

'And so what?' In spite of myself I was starting to get curious. 'You let your life be decided by the choosing of a card?'

'Not so simple. We must use our intuition, Constantine said we rely too much on the intellect when making decisions. Instead we should let everything flow, especially in the art of love. Let things change. The Greeks have a name for it: '*Panta rhei*.'

'Surely three years at university have taught you more than that,' I told her. 'Decisions must be based on facts and facts alone. Logic.' It seemed that she had really been taken in by this Constantine woman. Why had she gone to all that trouble with

Alison? And Janus whoever-he-was must have been part of that. The speech about bad faith and authenticity. I knew enough about existentialism to make some sense of it. But Alison was safe in her comfortable world. She didn't need to get mixed up with anything as shady as tarot cards. I, on the other hand, had never had that security or confidence in my own life.

'And guess what,' she continued, 'after Janus took off his mask—'

'My mask you mean.'

'He told me his real name was Jonathan.'

'Did you take off yours?'

'You bet. I'd had enough of the game.'

For some reason Alison telling me this broke some sort of spell that had been hanging over me. After the masquerade something had changed in my own mind. Of course tarot was nonsense but what Janus had said about the masks, how we meet the people behind the masks, the games people play – I had to agree with. I was still wearing my mask, hiding behind the different roles, but now I realised I should get rid of them. Be myself – take it or leave it. It was my blessing not to have a comfortable world behind me. I was creating my own world from working-class roots. I had much to learn about myself and my emotions. I realised Greece could be my teacher.

'Anyway, he wasn't too bad, he was quite handsome and he offered to drive me home.' Alison smiled, more her old self. 'In fact, I had a date with him last Saturday, but then he had to go to Athens on business.'

I was surprised by the speed at which things were changing but I wasn't too upset. A bit sad maybe. She had all the time been more like a distant star out of my reach. 'Good luck!' I said when we parted, and somehow I meant it.

The next weeks I tried to find out something about Constantine from my employers but my family were not the gossipy type and I drew a blank. Then, I had a day off and I decided to visit the monastery Moni Panagia Hozoviatissa. I had already seen it from the distance: a spectacular and brilliant white scion pointing out of the enormous cliff's sheer side. It looked like it had metamorphosed out of the rock itself. The path was through sunburnt fields and olive woods. It was a much longer walk than it first looked.

When I finally got there I was exhausted. A monk opened the door and led me inside. It was pleasantly cool inside the stone-flagged building. The sun beams were coming in through the window bars. I sat down in some kind of waiting room where I was offered fresh figs and cold water from a tray. The monk told me I was free to walk around the monastery but not to disturb the prayers. He left me with a leaflet about the place and its history. As I was reading in the empty room, the door opened and in came Constantine, looking cool and elegant in a grey silk dress.

'Hello, Michael, nice to meet you again. Refreshed after your walk?'

'Yes thank you, and hello, Constantine.' I was suddenly very alert.

Constantine didn't seem at all surprised to see me; on the contrary, she spoke as if we had an appointment. 'Remarkable place.' She waved her hand in a big circle. 'Did you know this monastery saved many lives during the war?'

'Really?' I tried to sound interested.

'My family included my mother, sister and me. Father was fighting in the mainland. We were starving and the fascists were hunting everywhere, so the monastery hid us and many others in its secret corridors.'

'That must have been frightening—'

'I was only six then but I still remember the fear and hunger. We owe everything to this place and those who risked their lives for us. Ever since I have tried to do my bit to make people value life and its gifts.' She paused for a while. 'Would you sacrifice your life for someone, Michael?' She was looking straight into my eyes. 'That is the question we all have to ask ourselves at some point. And if you can answer *yes*, you know your life has not been in vain.' Her eyes pierced me and I had no idea how to reply.

Writing this story now, surrounded by Old Testament heroes and villains, this moment at the monastery comes back to me; the ascetic room and its strong smell of incense that were burning in front of the holy icons. Only now do I fully understand what she was saying.

Then she took a pack of cards from her little handbag. I stared at the tarot cards, watchful like a snake in front of his snake charmer. Constantine offered me the pack. I pulled a card and returned it to her. The picture was of a man in ragged clothes carrying a stick on his back. It was The Fool. 'You are young and the journey is in front of you with all its possibilities, challenges and risks. Conquer the world but remember, freedom includes responsibility.' She spoke calmly and steadily. 'Use it wisely and it will reward you. It is your life but it is connected to the lives of others.' She offered me the pack again. This time the picture was of a sphinx-like, half-human creature on an eight-spoked wheel. There was a compass, a blind person, guards.

What a coincidence. 'The Wheel of Fortune,' I said.

'This is very interesting. You got the first card from the Major Arcana and now you picked the middle one. They have a strong message to you. Do you know anything of Greek philosophy?'

'Well ... some, Plato and Aristotle and so on, but not very well.'

'Well then, you know that basically the principles of good life are very simple. That's what the Greek philosophers tried to define to the *hoi polloi*, the crowd. The first principle was G*nothi seauton*, know thyself, and the second *meden agan*, everything in moderation. It is simple but also very difficult. The Wheel of Fortune turns and you notice that the life as you knew it doesn't exist any more. To survive you need lots of courage and self-discipline. Good things happen to good people, in the end. You can't choose what happens in life but you can choose your attitude to it.'

I was in goose pimples all over. I was charmed by her voice. To think I had once thought it hard. 'Yes, um ... thank you for this. I'll try to keep it in mind. Know myself and moderation—'

The door opened suddenly and a young Greek man walked in. He had thick dark hair and eyes as clear as a turquoise sea.

'Have you two met?' Constantine asked.

'I don't think so,' I replied. 'How do you do.'

'Actually, we have met.' And when he spoke I recognised his vibrant voice.

'You are Janus, the one with the double mask.'

'Yes. You were with Alison at Constantine's party.'

I noticed he talked of her as if her knew her very well – maybe he did. I had not heard from Alison since the night at the taverna. I had tried to call her but she was always out. I wanted to confront him about the events of the party but Constantine started to talk again.

'You must be confused now but I am an old woman, I have seen life and I dare say the truth. Make the right choices and if you don't, learn from your mistakes.'

Then they left and I was alone in the waiting room.

About a week later I finally met Alison, by accident. I had some letters to post and was heading along the sea boulevard on another baking hot day to the post office in Katapula, when I saw her in a hat and sunglasses. She was being helped out of a fishing boat by a man. Her companion I recognised right away. They walked right towards me.

'Hi, Michael. Great to see you! Sorry, I've been so busy with my social life I haven't had time to contact you.' Alison looked radiant and genuinely pleased to see me.

'Never mind. I've been busy too. How are you?'

'I'm really good. Let me introduce you to Jonathan.' She

turned to the man beside her and he looked at me with his mesmeric turquoise eyes.

'Hello, Michael,' he said.

I felt strange. Why didn't he say we had met last week? It was as though we were meeting for the first time and not the third. I shook his hand. 'Hello,' I replied.

'Sorry, I have to dash.' He paused to kiss Alison on the cheek. 'Errands ... but I can see my dove is in safe hands.'

I was alone with Alison again.

'Come on, let's find some shade,' I said and steered her to the taverna we had visited before. The first thing Alison told me was that she had fallen in love. I had already guessed.

'Jonathan is really sweet, interesting and ... mysterious. I was completely wrong about him.'

'Do you know why he pretended he didn't know me? I have met him twice before.'

'Twice?'

'Well, I also had the tarot treatment from Constantine.'

'Really? What happened?'

I told her about the whole incident in the monastery.

'He is sometimes ... a bit, in his own world. Absent-minded.'

'Well, I didn't get that impression of him before—'

'Don't worry. I think that's part of his charm. He's different from anyone I have ever met.'

But I did. My instinct said something was not quite right. I could not explain it but I felt it in my bones. As I was listening to Alison my mind was full of questions.

'Isn't that quite funny really,' she said twirling the sunglasses in her hand. 'I might start believing tarot and the future telling. Remember, I got the Lovers card and I decided to follow my instinct.'

'You're just having a holiday fling. You cannot be serious about this.'

'Why not? Jonathan is well-educated, handsome and well-off. I want to live by my feelings and see what happens—'

'You've only known him just over month. Do you know him at all? Are you now planning a future with him?'

'In fact, six weeks. Well, I don't rule it out, but mainly I just want to seize the day. Carpe Diem!' She was so sure of herself and reckless.

'Well be careful,' I warned. I even started to wonder if she had got into drugs – but maybe love was the worst of drugs.

'I am perfectly capable of looking after myself.' Alison closed her eyes and turned her face to the scorching sun. She looked happy and it felt criminal to spoil that.

A week later she called me. 'Why don't we do something fun tonight? Jonathan is in Athens and I'm free. Let's take a picnic and find a nice beach, swim and chat and get a bit merry.'

It sounded a good plan and we agreed to meet in Chora, the main town of the island, where we could take a bus if needed.

Chora was beautiful. All the houses were shining white with blue and green shutters and the streets narrow and neat. It had a serene and ageless atmosphere. This is how ancient Greece must have been, what attracted me to apply for a job here. My bag was heavy: I had water and wine bottles, some goats cheese and spinach pies, olives and fresh bread. I felt pleasantly excited.

I saw the familiar battered Opel stopping by the main square and Alison stepped out with a napsack and a blanket under her arm. I waved my hand to Stelios and walked toward Alison.

She said she knew a hidden sandy bay, a favourite of Jonathan's. They had gone there by boat – now we were to walk. The island was covered in criss-crossing paths made by the goats and we chose one that seemed to lead in the right direction. The air was full of scents, mixture of sun-dried herbs: sage, thyme and oregano.

Just as the sun was reaching the horizon, we were lucky and found the path down to our beach. It was as perfect a place as Alison had predicted. We spread our blanket down just by the edge of the rock and opened the wine.

After a couple of glasses the sunset had gone but the moon was rising and almost full, and we could still see fairly well. We were in a great mood: she was in love and so was I. Only the objects of our love were different.

We heard it before we saw it; the sound of a rowing boat. We were hidden against the rock and for some reason we instinctively stopped talking. The boat, silhouetted in the moonlight, hit the sand and out jumped a man. He lifted up a woman from the boat onto the beach. He wrapped his arm around her and they kissed passionately. Then as he pulled the boat up we saw his face. Alison took a deep breath and I squeezed her hand. It was Jonathan. There was something familiar about the woman.

We heard her saying: 'David, let's go swimming!' and they both took their clothes off and walked into the sea, hand-in-hand, naked. They swam away from us.

'What shall we do now?' I whispered. It all was so weird. Our acquaintance, the double-faced Janus, seemed to be like his name; a two-faced cheat using different names for his women.

Alison crouched next to me, trembling with emotion. 'I don't want to see him, but I'd like to tear him in pieces. Let's leave so that they can't see us!' Tears were pouring down her face and in the ghostly light I saw her cheeks were flushed.

We silently collected our things and almost crawled up the steep path, getting nasty scratches from the spiky bushes. She tried not to sniffle but I heard sounds of her sobbing. Finally, on the top of the hill, we stopped then sat down, and I poured us the remains of the wine. 'You heard it too, didn't you?' I said. 'She called him David. But it was Jonathan—'

'He's a lying bastard! I've been such a fool. I really thought he liked me. I've slept with him. This is the guy who is accusing people of hiding behind masks and playing roles. Be true to oneself – unless of course you fancy a shag on the beach.'

'It sounds fishy, I agree,' was all I managed to add. Part of me was pleased about this latest twist, but I also found myself sympathising with Alison.

'Maybe we should go to the villa to see Constantine and ask her about it?' I suggested. But Alison was sullen and withdrawn, in her own misery.

Soon after that Alison returned home to England. She rang me to say she was taking the ferry the next day and insisted she didn't want me there to say goodbye. I think her pride was hurt, but she promised to keep in touch.

I watched from a distance and saw the Opel parking at the side of the harbour. Stelios carried Alison's case. She now looked so tanned she could easily pass for a Greek. She gave him what I guessed was a tip before pulling the large bag across the deck. Alison didn't see me but I ached inside when I saw her and I knew I'd never felt as fond of anyone before.

I still had another month at my job. After Alison left I completely lost any interest in socialising. Whether it was the atmosphere of the island or the absence of Alison I couldn't say, but I was becoming more of a recluse. In the evenings I showered and lay naked on my bed listening to Leonard Cohen and Don Giovanni over and over again.

The days I spent with the family, often just me and the kids exploring the island. We would take a little picnic with us and discover safe bays to swim and sunbathe. They really liked me. I could even say they admired me. It felt good after all the shifty goings-on. For the first time I was observing a family life and thinking that could be a base for true happiness. I mooched around, sometimes just sitting for hours day-dreaming of Alison or, feeling restless, I would set off under the burning sky to the places we had visited – which almost amounted to the same thing. Her presence was everywhere. I wondered what she was up to. In the next four weeks I heard nothing of her and then my own time was up.

The day before I was to leave the island I got a letter from Alison, post-marked London.

Dear Michael,
It's not going to be a long letter. Too much to write, too much to explain, so I'll go straight to the point. Maybe you should sit down first ...
   Would you like to be the Godfather to my child? I would be honoured and you would be a great role model to him/her. I really messed up in Amorgos. I was so naïve and I was just a passing fling for Jonathan, the man with many masks. I considered an abortion but I realised I couldn't. You see, I was listening to my intuition. I was thinking of the masquerade evening, what 'Janus' said and the tarot. This is my Wheel of Fortune. At first it felt like the end of the world, but now the more I think about it, the more it feels like a beginning. I will look after this baby and I will find my place in the world. We had a special time in Amorgos, you and me, and I hope you will be part of my life still.
   As much as you want to.
   Looking forward to seeing you soon, in London!
   Yours, Alison xxx

It was like a bomb had dropped – the chaos this letter caused in my head. After the obvious shock about the baby, my thoughts turned on the single inescapable fact that Alison wanted to see me. That made me happy, hopeful.

On the departing ferry I leaned against the rail and watched until my family, who had escorted me to the harbour, were just black dots vanishing from view. Both kids had given me presents. I was touched and had promised to write.

I watched the hills of Amorgos, the sea turning deeper blue and in patches glowing surreal turquoise like Janus's eyes – because that's who I was thinking of, him: Janus.

Then I turned, hoping to find a seat but instead I found myself looking across the deck at Janus. Our eyes met. He was sitting on a bench with his arm around a girl. I felt angry, even violent. Did it stem from jealousy or resentment of Alison's treatment? I wasn't sure, but I told myself to stay calm and walked over to them. 'Hello, Janus. Or how should I call you? Jonathan? David?'

'Hello, Michael. Meet Penelope.'

I nodded at her – she could easily have been the girl from the beach.

'I think you have been confused with me and my twin brother.' He spoke in the same smooth tone I remembered.

That stopped me in my tracks. I studied him more closely now. 'Are you serious?'

'That's right. Jonathan never mentions me because he doesn't want to be seen as a twin. Jonathan has this thing about being his own man—'

'So, which one of you was cheating Alison? After all your talk of *be true to yourself* – ironic isn't it?'

'Well, Jonathan is always a bit of a bore, taking things so seriously. I think he rather fancied Alison. And he got really pissed off with me, when he heard that I had dated her too. Bit of a joke, you know.' He winked and smiled charmingly.

There was something darkly malevolent about that smile.

'What he says, it's true.' The girl, Penelope, spoke for the first time. I noticed her finely shaped ears. 'I'm not even sure which one is which but I think this is David, or is it Jonathan?' She looked at me as she stroked Janus's hair.

I didn't find any of this amusing. I stared at the top of their heads, and knew behind my own the blank upper windows of the top deck; the balcony view for this endgame. It dawned on me that both brothers had probably slept with Alison – that had been her wheel of fortune. And she had no idea of the trick or that one of the brothers still fancied her – or which one was the father of her child. I was in between them all, like the omnipotent writer. Mine the decision what to tell, to whom.

'So have you heard from Alison?' asked Janus. 'Do you know where she is, Michael?'

I turned my back on the two of them.

'Michael?'

I walked to the front of the deck and chose a solitary chair on the side of the setting sun. I had looked at Janus's face, the good and the evil. The past and the future. I glanced up at the windows of the top deck. The evening sun made them gleam with light. Could Constantine be watching me even now?

Chords from Don Giovanni turned in my head as I watched the coastline of the island receding behind the blue rim. I turned and contemplated the empty miles of sea. I was sailing away to an unknown future, to a new beginning. I had a strong sense of being alive and having the power to affect the future – or did I let the wheel of fortune just roll? Arriving at Amorgos, I had travelled lightly – no more than a boy. Now leaving, I was carrying knowledge and with it came a man's responsibility. *Panta rhei.*

I made the last mark with my pencil stub and put it in the drawer. I had told the truth as I knew it. I wondered if Alison would ever read my story. Soon it would be dawn and I sat, Bible open at the Book of Job, waiting for the Owslafa to arrive.

End of the World

In a reflex from a previous life Julia looked to her wrist, and then remembered she no longer believed in watches. It didn't stem the rising tide of indignation at his lateness, if he was late. They should have agreed to meet inside the library but she couldn't ring him because her phone battery was dead. It was December and cold. Julia shivered in her skirt.

In the three months since they had met, she and her lover had stolen every available moment together. Not easy with her two small children. Then there was the not insignificant problem of Spider. But compared with the real problem, well, even Spider was 'small beer', as her dad would say.

At last, Edward appeared at the far corner of the square. As he approached he had one eye on the raised stones that served as a pavement, and the other on his Blackberry.

'Over here,' she shouted. But he couldn't have heard her. She waved. His two-piece suit and smart raincoat were incongruous in this dreary backwater, discovered by her and Spider two or maybe three summers before. She noticed an infinitesimal increase of interest from a few shopkeepers leaning in doorways, looking up to see the new arrival, the fatted calf here on their turf. Edward, slim and immaculately dressed from crisp white collar down to shiny brown brogues, walked towards her with the nonchalant confidence of youth. Smart, short brown hair and a wide and open forehead. With the courage of despair Julia pinched herself; how much longer could it continue?

'Amazing, nobody knew where the library was. That's the internet for you I suppose. Wow! *Like* the skirt. You look good, love the eye-shadow. How much time have we got?'

'Minutes, maybe hours, depends...'

'Sorry?'

He looked confused. That's what she loved, his innocence.

Julia pulled her long blonde hair into shape – thick and luxuriant, it had always been her best feature. She shuddered when she recalled the first wrinkle she had seen under her eyes that morning.

'You're cold,' said Edward. 'Here.' He opened his arms to her and they embraced on the library steps.

The library was her special place. Recently Julia had started to spend more time there. She liked its quietness and the feeling of not being an intruder. Edward she had met whilst renewing her passport at the British Embassy, maybe the first time someone had ever picked her up in some place other than a pub. He was cultured, clever and five years her junior. She had been drawn to his middle-class *Englishness*, and he followed Test cricket.

'Don't worry, leave it to me,' he said. 'Let's find some warmth and what passes for coffee around here.'

Julia never tired of listening to Edward speak; all his words carefully enunciated in a cut-glass accent. Spider had been very keen for them to leave Torquay to move to this country. *We'll meet people like us*. Well they hadn't. They'd met people like Spider: Angus, Trigger, Rory, Mags (collector of pornography most likely), Spike and Horse (he had one). They weren't so much friends thought Julia, more people plunked together with no choice but to get on, like inmates in a prison. One day the governor would announce a pardon and they would all go home, wherever that was.

The café next to the library was open, unbecoming and empty. The moped leaning against the wall outside must belong to the waiter, surmised Julia who chose a chair by the window. The waiter looked like he'd rather be anywhere else and Julia wondered if she dared to ask him to turn down the volume on the ghetto-blaster which belted out Good Vibrations to white plastic chairs. Julia spotted Edward surreptitiously slipping his Blackberry into a pocket. She found his unease endearing – who did he think was going to steal it, the waiter? Julia reflected that the men in her life were mostly attentive when they wanted something. Spider would tell her she was a 'sexy piece of stuff' before they went to bed but afterwards was more interested in rolling a joint. He also had a habit of exhorting himself: *Go, Spider-Man!* So far she had always managed not to laugh at such absurdity but she knew one day she wouldn't be able to restrain herself. What would happen then?

Edward was different. He whispered her name when they made love. And right now was stroking her arm with his long, sensitive fingers. Too bad it was just another coffee rendezvous she thought, not a shared afternoon at Maya's cabin in the mountains.

'How's Maya?' asked Edward.

'She's meeting with some Reiki practitioners. They're going to concentrate on yoga and the Hoffman process.' Julia considered how much easier it was to talk to Edward; he was on her wavelength. 'It's a great place for high vibrations and sound healing ... you know, the mountain top. She wanted me to go but—'

'You're still going to tell Spider tonight? That was the plan, wasn't it? Then we'll leave together. How will he take it? I mean, he'll think it's the end of the world, won't he? He'll ... sorry, I didn't mean—' Her lover was nervous.

Julia studied the worn menu. The Portuguese phrases reminded her of an unfriendly exam paper. Was he mad? Did he really believe for a minute she would ever tell Spider, let alone leave him? She and Edward inhabited a make-believe world of knights, damsels, sunsets and impossible romance. 'For sure I'll tell Spider, maybe even tonight. That's assuming he's not spangled on whatever.' She eyed the sullen-looking waiter, 'Just two coffees, please.'

'I've got to be back at the embassy by five. My secretary thinks I'm interviewing someone about a passport application.'

'Any young mums desperate for passport renewals?' Julia knew she had no right to sound jealous and hoped he hadn't noticed. Edward liked to talk about work. It was strange for her to meet someone who had some. To think that years ago *all* her friends were like him.

'Just paper filing. I'm buried in bureaucracy.'

'The bureaucrat has the world as a mere object of his action.'

'What did you say?'

The waiter returned, clumsily clattering with the coffees which he slammed down on the table, spilling some. She wondered if this would be the last coffee they shared together.

'Not me, Marx.'

'No marks with me, but isn't it *pesetas* anyway?'

Edward reached for his wallet. 'You're not cross about me being late?'

She *was* bothered but her irritation had more to do with the ageing of her skin. She wasn't yet thirty but already many years in the sun meant she should use face creams. But they were so expensive. 'Of course I'm not cross. It's lovely to see you.'

They drank their coffees together in silence. A black cat tiptoed past the window, arching its back. She tried to remember what that signified.

'I'm pregnant.'

'What? But how's that possible?'

'At my age, you mean?'

Edward put his hand to the back of his neck. It was surprising how quickly he looked uncomfortable in his smart clothes. 'No ... I mean ... of course not ... Wow! We'll have to think about how we break it to my parents. That's good, isn't it? I mean assuming that I—' He ran out of words.

To be fair to him she guessed this was not the sort of thing one covered even on the extensive Embassy training programme: *How to handle a native girl who tells you she is up the duff*. 'It's all right, I'm not. But I could be. I just wanted to hear how you would react.'

'Well, certainly you had me ... uhm ... for a minute. Maybe it's for the best. I mean—'

'Of course you would be the father. Spider and I haven't enjoyed that side of things for—'

'We is closing at three of clock today,' shouted the waiter in his best English from the frame of the doorway, where he stood like an extra in a Western, waiting for something to happen. Tomorrow could be his lucky day, thought Julia.

'He doesn't like me,' she said, dropping her voice. 'You should show him who's boss.'

'Well I've never punched anyone before but if there has to be a first time, why not Spider?'

'I meant the waiter. We've still got nearly an hour.' Julia put her hand on his arm before replacing it under the table. 'They only tolerate us because of the hard currency we bring. Come tomorrow – if the meteorite doesn't get us the locals will. Time for a real drink. Join me?' Rather than wait for the waiter she marched up to the bar, her long hair fanned behind her.

'But it's hard to leave Spider.' The small carafe of wine was nearly finished. Julia placed her hand on Edward's leg.

'You mean you still love him?' He sounded horrified.

'No. He's hidden my passport.'

'Oh I see,' said Edward who clearly didn't. 'But why have you put up with it for so long?'

'You have to remember Spider is a painter. They live by a different set of rules.' Why, thought Julia, was she sticking up for him? Or was it because of the memory of the shocking, left-wing, idealist revolutionary with a striking stare who had once attracted her? Too late she had discovered Spider's interest in politics was passing, and that the attraction of opposites wasn't love. She looked to her wrist again. 'What's the time? My brother's plane is landing about now. You'll meet him tonight at the End of the World party. You're still coming, aren't you? You know where to go?'

'Esmeralda's.'

The afternoon's assignation had allowed her to temporarily

forget what day it was. Or rather, what date. The knowledge resurfaced like an unkind comment amongst friends; something you wish you could take back, but couldn't.

'If you're right about tonight what's the point of worrying about tomorrow? On the other hand if you're wrong, and I'm obviously very much hoping you are—' He turned to Julia for help.

No dice.

'What do you mean *if*... haven't I explained it well enough for you?' Julia sounded calm and certain. Meeting scepticism, incredulity, anger even, these were nothing new to her.

'But there is some reasonable doubt, surely? I mean it stands to reason—'

'It won't change now.' Julia sounded angrier than she had meant to. 'Look, I'm sorry. It's not your fault.'

'So tonight?' said Edward in a neutral tone, adjusting his perfectly knotted tie. 'But it's been predicted before?'

'Yes, Edward,' she emphasised as if chastising a simpleton, 'there were some mistakes last time with leap years in the calculation. This time we may not be so lucky. All the signs are there; look at what's happening with the economies, the riots, the weather. None of it is normal.'

The waiter re-appeared, staring unsmilingly at Edward.

'I think he wants us to settle up.'

'That's ridiculous.' The colour was rising to Julia's face. 'He should be open a couple of hours still—'

'We *are* the only customers.'

'Imperialistas Inglês!' the waiter cursed. To reinforce his point he banged down a small plastic dish. On it was a hand-scrawled bill.

'You heard that, Edward. Do something!'

'Julia, my job is to deal with incidents – not cause one. Just think.' He got out his wallet.

Outside, nothing had changed. The square was still empty, no impending storm clouds, just another rendezvous which had run out of time. Edward stood before the crumbling walls of the library, the sun in his face. They embraced and said their goodbyes. She realised the next time she set eyes on her naïve and sentimental lover, he would be coming to carry her away to start their new life together, if it got that far.

She returned to her yellow Volkswagen, parked under the shade of a lemon tree, and set off for Spider and home. Was it guilty conscience that made her check the driver's mirror a few minutes later? The road wound back down to the town below; a strip of dark-brown leather put out to dry in the wintry sunshine, empty except for a solitary motorbike weaving its way through the mountain curves. The sun looked as she felt; tired out. For expansive energy and yang she would have to wait for summer.

She decided to make a small detour on the way home to see Elina, her friend and spiritual teacher. Julia had met many healers and could now recognise the real article. Some of the fakes were very good. Elina was genuine. She had studied the Crystalline Consciousness Technique (CCT) with Mohan Guruji. What was more her successes were legendary. Famously one patient with terminal cancer and for whom doctors had given up hope, went to Elina for a consultation. After the crystal treatment – which Julia didn't fully understand, although she knew crystals were used to create an energy grid to remove blockages in the body's electromagnetic field – not only had the cancer gone into remission, but on the last scan it had disappeared from the body completely. The doctors were baffled. They said it was a miracle. Elina, with customary humility, had said it was the patient's fate to beat cancer. But Julia knew different.

She turned the Volkswagen into the overgrown drive of the converted stable-block. Good, no other cars. 'Anybody home?' she called out, stepping across the tiled floor.

'Hello, come into the light, my dear, where I can feel your aura.'

Julia walked towards a well-lit patch of floor near the east-facing window overlooking the monastery. Elina was over sixty years old and had been blind for the last twenty.

'Julia, isn't it? I can sense you are troubled, are you?'

'Elina, it's the day. December 21st.'

'Ah yes. The grand rhythm of the cosmos begins. The movement from our world of water to the sacred world of space.'

'You're not worried? Will it be sudden? Should I do anything? The children?'

'Child, relax. When you achieve complete surrender your freewill ceases to exist and you achieve pure consciousness, so you won't need to make decisions. Julia, you and your children will still have a role in the new world. Embrace it. True surrendering is a powerful tool to master.'

Julia felt positive vibes returning.

Elina talked about *at-one-ment*. 'Remember, it isn't all white light, it's about being able to face the darkness and not run away.'

Julia would have liked to have stayed longer but Spider would be wondering where she had got to. She left, putting something in the small dish by the door, not that Elina would ever dream of asking for anything. She was pleased with her decision to make the detour. Now she had nothing to fear, not even Spider. Driving home she understood her mistake was to worry too much. She was the queen of improvisation. She must let the pure stream of consciousness take over. Julia alighted from the car. Spider was waiting for her.

'Jinx! Where in hell 'av you been?'

If she had thought that after all these years together Spider had lost his capacity to surprise she was wrong. He stood in the drive to their house wearing his best suit, the one her mother had insisted on buying for their wedding. He was holding a shotgun.

'I hope that isn't loaded?' She tried to sound relaxed, to conceal her rising panic. Had Spider found out about Edward? Who could have shopped her? 'What's up?'

'Bloody bailiffs, that's what's up. Talkin' about repossession.

Ha' can they do that? The 'ouse is paid for, innit?' Spider snapped the barrel shut. He looked angry but her panic was subsiding – she knew his quixotic rhythms by now. In a minute he could be laughing. What Spider didn't know was that just over a year ago Julia had re-mortgaged the house. Even if the world didn't actually end tomorrow, it could look very different and she didn't have much hope for property prices, not in this country.

'Well, if you'd bothered to open some of the mountain of letters that have been piling up in the postbox you wouldn't be so surprised. Don't worry, I'll take care of it.' She sounded a lot more confident than she felt. Could they repossess? On the other hand at least it didn't look like Spider knew anything about her secret lover. 'Anyway what's with the suit? I seem to remember you swearing you'd never be seen dead in one again?'

'That's it, Jinx. Me lucky charm, innit.'

'Any news from Simon?'

'Whaddya mean?'

'Well he's flying in today, remember?'

'Uh, yeah, sorry, forgot. He rang ... said all fine an' he'll meet us in the pub. Oh yeah and I told 'im to wear a suit. That surprised 'im.' Spider laughed.

'I bet it did.' Julia started to relax. 'How's the painting coming on?'

They went to the shed in the garden to look at Spider's latest canvas. It was three metres by two and almost completely green. It looked as if someone had spilt a can of paint across one corner but that was Spider's trademark. Back in the Torquay days one art critic had described his work as 'thought-provoking'. One throw-away comment but it had kept Spider going for years. For a time he had cultivated the painter's look; long, straggly, unkempt hair, a beard, neckerchiefs. Now he had no hair at all and the brightly coloured shirts had been replaced by drab military fatigues. Until today.

'What's it called?'

'Re-birth, geddit?'

She didn't know what to say. 'Re-birth?'

'Yer, know. After the world's end, comes the re-birth like.'

The revving of motorbikes filled the air in the busy car park at Esmeralda's. 'I'll see ya inside. I'm just 'aving a chat with Horse,' said Spider.

'Fine, I'll see if Simon has arrived,' replied Julia watching Spider going over to join a group of guys collected like a colony of bats, attracted to the shady recesses found on the outside of pubs. It was less than four hours since Julia had said goodbye to Edward but it seemed days ago. Time was slow today.

She liked pubs – never more so than at Christmas. Opening the door of Esmeralda's on this 21st December she was greeted with music, chatter and the smell of beer. It brought back old memories of sneaking out from her posh boarding school to the village pub on a Friday night. Esmeralda had really gone to town with the decorations. Christmas music was playing. The only clue that they were not in England was the glide of slowly revolving fan blades above her head. Julia felt at home, at peace.

She quickly spotted her brother perched on a bar stool engrossed in some newspaper. He looked up as she came over, tanned face, perfect teeth – he'd had those done since last time they'd met. As a rule Julia had learnt to be careful about which friends from her previous life to invite. People who were in the habit of dressing for work often found those who didn't in some way threatening but it was Simon's talent to be effortlessly at ease and confident wherever he was, with whomever. He had the poise of a kingfisher on a branch, any minute set to dazzle with his charm and yet with all the time in the world, and whatever differences they had, she loved him.

'Hello, sis. Long time no see. Give us a kiss.'

She did. She was reassured by the feel of him, the familiar aftershave.

'No Spider? I was looking forward to buying him a pint. He told me I had to wear this, you know.' Simon was fingering the cloth of his suit. 'What's going on? Anything to do with this End of the World banner thing?'

She followed his gaze and saw for the first time the rainbow-coloured, hand-painted cloth hanging over the door.

'Esmeralda must have a Harvard degree in Marketing. The End of the World sells like hell.'

She hadn't intended to tell him straight away but now she started, missing nothing out: Elina's vibes, the Mayan calendar, the Giza plateau pyramids, four thousand columns of hieroglyphs which we were only just beginning to unravel. And there was more: 'The research proves that the Giza pyramids and the sphinx were laid out to point to a specific date—'

'And you got all this from the internet?' It sounded like he really was listening.

She heard a text message arrive on her phone but decided to ignore it. 'Look Simon, these people knew what they were talking about. What they foretold for us had already happened to them . . .' She tailed off.

Simon took a sip from his pint. 'So in a nutshell the Mayans were pre-dated by an advanced civilisation, superior to our own, that had almost certainly invented atomic power and space travel – they built the pyramids which point to the day when the whole process is going to be re-cycled. It's like a prophetic washing machine that takes ten thousand years to turn full cycle and now at midnight it's coming around to tumble again.' He looked at his watch. 'Time for a last pint?'

She could see he was trying not to laugh. 'Listen, sis, I've heard this before. I could show you some major landmark buildings in New York and demonstrate they all point in the same direction as your pyramids and sphinx.' Her brother hadn't changed, Simon was establishment, a corporate banker on a hunting trip, getting all his ducks in a row. He opened his arms expansively. 'Look, sis, you've been with this crowd too long. There are a number of central flaws in your argument, the whole Armageddon—'

Simon never finished his Armageddon sentence. Two things happened: First: she remembered to check her text message. It read: *Can't make it tonight. Embassy training all C Rank and above. Back in a few days. Love you Edward :)*

He tried again: 'As I was saying, the trouble with Armageddon theories is that they pre-suppose—'

Second: a flash of bright white light followed by the sound of splintering windows and shattering glass. Then darkness except for the kaleidoscope of Christmas lights. Out of the gloom a set of fan-blades winged silently by like a large caged bird freed after captivity. It was difficult to breathe – where had all the air gone? For a split second she had a crazy notion that this was some stunt of Spider's. Sounds of people screaming which slowly faded away. The pub was full of smoke but she couldn't see anybody. So this was what it was like. No tidal wave. No meteorite blotting out the night sky. The world finished with a bang and Slade playing on the jukebox.

She remembered Elina's parting advice – was it really just this afternoon? 'Julia, remember, sacrifice your life before you sacrifice your faith.' So it had finally come true: first the white light and then the dark. Was it getting darker? The bar seemed a long way off. She felt sad. But she wouldn't run away. Where was Simon? No one could say she hadn't tried to warn them. She reached for the table, feeling tired, slipping to the floor. She was on a cloud. The children? What was it Elina had said about complete surrender?

The last thing she remembered was a ghost-like figure, arms outstretched, coming towards her, calling out to her. It came from out of the orange and red flames that curled like serpents' tongues to the skies. She welcomed her destiny, her complete surrendering...

Whiteness everywhere. Silence. No movement in her hands,

some sort of bed. Weightless. Was this how pure consciousness felt? And a bird singing somewhere and was that the sun streaming in through a window? Was this heaven? A voice, a long way off.

'She's awake!' Spider shouted.

'I'm alive,' she whispered. Her throat felt like sandpaper. It was an effort to talk.

Simon lent over her; 'Sis, you're fine. You've been out for days. You're going to be good as new, thanks to Spider.'

'Spider?'

'Yes, sis. Some local nutter, a wannabe terrorist, chucked a home-made bomb from the back of a moped. Random attack – just out to get some English.'

As her focus widened she saw Spider in the room. He was grinning.

Simon continued: 'Everyone else got out but you stayed put ... must have been shock. Spider went back in for you. The fire had started to take hold by then, really ablaze. We called him back but he wouldn't listen.' Julia was struggling to understand. 'He carried you out like a babe in arms. The guy deserves a medal.' And this was Simon talking. 'He's a hero.'

Spider's face loomed into view, eyebrows singed. 'Ello, gorgeous.' He smiled, showing his silver fillings. 'Elina was here – she's got more front than Brighton that one. Anyways, she's got a new date; next year, innit? Best check the Mayan calendar double proper, I says. There's a real danger I imperil my good name. Oh yeah and some nosey parker toff from the Embassy turned up. Well out of order. Won't be showing his face around here again. Some other benders too, apparently they can repossess the house but I never liked that place anyhow. We can start again. Trigger's got a caravan we can lend. Horse reckons the happening place nowadays is Bolivia. And I might have got a buyer for Re-birth. Good to have you back, Jinx.'

Everything was worse than before. Julia felt a tear rolling down her cheek.

'Cheer up girl, it's not like it's the end of the world, innit?'

She couldn't speak. The picture of the black cat with the arched back in the café window came back to her. Now she remembered the portent: *Prepare for a long journey.*

The Forgotten Present

1976

'Anybody want the sport?' asked the boys' father.

'Rather!' said Tom, and just managed to snatch the paper ahead of his twelve-year-old twin brother.

It was summer and the start of the cricket season. The boys were keen to read about their heroes' exploits but yesterday there hadn't been any on account of the rain, which was forecast to continue.

Ralph Castle, financier, entrepreneur and man with connections, sat at the head of the table. He was young to have such a house and children. While most of his contemporaries were still struggling with their first flats, Ralph had bought Candleford, aided by a successful foray onto the Far East stock markets and some financial support from his father. Candleford was Georgian, and lavishly furnished over three floors. It boasted forty-six windows – one afternoon the boys had counted them.

The house was reached by a gravelled drive past a couple of large trees and a tennis court. The twins went to preparatory school and their sister Fiona stayed at home. Now it was the first week of the summer holidays.

'I was thinking of inviting the Cummings for the weekend. If this rain clears up we can get in some tennis and if it doesn't, billiards.'

'More coffee, Ralph?'

'Thank you, darling.' Ralph looked fondly at his wife Elisabeth. 'And boys, we've got to have a quieter day than yesterday. Was that a game of cricket I saw in the hallway? One of these days you'll do some serious damage.'

'But Father, we're not playing with a hard ball,' said Tom.

'He knows that. Wombat!' said Gerald.

'I was just saying.'

The volume quickly started to rise in the dining room, with its views through tall windows onto the garden.

'Ssh!' said their father in a tone that the boys knew well. Minutes passed and the only sounds were the rustle of turning newspaper pages and the sonorous tick of the grandfather clock in the hall.

'If the Cummings do come I think we may have to suspend the cricket. You can listen to it on the radio.'

'There isn't any.'

'What are you saying? There's one in the drawing room, the sitting room—'

'Father, I meant there isn't any cricket. It's raining at Lords as well.'

'Oh, I see,' said Ralph, as he began the elaborate ritual of lighting his pipe. 'Well think of something else. You are Castles after all. Empires were built on the Castle spirit.' Ralph was packing his pipe with fresh tobacco. 'What about your Christmas present, which cost me an arm and a leg?'

'What, Subbuteo?'

'Mastermind is boring.'

'No I mean your main present.' Ralph set down his tobacco pouch and observed the boys.

'But we didn't get any other presents.'

'You didn't?'

'Just the Mastermind.'

'And the Subbuteo, actually just a new Subbuteo team.'

'Well we did get the pet mouse from cook that we took to school but matron confiscated it.'

'Probably put it in the porridge.'

'A big heavy box, in blue paper?' Ralph struck a match and the tang of sulphur hit the air.

Nobody spoke in the dining room. The boys exchanged excited glances, as the enormity of the news began to sink in.

'You mean there is a present from last Christmas we haven't yet opened?' Tom spoke slower than normal. 'Wacco!'

'Wizard!'

Ralph Castle had got his pipe going now and small clouds of smoke drifted across the dining room table.

'Darling, you know what I think about your pipe in the dining room. Can't you go into the drawing room?'

'We're just on our way, aren't we, boys? Now we've got to put our thinking caps on. We have some serious searching in front of us.' Candleford was a big house and Ralph divided it into three sections; one searcher for each floor. They knew what they were searching for – a large box, wrapped in blue paper.

Thirty years later

'Dad, do you like it that Uncle Tom calls you Gerry?' The questioner was Felix, the son of Gerald and Amanda. The family were travelling to Candleford in a bullet-grey Volvo estate, X-Country model. Gerald was driving.

'I do, Felix,' said Gerald, glancing in the driving-mirror at his ten-year-old son sitting alone on the back seat. 'In fact I would quite like it if your mother called me Gerry as well.'

'And I've lost count of the times I've told you, if you wanted to be called Gerry you should have thought of that when we first met and not introduced yourself as Gerald. Now watch out, you're driving in the middle of the road,' said Amanda with a reproachful look through her glasses.

'I learnt to drive on these country lanes. Felix, did you know the reason you drive a little into the middle is that it gives you a better line of sight,' Gerald swung the Volvo, with just a little more zest than was necessary into the corner, 'around left-handers like *this one*?' Amanda reached up to grasp the roof-support handle. To compound matters an oncoming tractor forced Gerald to swerve almost onto the verge. Hedge branches rasped against the windows.

'Careful, you idiot!' exclaimed Amanda.

'That's tractor drivers for you,' said Gerald dryly. 'I'm looking forward to seeing Tom. I can't remember the last time all three of us were together – Fiona will be there of course and also this guy is coming down from Sotheby's. Could be quite a party. Sorry, Amanda, I forgot you don't like parties *or* country lanes.'

'Don't be ridiculous. It's just bad drivers I don't like.'

'Well, son, I don't think it's going to be as much fun for you, all boring grown-up stuff. Still, you can explore the house.'

'How much further to go, Dad?'

'Home straight, now. Look! Another orchard that's been chopped down. Do you know it's been three years since we were last here?' He glanced across to Amanda. 'We should have made more visits to see Father.'

'I never stopped you. Eyes on the road!'

'But you were never very keen.'

'Some of us really are committed to our work. I mean you're not the only one with a career.'

'I wonder if Tom will bring a girlfriend?'

'Who was that awful Marxist last time? Sara or something?'

'Great opinions and legs to match, I seem to remember.'

'Typical Tom. He's hopeless.' Amanda spoke with the customary irritation that showed in her voice whenever Tom was mentioned. 'That man will never settle down.'

'Oh, Tom is a good sort,' said Gerald, motioning his head in the direction of the back seat, as if to indicate to his wife not to criticise his brother in front of Felix.

'You watch the road, and your hands should be at ten to two on the wheel.'

'As Father would say, the pursuit of perfection is the enemy of good enough.'

'You're not half the man your father used to be.'

'You've been listening to my enemies again.'

'I didn't know you had any friends.'

*

The Volvo swept confidently into the Kent village, whose most famous inhabitant – Ralph Castle – had passed away in his sleep the preceding week, aged seventy-eight. The last of the autumn leaves clung to the trees not wanting to let go, like spectators at a cricket match sitting under umbrellas.

The dining room at Candleford hadn't changed in thirty years; mahogany furniture and yellow wallpaper decorated with pale blue coats of arms. Gerald, in a blue-striped shirt and a matching blue silk tie and polished brown shoes, studied a series of family portraits hanging on the wall. Back in those days the Castles dressed for Sunday lunch. He was oblivious to any other presence in the room, absent-mindedly running his hand along one of the high-backed Windsor chairs positioned at either end of the table.

'Hello, Gerald,' said Fiona who had stepped into the room a moment earlier, and had been observing her brother. 'Give us a kiss.' She was a tall and elegant woman with long, streaming and raven-black hair.

'Hello, Fio. I was just remembering all those Sunday lunches we had here.'

'Battles might be a more apt description.'

The two affectionately embraced. She was only two years younger than Gerald but appeared under thirty. Fiona's husband worked in New York and she divided her time between America and London, where she had her own job in chambers.

'You're still the only person who calls me Fio.' She picked up an old photograph of the three of them as children wearing fancy dress clothes. 'When did you get here?'

'Couple of hours ago. I've been trying to explain the concept of conkers to Felix, and Amanda's been busy ... well, you know Amanda. It's nice to see you, Fio. You radiate style as always. Long hair suits you. Still happily married across two continents?'

'You bet. Todd is so much into his work he wouldn't know whether I'm in the living room or London. Of course, no children, but I would probably have been a poor mum anyway.

And the money I'm on; I *really* don't think anyone is worth that much. What was her phrase?'

'Silly money!'

They both laughed at the recollection of their mother Elisabeth who had been a constant moderating influence on their idiosyncratic and extravagant father.

'Poor Dad,' said Elisabeth. 'He never got over Mum's death.'

'He certainly lost his Midas touch; taking loans and selling the tennis court to the developers. There's no danger of finding any "silly money" kicking about here. I got a letter from the lawyers last week. The house is worth close to a million and the re-mortgages and taxes are—'

'Let me guess. Close to a million?'

'Even when Father's luck deserted him he could still balance the books.'

'When does Tom arrive?'

'Any minute now. I offered to collect him from the station but he said he'd rather walk through the orchards. Also, there's a man from Sotheby's, probably on the same train.'

'Sotheby's?'

'Amanda's idea. I'll explain later. Are we too early for a drink? Can you stay for the funeral? I don't expect it'll be any more than a handful of mourners from the village.'

'That's the advantage of dying young; you get a better turnout.'

'Thirty years ago he was minted. He would have had kings of industry and nobility.'

'Well you never know, maybe a mystery lover?'

'Father? I don't think so, he was like a swan, mated for life.'

Footsteps on parquet floor echoed from the corridor off the dining room. Amanda's voice, sure and slightly hard, preceded her: 'How about that watercolour above the fireplace? Horrible picture but it could be worth something. I could send a photo to my dealer friend.' Amanda, now in a tracksuit, entered the room.

Short hair and a figure that was testimony to years of self-control lent her a lean, almost boyish appearance. She had a clipboard in one hand and a digital camera in the other. 'Oh hello, Fiona, when did you arrive? I mean, how do we know we can trust this Sotheby's expert?'

'Just half an hour ago. Is Felix around? I've got a small present for him. And Todd wants to know when you are coming out to New York for a holiday.'

'What would be the point, we'd only argue.' Like a soldier on retreat, she directed a tired look in Gerald's direction. 'As for Felix, he's somewhere, exploring the house.' Amanda had the appearance of someone whose mind was elsewhere and was already turning away. 'I've met Mary – some sort of housekeeper. She says she'll bring us a supper at eight o'clock. I wonder if there's any of the best silver left or did Ralph sell that off as well? I'm sure there was a pair of Georgian candlesticks in that room before the study. What do you call it?'

'The Range room?' helped Fiona.

'I'm just getting the final list ready. I should have it printed in half an hour. I've left a blank column for the evaluations, if that Sotheby's man ever shows up.'

And with that Amanda was gone.

'Very organised, my wife. Not changed, has she?'

'Like a football manager before the Cup Final. I'm sorry, I shouldn't—' Fiona tried to smother a laugh.

'It's all right,' said Gerald, his features expressionless. 'I don't mind it at all, really. Sometimes I forget, but Amanda wasn't always like this. I think after Felix came along she changed, she'd do anything for the boy.' He moved to the window with a view to the front lawn. 'Do you know, I think the happiest years of my life were spent in this house? Do you remember that summer we played tennis every day?'

'How could I forget? Virtually a professional umpire before my fourteenth birthday. You were Björn Borg—'

'Tom was more McEnroe than McEnroe.' Gerald laughed for

THE FORGOTTEN PRESENT

the first time that day. 'When we sell we should make sure it's a real family that gets Candleford, not a nursing home.'

'Not many families could afford the renovation this place needs? What's with Amanda's clipboard?'

Gerald explained Amanda's system for allocating the family 'heirlooms' as she called them.

'And the man from Sotheby's?'

'To help us make some informed judgements, otherwise how do we know what some items are really worth?' Gerald raised his eyebrows whilst quoting his wife. 'That's the official line. The truth is, Amanda just hates the thought of losing out.'

'For me it's just sentimental value. I was hoping to have Mum's dressing table. Do you think that would be all right?'

'Well doesn't that rather depend on what the Sotheby's expert values it at?'

Fiona's face fell.

'I'm only joking, Fio. Of course it's okay. Amanda doesn't make all the decisions, you know. Look who's here at last.'

Brother and sister rushed out of the house to meet Tom strolling up the drive.

'Golly, you're looking very artistic these days, Tom,' said Fiona. Tom wore his hair long, and had a soft velvet hat and a long scarf that fell down as far as his cowboy boots. 'It's hard to imagine you're identical twins any longer. Gerald has put on weight, yet I think it suits him.'

Tom smiled before replying: 'And you're looking, what do they say over there, knock-out?' Before turning to his brother. 'Good to see you bro'.

'On your own?' asked Fiona.

'Well the night is young. There was a real stunner on the train who got off at our stop so I thought I might check out The Ship tonight.'

Fiona laughed, threaded her arms through her brothers' and led them towards the house. 'I still remember, Tom, when you tried to sneak a barmaid upstairs during one of Mum and Dad's parties. Dad intercepted her in the hallway, with something along the lines of "My dear young thing, have we been properly introduced?"'

The three disappeared into the house, unaware of the flaking paintwork around the door, instead interrupting each other with recollections of times long gone, when they were young and their whole lives, loaded with promise, had beckoned before them.

Amanda had the inventory ready. The list ran to five pages and catalogued items room by room. From her laptop and portable printer she had created copies for each of them.

'So we just go through this list and tick what we want?' asked Fiona. 'Why the evaluation column?'

Amanda explained the correct procedure – the evaluation was an indication for decision-making purposes only. The person who had first pick would then get pick number six, number two would then get number five, whereas the person who had third choice would also get fourth.

'It all sounds very compli—' Fiona corrected herself, 'well thought-out.'

'It's perfectly simple,' said Amanda tersely. 'And we're not starting anything until the Sotheby's expert gets here. Nobody has any idea of the value of any of the paintings, or the Chinese vases. The silver, I suppose, is hallmarked, but still—'

'Can we get Gerald to choose a wine bottle for supper from the cellar or are they already catalogued?'

Amanda looked at Fiona sharply. 'No, I didn't have time to do that. Anyway I don't suppose there's anything valuable there.'

The doorbell rang. Felix came into the room. 'There's someone at the front door. Should I open it?'

'If that's Sotherby's, they're late.' Amanda frowned.

'Only way to find out,' said Tom, following Felix out. He returned with a wide grin and an ash blonde. She was in her mid-thirties, wearing long cream leather gloves, a close-cut green jacket and a deep red skirt patterned with black embroidery. The overall appearance was of an exotic migratory bird. Tom announced: 'Miss Gregson.' There was a pause. 'From Sotheby's. She was on the same train as me.' He winked at his brother.

'But we were expecting—' blurted out Amanda.

'Yes, people often do. Not everybody from Sotheby's is over fifty and male with steel-rimmed spectacles.' The new arrival delicately peeled off her gloves as she spoke. 'No grey hair, not yet anyway. I'm Miss Gregson, how do you do?' She had a resonant, sensual voice, at odds with her light build and slender features.

'Well it's—'

'Of course.'

Miss Gregson laughed as the brothers started speaking at the same time. Soon they were all laughing with the exception of Amanda who restored formality with a conclusion of the introductions: 'That just leaves Gerald my husband and his brother Tom, who let you in.'

'Tom and Jerry,' Miss Gregson laughed again.

'Yes, Father had a good sense of humour,' said Tom. 'You and he would have got on well, but Miss Gregson won't do at all. What can we call you?'

'And here, let me take your coat and bag,' said Gerald.

'Thank you, and forget the Miss Gregson, Jill will do just fine,' said the evaluator from Sotheby's with an easy confidence. 'My, what an exciting place this is. If this room is anything to go by there has to be hundreds of items. It's going to take me some time. Where would you like me to start?' she asked taking a spiral notebook from her worn leather satchel.

'How about a cup of tea?' said Gerald.

'The main sitting room,' said Amanda. 'There are a couple of watercolours. No one seems to agree on what they're worth.'

'Why didn't you pack the brown shirt I bought you?' Amanda asked Gerald. They were upstairs in the blue bedroom. 'Anyone would think Tom was a writer or something big in the art world, the way he dresses.'

'I guess he does do pretty much as he chooses,' said Gerald, putting on some aftershave. 'He's evidently taken a shine to Jill.'

'And that's another thing. I don't know why that Sotheby's woman has to join us for supper. She's not family. Here, fix these pearls for me, *please*.'

Earlier on, as the size of the evaluation job had become apparent, Gerald had offered to ring a local hotel and book a room for Jill. She had replied: 'That won't be necessary. I have a sleeping bag, a Sotheby's evaluator has to be prepared for anything.' Gerald had offered Jill the yellow room. Now he stood behind his wife to join the clasp on her necklace.

'Fiona likes Jill – says she reminds her of Mary Poppins.'

'Yes, our Miss Sotheby's – that's another one who behaves just as she chooses.'

'That's done.'

'Thanks.' Amanda checked her look in the mirror. 'So remember, if Tom chooses one of the large Chinese vases then we must make the other vase your next pick because if you don't, Tom could snaffle up the pair.'

'Tom grew up with those vases, like we all did. He has every right—'

'Of course he has,' interrupted Amanda. 'That's why you have to think on your feet. And whatever happens we must get your grandfather's embroidered fire screen.'

'Fire screen, right.'

'I don't trust that woman.'

'Who?'

'Your sister, who else? All that we'd-love-to-do-something-for-Felix. Well if they like children so much why didn't they have any? Her precious career, that's why.'

'I couldn't understand it when you said to Fiona that all we would do on holiday is argue.' Gerald made an attempt to soften his voice. 'You don't really mean that, do you?'

'We can't even agree about the Chinese vase. That's the trouble with you, Gerald. You never listen to me.' Amanda consulted her list again.

'What, never?'

'I know Tom puts on that laid-back *I'm not materialistic* air but he will be calculating exactly what our moves are going to be.'

'Sometimes, Amanda, I wonder: are we right for each other? Is this what we dreamed of when we started out?'

'Don't be silly. No one gets what they dreamed of. If they did every bird singing in the garden would be a robin and every day would be your birthday. Besides, after the last marriage counselling session you arranged, I consulted with my work colleagues and—'

'You did what?'

'You heard. They said our marriage is perfectly good enough.'

Gerald was about to reply to her when they heard the gong sound for dinner. 'Good old Tom,' said Gerald.

'And that's one thing I'm definitely not having in *my* house ... the gong.' Amanda lent over to give Gerald a kiss on the cheek before descending the staircase. Gerald paused for a moment, put his hand up to touch his cheek, and then followed.

Jill was in a long dress of Fiona's – a perfect fit.

'Cute doll,' Fiona said to Tom.

'Isn't she lovely?'

'I take it you're no longer planning a visit to The Ship tonight?'

'A voice to die for,' he whispered back, his eyes on stalks. Jill had let down her hair, which fell in blonde ringlets below her shoulders and Tom's gaze followed her everywhere. Gerald came around offering champagne from the silver tray their father had always used. They were gathered with their backs to the fire in the large sitting room.

'What a lovely room this is,' said Jill. 'I was sorry to disappoint you about the value of those Chinese vases. I'm sure your father was thinking of this room when he bought them.'

'For something so modern you mean,' said Amanda with a trace of bitterness. 'Well, now I know their real value they've come right down my list, I can tell you.'

'And what's top of your list,' asked Tom, 'dear sister-in-law?'

'That would be telling.'

'Well, clearly.' Tom looked to the ceiling.

'You, Tom, really are insufferable.' Amanda raised her voice. 'Don't expect any help from us when you run out of money again.'

'Amanda is only concerned that nobody gets disappointed,' said Gerald. 'Tom, how about proposing a toast?' Tom was just clearing his throat in readiness when Felix poked his head around the door.

'What's the matter, darling?' said Amanda gently. 'Would you like me to come and find you you a good book?'

'I thought you were practising billiards?' said Gerald.

'Mum, let me show you what I found.' With some effort the boy pushed into the room, along the carpet, a very large and evidently heavy package wrapped up in blue wrapping paper. It was tied with a silver ribbon.

'Where did you find that?' asked Amanda.

'I'm more interested in *whose* it is. Is there a label?' Fiona was on her knees, her head level with Felix's.

'It's very heavy,' said Gerald, lifting it onto the mahogany coffee table. 'Isn't this exciting?'

'Finders keepers?' asked the boy.

'Yes, like treasure trove you mean,' enthused Amanda. 'Why not?'

'It was in the little room in the attic,' Felix was jumping up and down with excitement, 'under a table in a big box.'

'That explains it,' said Tom. 'You know what this is?'

'Not till we open it,' said Fiona.

'It's the missing present! Do you remember, Gerry, that summer when it rained and we hunted through the house? We searched for days.'

'Where?' replied his brother. 'What little room in the attic?'

'Used to be the maid's room,' said Tom. 'Probably the one place we assumed it wouldn't be.'

'Tom, you're right. And you were still trying to find the wretched box long after the rest of us gave up,' said Gerald. 'So the forgotten present really existed. I assumed it was just one of Dad's games.'

'Such a good hiding place, even he forgot it. I never doubted it existed.' Tom spoke quietly and slowly as if recalling his younger self. 'Not for a minute.'

'Father assumed it must have been one of the summer visitors who walked off with it,' remembered Gerald. 'Wasn't Thierry from France the number one suspect?'

'Well it's here now. So unless Thierry brought it back, Dad was wrong for once,' said Fiona who was carefully examining the present. 'The label says: *To Tom and Gerald. Happy Christmas. Your loving Father.* Well, don't you want to see what it is? Talk about *déjà vu*, this feels just weird, us and Christmas presents in the sitting room.'

'Yes. Expect Mother and Father to poke their heads around the door any minute,' said Gerald.

'You know the rules, no presents opened until the breakfast is cleared.' Tom, possibly feeling the effects of the whisky before his champagne, gave a passable imitation of his father, good enough to start Fiona and Tom giggling. Amanda gave them both a disapproving glance which made Tom laugh even more. Gerald decided it was time to open the present.

'They don't make wrapping paper like this any more,' said Jill, who seemed as excited as any member of the family.

Tom pulled off the last of the thick blue paper. 'I expected dust but there isn't any.' The paper revealed a wooden box, with a loose lid. Tom delved inside the box, which was full to the brim with wood shavings. 'There are two items here.' He gently fished out something green, about eighteen inches long.

'A train,' said Felix.

'Not yet it isn't,' said Tom. 'I think this is just the tender.' He placed the truck on the coffee table before rummaging through the wood shavings again. 'Now, this baby feels a whole lot heavier.'

'It *is* a train!' exclaimed Felix. 'A jolly big train!'

'Gerald, you should spend more time with Felix,' said Amanda, 'and share a proper hobby.'

'Dad loved those trains,' said Fiona, 'he spent hours up in the attic, *alone*.'

'It's very heavy.' Tom carefully placed the train on the dining room table. The train was nearly two feet long, painted in enamel green with gold chimneys. There was a large copper boiler. Both tender and train were hand-painted with accurate detailing. *Castle Conqueror* was engraved on the side of the engine boiler.

'Wow!' said Fiona, 'A real steam train.'

'But Castle, means it must have been a special commission,' said Tom.

'It's enormous!' said Gerald. 'On the other side it's got the name *Lionel Trains*—'

'Well, if Ralph were still alive,' interrupted Amanda, 'I think he'd have wanted Felix to have it. I mean—'

'Lionel? Did you just say *Lionel*?' said Jill.

'I've heard about Lionel Trains but I've never seen one.' Jill turned around the engine to look for herself. 'If this is a real Lionel. Well, I think there are only a dozen or so in existence. And they were all hand-made, special commissions, very special indeed.'

'Wow!' said Tom

'I need to get a second opinion,' said Jill. 'But I'd say: get champagne.'

'So it's valuable?' said Amanda . 'More than the Russell Flint?' Amanda was referring to the original watercolour in the master bedroom that Jill had valued at a conservative seven thousand pounds.

'Trains have a singular appeal. And a genuine Lionel.' Jill took out her own pocket camera. I'll take a couple of photos and send them to someone who specialises in trains.'

'How quickly can you find something out?' There was a rising excitement in Amanda's voice. Jill concentrated on the photograph she was taking.

'And this *someone*,' Tom said, 'does he always return your mails at eight o'clock at night?'

'If I know Russell he's just about to have breakfast,' said Jill matter-of-factly, moving the train on the table to get a sideways angle. Tom seemed surprised. 'In New York,' she added pulling a small laptop from her satchel.

Supper was finished. The train and its boiler had been positioned on display on the long mahogany sideboard in the dining room. The beef goulash provided by Mary from the village had been acceptable but all agreed that it was the fine wine that had saved the day.

'Well done, Gerry. I think you and Jill did an excellent job in liberating such a fine wine. To the *Liberators*.' Tom raised his glass and both brothers smiled at the recollection of their father.

'A good wine should be decanted, Gerald,' said Amanda, whose glass remained almost full. 'Your father would have done so.'

'Well, some experts would say that for a Chateau Latour seventy-five, decanting would make no difference. What luck we found not one but two bottles.' Jill met Tom's eye, who was quick to fill her glass.

'Well for some of us there's more important things to life than drink,' said Amanda, her glance to Jill a withering moral scorn. 'I suggest it's time we started work on the list.'

'Yep, time to divvy up the loot,' agreed Tom with heightened colour in his cheeks. Amanda had earlier said they couldn't start until they had some idea of the value of the train. 'I mean if it's going to be valuable.' But Fiona had pointed out that the label said it was a present for Gerald and Tom, so it was something they should sort out between themselves later.

The brothers and sister started to take their pick of the family heirlooms. As expected, Amanda (or officially Gerald) had the Russell Flint at the top of her own list. Fiona chose the dressing table, Tom the grandfather clock and so they worked they way through Amanda's carefully put-together catalogue. At the start there had been noticeable excitement in the room but this gradually dissipated. After the top thirty items had been allocated, a cigar break was announced by Tom. It seemed everyone except Amanda was starting to lose interest.

While Tom went outside and Gerald went hunting in the cellar for some single malt, Jill and Fiona were in the kitchen making coffee. The Sotheby's expert and the sister had formed an immediate bond. 'You don't like her much, do you?' Jill said.

'Oh dear. Is it that obvious?' replied Fiona. 'It makes me so angry to see Gerald pushed around like that. Tom was always more the mischief-maker of course, but Gerald was still his own man and now Amanda—'

The kitchen door opened and Tom came in, the top two buttons of his shirt undone and glass in hand. 'So this is where you've been skulking. Come on, Fiona, it's not fair if you keep Jill to yourself. Anyway there's a *ping* just come from the laptop. Sounds like New York has got out of bed at last.'

'Coffee. You may need it before the evening's out.' Fiona placed the tray on the dining room table away from Jill who was engrossed in her laptop.

Gerald returned from the cellar, holding aloft a dusty whisky bottle, 'I knew it! Father had taste. Twelve years old, and that's before they bottled it—'

'Shh!' Amanda gestured towards Jill at the other end of the table.

Fiona mouthed the words 'New York'.

'Phew!' exclaimed Jill. She had everyone's attention. 'Okay,' she said. 'Prepare yourselves for a shock, everybody.'

'Good or bad?' asked Amanda, her fingernails drumming on the table top.

'This mail is short but nonetheless exciting. Rufus does somewhat murder the Queen's English. I'll read you exactly what he's written: "Lionel Trains are the Gold Standard in the industry, rumour has it they sometimes casted chimneys from gold. The key question is whether this is an original Lionel design or one of his apprentices. No record of a Castle Conqueror, so a custom job. Value will vary a lot depending on rarity, could be anything from twenty to a hundred thousand depending on condition. Of course, provenance would add to value considerably. News of a new Lionel find will start a feeding frenzy, Rufus."'

'How can it be worth so much, it's not even antique?' asked Gerald.

Jill explained that rarity was a bigger indicator of value than age. 'A Charles II halfpenny, nearly three hundred and fifty years old, is worth today around sixty pounds but the 1933 British penny could fetch around one hundred thousand pounds, because only eight were ever made. So rarity and provenance are what counts.'

'Provenance?' asked Tom.

'Well, you can say "Winston Churchill slept in my bed", but the question is, can you prove it? If you have a letter from Winston and he writes "What a pleasant night's sleep in your four-poster", then you've got great provenance. I wonder. Did we check the box thoroughly?'

'You mean—?' asked Gerald.

Tom was already emptying the wood chippings of the box onto the table. 'Nothing! Except, hello! What's this?' Out from the bottom fell a cream envelope.

'Looks like a brand new envelope,' said Amanda. 'Is that really old?'

'It's only light that fades. You read it,' said Tom giving the envelope to Gerald.

Gerald, also nervous, passed it to Jill. 'Sure?' she asked. They nodded. Jill started to read the type-written words. '"Dear Mr Castle, please find enclosed by special commission the Castle Conqueror steam locomotive: five-inch gauge, superheated copper boiler and twin outside cylinders, Walschaert's valve gear and Alco diesel two cylinder engine with steam brakes. Twenty-two carat gold chimneys. Two years guarantee. Signed Mr Lionel Cohen 1974, Lionel Manufacturing Company." There's also a handwritten PS. "Hope you approve of the name. I took the liberty of adding in Conqueror. Trust your sons approve. Lionel."'

Jill put down the letter and studied for a moment another piece of paper from the envelope. 'Bingo! And that's not all, we also have a boiler certificate.'

'And that's a good thing?' said Amanda.

'I would say that's a very good thing,' replied Jill.

'You bet it is. Give that girl a cigar!' said Tom.

'I don't smoke, thank you, but another glass of champagne would be very nice. I think Rufus still has some work to do.' Jill smiled at the brothers. 'You get the champagne and I'll write the email.'

'Well, Fiona, this is hardly fair for you.' Gerald put his arm around his sister's shoulder.

'It's not as if it's *my* present. One thing I've learnt is that money doesn't bring you happiness. God knows I've got enough – money I mean. Sorry, that didn't sound like I meant it to.'

'Easy for you to say, but I'm sure it helps,' said Amanda. 'Just think what we could do with a hundred thousand. We could buy that cottage we've always dreamed of.' The lines had momentarily vanished from her forehead and Amanda seemed genuinely happy. Her eyes were shining brightly and she was speaking faster than normal.

'Say that again,' said Gerald.

'I've always said a cottage in the south of France—'

'No, Fiona is right,' said Gerald, pausing. 'It's not as if it's *my* present either.'

'Don't be silly, she meant it's not *her* present.'

'Listen, it's coming back to me. Tom, you remember my Gray-Nicolls cricket bat, the first one we played with a hard ball?'

'Size six. Of course I do,' said Tom. 'You cracked the window in the hallway the first day you got it—'

'Cricket bats. You'll drive *me* bats! What relevance is there?' Amanda's smile quickly vanished and was replaced with eyebrows knitted together in a well-practised frown.

'Tom, think back ... when we couldn't find the forgotten present, Dad felt so guilty he bought us another present, the cricket bat.'

'So what?' said Amanda, who took a deep breath to cover her impatience.

'Because don't you see – it's my bat? Tom said that he would rather carry on looking for the missing present if it ever turned up and I said fine, he could have that and I would have the cricket bat. That was the deal. Felix, are you listening?' Felix emerged from behind the door. 'Son, I'll explain later what all this is about. Right now the important thing for you to remember is that a deal is a deal; I got the bat and Uncle Tom got the train. No Castle ever breaks his word and I won't be the first.'

'Ping!' Another mail arrived on Jill's laptop.

'This ratchets up the tension another notch,' said Tom. 'How's everybody's glass?'

Everybody was watching Jill at her computer. She read: '"Provenance changes everything and Lionel Trains are in demand. A one-off Lionel sold to an anonymous Japanese buyer three years ago for four hundred thousand pounds but that was slightly used. An unused Lionel Cohen, authenticated, with original boiler cert, I would say anything upwards from six hundred thousand. That's pounds not dollars – usual caveats apply. Lucky you, Rufus".'

The only sound in the old dining room at Candleford was Tom carefully placing the whisky bottle down on the table.

'Hold on. No one seriously expects,' Amanda spoke quickly, the colour rising to her cheeks, 'you to swap a crappy old cricket back for half of six hundred thousand—'

'Less of the *crappy* thank you,' interjected Tom. It was a

Gray-Nicolls. What would be the going rate for a Gray-Nicolls, Jill?'

'It isn't a laughing matter.' Amanda was not trying to hide her annoyance. 'You're loving this, aren't you, Tom? I bet you don't even remember the arrangement, do you? Anyway, Felix found the train, not you.'

'I certainly remember the bat.'

'Hah hah, very droll. The trouble with you, Tom, is that you bank on people feeling sorry for you. It's the only thing you're any good at – putting aside your rogue-male appeal to a certain type of gullible woman. It's your substitute for hard work and application, isn't it?' And Gerald has always felt sorry for you, but not this time. This time he's not playing, that would be taking things a step too far.'

'Do you know, Amanda, you're absolutely right. I completely forgot the arrangement.' Tom moved closer to his sister-in-law. 'For all I know, Gerry is fabricating the whole thing.'

'Get back from me. No court of law would uphold the words of a twelve-year-old.' Amanda was sounding fierce. 'I'm right, aren't I, Fiona? You're the lawyer. What do you say?'

'Uhm, I think the bigger issue might be the nature of the agreement, very difficult to prove.' In contrast to Amanda, Fiona's voice was calm. 'Without witnesses a verbal agreement wouldn't have much standing. Sorry, Tom.'

Gerald put down the train which he had been examining as the discussion had become heated. 'There is one game of cricket I often remember. Father inadvertently gloved his ball to the wicketkeeper and declared himself "out caught" which lost us the game. I was furious. Nobody else saw a thing and we were all set to win the match—'

'Yes, and this is vitally relevant now because?' said Amanda whose irritation was starting to take control of her manners.

Gerald ignored her. 'After the defeat, when I was sulking in my bedroom, Father came in and reminded me of who I was. Father was right. Our family has the code of the Castles and it's not like shoes you choose to use or not depending on the weather, it's more like the feet you walk with.' No one seemed to pay any particular attention to what Gerald had just said but he didn't seem to mind. He looked like a man who'd made a personal discovery.

'Tom will gloat about this for years if you let him get away with it.' Amanda's anger was now directed at both brothers.

'You're quite serious, aren't you, Gerald? You'd give away hundreds of thousands of pounds for the sake of a principle?' Jill leant forward with both arms on the table and sounded more engaged than at any point hitherto that evening.

'We'll take you to court.' Amanda was almost shouting. So her hair had come loose which, combined with her rising voice, leant to the appearance of someone wild and out of control. The others seemed embarrassed. Nobody spoke. Instead they just stared at her.

'Okay, Gerald,' said Amanda, dropping her voice to a quietly menacing tone. 'Let me tell you how it's going to be. It's simple. You have to choose. You either do the sensible thing and forget this ridiculous so-called pact between two twelve-year-old boys or you can forget me. Because what I'm not going to have is me and Felix being forced to watch whilst Tom burns our inheritance.'

Gerald moved a few steps towards the windows, then wheeled around to face his wife. The other three took turns to look at Gerald and Amanda, confronting each other, across the elegant dining room, like some static tableau of an old family drama.

Tom broke the silence. 'Gerald, I may be many things but greedy is not one of them. Amanda's right, so of course I'm ready to go halves—'

'There'll be no halves. What you do with your inheritance is up to you,' replied Gerald. 'Still, there is a way you could make it up to me.'

'Anything, you say it.' Tom looked like a man pinching himself to confirm that he wasn't dreaming; the winning lottery ticket really was in his hand.

'It was on your list and I wish I'd put it on mine ... the dinner gong.'

'Deal.'

Amanda stormed from the room, slamming the door behind her. 'Is there any champagne left in the cellar?' asked Gerald.

The next morning Fiona was alone with Gerald in the dining room, toast and coffee on the table. Sun streamed in through the long windows. Gerald was half reading the newspaper. 'I'm pleased I got this table,' said Fiona, I shall think of them both every time I sit at it.' Fiona was in her mother's chair facing the hall end of the table, where for so many years their father had sat. 'We had some laughs here, didn't we? Do you remember when Dad pretended to read that telegram from the Queen?' They both smiled at the memory from long ago.

'Absolutely, and I'm looking forward to having a few laughs again soon,' replied Gerald.

'I expect Tom has quite a hangover. That was some celebration,' mused Fiona, sipping her coffee and gazing across the lawn. 'Were you drinking to drown your sorrows?'

'Oh, Fio, don't you realise that yesterday was a day I'll never forget. It counts as one of the most memorable of my life. I lost a wife and I won my life back.'

'I thought you seemed to be bearing up pretty well,' said Fiona with mock seriousness. 'I must admit I thought she was bluffing when she threatened to call a taxi in the middle of the night.'

'That's Amanda for you; doesn't drink, doesn't bluff and there are a few other "doesn'ts" you won't want to hear about.'

'What a picture she was. You could grow corn in those furrows on her forehead.' Fiona had a hand across her chest as she attempted to control her laugh. 'Oh, we mustn't. And poor Felix, I do hope he's all right. He seemed half asleep.'

'Well he was. Don't worry, Felix is a Castle. He's a survivor and Amanda is a great mum.'

'Wouldn't Dad have just loved to have been there yesterday evening?'

'Rather, but in a way he was, wasn't he? His unseen hand was shaping our destinies. And as for me, today feels like my birthday.' Gerald had the satisfied demeanour of a centurion who had just saved the Test match. 'Yes it was rather what Father would call a Castle-defining moment.' He picked up the newspaper.

'Perhaps I'll take up a cup of tea to Jill – she's nice, isn't she?'

'Well, she's different. I'll give you that.'

'Was she in the Yellow Room?'

'Uhm, actually, I think you might find her in the Blue Room.' Gerald peeked a glance at his sister from behind the sports pages.

'The Blue Room?' exclaimed Fiona. Gerald was back engrossed in his reading. 'But that's always been your bedroom.' The surprise in her voice had turned to warmth.

There was a tranquil quietness in the long dining room at Candleford, save for the the profound tick of the grandfather clock that could clearly be heard from the hallway and Gerald searching for the cricket scores in the paper. Outside, a small bird flew down to land on the window sill. Gerald glanced up from his newspaper. 'Fancy that, a robin. Makes one think of Christmas.'

Millionaires

'Millionaires in a week!' Tim, stood up, glass in hand. 'Let's drink to that.' The others rose in unison, four men in black dinner jackets, two with bow-ties undone, all of them rich and soon to be a lot more so, calculated Tim. He was proud of his membership at Worth's; only an exclusive group knew of the discreet door in a side street between Trafalgar Square and Covent Garden.

There was an uncoordinated chorus of 'Cheers' and 'Millionaires!' before they collapsed back into their plush upholstered chairs. The scene in the private dining room was illuminated by the light of two massive silver candelabra on the table, evoking a Renaissance painting of Faust. Tim had always appreciated art. Soon he'd be able to make a few well-informed investments. He made a mental note to find and cultivate an art dealer.

'Who dares sins!' shouted Frank, the silver-haired production director; at forty-seven, a handful of years older than the others.

'Who dares sins!' intoned Massimo. The sleek, well-groomed director of finance in a striped shirt took up the mantra, banging his fist on the polished mahogany table. Not yet drunk but well on the way – Tim knew the signs. He tilted his heavy cut-crystal glass against the candlelight and watched the refracted patterns of light kaleidoscope through the whirls of amber liquid. Looking around the table he felt warmth, almost affection, for the three co-owners of their company, Oxyron. He had carefully handpicked each one, before setting about wooing them away from their unsuspecting former employers. All hard workers, no golf players.

'And the dare is ... the dare is—' Frank paused as he eyed them all, 'how to get the most fun out of the money?' He banged his glass on the table. 'Tim?' The others were quick to follow suit, and soon the glasses were rhythmically striking the table.

Tim smiled, waiting for the noise to subside. 'Let Massimo go first.' All eyes turned towards the Italian, expecting him to say something. They'd kept going when they could have sold out, waiting for the big one, the Initial Public Offering. And now the graft was about to pay off. Oxyron's reputation in providing technology platforms for the latest generation of mobile phones had made them one of the big players in the market. The soon-to-be-listed company employed close on two thousand people. Not bad for a start-up from a rented garage in Croydon. He still remembered negotiating the rental agreement for twenty pounds a week.

'Oh that?' said Massimo as if he had more important things to think about. He went on in a bored tone, 'I'm going to get myself a forty-four foot Swan sailing yacht and hire a gorgeous professional female crew to show me around the world.'

Strictly speaking they had a week to wait for their money, but it was in the bag, agreements had been signed and witnessed. Only the end of the world could stop them collecting the following Friday.

Massimo continued: 'I've got so far as a short-list—'

'What?' asked Frank. 'Girls or boats?'

'And it's not cheap I can tell you. If anyone's interested to see photographs?' Massimo pretended to search for supporting pictures from his breast pocket.

And he could afford it. As CEO Tim was due between fifteen and twenty million pounds, depending on the uptake from institutions. He calculated that no one around the table was going to cash in less than five million. They deserved it, every penny.

'Bollocks!' shouted Frank. 'Your wife would never give permission. She hates sailing.'

Tim knew Frank was the biggest drinker in the group, which made him a potential liability. But he was also the one who had squeezed suppliers to get their production costs the lowest in the industry. 'What about you, Frankowski?' Tim used the nickname Frank had been given after recruiting so many Polish immigrant programmers.

'I'm going to buy a couple of pubs,' said Frank filling his glass, 'and brew the best beer in Devon.'

'Like Denise is going to say yes to that,' said Massimo, looking like someone wanting to get even. 'She thinks you can't handle your drink as it is.' Taking an appreciative sip of the single malt, Tim reflected that he, of all people, knew how to enjoy the finer things in life and this was just the prelude.

'Chaps.' There was an instant silence in the room. Tim had noticed this before: when Paul spoke others listened. Paul was the company lawyer, sharp as a knife, silver-rimmed spectacles and short black hair. 'It's a show-stopper.'

'What do you mean?' James sounded indignant.' Show-stopper? What is?'

'Well don't you see?' answered Paul, in the same quiet voice he usually reserved for suppliers when explaining that they didn't have a leg to stand on. 'We're getting only half of what we're entitled to.'

The room was silent.

'Well sorry but I got us a damned good price at fifteen pounds a share,' said Massimo. 'No lock-in clause remember?' His chin was jutting out. 'I'd challenge anyone to have done better.'

Tim quickly nodded in agreement. It certainly was a good price. The figures had been massaged to give the best possible valuation and he felt no loyalty to hang on to his shares. He'd get out when the going was good and reckoned on Paul to do the same. 'John, it is a fine price.' Paul spread his hands in a placatory gesture. 'But would you have accepted seven pounds fifty?' he asked, carefully selecting a piece of Stilton from the cheese board.

'No, of course not. That would be daylight robbery.'

'Exactly. A show-stopper. But we're all married, so under British law—' As if to make the point he divided his Stilton into two halves, placing one on a dry biscuit. 'We all lose exactly half.'

'But we can't do anything about it,' said Frank. The others were nodding their agreement. 'Richer or poorer, we're married. We can't change that, not cheaply anyhow.'

Tim said nothing. Paul was being Paul, taking his time, inspecting the whisky in his glass.

'Have you heard there are three rings involved in marriage? The engagement ring, the wedding ring and the suffering?' Massimo was attempting to lighten the mood, but no one else was laughing. Paul had given voice to the thought that they all recognised. The idea was not new, the execution was the problem. Paul had only brought the elephant into the room, so far.

'But there's no way around it, is there?' Frank sounded resigned.

'You're sure about that?' Paul spoke like a poker player raising the stakes.

He had everyone's full attention now. Tim was not surprised Paul had been thinking about the problem. Last month the lawyer had confided in him that he suspected his wife of having an affair.

Paul explained. 'What if we were each in possession of a document that relinquishes any ownership claims from our respective wives, like a premarital agreement. Plenty of people sign them before they are married so why not now?'

'But why would they sign it?' asked Frank.

Massimo nodded. 'I can think of five million reasons why not.'

'That's what we do best, isn't it?' said Paul. 'Investors, inventors, suppliers, workers – we get them all to toe the line, eventually. So why not our wives?'

'If she's drunk, she might sign,' tried Massimo.

'If she thinks she's signing something else.' Tim's turn.

'But will a tricked signature stand up in a court of law?' asked Frank.

'In the end it's not what's *right*, it's what practicable,' said Paul. 'Remember Lipasti?' Lauri Lipasti, the Hungarian inventor, had worried them all with a strong patent infringement action, but he'd got cold feet after threats of intractable delays and huge legal costs, allowing them to buy him off. That brinkmanship, led by Paul, had saved them millions. 'Lipasti worked that out. And so will our wives.'

'But we had a plan for Lipasti,' said Frank.

'That's right, we planned.'

Now Tim got it. He didn't know what it was for sure but this was far more than an exploratory probe – Paul already knew where this conversation was going. Like an astronomer picking out the shape of a constellation from the night sky. Nothing they said had surprised Paul, so far they'd just been joining up the dots. Far from irritated, Tim was curious to see where this exploration was going.

'Still, I mean ... Judith?' Frank was biting his lip.

'Well okay, guys, where is the best place to hide a tree?' asked Paul.

Tim saw the idea a split-second before the others. 'Of course,' he said, 'in a forest.' Trust Paul to come up with it. The man was a genius. It really could work.

'Exactly.' Paul smiled. 'That's what we do. Get a bunch of documents for our wives to sign, all of them meaningless. Then when their eyes are starting to glaze over, we slide in the *big one*. They won't even notice what they're signing.'

'A throw from left field,' applauded Tim. 'They won't see it coming. 'He was starting to feel the familiar flutter in his stomach. 'It's just like we've made a second IPO. Not only do we double our return – there is no incremental cost to factor in. Are we all in?'

'I'm really not sure—' Frank now held a hand to his forehead. 'Lipasti was easy to put one over. But my wife, she's not so soft ...' Tim realised the trouble with Frank: he was that bit older than the rest of them, a throwback. He didn't have an eye for the main chance as they did. Well, they didn't need him to make the plan work.

'Come on, Frank,' said Paul 'It's just a signature; besides, you don't have to exercise the option. It's just there, insurance. She never need know.'

'So it would be just a secret between us?' said Frank.

'That's right, Frank, just insurance.'

'Okay, count me in.'

'Simple. Ingenious. Priceless.' Tim felt like a proud horse owner in the winner's enclosure after winning a turf classic. 'Gentlemen, we just netted ourselves a few extra million. Not bad for an evening's work. Let's get that man a cigar! And cognacs all round. Waiter!'

After a further hour and many more toasts, they left the table covered with empty glasses and cigar stubs, to pick up hats and gloves from the club steward. Tim noticed the cloakroom hooks were bare – they must be the last to leave. 'Drat! I forgot my phone,' he said and nipped back into their private cabinet room. He eyed-up the ninety-pound tip left in notes on the silver tray. Checking the coast was clear, he pocketed fifty.

Tim had woken with a hangover and the uneasy feeling that accompanies an important but so far not completed task. Pulling one over on the doppelgänger – the name he'd given his wife – was not going to be easy. They'd been married twenty years. But his resolve was clear. It was too good an opportunity to miss. After three coffees and a couple of paracetamol he was feeling a lot better as he looked out onto the garden. He was no gardener, but nonetheless Tim thought this one could be bigger, more impressive somehow.

'Don't forget I'm off to see my sister next weekend,' the doppelgänger called through from the conservatory.

A slow wide grin spread across his face. Sisterly visits came every month or so and meant a weekend of freedom! Just what he needed, a couple of champagne nights with the intriguing

Chantelle. 'That's fine. Friday is the IPO day but we can always celebrate when you get back.'

'You're sure you don't mind?'

'No, no, darling, that's fine. Oh, I forgot to mention we still have some more papers for you to sign, later in the week.'

'For me?' The doppelgänger came through into the kitchen. At fifty she still managed to cut a graceful figure, Tim thought, but there was something about the skin of a woman her age – it just didn't have the same tone and elasticity of a younger woman, and the streaks of grey hair were starting to get more obvious.

'As a co-owner of the company.' He tried to remember what she had looked like when they had first met. 'You know what these accountants are like.'

'Fine.' She was stroking the back of his neck. 'I thought we would have fish for lunch.' His skin crawled. He hated it when she did that. 'Could you get some white wine, darling?'

Down in the cellar, relieved to be on his own. Tim was pleased with the way he'd dropped the signings into the conversation; casual and realistic, with just the right emphasis. He wondered for a minute how the other chaps were getting on. When it came to the crunch they were on their own. He texted Chantelle: *Get ready for Tiger next weekend!*

He'd decided that as soon as he got his hands on the millions he would leave. There was nothing to be gained by kicking his heels around this worn-out marriage. That was the up-side of having no children – no tricky explanations. As for friends, well, he had always found them easy to make. With the money he would have there'd be a whole new social world opening up for him. Sailing and hunting, opera and travelling – not the life the doppelgänger appreciated anyway.

Seeing his reflection in the cellar's passageway mirror, he gave himself a small nod. Not bad for a boy who had come up through grammar school. It was a shame his dad couldn't have lived to see the day.

*

They drank copiously that evening but Tim managed to avoid contact in the bedroom, happy to save himself for next weekend. And gradually, as if a co-conspirator in his grand scheme, the clock wound its way down on the last weekend of his old life. Now the countdown changed from weeks to days, four to go. He set off to work whistling. Leaving his black Mercedes in the reserved parking space looking like a huge, polished, stag beetle shining in the sun, Tim leapt up the steps to Oxyron's main entrance, two at a time.

'Morning, Mr Witherspoon,' greeted the security chief.

'Same to you, Ralph.' He raised his hand in a cheery recognition. 'Good to see the Arsenal's results aren't getting you down.' Tim felt an end-of-term atmosphere entering the office on this particular Monday. Perhaps others misinterpreted his smiles; employees' individual motivations had little relevance for him this week, still less the week after. Despite that, knowing his role – the interested boss – he played it well, stopping to say hello and glad-handing colleagues on the way to his wood-panelled inner sanctum.

His secretary appeared with the coffee just as he spread the pink pages of the *Financial Times* across his desk, the size of an aircraft carrier. Janice looked after him better than his wife.

In the morning post there was an internal envelope and he recognised Paul's immaculate copperplate handwriting, *For the personal attention of ...* Inside were about ten letters for signing. The agreement was entitled *Covenant of Variation*. It waived all ownership rights for their spouses to Oxyron shares. The other end of year documents were imprinted on heavily embossed thick cream paper and looked imposing. The important one looked more ordinary on a sheet of plain paper – nice touch, thought Tim. It must have been a long working weekend for Paul. There was a handwritten post-it note *My advice is to get witness signatures and your own in place first. Good luck!* Tim understood the reasoning; much easier to sign when two had gone before you.

Holding this stack of documents in his hands his confidence in the whole scheme grew. He picked up the phone. 'Hello, Massimo. Good weekend? Did you get your envelope?'

Then he rang Frank, who was nervous as always, but he agreed: 'D-day tonight.'

Tim had time to change twice before the doppelgänger came home. In the end he decided the best thing would be to just look and act *normal*. His first thought had been to prepare for a champagne celebration; *just a few papers to sign first, darling*, but then he reckoned that a low-key approach might be better after all. A last-minute phone call to Paul had confirmed that great minds think alike. Reassuring, especially since Paul's wife was likely to be more suspicious than his own.

He tried to put a finger on how he felt, like ending it with a mistress – you knew you had to do it but it wasn't going to be easy. When at last he heard the door open he called out: 'Bus late again?'

'I've always got a book. You know me.'

Too true, he thought. He knew her as well as his favourite chair. They never discussed her work. His wife had been given the title of office manager as compensation for years of service and that was just what it was, *work* as opposed to what he had: a *career*.

Tim sat at his desk, papers about. Initially, he thought it would be a good idea to have the computer fired up so that he could pretend to be concentrating on something else when she was signing but now at the last minute he considered this might allow her the freedom to make a closer perusal of the papers. 'I wonder, could you just sign a few papers in here?' She came through from the kitchen. Here goes, he thought.

'Why don't you leave them?' she said without looking at him. 'And I can do them later.'

That sounded disastrous – like she might even plan to read them first! 'Well, if you do it now I can put them in the case and the job's done. I could make you a gin and tonic when we're finished. It'll only take five minutes.' Was he overdoing it? Shutting his laptop he stood and offered his seat. 'Here, I'll show you where to sign.'

They started, the meaningless year end documents first.

She looked briefly over the first one. 'I can't say I understand any of this.' He froze. Was she already suspicious? 'But then I suppose I'm not supposed to.' He managed to force a polite laugh. His plan was to place the deed of variation second from the end. 'I could be signing my life away here and I'd be none the wiser.'

Tim felt his heart beating against his chest. He concentrated on taking normal breaths. 'These lawyers have to justify their fees.' He got this out in what he hoped was a passably normal voice. It was a phrase that he had rehearsed earlier to fill any embarrassing silence.

She hadn't looked up once. It was now or never. He slipped the deed of variation across the desk to her. It was just as Paul had suggested, with two sprawling witness signatures already on each page. The words from the paper seemed to dance on the page and shout: ... *waive any claim to proceeds from the sale of Oxyron shares* ... Time stood still. Inside his head he heard Massimo's voice. 'I can think of five million reasons why not ...' But she didn't even pause. Just glanced at the paper before signing it on the dotted line.

Bullseye.

Cut and dried. Ten million pounds with that one stroke of a pen – unbelievable! Try explaining that signature away in court, he thought. It was as much as he could do not to shout YES! and punch the air in triumph. As a poor substitute, and not for the first time that week, he winked secretly at his reflection in the mirror. 'I'm glad we got that out of the way.' He put the signed papers into his briefcase. 'Now are you ready for that G & T?' Wait till he told the guys. He'd done it.

*

At last it was Friday. The flotation was scheduled for noon and the four musketeers were due to meet in the Oxyron boardroom just before. Paul and Massimo were already there when Tim arrived. He cast an appreciative eye around the room. Champagne bottles sat in silver buckets around the long table. 'Where's Frankowski?' he asked.

'Don't worry, he's on his way,' said Massimo. 'I think that's him now.' Outside the boardroom was the sound of running footsteps.

'I've not missed it, have I?' Frank burst into the room. He had a bundle of papers in one hand.

'Got it!' He waved the papers. 'Nabbed her as she was going out the door this morning, just as you said, like falling off a log. She didn't suspect a thing.'

'Well done,' said Tim. 'Better late than never.'

'You'd better start opening a bottle. It's two minutes to twelve,' said Paul, who glancing at his Rolex, strolled over to turn up the radio.

Tim started to unwind the metal wire from the cork of the nearest champagne bottle. 'Massimo, let's have some glasses.'

'And now the twelve o'clock news. President Obama—'

'So we've done it?' said Massimo, rushing over with some glasses. 'Time for a toast?'

'Hold your position,' said Tim. 'Couple of minutes yet.' He felt like a fighter pilot who'd returned unscathed and triumphant from behind enemy lines. They were the few. When the doppelgänger returned home from her sister's next week, he would have already instructed solicitors. Life was beginning. They listened for a couple of minutes as Tim filled the champagne flutes.

'And now the financial news. Gas prices are set—' There was silence in the boardroom. 'High-tech company Oxyron founded by entrepreneur businessman Tim Witherspoon, today becomes a public listed company. Trading in shares is expected to start briskly at around eighteen pounds fifty amidst widening interest in this—'

'Eighteen fifty... EIGHTEEN FIFTY!' Massimo shouted. 'Did you hear that?'

Tim raised a glass: 'Here's to us! We faced down the showstopper.' He beamed at the others. 'The show goes on. To Victory.'

'Victory.'

Champagne corks popping, Tim felt a childish desire to check his share account right away just to see it, but Paul explained it would be a couple of hours before the shares were registered, hopefully that afternoon. No matter. Now was the time to celebrate.

They were still celebrating nearly four hours and quite a few champagne bottles later. It seemed, thought Tim, that at the moment of triumph they wanted to stick together. Massimo was showing the others boat brochures.

Tim took the opportunity to log in to check his personal share account at the bank. At last the transaction had come through. The shares were registered! He connected the screen to the beamer so they could all read the numbers a foot high on the wall. One million, two hundred thousand shares at eighteen pounds forty pence each. He checked the time. He wanted to remember it: fifteen fifty-two. He would instruct his stockbroker to sell first thing on Monday. The others wanted to see their own accounts.

Tim felt the smallest pangs of guilt, although it wasn't as if he would be taking everything. She could keep the holiday home in Spain, which she'd inherited in any case. But the serious money would be his. After all, he was the one who'd earned it. Paul turned to him. 'We did it.'

'*Gentlemen.*' Tim had to repeat himself a couple of times to get their attention. When at last he had it, he raised his glass. 'Welcome to the millionaire's club.'

To Catch a Thief

'You see, the problem is that until recently it's been very difficult to detect. But now,' added the bank inspector, leaning forwards, 'we have some new software, from America.'

'But this is just a random check. I mean, you don't suspect anybody from this branch?' Adam Jones racked his memory regarding the security lectures on his grad-scheme, fast-track training. 'Don't keep your pin number in your wallet' – a bad habit for a bank manager, he knew, and still he hadn't kicked it – was the only thing he remembered.

The inspector had arrived without an appointment just when the bank had opened its doors that morning and asked directly for Adam. The inspector had been friendly enough. Head Office had given him one of Adam's business cards but he had insisted Adam ring a telephone number to confirm his identity. And now here he was chasing a . . . 'What do you call it again,' asked Adam, 'the sweeper thing?'

'A weevil-sweeper. It trawls through the bank system identifying accounts where there has been no activity, or to be more specific, no withdrawals.' The inspector spoke with the intensity of someone in love with his work. 'And then it starts to make its own withdrawals.'

'But surely someone would soon find out?'

'That's what's so clever about the weevil-sweeper software. As soon as an account is re-activated, then the weevil stops working. It goes back to sleep.'

'But we don't even have an IT department in Farbourne. There's only a handful of us.' The manager furrowed his brow. 'I mean, we're just a branch office.'

'Don't worry, sir. My job is a bit like a chase for wild geese. We reckon that the weevil-sweepers could be costing the banking industry up to a billion pounds per year.'

'But you don't know?'

'That's right. It's the nature of the beast. Must say, it's quite fun to be on their trail. I enjoy it.'

As he spoke, the inspector tapped the sides of the aluminium briefcase on his lap as if, thought Adam, it contained a giant weevil-sweeper trap. 'Have you actually caught any yet?'

The inspector, who couldn't be more than twenty-five years himself, looked suddenly sheepish and took off his glasses. He spoke quietly but earnestly as he polished them with his tie. 'But that's not to say we're not going to. I mean, there is no doubt the weevil-sweeper exists. If I could just have a little time with each person with access to the system.'

Adam felt noticeably more relaxed. 'Well of course, feel free to talk to anyone you want. I'll get my office manager to draw up an interview list for you. But I can't see how it's going to help. I mean, it's hardly likely they're going to admit to stealing from the bank, besides which you say you don't even have any proof.'

'Well perhaps we could start with you, sir?' The inspector opened his aluminium briefcase and slid out a card printed with a paragraph of text which he showed to the manager. It looked meaningless – just random words and numbers.

'Me!'

'If you would just like to type this sample text into your computer.'

'What does this prove?'

'It's a simple recording, sir. It records the way you type. Every computer user has his or her own idiosyncratic way of pressing the keys – thousandths of a second differences in the speeds between certain letters. It adds up to give a keyboard fingerprint, if you like, that is quite unique. And this is what our sweeper-tracking software is using to build up a picture of users on the system.'

'Wouldn't it be just easier to see what IP address the weevil-trackers, weevil-sweepers or whoever are using?' Adam noticed he pronounced the words with distaste.

'If only it were that easy, sir. But you see these people are using multi-layered proxy services, hide-my-IP programs and heaven knows what else. But it's true sometimes there's a loose brick in their firewalls and then if we're very lucky we might catch a glimpse of them through the wall, so to speak.'

'Which is why you're here today?'

'If you *could* just type that paragraph, sir?' insisted the inspector, handing him the piece of card. While the PC booted up the inspector produced a small black box from his aluminium briefcase. He deftly dropped down on one knee, presumably to make a connection to one of the many inexplicable ports on the back of the computer. 'That would be a great help, sir.'

'Give us a chance, I've just got to wait for the computer first.' Adam concentrated to write the text. He noticed a green light was now flashing on top of the black box which didn't make concentrating any easier. The paragraph had to be typed three times before the bank inspector was happy, and Adam was a slow typist. 'Quite a unique fingerprint, I imagine,' he said as he finished. His quip with the inspector had been received deadpan; the inspector just pushed the thick black glasses up his nose. That was the problem with nerds – no sense of humour.

'Would you like to use one of the negotiation rooms to interview the rest of my staff?'

'Don't go to the trouble, sir. I'd rather just have a chat with people at their work stations. More relaxed and informal, if you see what I mean. We don't want to unsettle your staff unnecessarily.'

'Fine, as you wish. By the way, I think Yvonne, my office manager, is the one person you can definitely cross off your list.' Adam laughed: 'If I was running a football club instead of a bank she'd be happy cleaning boots, no ambition whatsoever.'

'Not so much your young talent then?' The inspector glanced at the manager.

Adam Jones sniggered. 'You're not wrong there.' He gave the inspector a friendly punch on the arm, before adding:

'Confidentially, that's my remit here, you could say—' he chose his words carefully, 'to recruit young professionals. I've got orders to brighten the place up. You'll see what's needed when you meet my office manager.' He chuckled again. 'But a list of employees to interview – she should just about manage *that*.' He picked up the phone. 'Yvonne, get in here, will you?'

Looking middle-aged with a hint of grey hair over horn-rimmed spectacles and notepad in hand, Yvonne came into his office. Adam felt embarrassed to be associated with her in front of this sharp young inspector from head office. He'd think of a way to force her resignation shortly, just as soon as the new wave of recruits was trained up. 'By the way, Yvonne, have we heard anything from that graduate I interviewed a couple of weeks ago, what was her name – Sadie? Madie?'

'Madie Maitland. Nothing since the interview.'

'She'd probably call me in any case. Now I've got a job for you to do.' Yvonne listened as the bank manager patiently explained that he wanted her to draw up a list of staff for the inspector's interviews. 'Any questions?' he asked, already looking through the day's meetings in his diary.

'I was wondering whether you or the inspector would like a cup of coffee?'

Adam shook his hand and the inspector replied: 'I think I'll just get started right away if that's all right.'

Yvonne wrote six names on the piece of paper. After a moment's deliberation she added her name to the bottom. She could *just about manage that*, she thought. In her position she liked to keep abreast of developments, particularly when there were new faces visiting the branch. When someone shut the door behind them going into the manager's office, she had usually already pressed the telephone conference button which acted as loudspeaker to her own telephone headset. There wasn't much that happened in the branch that she didn't know about.

'Any chance of that coffee?' The inspector was entering

Yvonne's office, next door to the manager's. 'Yvonne, wasn't it?' The young man seemed more relaxed now that he was out of that snake's presence.

'Nothing but ghastly machine, I'm afraid.' She led the inspector across the open plan part of the office. 'I'll show you. And then you can get started on your first interview.' She passed the inspector the interview list. 'I thought you might like to see Devlin first. He's our assistant manager.' She took a few steps back, trying to sound off-hand. 'He has his own office. I'll just check he's free.'

Yvonne left the inspector at the coffee machine and walked briskly to the next office, entering without knocking. As she expected, Devlin was engrossed in the football pages. In less than sixty seconds she gave the assistant manager a summary of the surprise visitor and his intentions. While listening, Devlin put his various papers on the desk in a semblance of order, stashing the tabloid in the waste-paper basket. 'An inspector should be fun.' He straightened up his tie and added in a near whisper: 'I'll let you know how the interrogation goes.' At the same time he pulled his forefinger across his throat.

'Make sure you do,' she replied. Yvonne had more than a passing interest in the inspector's interview technique; she had been robbing the bank, so far undetected, for twenty-eight years. Leaving Devlin's office she nearly collided with the inspector carrying his aluminium case and a coffee.

'Oops, look out,' he said, just managing to avoid spilling his coffee. 'That was a close shave.'

'I must be more careful.'

'Saving yourself to last I see.'

'Sorry?'

'You put yourself last on the list—'

'Yes, a few loose ends to tie up this morning. We're often busy around the last days of the month,' Yvonne's husband of twenty years had been spending a lot of time at work and she was thinking it was high time to arrange a holiday, 'since we have to compile profit and loss accounts for all our customers at the end of the month, you see.' She added in a business-like voice: 'But look forward to chatting with you later.'

Security might be slack in the branch, but the Bush Telegraph was fully functioning. Within minutes of the inspector starting his first interview, news of the surprise visitor and his secret mission had spread like a forest fire. Yvonne was thinking it could be a long morning.

'Sorry to disturb you, Yvonne, but is there any chance of some help with the Marston deal?'

She looked up to see Tony. He was the *one* new recruit she could find time for. 'What's the problem?' In his hands he held a number of brown cardboard folders, pages spilling out.

'I've got to get everything signed off today and—'

'Bring the papers in here and let's have a look at them.' Yvonne knew of her reputation as a safe pair of hands, not that she got any official recognition for her mentor role. At any rate helping Tony was infinitely preferable to sorting out the daily botch jobs made by the giggling and incompetent recruits that Adam Jones favoured.

'I've spent all yesterday checking and re-checking,' he explained. 'After all the invoices, royalties and fees paid, I've still got a surplus of seven thousand three hundred and seven pounds unaccounted for ... could you take a dekko?'

'And you're certain all the fees and commissions have been paid?'

'Sure, look.' He was pulling out papers onto the table. 'I double-checked, triple even ... Yvonne?'

Yvonne was looking out of the small barred window to the inner courtyard, remembering an almost identical discussion she had had with the then office manager, David Beardwell – was it really twenty-eight years ago? Her eye was drawn to a faded postcard of the Colosseum stuck on the side of the window frame. Normally, she would have told Tony 'leave it with me' but today being the day it was, she decided it might be time for a new approach, a changing of the guard. 'Well, Tony,' she turned around to check no one else was in earshot. 'Nothing for it but to set up a Janet Raine account.'

'A what?'

'Every so often this happens in the bank; no surprise, the millions we deal with. Easiest thing to do with money that is not accounted for. *Randoms* I call them. I put them in an account under a fictitious name and then if anyone comes asking for it you can quickly pay it back and if they don't ... well then ask no questions, get no lies.'

'Isn't that breaking, like a hundred-and-one banking statutes?'

'You're not taking the money, just ... storing it somewhere safe. You could say you're protecting the interests of the bank. Like a guardian angel. Only don't throw away the key.'

'The key?'

'Something put by for a rainy day.'

'Ah, I see, Janet Raine.' Tony swallowed. 'But isn't it risky?'

'Tony, have you ever wondered why so many people work in the banking industry? Our bank employs thousands of people up and down the country. Why don't we do it all with one enormous computer?'

'I don't know,' said Tony. He seemed out of his depth. 'Why don't we?'

'Because we need the little people, the likes of you and me, to cover up the traces, tie up the loose ends. We are, if you like—' she remembered the analogy that her own office manager had used, 'we're like the slaves in the Roman empire, we do our job properly and the senators don't even know that we're here.' For years she had heard nothing from her mentor after he had left the bank. And then one morning the postcard, unsigned: *Happy Rainey days.*

'So I mean this is not you talking theoretically? I mean, you have your own?'

'*Randoms*? Yes, some.' The last time she had checked her Janet Raine account the balance was one hundred and fifty-seven thousand and six hundred pounds. 'And the way I see it the big men still earn a lot more for doing a lot less.' She remembered how similar her own responses had been twenty-eight years ago.

'But what about the inspector? I mean, we heard that—'

'Our inspector has got much bigger fish to fry. He's on a weevil-sweeper hunt—'

'A weevil what?'

'Tony, don't you have things to do? New accounts to open?' She moved over to her PC. 'And Tony, one last thing.'

'What's that?'

'If you ever had this conversation with anyone, it wasn't with me, understand?'

She looked up to see the inspector outside Devlin's door, looking for the second name on the list. She waited until the coast was clear before slipping into Devlin's office. 'You're still here then?'

'What a lark. More like a typing test than a full-on thumb-screws interrogation. Shame.' Devlin grimaced. '*Weevils* or something, never heard anything so ridiculous.'

'Nothing tricky then?'

'He's just a kid, another one fresh out of uni. They'll have to dig up someone a lot smarter than that to catch you Yvonne—'

Yvonne smiled, thinly. 'Oh I nearly forgot, Dev. Could you get me an authorisation code for this loan extension? I've had the outline approval a long time but I'm going to arrange a little holiday. I'll get the boss's signature later but he's busy right now.'

Devlin made a quick perusal of the forms. 'Ah, I take it you use your maiden name at work.' She nodded in agreement and he read on. The loan involved heavily re-mortgaging the house Yvonne owned with her husband. 'You know you don't have to *buy* the hotel!' Devlin exclaimed. 'They'll probably rent you a room—'

'My husband's been thinking of giving up work,' at least that much was true, 'and I thought something spectacular—'

'Hey, you don't have to explain anything to me. It's your house to do what you want with.' The assistant manager signed the forms, stamped them *Approved* diagonally across the front page and fished out an authorisation code from a folder. 'There you go, Yvonne.' She kept her private accounts at the bank, as many employees did, but for borrowing they had to go through security procedures. She didn't need the money but she knew her husband would. A smile stole across Yvonne's face as she pictured his surprise when he found out.

'Remember, you still need to get the manager's signature on that.'

'Dev, you're a good chap. It's nice working with you.'

Devlin looked bemused. 'You're talking like it's your holiday already. Back to work on Monday. Sorry to disappoint you.' On her way back to her desk she saw the inspector and his box with the flashing light at Anna's desk. That meant he was already at number three and moving quickly down his list.

Yvonne still had a lot to do before the morning was finished; hairdresser's appointment and a call to the florists. As for the manager's signature, it was something she had got very good at. Time to check her own accounts. She always enjoyed logging in as Janet Raine. It reminded her of when her own career had really taken off, ten years ago.

She hadn't been looking for an affair. It had sneaked up on her from around a corner, or rather over a stack of books at a Manhattan book shop. She hadn't any time for guilt, just Brett. Two glorious days and nights and her husband didn't notice a thing. He had been wrapped up with his company takeover, she with her lover. It could have easily ended there – a holiday romance. But Brett had become very excited when he heard that she worked for a bank. In the middle of the night he had found pencil and paper and explained to her all about the weevil-sweeper. He had promised to send her a floppy disc with the program and much to her surprise it had been waiting for her on her return to work at 125 Farbourne High Street.

Every year she paid her IT consultant ten per cent of her winnings while Brett kept her up to date with new software versions. Her meeting Brett had come at the opportune moment. The advent of spreadsheets had put income from *randoms* on a steady decline, yet thanks to the weevil-sweeper, *sweepings* showed a year-by-year steady growth.

She was happy to see a summary of her *randoms* and *sweepings* investments. With the latest interest the bank generously paid across her accounts, she was sitting pretty on one million, three hundred and sixty-seven thousand pounds. Who said crime didn't pay? But now there was a bank inspector visiting their branch. In some ways she had been expecting him for twenty years. Strange that he chose today of all days.

'And now the financial news. Gas prices are set—' Yvonne turned up the radio which had been murmuring quietly on her desk. 'High tech company Oxyron founded by entrepreneur businessman Tim Witherspoon, today becomes a public listed company. Trading in shares is expected to start briskly at around eighteen pounds fifty amidst widening interest—'

'I wish I'd got some shares.'

Yvonne jumped.

One of the new recruits was walking past her office. 'They reckon they'll shoot up. Did you cash in, Yvonne?' She laughed and walked by, not waiting for an answer.

New recruits saw teasing her as fair game in the office, encouraged by Adam Jones himself, no doubt. Yvonne didn't object. Of course she could have replied: *Well yeah, just over a million shares as a matter of fact*, but she kept quiet. Best not to rock the boat. She was acutely aware that this would be her last day at the bank. And that reminded her. It was time to make the most important call of the day. She picked up the phone. 'Hello, Elizabeth, it's Yvonne here. I was wondering if I could call in a favour.' Her old contact worked in cash management, a head office section responsible for clearing share payments. 'I've got a client who's having some liquidity problems and I've promised him same day payment on shares ... as long as he sells of course. What do you think? I wouldn't ask if it wasn't—'

'How much are we talking about?'

'Around twenty million.' Yvonne heard a whistle on the other end of the line.

'Dollars?'

'Sterling.'

'You know really I should wait till Monday—'

'He's a key customer, for the bank and for *me*.'

'Okay then, but the shares have to be sold by four o'clock latest otherwise I won't be able to work anything today.'

'You're an angel, Elizabeth. I owe you.' Yvonne put the phone down. Four hours exactly. The bank had a user tracking program that would tell her the minute her husband logged on. She knew he wouldn't be able to resist witnessing the shares in the account. Once Tim had checked the money was in she would move swiftly. But he had to do it by four o'clock. For the second time in five minutes she looked at her watch.

'So I get to the end of the list.'

She jumped again. It was the inspector.

The first indication something was seriously wrong was when he turned on the computer. Instead of the familiar bank logo sign he saw a message *Thank you for your generous donation to the Tsunami Relief Fund.* He clicked the X to close the message box only to see another more worrying message take its place: *Adam this time you really fucked up. Call security before they call you.* There was a number on the screen. In panic his first thought was to shout for Yvonne – then he remembered she still wasn't in. Very unusual for her to be late – at her age and with her looks, the least she could do would be to arrive on time. Bus problems no doubt. Monday morning had not started well and when the phone rang, Adam Jones had a terrible premonition things could be about to get worse.

*

At that precise moment Janet Raine was at Heathrow terminal four's first-class check-in. Dressed in a chic designer outfit, she was pleased to note that her new hairstyle had survived surprisingly well through a passionate weekend with more champagne than was probably advisable. The last words of her younger lover had been: 'You look a million dollars.' Where did that leave the other *thirty-five* she wondered? For years their relationship had been restricted to a weekend once a month. Her sister had provided a very convenient alibi.

There were police at the airport but she was fairly confident that they weren't looking for her. In any case, even if they were, she was now a redhead, looked about forty and unrecognisable from the Yvonne Witherspoon from her previous life. If Tim himself were doing the check-in, he wouldn't recognise her. And she had a brand new passport in her handbag. It wasn't just money she had put by for a rainy day.

Adam Jones answered the phone with none of his customary panache. 'Hello, Adam Jones, branch manager, speaking. What is it?'

'This is Mr Morgan from security speaking. Are you alone in your office?' The voice was icy cold. 'Mr Jones, I am ringing to inform you that we have a level nine security breach at the Farbourne branch. I repeat: a level nine security breach. You are to listen to me very carefully and answer my questions truthfully and carefully. Am I understood?'

Adam had to clear his throat before he could speak. 'Yes.'

The voice at the other end of the telephone continued. 'Has anyone besides yourself had recent access to your computer?'

Adam remembered the inspector and his box with the green flashing light. The only way this could be scarier would be if this conversation was happening in the dark. 'Well, yes, there was someone. I thought he was one of your lot, I mean, he said was a bank inspector. We phoned you to check him. His name was—'
Adam searched for the card on the desk and found it. 'His name

was ... his name was—' He could hardly bring himself to pronounce it. Hadn't he read the card at the time? 'His name was Inspector Oaks ... H. Oaks actually,' the manager added lamely. He needed to sit down.

The voice on the end of the line was uncompromising and Adam was dreading the next question.

'And Mr Jones, what I hope you're not going to tell me is that this inspector, this Inspector Hoax, please don't tell me he had access to all the PCs in the branch?'

Silence.

'Mr Jones?'

'Your tickets, madam. And please feel free to use the VIP lounge. Have a pleasant flight, Miss Raine.' Janet, aka Yvonne, aka the doppelgänger – she had once overheard her husband let slip his name for her to a crony – was looking forward to her new life. Originally it had been her plan to leave the house and Spanish flat to Tim but when she had seen the clumsy attempt to cheat her out of her shares she had decided to leave him penniless. But it had been a race against the clock. Only after the tracking program on her computer had reported Tim checking his shares account just before four o'clock had she given the 'sell' instruction, with six minutes to spare.

She figured it would be Monday morning before he realised anything was amiss. If Tim wanted to liquidate any assets he would find the flat in Spain sold and the house now re-mortgaged up to the hilt. Poor Tim would have trouble settling the credit card bill at the end of the month. Maybe his latest mistress would help him out. Not Yvonne's problem.

Adam Jones was sitting cross-legged on the carpet next to his desk. The receiver was dangling between the desk and floor and he could still hear sounds on the line. There was a commotion in the outer office. He saw a vaguely familiar face remonstrating with some of his staff, the boss of that new company Oxymoron or whatever it was, looking like he was trying to force his way into Adam's office.

'Penniless ... the thief ... twenty years.'

From inaudible commotion, Adam seemed to suddenly be able to overhear snippets, then suddenly he could hear every word.

'The only thing I got is a bunch of flowers ... and she worked here. Where is she? She's stolen my money. You've stolen my money. Thieves, the lot of you. Where is the manager? I'm calling the police.'

So this is what trapped between a rock and a hard place really means, thought Adam. He had always wondered. He decided to crawl further under the desk.

Yvonne watched England vanish behind clouds beneath her. She accepted a glass of champagne and wondered if for the sake of tradition she should send Tony a postcard from Rio de Janeiro.

Two weeks earlier

Madie Maitland had been nervous about the job interview, maybe because Farbourne was just the perfect place for her to get a first job after graduating. But so far she thought it had gone quite well.

'So what we need in this branch is some young talent,' said the interviewer, 'people who are really committed and who have ambition. I wonder, Yvonne, how about a cup of tea for myself and Madie? You would like another cup?'

Madie nodded and the older lady who looked a bit of a battleaxe left the room. She took it as a good sign she had been offered a second cup of tea even if it tasted awful. *Just don't say anything stupid. It's in the bag,* she told herself. She was alone in the room with the bank manager. He was younger than she was expecting and seemed really interested.

The manager stood up. She liked him and the atmosphere of the bank which was bustling with a quiet efficiency. 'My door is always open except for personal meetings,' he said shutting the door. 'So where were we?' he asked, coming back to lean on the desk in front of her.

'You said you were looking for committed people with young talent and certainly this is just the sort of position—'

'Committed to the bank,' he interrupted. 'And also I want,' the manager reached towards her to pluck a hair from her shoulder, 'real *personal* commitment.' He dropped his voice. 'Do you have a steady boyfriend?' leaning forward as he asked the question. She was enveloped with the smell of heavy aftershave. The way he was emphasising the words started alarm bells ringing in Madie's head.

She flinched. She regretted not choosing a longer skirt for the interview or even smart trousers like those of the office manager. Too late now, she crossed her legs and saw the manager's eyes follow the movement like a kitten watching a ball on a string. 'Sorry, I don't understand what my boyfriend has to do with anything?'

'Well it's just that someone in this position might be—' For a second his hand brushed against Madie's knee, 'working quite late.'

She moved backwards in the chair.

'Madie, do you know how many other applicants we had for this position?' She assumed the question was rhetorical and cast an obvious look to the door.

The manager ignored it. 'Over two hundred. It's a difficult decision for me to make. If you really are serious about this job, give me a ring on this mobile number.' He handed her a card. 'And we'll arrange a follow-up interview. Just one to one.' His tongue darted out to lick the underside of his top lip and he briefly touched her arm again – presumably to show there was no misunderstanding, thought Madie, watching him return to his chair. His timing was split-second as he made the other side of the desk just as the door opened and the office manager entered with two cups of tea.

*

'It makes me sick to remember it,' said Madie pouring two large glasses of white wine. 'To think a young manager can get away with that sort of behaviour.'

'And it's the branch on Farbourne High Street?' Her boyfriend pushed the thick black glasses up his nose, a sign she recognised that he was taking things seriously.

'Yes, that's right. But what should I do? He was very sneaky – if I make a complaint he'll say that his office manager was there the whole time.'

'Well let's see if I can find out anything about this guy. Who knows, he may come to regret the day he put a hand on your knee. Did you say he gave you a business card?'

'I was just about to throw it away. It's there on the table.'

'You never know, it might come in useful.' Her boyfriend photographed the card with his phone before putting it into his aluminium briefcase. 'Maybe I should pay him a visit, our Mr Adam Jones, Branch Manager?'

Madie imagined him confronting the manager and tried not to laugh. But he was already making her feel better. 'Don't be silly, if I had wanted an old-fashioned hard man I would have a rugby player for a boyfriend, not some computer geek.'

'Well be warned.' He had his laptop open, fingers gliding over the keyboard like a man reading Braille. 'This geek is about to pull your kit off, darling. Just after I've sent one mail.'

The Neighbour

When friends stopped by I sometimes said *Welcome to the White House*. Well it was, and we had a flag pole. Not that we had so many visitors these days – hardly surprising when Marlene, that's my wife, treated every visit like it would be the opening of Congress. I mean, I wouldn't have been surprised if folk started putting in visa applications, it was that much of a big deal. But hey, God bless America! That's one reason I moved here – to escape the uptight, politically correct dudes from back home in Sweden. That was twenty years ago but if I really wanted to escape, what possessed me to get hitched up with a broad like Marlene? I mean, she wasn't even pregnant *or* rich.

Anyway, I was thinking about all this one particularly angst-ridden Friday evening when I was sneaking a cigarette in the backyard. I had taken a day off work to help prepare for the big party – the bill was going to come in around two thousand bucks, dough we couldn't really afford. Marlene had asked if they would be all right without me in the office – sweet and touching but totally out of touch with reality. That was Marlene for you – she still didn't know exactly how low I had sunk in the latest *reorg* – who on earth invented that terrible phrase? It surprised me that anyone at all even remembered my name at work; the fact that it was also stencilled on my office door I saw as a temporary oversight; no doubt I would soon be in the *more creative* open working space. When people moved out there, everyone knew there was never any coming back, like factory chickens just one short step away from the guillotine. You could almost smell the bunched rosemary and sizzling olive oil when you walked by *the void* – as I called it.

And what was I doing in the stationery business? My heart was in the automotive industry, always had been since my first summer job working on the Saab 99 assembly line at Trollhattan.

Stationery was just another wrong turning in my life. Anyway, where was I? Friday. The party and the weekend that was going to change my life. If I'd known it then I would have been happier and probably would never have made the party and then it wouldn't have been *that weekend* – but I'm getting ahead of myself.

Oh, I forgot to tell you that Chelsea was well sore with me because nobody who was anybody was coming to her graduation bash. This, for some surprise reason, was meant to be all my fault, like I wouldn't have anything more important to do in life than arranging a list of celebrities to come to my daughter's graduation party – like celebrities wouldn't have anything better to do than queue up to buy their own stationery in bulk. Instead I was more concerned about the oil leak on my classic Volvo estate – one of the best things that came out of Sweden – that was going to be another one thousand bucks. I put the cigarette butt out in the Miller Lite can, and went back into the house, feeling noticeably less relaxed than five minutes previously. That was the trouble with my life; the more I thought about it the more it depressed me.

There was a lot to do. I reckoned if I did two straight hours I could get a good way down Marlene's list of *imperative tasks* before tonight's Patriots' game that kicked off at eleven. I went in the swing door at the back.

The kitchen looked like it had been hit by a bomb or a minor earthquake, or both. It always killed me this; how does tidying up make so much mess? Marlene was there with some letters in her hand; that was worrying. The most mail we seemed to get these days was reminders on top of the regular bills, the reason why I had earmarked mail collection as another of my daily chores. I looked at the kitchen table; no final reminders there. I let out a small cheer of congratulations to myself: *Did it again! Survived another week!* Marlene had in her hand a small envelope, but I could relax, I could see real handwriting on the front.

'Wuddaya know, we got an invite to Don Morillo's party? It's tonight. They must be short of numbers.' Marlene had now transferred her attention to her recipe book. 'Anyway, why would he invite you?'

'As a matter of fact I was having a chat with him just the other day and he mentioned it,' I lied. 'What time are we going?'

'You can't be serious. Do you remember last year?'

Was it a year already? I looked over to my neighbour's place – what a realtor would call *a tastefully extended and well-arranged property* with an indoor and an outdoor pool and God knows how many bathrooms. Last year Marlene had wanted to call the cops on account of the noise across the way. In the end someone else had saved her the trouble. So *yes*, Don Morillo the DJ was my neighbour and *no*, we hadn't been invited to his party before. We exchanged pleasantries about once a week over the fence. I occasionally saw him heading off downtown in a flash new convertible – he changed them more often than his girlfriends, which was impressive. And you know the way some people are permanently smiling whatever the weather? Well, Don Morillo was one of them with this painted-on, all-American, cheesy grin. I wasn't sure whether I hated or admired him.

'Anyway it's impossible.' Marlene was throwing me her *really-this tops-Apollo-13* look. 'We still have loads to do for our own party. I haven't even started making the desserts. I suppose other folks just order in catering. If only we—' Marlene was surrounded by unopened shopping bags and foods in various stages of preparation. For some reason we had Christmas lights on the table. It was the middle of June. Any minute now she was going to say something along the lines of 'if we had a bigger kitchen'.

'Mom, I can't believe it. Dad bought the totally wrong soda. I explicitly told him *Whites*, I said. *Whites*, you heard me, didn't you, Mom?' Marlene was interrupted by my eighteen-year-old daughter who came into the kitchen with a you're-for-the-high-jump glance in my direction. Marlene described Chelsea as a girl with presence. She had that, and then some – she was fat. But whose fault was that? In this house there weren't too many scapegoats and the main one started with the letter E – did I tell you that my name was Erik? And since when had my only child started talking to me like I was the house boy and looking at me like I was nobody's cat?

'You know that Julie Jacobs has a retired pro-ball player coming. I'm going to be the laughing stock of the school. What did I do to deserve such a total wasted—'

'Tell me about it, hon. If we just had a proper kitchen like most folk. I mean, Ann Jones—'

And didn't my wife also just say *impossible*? Since way back, if there was any word that was sure to motivate me it was that. *Plus* I had a party invite, and I mean they were as rare for me as walk-on parts were for Jack Nicholson. I grabbed my favourite black-and-white sports jacket and was out the house with the swing door crashing loudly behind me without a backward glance. The last backward glance I had was when I was eighteen and I was finishing with this girl and it cost me an extra six months in a doomed relationship – so the point is this: I screw up probably more than the next dude but I rarely make the same mistake twice and what you can't do is tell me something is impossible.

Walking across to the sound of my neighbour's party I had the feeling when me and Magnus skipped double chemistry and there had been hell to pay after. I'd been grounded for a month – it had been worth it though as we'd got the bus into Stockholm to see *Butch Cassidy and the Sundance Kid* – after that movie Magnus made me call him 'the kid'. If it wasn't for that movie I probably wouldn't have come to America in the first place. Anyhow that's how I felt walking across to Don Morillo's extensive and well-arranged yard: to hell with the consequences. 'You know, when I was a kid I always thought I'd grow up to be a hero.'

'What was that?'

There I was talking to myself. Lost in my thoughts I was

already standing in Don Morillo's yard and this mysterious-looking girl in a small bikini with big sunglasses was looking at me. 'Just a line from an old movie. You know, *Butch Cassidy and the Sundance Kid*.'

'Never heard of it,' she said and went back to her nails. That decided me. This was not my place: different generation, different values, different everything. Period.

Maybe my dad had been right. When he said goodbye to me as I was leaving Sweden he said that my trouble was that I was always running away from something. *Should I stay or should I go now?* I saw a stack of Buds sitting in a pile of ice cubes and I thought 'ten minutes'. By the way, that was the last time I ever saw my dad. He refused to travel to the country that had assassinated JFK and he was a man of principle; sure, it's fine to believe in something, but what sort of parent puts his dislike for Lee Harvey Oswald ahead of his love for his son? I was saving up money to buy a flight back home when one day he walked to the tobacconist and keeled right over. Dead before he hit the ground they said. Dead at fifty-six; only ten years older than me now.

'So who are you? How about a Bud?'

It was the girl with the nails and I looked over my shoulder at an expanse of mostly young and partying people, but it looked like this babe was talking to me. I realised she was asking me for a beer. A minute later I was back with two cans. 'Cheers,' I said. I liked the sound of an opening beer can. Like a fountain on a hot day, it signalled hope.

We looked at each other. At least I think she was looking at me; as I said, she had these enormous sunglasses on. I realised she was maybe three or four years older than my daughter but a lot thinner.

'So what are you looking so glum about?'

'It's the car. It needs a service.' When was the last time I talked to a girl this age who wasn't my daughter? Boy, that sounded lame. 'It's a Volvo,' I added – like that would throw a whole lot more light on anything. But strangely this seemed to make some sort of impact.

'Volvo,' she said dreamily, like she was remembering something. I wondered was she on drugs? Something I had tried but with very little success. Me and drugs was a bit like me and Suzy Torseke at school; we had the potential but we never clicked. Anyway back to the here and now, after about fully half a minute when the nail girl was looking at the heavens and I figured either the conversation was over or she had fallen asleep, she added: 'Say, would you be ... *the neighbour?*'

I decided it was time to move on. 'Catch you later,' I said, trying to sound relaxed and cool which I certainly wasn't.

'That'd be nice,' she replied like she meant it, but the conversation was now over. I cast a backward glance and she was doing her nails again. Me and a backward glance; what was that all about? I made my way past the swimming pool and some people nodded at me but most had their eyes locked onto more interesting stuff. I was thinking I might say hello to my host and thank him.

'Hi, dude, chuck us a Bud, will ya?'

Again – that was the second time in ten minutes someone had mistaken me for a waiter. I frowned and then remembered the sports jacket. I passed the beer over to the jock, tempted for a minute to ask him for ID. 'Not the waiter. The neighbour,' I added.

The jock just kept looking at me, like I was pulling a fast one. 'So you are the Don's neighbour?' I didn't usually get the feeling at parties I was the clever one – usually it was the opposite, like I was the uninvited guest. But smart one? I kinda liked it.

'Sure, right over there, other side of the fence. You can even see my Volvo from here.' Right now I was pleased that I'd cleaned it, like I did every Sunday morning – my father may be dead but it was my way of remembering him.

'Cool, man. Pleased to meet you. If you ever want any tickets for the game, just give us a call.' And then the jock was off, being pulled into the house by a cute blonde whose legs disappeared up to the sky. I looked at the card. *Dale Cougar, quarterback*, and a phone number. Of course, now I recognised him ... twenty points in a superbowl final. I said goodbye to my jacket forever and tossed it onto a chair. Time to move on.

I had this crazy notion of talking to a girl. I remembered vaguely having felt like that before. No one was more surprised than me when some beers later I was surrounded by not one, not two but three gorgeous-looking chicks. I mean this sort of thing didn't happen to me, not ever. And these babes just wanted to hear the everyday stuff, my boring life; they loved it all.

'Hey, come over here, Cindy. You won't believe who's here. It's the neighbour, you know, Don Morillo's neighbour with the Volvo.' I'd always had a sneaking feeling that I'd paid over the odds for that Volvo, maybe that slimeball dealer knew something that I didn't, until now. But my dad had just keeled over and I wanted a reminder of Sweden – blue had been his favourite colour, it was like an omen.

I saw this classy-looking girl walking over and after four or maybe five Buds even I knew she was Ivy League. I looked around to see some cameras or guys laughing but there wasn't, just me alone with four gorgeous girls. *Summer of '69* came on the radio. Me and 'the kid' had been to see Bryan Adams one day live, a small gig at Central Park in Stockholm before he became A-list and I got within twenty yards of the stage and I saw all those girls, dancing, T-shirts waving over their heads and I had this clear thought, why couldn't that be me just for one evening? Well tonight, this was my Bryan Adams night.

Then I woke up – that's what you might expect to read next, like get real, get down to earth. Well, the crash did come, but not in the way you would imagine. I was with this latest girl Cindy, 'somebody in TV', she said. The bomb dropped something like this. She leans over and asks me straight up: 'Say, how does it feel to be *the neighbour*?'

'Well, you know—' but then I stopped. It was like some

synapse connected in my head, like the day when the bus inspector was walking up the bus and me aged twelve, I realised that the game was up; no ticket, it was the uninvited guest feeling again in spades. 'What do you mean, *the neighbour*?' I asked. I already had this hollow ball of dread in my guts waiting for the answer.

'Well you're just about as famous as me, you dumb ass. I mean everybody knows *the neighbour* from Don Morillo's show.' Her emphasis sent alarm bells ringing louder than the swimming pool shrieks into the night air. In five miserable crushing minutes it all came out, like how the Don in his morning show mentions me every time he comes on the air; he's talking about my important job – *not*, working in a stationery company, and my perfect family – *not*. Cindy was more tactful than that but you get the picture. Although most of all, the bits he likes the best, me and my Volvo: the way I clean it every Sunday; everyone else goes to the game and Erik the Swede is cleaning his Volvo. It's true I take mighty good care of that car, and sure I wax and polish that paintwork till I see my reflection like a mirror, but I already told you what that's all about.

I felt sick, like I wanted the ground to open up wide and swallow me whole; here lies the neighbour, the biggest joke in town. I was ready to go home and Cindy figured it out pretty quick: 'Hell, you didn't know any of this, did you?' She read me the way other people read books. I shook my head, no words. She couldn't believe it, that I wasn't in on the joke, and I had to explain that Marlene always chose the radio in the house and Don knew that in the car I was a sports fanatic. And me and my daughter hardly spoke. Then just when I thought there couldn't be any more turning points in this crazy evening along came the next one. A real U-turn this one. Get this.

'Listen, Erik.' For the first time someone was calling me by my real name, which I kinda liked. 'You should be proud. What the Don doesn't get is that he's laughing at you and he wants us to laugh along, but the rest of us, we're on your side. Don Morillo thinks it's funny to take a snook at the little guy but inside we're all little guys too and we often say, me and the girls, that if we ever meet you, we're on your side. You know, all for one and one for all. I've always wanted to meet you to tell you just that, you know.'

I was touched. Once again I didn't know what to say. 'Cindy, would you like to come to my daughter's graduation party tomorrow?'

'Sure,' she said and leaned over and gave me a real belter of a kiss, full on the lips. Wow! I was trying to remember the last time I'd been kissed like that. Had I *ever* been kissed like that?

'You tell me the time. I'll be there. Now come on, there's a friend I want you to meet.'

You're not going to believe this but I was actually almost relieved when it wasn't another drop-dead gorgeous blonde. Hank was a big fella about my age, smoking an expensive-looking cigar. And now I introduced myself as Erik the Neighbour. As I had already figured out, this Cindy chick was smarter than she looked, because Hank was just my kinda guy. Me being the neighbour had a big impact on him, you could see, especially the Volvo connection because it turned out he was in the car business. He talked about a new business idea he had; exporting quality used cars to Latin America. He wanted someone who was ready to travel. He was talking about the growth possibilities when I had to interrupt him: 'Hank, did you just say Bolivia?'

'Well yeah, not everyone's cup of tea. Sure you don't have to go there but—'

'Kid, the next time I say let's go some place like Bolivia let's GO some place like Bolivia.' I had a feeling of *déjà vu*. But I had to put Hank in the picture. My whole childhood I wanted to go to America but only when I watched *Sundance* years later I realised that I'd got it wrong; it was Bolivia all along where Butch and Sundance ended up. Me and omens – sound familiar? Bolivia was an omen. And you know how it is some people you just click

from the first minute that you meet? Like you already knew them a lifetime? Well, that was how it was with me and Hank. His last words to me that evening were: 'Erik, I hardly know you but you got the job,' and he gave me his card. I accepted that job at the drop of a hat, nearly pulled his arm off in fact.

By the end of that evening I had a whole bunch of cards in my wallet. It seemed everyone wanted to shake my hand and I got quite good at playing the neighbour role. I developed my dumb Swede routine: some corny lines like *you can always tell a Swede but you can't tell him much* which they lapped up, and then I would be the real Erik and they liked me for that too. When I left the Don's place my cup was overflowing with happiness. What a night! I still wasn't totally clear what Hank's job offer was but it was something to do with Bolivia and that sure had the stationery business licked. At least I didn't have far to go to get home. I started laughing at that, so I must have still been a bit drunk.

There was a note waiting for me on the kitchen table: *Gone to bed. You are in the spare room.* I dreamt that me and the kid were robbing a bank together in Bolivia and we were about to rush out through the door. Magnus says to me: *'For a moment there I thought we were in trouble—'*

I was woken by a loud noise. 'Erik, have you any idea of what time it is?' Even in my hungover state I was able to figure out that this wasn't a barrage of rifle fire from the entire Bolivian army but Marlene shouting up the stairs. 'The party starts in two hours and you've still got chores to do.' Chelsea passed me in the hall. She gave me a look like *I* was the teenager.

I needed coffee.

'This is no time for coffee. Make sure you put on a decent shirt, the blue one will do. And you've got to sweep the yard—'

Now I knew for a fact that the yard didn't need sweeping. Some things never change. Did last night really happen? Did it change anything? I guess the answer to the last question was really up to me. Period.

'Marlene, wait up. I've got something to tell you.' My voice was low-key, like it wasn't even mine. Marlene must have also noticed something was up because she stopped yelling. 'Marlene, just wanted you to know that if you ever shout at me again like that, it's no problem. I'll leave this house and I won't come back. We've not been nice to each other for years but I reckon we still have something worth fighting for. You've got to start treating me like I'm your best friend, start looking at me like you love me and even tell me that once in a while because I love you and I never hear you criticising what clothes Tracey wears' – that was Marlene's best friend – 'so you can cut that out as well. Didn't we say love 'n' cherish in church on our wedding day? Those are the rules. You're still my princess and I'm your man if you want it. If you don't, that's fine too. Your call.'

Where did that come from? I kept it real friendly and went out to the yard to drink my coffee. It was going to be a beautiful day. The next couple of hours before the party started Marlene kept her distance from me and now and then I caught her looking at me a bit strangely. Chelsea just looked at me as if I was mad.

Uncle Herb from Texas was the first to turn up wearing a Stetson and all – he wasn't really an uncle but an old friend of Marlene's mum. Then came the usual gaggle of Marlene's friends from the department store – the noise they made – it always amazed me that anybody got served in that store. Chelsea was standing by the door receiving the guests and doing her best to look happy. About an hour later when we already had a pretty good turnout including some long-lost cousins from Connecticut, Chelsea comes rushing over, looking flustered.

'Dad, you won't believe who's at the door. Cindy Londraris. Cindy Londraris! I thought she must have got the wrong address but she swears it isn't, says you invited her.'

'Cindy Londraris?'

'Yeah, from *Friends*. Dad, she's *totally* famous.'

Now Chelsea was standing on one leg and gesturing furiously with her head in the direction of the door. Well I had no idea who she was talking about but I went to the door anyway and there was Cindy from last night. I hardly recognised her; 'Hi, Cindy,' I said, 'hardly recognise you out of your bikini. Glad you could make it.'

'My new best friend Erik. I wouldn't miss this for the world. Now I want to meet the queen of the ball. And I saw Dale Cougar parking his coupé round the corner. Did you have to invite him?'

'Cougar. Does she mean the Cougar? Quarterback Cougar?' Chelsea was hovering behind me like a cat on a hot tin roof.

'I suppose so,' I replied. Now I thought about it, I remembered inviting quite a few of the guests from last night. Dale showed up – he even had an autographed ball for Chelsea's graduation present – she was so chuffed. 'But you don't even like football,' I said.

'Daaad, pleeeazze.' She looked at me differently now, like I was some kind of father again. Later on I heard her on the phone to her friend Julie Jacobs: 'Cindy Londraris said to Dad hello, my new best friend, can you believe ... I was so totally excited I could scarcely draw breath—'

It wasn't long before the party had spilled out into the yard. Marlene was videoing away: wannabe Uncle Herb was demonstrating to Dale Cougar how to throw a home run; Hank turned up in a 1959 Cadillac Eldorado Biarritz, deep purple with BIG fins; and right at the end I thought Chelsea was going to have a heart attack when some latest hot actress showed up – it was the girl with the nails – I didn't even remember inviting her. She had a nerve, especially as she was followed by paparazzi who pitched base at the end of our drive. I made a mental note to take them out tea later, extra publicity for Erik the Neighbour – terrific, that's all I needed. But Chelsea was as chuffed as hell. I went out to the yard to have a chat with Hank. We needed to talk some more about Bolivia.

Marlene was there, looking happier than she'd done in years and threw me a you're-on-a-promise look, that I'd forgotten the last time I'd seen and this was when I was still wearing the surfer's shirt she'd always hated. Cindy was talking away to Chelsea about some fitness club she could get her membership with that sounded expensive. Still, if half of what Hank promised came to pass I shouldn't be too worried about bills from now on.

And right now it's fair to say that I wasn't too much worried about anything. I was already looking forward to my speech to the chickens cooped in the void, when I told them I was out of stationery altogether. I had a fresh start in front at home and a quality used convertible on the way – Hank said that it came with the job.

It was time to move on. Thinking that reminded me of the last birthday card my dad ever sent me, the year he died. Normally he didn't even remember. On the card was a picture of a man in a suit and hat, carrying a briefcase and running past a row of houses, with a big grin on his face. The caption on top read: *Despite being in his early thirties Erik still found it highly amusing to ring people's doorbells and run away.* My dad had added on the inside: *Happy Birthday Erik (Keep running!).* Weeks later he was dead. Now after twenty years stuck in a rut I was listening to my dad once more, I was on my way. Erik the Swede was up and running again. Perhaps I could even twist Hank's arm for the Saab 900 Classic, straight shift in electric blue with a white canvas hood. I *would* sell the Volvo, maybe I could even find a buyer in Bolivia.

The Verdict

''Ere, you'd best look sharp,' said the clerk of the court, poking his head into the small cubicle he shared with the usher, 'rumour 'as it his lordship's starting on time.'

'And me the last to know,' said Perkins, quickly folding the cricket pages. 'The Caribbean, now that's where I'd rather be—'

'Well I reckons you've got 'arf a minute to be in Court One.'

'Blimey!'

Twenty seconds later Perkins was in the main courtroom, his eyes fixed on the handle of the door behind the dais. 'All rise!' he shouted as the handle started to turn.

The judge emerged to a chorus of scraping chair legs, and walked the few short paces across the dais, a wig of white hair capping his wide and open face. After a swirl of black and purple robes and a nod to Perkins, he sat in his high-backed oak chair. 'Crown versus Woods,' said the judge. 'Counsel, you're all set? No submissions? Excellent, just—'

'Your Honour, permission to approach the bench.' Mr Northcroft, for the prosecution, hadn't sat down with the rest of the court and started his walk towards him. Whilst the prosecutor's pugilist features, square-jawed and with a dark blue shaving shadow above a starched white collar, were well known to the judge, the defence barrister, Miss Lantern, was a new face to him. He estimated she was mid-thirties and her gown and barrister's wig accentuated a tanned and slender appearance. He wondered how she would do up against Northcroft, a man who didn't pull any punches.

'Permission denied,' he said, as he opened his file of papers. He would be strictly impartial; well, almost. 'Let's hear it from there.' The judge was aware of Northcroft checking his stride in surprise and Miss Lantern failing to suppress a smile.

'Your Honour, I would like to request—' Northcroft was

starting to justify the need for a two-day postponement, by which time a key prosecution witness would have returned from an 'unexpected and unavoidable business trip'.

The judge stopped listening. He already knew what he was going to rule on this request. He discreetly removed the bluetooth earpiece he had forgotten to pocket earlier. This morning in chambers he had been warming up to the music of Arcade Fire, a present from his daughter Julia. She was currently holed up somewhere hot with Spider, a youth with a penchant for tattoos and C-class drugs.

Northcroft had finally run out of steam with his pleading and fell silent.

'Request denied. My jury is selected, sworn-in and raring to go. Aren't you, jury?' In fact they looked like every jury on the first morning of any case, a bit at sea. A few of them nodded. At least they were awake. He knew three or four weeks into a case they would have found their sea legs, except that he didn't expect this trial to last that long. It was an old trick for felons to ask for trial by jury to enjoy some extra months of their own pleasure before the inevitable submission to Her Majesty's. 'But first, Clerk of the Court, if you'd like to read the charges.' The judge raised his voice: 'And defendant, if you could stand up please.'

There was a pause before Woods slowly stood, arms folded across his chest. The clerk of the court turned towards the benches: 'Members of the jury, the defendant Keith Woods is charged on this indictment with attempted murder in that on the twenty-fifth of May he attempted the murder of Captain Crane. To this indictment he has pleaded not guilty. He is further charged—'

'And Sergeant,' Northcroft took a step towards the front of the court, 'could you just repeat that for the jury?'

The policeman read from his notebook, as he had done for most of the previous thirty minutes. 'Captain Crane was lying on the ground. He said, "He stabbed me ... for Christ's sake get an ambulance."'

'Your witness,' said Northcroft with what the judge detected as a smirk in the direction of Miss Lantern and her young pupil barrister. Northcroft strutted back to his corner like a man who had just banged some solid pre-emptive nails into the coffin of the defence case.

'Anything in cross-examination, Miss Lantern?'

'No questions, Your Honour.' The judge was disappointed, but not surprised that the defence counsel hadn't come back in cross-examination. Northcroft knew how to prepare a witness, and he'd taken the sergeant through the facts, point by laborious point, with painstaking clarity. The facts told their own story: Woods at the bus stop attempts to rob a law-abiding citizen on his way to work, pulling a knife on Captain Crane who was lucky to escape with his life. When the victim is a decorated British Army officer and the defendant is black and unemployed the jury is starting to make up its mind. No wonder Miss Lantern and her pupil looked subdued, he thought, and Northcroft was bristling with all the confidence of a barrister who'd won a lot more cases than he'd lost.

'That's it, Sergeant. You may stand down.' The judge nodded to the policeman. 'Righty ho, Prosecution. I think we'll have time for your next witness before lunch.'

After fifteen minutes of the next witness, Mrs Levy corroborating the sergeant's evidence, members of the jury had stopped watching the accused in the dock and instead started to cast glances in the judge's direction. From his experience he knew what this change signified; jurors were already starting to think a guilty verdict.

Northcroft was concluding: 'Thank you, Mrs Levy, for re-living what must have been a very unpleasant and frightening experience,' he wheeled round to face the jury, 'when confronted with such a dangerous and violent criminal—'

'Objection!' interjected Miss Lantern. 'The defendant—'

'Sustained,' said the judge. 'Mr Northcroft, next time I'll have you for contempt.' He turned to the jury benches. 'Ladies and gentlemen of the jury, it is for you to decide as to whether the defendant is guilty or not guilty. That is why of course we need *you* to reach a verdict, not the prosecution counsel.'

The witness was on the point of leaving the stand when Miss Lantern stood up. 'Your Honour, may I?'

The judge nodded. 'Mrs Levy, I'm afraid we still need your help on a few questions.'

'Mrs Levy, what was it that you heard whilst waiting at the bus stop?' asked Miss Lantern.

'He said, "You evil snake, you won't get away with this." And then the fight started. I remember snake as being unusual, maybe— ' She cast a look at the man in the dock. 'Anyway I've never seen a man so angry—'

'Thank you, Mrs Levy,' interrupted the judge. 'If you could just keep to answering the questions that are put to you. Any additions, Miss Lantern?'

'Uhm ... I'm not sure.' Defence counsel was consulting her notes.

'Your Honour, I fail to see where this is taking us – except to delay lunch, that is.' Northcroft nodded towards the courtroom clock. 'The hour, Your Honour.'

The judge glanced up from his notes. 'Hmm. Take your time, Miss Lantern. Let it never be said that our appetites got in the way of our legal duties.'

'Thank you, Your Honour.' And to the witness: 'So, Mrs Levy, did you hear what Captain Crane said to the defendant Mr Woods, just before the attack?' Mrs Levy's expression was attentive. Northcroft was noisily starting to collect his papers.

'I remember exactly, the bus was late and people started talking about it. The gent, sorry, Captain Crane said: "There's a strike on the depot", and then something else I didn't hear, an argument started and then the gent, the one who was stabbed, said: "You can say goodbye to June." I was thinking that's all right because I'm on holiday from the twenty-seventh; I mean, I won't be relying on the bus like. That's when that man there,' she pointed at Woods in the dock, 'got all heated and started talkin about "evil snakes". And then the smart-dressed gent collapsed to his knees, calling out, right in front of me. The last time I'd seen an argument like that was New Year's Eve, ninety-ninety seven—'

The judge smiled, appreciatively. 'Thank you for your appearance today, Mrs Levy. You have been a model witness. Do feel free to join us in the canteen for lunch.' He turned to the jury. 'Mondays is one of the better days, the stew is really quite palatable. May I remind you not to discuss the case with anyone, not even each other, during the breaks. We'll reconvene at one-thirty.'

'All rise!' declared Perkins.

As the others filed out of Court One, Perkins found the clerk of the court in the corridor. They consulted in low voices. 'Guilty's at seven-to four, six-to-one for an acquittal,' said the clerk of the court, 'and fifteens for case suspended.'

'I'll take an acquittal at sixes,' said the usher, checking the coast was clear as he slipped a fiver into the other man's hand. The clerk palmed the money and suddenly froze as the judge, taking large strides in the direction of the canteen, stopped in front of the two men.

'Ah, Perkins, just the man. Could you have a chat with one of your contacts about the air conditioning in Number One?'

'Yes, Your Honour. They're predicting a heatwave—'

'Good for the fast bowlers but not for us, eh, Perkins?'

'Leave it with me, sir.'

'And Perkins, I hope that wasn't our petty cash you're handing out.' The judge patted the court usher on the back and walked off, adding as he went, 'We're almost out of coffee, you know.'

'There's not much gets past his lordship's attention round

'ere,' observed the clerk of the court. 'If he knew we was betting on the verdict that'd be both of us down the job centre in two shakes of a lamb's tail. All right for you, you're still a young man, but me—'

'Who's to say he doesn't?' said Perkins. The two men watched the judge marching off to the canteen.

'Just be careful. That's my advice.'

'Anyway, you're right,' said Perkins. 'I'm a young man and there's such a lot of world to see.'

The judge had rarely seen a defence team so much up against it. After two days the prosecution had brought six witnesses and now there was just one to go. Still, it was Wednesday; he'd make sure they didn't run late. 'Anything in cross, Miss Lantern?' he asked, more out of politeness than in expectation.

'No, Your Honour.' Miss Lantern muttered under her breath to her young assisting pupil, 'What odds, Captain Crane, for Archbishop of Canterbury?'

'Next witness,' called Perkins.

'Why not ask him yourself?' whispered the pupil, nodding in the direction of the door as she polished her large glasses. The prosecution's last witness was the victim himself, Captain Crane, who marched to the stand in full military attire, medals across his dark green tunic and a shiny officer's cap under his arm. Again the judge saw Northcroft's stage directions in this piece of theatre.

'Very pleased you could join us today, Captain,' said the judge. By greeting a witness he was breaking with his own personal tradition. 'The business trip went well, I trust?'

The captain stiffened. 'Yes, sir ... it did, sir.'

'Thank you, Captain, and in fact in this court it's *Your Honour*. Save *sir* for the barracks.'

'Actually I'm retired, sir, I mean Your Honour.'

'Yes, indeed you are. Clerk of the Court, swear him in.'

Northcroft started with a preamble about the impeccable

credentials of his witness. The prosecutor appeared to be enjoying himself: 'So you had absolutely no idea why Mr Woods, a complete stranger, took it into his head to assault and rob you that May morning?'

'None, sir, I'd have thought it was the sort of thing that might happen in London but not amongst the good people of Kent,' the captain replied confidently, turning to the jury.

'Your witness,' said Northcroft.

Miss Lantern had more background questions about length of service, reasons the captain had left the army, and so on. As she spoke she circulated the courtroom, gradually getting closer to the captain. Northcroft seemed agitated. 'Your Honour, I really don't see how this interest in my witness's career throws much light on the reason why the accused committed this unprovoked attack in broad daylight.'

The judge frowned. 'And you are sailing uncomfortably close to the wind with your choice of words, Mr Northcroft, but yes, let's see this leading us somewhere sharply, Miss Lantern.' But he wasn't prepared for what happened next. Miss Lantern, who was now within a yard of the captain in the witness box, suddenly stumbled, and her papers launched like startled pigeons into the air. Her hand flicked outwards and struck the captain's water glass, which dropped from the witness stand rail.

'Miss, are you all right?' Perkins was quick to come forward to help.

Miss Lantern picked herself up, ignoring the papers. She only had eyes for the witness. 'Wow, how did you do that?'

'Do what?' the captain replied.

'Catch the glass. It was truly amazing.'

'Oh that! I've always had great reflexes. They called me "Slippy" at school. You know, as in cricket slip catcher,' he explained proudly, holding up the glass of water in his hand for all to see.

'So *Slippy*, one thing I don't quite understand is how a man with such amazing reflexes and military training falls victim to a civilian coming at him with a knife ... Captain?'

For the first time the judge noticed the captain looking at his prosecution counsel before answering – an interesting *tell*. 'Yes, but I wasn't expecting ... I mean I was caught unawares,' he added lamely.

'Okay. I think that's the case for the prosecution,' said the judge. 'Tomorrow we start the defence. Court adjourned.'

'All rise!' said Perkins.

The courtroom swiftly cleared leaving Miss Lantern and her short-haired assistant collecting the papers, strewn about the floor.

'Are you okay?' asked the pupil.

'Sandra, I'm better than okay. We've fired our first warning shot across the bows,' Miss Lantern said quietly. 'The captain and Northcroft are rattled.' Packing up on the other side of the court, the prosecution team were speaking in loud voices. 'I wonder,' said Miss Lantern, 'if we can persuade the usher to let us have access to the judge's famous espresso machine?'

'The judge is quite a studmuffin, isn't he?' said Sandra. 'Did you know he's also meant to be something of a chef de cuisine?'

'Really? Judges usually flatter to deceive,' said Miss Lantern, showing no trace of interest. 'It would help things if our client would speak to us.'

'The prosecution witnesses today were all so convincing.'

'Many a slip and all that. True, I've often lost from better positions than this. But we've got—'

'Hello, girls.' Northcroft, briefcase under his arm, had crossed the court. 'Still planning to turn up tomorrow, Miss Lantern? After all, you can't win them all. Maybe we should discuss plea bargains ... over dinner ... after a few concessions, naturally.' Northcroft dropped his gaze to the hem of Miss Lantern's skirt.

THE VERDICT

'Who could refuse such a sneer?' Miss Lantern replied, smiling.

'Ah does that mean ...?' He moved a step closer.

'I'd rather chew fresh lemons.'

'Well, then again, maybe your best bet will be the old man.' Northcroft smirked. 'In fact why don't you send him your meek little pupil – a pretty girl like her.' Northcroft turned his attention to Sandra. 'You might even get your client off with diminished responsibility and what – five years?'

'I take it that you're not aware that this meek little pupil, as you quaintly call her, has fenced for England, so be careful whom you challenge. And by the way, the judge was born in fifty-four which makes you three years his senior, I believe.' She picked up her own briefcase. 'Good day, Mr Northcroft. See you in court.'

Miss Lantern and Sandra left the court. 'But I never held a sword in my life,' protested Sandra when they were on their own. 'And ugh, did you see that leery grin of his?'

'Sandra, in this job you have to learn something about bluffing. And by the way, it's foil or épée. Anyway, good news; things might not be as bad as we thought.'

'How come?' asked Sandra as they approached the court chambers. 'If I was sitting on the jury I would know my verdict already.'

'Because, Sandra, no one suggests a deal when they're sitting on aces. Come on, we have to try to coax something out of Mr Woods. There's something he's not telling us.'

'Not telling us? He sits there without saying a word. He's completely dumb.'

'And that's another thing, Sandra. We've got to work on your positive attitude.'

The judge emerged whistling from his chambers. 'Bad luck knocking over that glass in court, Miss Lantern. You should learn to be more careful.' He chuckled and then turned around to add over his shoulder, 'Feel free to use my coffee machine. Perkins will show you how. And I agree, think positive. Cheerio.' He departed towards the car park, whistling. Miss Lantern's eyes followed the judge until he disappeared from view.

'Do you think the court is bugged?' asked Sandra.

'Huh, he can just spot a fellow coffee addict,' said Miss Lantern. 'Good stuff, Sandra, nice to see you haven't lost your sense of humour. Okay, let's find out where the artful dodger is skulking.'

'Sorry?

'Aka Perkins, the court usher.'

'What did the judge mean about the glass? You didn't do it on purpose, did you?'

The judge, on the way to his car, reflected that he would have liked to stay longer talking to Miss Lantern and her owl-like pupil, to congratulate them on the glass stunt properly, but he was more bashful than many people realised. Also, he had to appear strictly impartial, besides which he had an evening appointment and a train to catch. The idea occurred to him to make a change to his schedule, which was maybe overdue. He wound down the window and contemplated who would sound best on the drive home today: Mark Knopfler or Chrissy Hynde?

'Judge, will you be taking your supper in the conservatory?' The asker was thirty, curvaceous with long brown hair – and naked.

'Penelope, how long have we been lovers?'

She smiled and hesitated as she reached for the bathrobe, taking a grape instead. 'Well, you picked me up in the Selfridges' sale and it was spring green that season so it must be eighteen months now.'

'I'm afraid, Penelope, that this will have to be the last of our Wednesdays. I think I'll be … travelling for the foreseeable future.'

'I always knew a judge was too good to be true.'

'You don't mind?'

'Why should I mind, it's been great and we've still got sixty minutes before the last train.' Penelope took another grape, leaning towards him. 'So what will you have, judge, duck foie gras terrine or me?'

He appreciated her lovely shape and laughed. 'What made you think I wasn't a judge?'

Penelope sighed. 'Because no judge would ever wear Sex Pistols boxer shorts. Let's get them off. If this *is* going to be the last time I want you to remember it.'

'Morning, Your Honour.'

'Ah, Perkins, just the man. Let's have a chat, shall we? My chambers.' The judge grinned. Occasionally he pretended to be serious just to keep up appearances, but not today. He opened the door for the usher and went over to his prized Savinelli coffee machine. 'I think we might start with counsel this morning, speed up things a little.'

'Brokering a deal you mean?'

The judge handed Perkins a note. 'And if we could send a dozen red roses to Kensington.'

'*A dozen*, Your Honour?' The usher stood his ground.

'Perkins, as you know I have my quirks, and if I wanted an African Grey in your place, well ... I'm sure it could be arranged.'

'Sorry, sir. A dozen it is, to the usual address.'

He smiled as Perkins trotted out. He loved this job and everything that went with it. Before counsel arrived he would just have time to set up his morning playlist; something uplifting. Right now it seemed there were three reasons to be cheerful: great coffee, The Who at their zenith and the opportunity to talk to Miss Lantern once again.

'Ah, Northcroft, please do come in. Any sign of the defence team?' The judge beckoned the barrister to an armchair. Northcroft strode in and sat like an oil baron ready to discuss quotas. It was his case to lose and he knew it, thought the judge.

Miss Lantern and her pupil joined them and he outlined his ideas.

'So you're saying that if my client pleads guilty to armed robbery,' said Miss Lantern, 'the CPS would drop the attempted murder charge?'

'I think the Crown Persecution Service would be agreeable,' said the judge. 'I'm assuming you are going to run your client as a witness?'

'We have a client problem, Your Honour.' Their eyes met. 'He doesn't care whether he wins or loses.'

'Of course, your client has the right to remain silent,' the judge maintained eye contact, 'but you know I am duty bound to point out to the jury that inferences can be drawn, rightly or wrongly?'

Northcroft added: 'But we'd still expect a heavy custodial sentence to go with a guilty verdict' with his own look to the judge, who wondered whether Northcroft sensed forces outside his comprehension at work. The judge nodded curtly in tacit agreement. That Northcroft really was a devious animal. Pleas were up for discussion, but not sentencing – that was his remit.

'I don't know,' said Miss Lantern, 'if we could revert, Judge. A few hours to talk with our client?'

'That's fine.' The judge relaxed in his chair. 'Shall we agree at one o'clock, prompt?'

'Can't we just put him in the witness box anyway,' said Sandra, quietly to Miss Lantern, 'and simply hope … for the best?'

'Second Lantern's rule: *Don't put someone on the stand if you don't know where it's going*,' said Miss Lantern, sorting her papers as she surveyed the court. 'You've seen it yourself – ten minutes in his company and you start to feel he deserves everything he gets.' She glanced up at the clock. It showed one sharp. 'But you heard him – he refuses to speak anyway. You gave Perkins the message?'

'But the jury will think he's guilty.'

'Wagons roll!'

'All rise!' shouted Perkins and immediately approached the dais, presenting a folded piece of paper to the judge.

'Thank you, Perkins.' The judge read: *My client is standing by his Not Guilty on both charges. We're staying positive. J.* Northcroft watched the judge enquiringly. He shook his head to indicate no deal was to be brokered. Although it was still technically possible right up to the moment before the jury were sent out, the opportune moment had passed. The Crown versus Woods would go down to the wire.

The defence's first witness was a psychiatrist who testified that Woods, a man of blameless character, didn't fit the typical mould of violent robbery. 'Anything in cross?' The judge didn't expect Northcroft to hesitate.

'Thank you, Your Honour.' The prosecutor started to pace back and forth before the jury, a finger pressed against his temple in the pose of a thinker. The judge sensed a theatrical turn in the making. With some barristers it could be good entertainment but with Northcroft he suspected it could be just embarrassing.

'The defence team have taken us on a long and interesting run with the hounds,' said Northcroft waving his arms in a speculative manner. 'But to cut to the chase—' He loudly clapped his hands, which made a couple of the jury sit up in alarm.

The judge felt like groaning.

Northcroft continued: 'Doctor, in your considered opinion as a qualified psychiatrist wouldn't you expect an innocent man to want to testify, to proclaim his innocence?' Northcroft faced the jury. 'Isn't that what any innocent man or woman would do? Isn't it what we would do, eh?'

'Objection! This is a matter of opinion,' said Miss Lantern.

'Over-ruled. As you are aware, Miss Lantern, that is what we ask expert witnesses for, their opinions,' said the judge. 'Doctor, please answer the question.'

'Well—' The witness cleared his throat and paused. 'Yes, in

most circumstances an innocent man would, but that is not to say that in exceptional—'

'Thank you, doctor. You only voice what I'm sure we are all feeling,' said Northcroft. 'No further questions.'

The next witness for the defence, a bystander from the bus stop, started: 'I remember that week all very clearly. We had the police arresting a pickpocket in the butcher's and then two days later the attack—'

'But Mrs Borodowski, could you describe how the defendant seemed after the attack?' asked Miss Lantern.

'Well, surprised. I mean he seemed *really* surprised and not at all violent. A nice man I had him down as, before it all happened.'

The judge could see that Miss Lantern was making the best of the limited material at her disposal. She was trying to use this expression of surprise to create doubt in the jurors' minds, but it was like trying to bake a cake without eggs. He nodded to Northcroft, who stood in readiness for his cross-examination. 'So, Miss Borodowski, you work in a butcher's in the town, I believe?'

'That's right, I've been there—'

'And you witnessed the police arresting a pickpocket on the premises?'

'Yes. But I don't see—'

'And how did he react, this pickpocket, surprised?'

'His jaw fair fell open, I can tell ya. He had no idea—'

'Objection!' shouted Miss Lantern. But it was too late, realised the judge. It would take a minute or so for the penny to drop with the jury but they would soon understand what Northcroft was getting it.

Woods sat with his head bowed in the dock like a man who had given up. A couple of times since lunch the judge had caught Miss Lantern looking at him. She was in a tough spot and there was nothing that could be done about it. He decided to call a halt early. At this rate he would be starting a new trial before the end of the week. A guilty verdict appeared the only outcome. A shame he couldn't carry a light for Miss Lantern.

Back in chambers, the judge picked up the phone and selected his daughter's latest number, more in hope than anticipation. Often he found himself listening to the recorded message from a Spanish or Portuguese operator –they sounded the same to him. This time he was lucky.

'Yes, I'm fine,' she told him, 'battery's a bit low ... it's very hot.'

'It's surprisingly warm here as well,' he told her, hearing his voice echo on the line.

'Sorry, Dad, have to be quick, we're waiting at the bus stop. Spider has taken the Volvo in for the MOT ... it's the brakes. Do you know the latest cricket?' And then he lost the connection. Still, he was pleased to hear that his old Volvo was still going, thousands of miles away.

Perkins materialised in front of his desk with some papers for signature. 'That was my daughter wanting to know the latest cricket score. You and she have a lot in common.'

'Sixty-eight for one, Your Honour.'

'Leave those on the desk, will you? Thanks.' And then, in an effort to strike a sufficiently nonchalant tone he added, 'So, Perkins, how are their spirits holding up in the defence team?'

'Rumour has it that the accused is keeping as quiet as the third umpire on a flat pitch.'

There was something about the phone call with his daughter that he could not get out of his mind. 'Okay, Perkins. Well, people know where to find me.' He knew better than to enquire about the provenance of the usher's sayings and he said goodnight.

And then a moment later he remembered. He leapt out of his seat and called down the corridor: 'Perkins, come back, will you?'

He scribbled quickly. 'By hand for the defence counsel, and you never saw this note, right?'

'Saw what?' said Perkins touching his finger to the side of his nose melodramatically and was gone for the second time. The judge sighed. It was out of his hands now.

Perkins found Miss Lantern alone by the coffee machine. 'How about I fix you a proper espresso from the judge's machine?'

'That would be very nice, Perkins,' said Miss Lantern.

'And by the way, good luck.' The usher reached out to shake her hand and slipped the note into her palm. Dropping his voice he added, 'I'll be in quarters if you need me,' moving off as Sandra appeared.

'Curiouser and curiouser,' mused Miss Lantern.

'What's that?'

But Miss Lantern was reading: *Captain. Bus stop –WHY?* 'Sandra,' she said, 'there's good news and bad news. We've been very stupid.'

'That was the bad news?'

'No, that was the good news. The bad news is that we've got a long night in front of us. Why didn't we see it before?' She tore the piece of paper into small pieces and put them in her pocket. 'Why was the captain at the bus stop in the first place?'

'Because his car was in for a service?'

'Yes that's just what he *will* say, and then it's goodnight Vienna.' Miss Lantern was drumming her fingernails on the side of the coffee machine. 'We need to find a date when the captain has cast-iron proof he was nowhere near the depot—'

'But we can't get him back into the witness box. The prosecution's turn has gone,' sighed Sandra. 'I mean we should have thought of it before.'

'Lantern's rule number three, Sandra. The answer is in the law.'

'What do you mean, the law?

'Halsbury's Statutes. I believe the judge has a full set. We'll start with rebuttal witnesses. I think Lord Scarman is the authority ... Arbuckle versus Crawford, wasn't it?'

'Can we use the judge's library?'

'And his coffee machine. Now where did that usher disappear to?' Miss Lantern started in the direction of the usher's quarters. 'Perkins!'

The judge stood in the favourite room of his house. He could knock up something quickly, say, a quick scallops beurre blanc and invite some friends to drop in for a snack by the pool. It was warm enough. But tonight, although a touch lonely, he didn't feel like being a host. Music was the best antidote to loneliness he had found; some early Pink Floyd maybe. He needed something as the house was as quiet as a monastery. As he picked up the picture of his deceased wife from the Aga he remembered her voice. 'Come on, Jonathan. Attack the bowling.' Allison, ever the cricket fanatic.

Sirloin steak, good wine and Pink Floyd's *Wish You Were Here*, after which he would think about planning something for the coming August Bank Holiday weekend. He was as free as a bird. Later he found just what he was searching for; Muse in Concert, outdoors at Leeds Castle. Now that could be something. He poured himself a last glass of St Emillion – he wanted a clear head in court tomorrow – and decided to buy a ticket. His finger hovered over the keyboard, one or two?

'So help me, God.'

The judge was curious about the latest defence witness, if only because Northcroft plainly didn't take to being surprised. In addition to this last-minute witness there was now a large screen TV facing the jury and the judge's dais. He was aware of a heightened tension in Court Number One. The witness confirmed that he was the manager of the cash depot where Keith Woods, the defendant, was working as a night security guard. The depot was responsible for storing cash deposits from banks for short periods.

'And with your permission, Your Honour,' said Miss Lantern, 'I'd like to show a CCTV recording from the depot.' The film, poor quality grainy black and white, depicted someone entering the main reception area at the warehouse. Miss Lantern had pointed out that the video was clearly dated May the fourteenth.

'And your point, Miss Lantern?' asked the judge who had been hoping for, if not exactly Coppola, something more engaging.

'From this film we see the defendant clearly talking with Captain Crane and yet we heard the captain tell the court that they had never met before.' All eyes were on Miss Lantern, even Perkins, who was staring at her like a batsman watching the bowler's arm.

'Objection!' shouted Northcroft. 'There is no evidence that this is Captain—'

'Miss Lantern you are on pretty thin ice here. We can see the defendant plainly enough but the other man ... it *could* be Captain Crane but it could also be just about any man in the country around six feet tall, including me.' He paused before glancing in Northcroft's direction. 'Of course, the prosecution have an option to call a rebuttal witness. Anything else for the defence? You're not calling the defendant?'

'No, Your Honour.'

'Okay. Members of the jury, this is something I shall go through with you in my summing up. So unless there's anything else to add from the prosecution side?' The judge considered how much time to give Northcroft. He had a pretty good idea of where Miss Lantern was going, she wanted the captain back in the stand, but it was Northcroft's call. Miss Lantern had put out the bait – would the big greedy pike go for it? He remembered the last time a witness for the prosecution had been recalled; a messy divorce case that quickly became messier. Rebuttal witnesses had a curious wont to muddy the waters.

'Permission to call a rebuttal witness, Your Honour?'

He'd gone for it. The judge kept a poker face and answered:

'Permission granted.' He saw the faintest flicker of a smile play on the edge of Miss Lantern's lips.

The captain took the stand. 'Captain, may I remind you you are still under oath.'

The captain nodded and Northcroft began. He had irrefutable proof that the captain was out of the country on the fourteenth of May – the date of the CCTV picture. The captain, with the help of his diary, confirmed he was definitely out of the country. Northcroft raised his eyebrows at the defence corner. His look seemed to ask: 'Is that the best you can do?'

The judge raised his eyebrows, inviting Miss Lantern to cross. 'Just a couple of questions, Your Honour.' Miss Lantern nodded at Perkins who was not standing in his usual place but was by the door. 'Captain, as a serving officer in Afghanistan did you sometimes have to send your men into a combat situation?'

'Well of course. That's what you do every day in counter-insurgency situations. The Official Secrets Act forbids me—'

'I'm not asking for details. But Captain, is it just possible that under pressure you might get the directions the wrong way around, send the soldiers under your command on a wild goose chase? That you could make a right pig's ear of it?'

'Don't be ridiculous. That would be a court martial offence. You civilians have no idea. We are elite specialists, we don't make decisions without factoring the outcomes.'

'Objection, Your Honour,' interjected Northcroft.

The judge felt compelled to point out; 'Miss Lantern, I'm afraid I'll have to warn you that under rules of rebuttal evidence I am struggling to see relevance here.' As he was speaking the door of Number One Court opened and in strode a workman wearing blue overalls – as if he had come directly from a garage repair yard, thought the judge. He was carrying a large brown book under his arm and was followed by Perkins.

'One last question,' said Miss Lantern. 'So where was the bus going that day?'

'You what?' barked the captain.

'It's a simple enough question. Where were you going on the bus? You're a captain in the army, an elite specialist, you don't make decisions without—' she checked her notes, 'factoring the outcomes. So where were you going? Will you tell these good people of Kent why you were at the bus stop that day?'

'Objection, Your Honour!' shouted Northcroft. 'Counsel is badgering the witness, a man of proven integrity and a decorated officer.'

'Objection sustained,' agreed the judge. 'It's my duty to warn you that you don't *have* to answer that question, Captain.' The judge couldn't remember when he had last enjoyed himself in court so much. Miss Lantern at last seemed to have got under the skin of the captain – who was now clenching the rail of the witness box and focused on his inquisitor with a mix of undisguised dislike and hostility. His demeanour had lost its earlier cockiness.

'Well that must be because my car was in for a service *that day*,' the captain explained in a tight voice, like he would be talking to a seven-year-old, thought the judge, who saw Miss Lantern exchange looks with her pupil.

'Your normal service garage?'

'Well certainly.'

'And your car ... that would be a silver Audi, registration AC4 RT?' Miss Lantern read from her papers.

'Well, yes.'

Was the captain starting to sound less certain? wondered the judge. And again he saw the tell from the witness, a checking glance to Northcroft before answering the question. The judge found himself leaning forward in his seat. He realised Miss Lantern had cooked up a plan.

'Objection,' interrupted Northcroft.

'Well I think now that we've started,' said the judge, 'we may as well see where this is going.'

'According to our enquiries the last service for your car was in February and there has been no recorded entry since.' At this point Miss Lantern turned her attention to the man in overalls who had just walked in. The captain also stared towards the door. He turned pale and asked for a glass of water.

The judge couldn't remember his court so quiet during a case, like an arena of spectators listening for the starter's gun. Everyone was watching the witness stand. The captain looked lost behind enemy lines. At last he spoke: 'It's true I wanted to talk with Woods. That's why I followed him to the bus stop.'

'He threatened me.' Woods stood up and was talking to the court from the dock. 'He said if I didn't go along with a raid on the depot I'd lose my job. The bus stop was a put-up job. He put my hand on the knife and stabbed himself. I've kept quiet because he said at the bus stop that my daughter would be next—' Except for the words 'Not Guilty' three days earlier this was the first time the judge had heard the defendant speak. He was struck by the deep and believable voice.

'Objection!' Northcroft was on his feet. 'Your Honour, this evidence is not admissible. The defendant is not under oath.'

'Sustained. I'm sorry, you've had plenty of time to prepare your witness.' Miss Lantern appeared disappointed. Northcroft relieved. He pressed on: 'But I think in terms of common courtesy, although the defendant has chosen not to speak, we will give him the courtesy of at least finishing his sentence. Mr Woods, you were about to tell us the name of your daughter?'

'June. It's June.'

The judge nodded his head to the witness as a sign to sit down and turned to address the jury. 'Members of the jury, I must ask you to disregard the last comments from the prisoner in the dock. He hasn't been sworn in, he was not under oath. This is not admissible evidence. Am I clear on this point?'

The foreman of the jury, appreciating the seriousness of the moment, stood up to confirm. 'Yes, Your Honour.'

'The day is late and I know, members of the jury,' the judge gave a wide smile, 'you are keen to start your bank holiday weekend so

I think we still have time to hear closing statements and my summary of evidence very shortly. But to help me in my preparation there's one piece of earlier evidence I would like to check, and this *is* admissible.' He glanced at the jury. 'Could we ask the the court reporter to check the court record. There is one witness's comment I would like to confirm for my notes; Mrs Levy's testimony, what she heard before the incident.'

There was some delay before the court reporter found the evidence Mrs Levy had presented four days earlier. She read out in a voice the judge thought was as clear as a bell: 'Here we are: "There's a strike on the depot." Then the gent who was stabbed said: "You can say goodbye to June"'.

The judge heard a gasp from someone on the jury benches. 'I see, thank you. Sorry, I don't know your name, court reporter?' he enquired.

'Moira. Moira Cliff, Your Honour.'

'Thank you, Moira Cliff.' The judge suspected that the trained stenographer had written the question down before she had even realised that it was addressed to her.

'This is the phoney war, waiting for the jury,' said Miss Lantern. 'And however long you do this job, you don't get used to it.' The defence team were standing at the coffee machine.

'I still don't understand, why did Captain Crane incriminate himself?' asked Sandra. 'Did you know he would?'

'No, I only hoped. It was the judge who pushed him over the edge. The way he emphasised you don't *have* to answer the question.'

'You mean the captain wanted to show he couldn't be pushed around, even by a judge.' Sandra pressed the button for a coffee from the machine.

'I wouldn't be surprised if he wasn't onto Crane from the start. Our judge is ... something else.'

Sandra turned to face her mentor. 'But you still think that judges ... what was it, *flatter to deceive?*'

'They're predicting record-breaking temperatures for the weekend,' replied Miss Lantern.

'I think we might get the five o'clock train if we're lucky.'

'Don't count on me. I'm in no particular rush to get back to the smoke. Maybe it's time to spend some time by the sea, I could get used to life in the country. Anyway, remember Lantern's rule number one.'

'Oh yes, you never told me.'

'Did you see the look on the jury's faces when the name June came up?'

'Did you see Northcroft's?'

'Speak of the devil.'

The prosecution counsel walked up to the coffee machine. 'That was some stunt you pulled in there, ' said Northcroft, glowering at the two women. 'Remember, it's not my witness that's on trial here.'

'Not yet,' said Miss Lantern, sweetly.

'I'm still not sure how the judge managed it but that was the clearest case of jury manipulation I've ever seen.'

'I'd say that's the least of your troubles. Your main witness has now admitted to committing perjury in court,' replied Miss Lantern calmly. 'I'd say: expect papers.'

In his chambers the judge was writing up his case notes and trying to ignore the sunlight that cast an ever-diminishing arc on the carpet under the window, when there was a knock on the chambers door. 'Enter!' he shouted and in came his usher. 'I hope it's important, Perkins. I'm keen not to be here a minute longer than is absolutely necessary. I might have a fair amount of ducking and diving to do when we wrap this one up.'

'Latest from the jury – they want to know if they could find the captain guilty.' The judge laughed. Perkins continued: 'I had to send the clerk of the court in to have a word.'

'Good man. Won't be long now. You look quite happy, you

wouldn't have anything riding on the verdict, would you? No. Don't answer that.' He glanced at his watch and then out of the window at the blue August sky. 'Second thoughts, Perkins. It's getting late, some dishes best served cold and all that. Maybe we'll hear this first thing on Tuesday. Oh and Perkins, get the foreman to write down the verdict, we don't want any change of mind—'

'Oh, I don't see there's any danger of that.'

'By the way, did you give that note to Miss Lantern?'

'Oh, she asked me to give you this, Your Honour. Sorry, I forgot.' Perkins handed over an envelope and laughed. 'So many notes I'm starting to feel like a pigeon.'

The judge read and smiled. 'If you wouldn't mind one last flight, Perkins. Tell Miss Lantern I have the legal statute she can borrow for the weekend. If she would like to drop in here.' He bent down to continue writing on his laptop.

'Statutes. Right you are, Your Honour. In fact she owes me.'

'Miss Lantern owes you, Perkins?' He stopped writing.

'Bit of overtime, sir. The man in the overalls, the garage – he's my brother-in-law.'

'I didn't know he worked in a garage?'

'Oh he doesn't. He's fruit and veg. Down the market. Miss Lantern said to bring the order book, she was very specific about that, and for overalls my cousin Reg—'

'If I hear any more of this I'll have you suspended. Perkins, are you still here?' The next time he looked up from his laptop, the door was closed and Perkins had vanished.

'So what do you think the verdict will be on Tuesday?' Miss Lantern was walking down the court corridor side-by-side with the judge.

'Miss Lantern, you can't possibly expect me to comment on a case with no prosecution counsel present,' he laughed. 'But rumour has it that the clerk of the court has closed his book and Perkins looks like a man who's lost a sixpence and found a pound. As you know, Miss Lantern, you can never second guess a jury—'

'I'm in danger of forgetting my own Lantern's rule number one.'

'Which is?'

'*First fun. Work second.*' Just don't tell my pupil, she's still trying to work it out. And now we're adjourned, forget Lantern, it's Juliet and thanks for the offer of a concert ticket. I was delighted to accept.'

He held the door open for her as they emerged outside into the still-hot afternoon sun. 'Yes, I did wonder about the J—' He stopped abruptly and appreciated for the first time Miss Lantern without a wig, her short haircut accentuating her elfin-like features.

'I notice that when the verdict is a close call like this, I often can't sleep that well. I could be up all night – and there's the heat,' she added with a sideways glance in his direction.

'I've already seen men underestimate you at their peril,' he said. 'I hope you have a swimming costume with you.' He was reminded of a deer in the forest.

'Will I be needing one?' She paused on their way to his car, the last remaining in the car park, before continuing: 'Don't think I'm saying *yes* because I think I owe you one. I don't even like classical music!'

'You don't?'

'My ex was mad about Mozart and he used to drag me to concerts all over the place. But I found even if I didn't get into the music it was still a good time for me to be with my thoughts.' They'd reached the car. 'So you don't have to worry—'

'So classical music isn't really your thing, Juliet,' said the judge, thinking he liked the name.

'Well no, and to be honest I'm afraid I'm not very refined. Eighties pop is more my thing. You must promise not to tell anybody, Judge.'

He opened the passenger door, walking to his side. 'It's a

promise,' he said, trying to keep a straight face and ticking another box.

'I knew you'd laugh.' She casually threw her bag into the seat behind her. As he fastened his seat belt he took the opportunity to study her profile close up and for the first time noticed her smile lines reach all the way from her lips to the edges of her eyes. He pressed a button and the roof started to fold back as the car was already gliding from the car park.

Perkins was making his way home on foot and at the car park exit turned to give the Jaguar a mock salute as it glided past. 'Good chap, Perkins,' said the judge, as he pressed another button on the car stereo. He saw her lips moving in reply but whatever she was saying was drowned out by The Undertones launching into the opening bars of *Teenage Kicks*.

The Lonely Spy

The phone was standard issue, the old-fashioned type, and it was ringing. Anthony looked around the office to see if there was anyone else there to answer it. There wasn't. 'Whitehall eight three eight three,' he read from the number in the middle of the dial.

'Someone has borrowed the file,' a woman's voice informed him.

'Sorry, what was that? To whom did you wish to speak?'

'Someone has borrowed the file,' the voice repeated. And then the click and burr of the empty line. Anthony replaced the receiver. On the other end of the line, the woman picked up her hat and gloves and walked slowly from the room. At the door she paused, leaned on her walking stick and put her other hand to the light switch, before turning her back on the room, leaving the lights on.

'Where is he hiding?' Aldo didn't care that people were staring at him as he strode past work stations towards the editor's office. 'Under a very large stone I bet. Wait till I get my hands on him!' He had read the memo less than a minute ago. It had stitch-up written all over it.

'I'm sorry, you haven't got an appointment.'

He ignored the secretary and opened the door. 'I heard Jamie is leading on the election. Tell me it's not true. No one on this paper, strike that, *any* paper, has an election record to touch mine: Callaghan seventy-six, Thatcher seventy-nine, Thatcher eighty-three, Thatcher eighty-seven.' He'd not slept two days before that front page. 'God! I was bored long before the electorate. Then Major ninety-two—'

'Aldo, it's true,' said the editor quietly. 'Jamie is front man on the election.'

'And then Blair ninety-seven. Now there was a scoop. Remember when I – what did you say, Derek?'

'The paper needs to stay a step ahead to be avant-garde.'

'*But there's not a day passes that I don't feel young* – Mark Twain, and *he* was a good deal older than me, I can tell you. But Jamie Nonce for chrissakes? He was still in nappies when I was interviewing Thatcher.'

'My point precisely. It's one of the reasons I'm putting you on a special feature. Your new assistant and I were just discussing it.' The editor motioned his head and Aldo turned around to see a girl of about twenty-five sitting at the small meeting table.

'Aldo Court,' he introduced himself. 'Good afternoon.'

'My privilege to work with such a—'

'You can't be serious.' He turned back to the editor but this was starting to feel like a lost cause. 'I needed this election.' His bravura was ebbing. 'This election needs me,' he added limply.

'Sit down and listen to me for a change!' The editor pointed firmly at the meeting table. 'If you'd just give me a chance to elaborate on my plans.' Aldo saw the familiar pressing together of the fingers of each hand in cat's cradle formation. This was a rehearsed talk. He sat down.

As the editor went into the story from behind his desk, the young reporter started busily writing in her notebook. Aldo himself glanced around the smartly furnished office, glass-topped tables and *objets d'art*. Time was when it would have been ashtrays and bourbon bottles lifted from the red-eye out of JFK. 'The key will be to preserve the sense of history but make it, you know, exciting.'

The trouble with growing old, thought Aldo, as the editor elaborated, was that you started to matter less, if you ever mattered at all. Maybe it was time to get out now while the going was still good. He wasn't too old to get back into shape, join a gym maybe. 'So what do you think, Aldo? We need an old-fashioned newshound with a nose for a story. Could you get your teeth into it, nail the Fifth Man legend once and for all?' The editor was pitching *at him* – invariably a bad sign. 'You find him or we bury the ghost. We print either way. It's right up your street.'

The girl put down her pencil and turned her attention to Aldo. The two of them waited for his answer. He let them think he'd lost his lines for a moment, before starting: 'So what are we looking at? Another spy from the cold war era ... probably living it up in a retirement home in East Anglia.' Aldo stood up and started pacing. 'The only spying they'll be good for now is reading their oppo's dominoes. Our man probably doesn't even remember what the domino dots, represent – likely as not he thinks it's a new super code – like Morse but just dots, no dashes. Heh! I like that. Anyway, that's assuming the fifth man or woman even exists, which I very much doubt. Next thing you'll be calling me a turkey and have me voting for Christmas. Sorry, I mean, who cares—'

'But Aldo, that's your art,' the editor interrupted before picking up something from his desk. 'You can make people care. You know the political history. And besides, we do have one lead.'

Aldo suspected something like that. Years on the job had taught him to be vigilant; lightning didn't come out of a blue sky. He stopped pacing. 'What sort of lead?'

'We received a file. It was marked for the personal attention of the editor and hand delivered yesterday, anonymously.' The editor picked up a black-and-white still from his desk and passed it over for Aldo who sat down to inspect it. The photograph showed two men shaking hands outside an office.

'Well hold the front page!' exclaimed Aldo, trying to sound ironic. Underneath the caption was a post-it. In handwriting he didn't recognise: *Portland; the one that got away.*

'Look closely. That's not *any* office. It's ours, this newspaper's. And I don't believe in coincidences. Archives has already corroborated the material. Whoever our mystery source was, it stacks up. The man in that still is the mastermind, Gordon Lonsdale. He ended up in Russia with all the others, except one.'

'The one that got away, you mean?'

'Right. Readers are bored of Muslims and terrorists; a real old-fashioned British spy will be a breath of fresh air.'

'You want me to dig out the dirt on some retired agent, track him down and confront him in his lair in some dank Moscow tenement block before casually asking: "By the way, old chap, do you think you could let me know the name of the fifth man – my editor would much appreciate it?" Do you really think he would tell me? I mean, don't we have James Bond for that kind of thing?'

'Everyone tells you everything, Aldo,' said the editor, still pitching. 'You know the ropes, prove you've still got the magic.' They were interrupted by the phone. 'Talk amongst yourselves.'

Aldo, picking up his reading glasses from his jacket pocket, took a closer look at the photograph. One man was clearly identifiable but the other was in shadow with his back half-turned. 'Could be anybody: the prime minister, Clint Eastwood,' he muttered, 'or even me when I was in my prime.'

'Actually,' said the girl leaning forwards, 'it's more likely to be Peru than Moscow.'

'Come again ... uhm?' Aldo observed the woman more closely: hair up, glasses and smart executive suit. On the plus side she did seem genuinely friendly. He'd had to work with a lot worse.

'Judith. My preliminary research indicates the last sighting of Gordon Lonsdale was on a plane to Lima.'

'You're sure about that? Peru as in South America?'

'Last time I looked it was. But shouldn't we tell him?' She nodded in the direction of the editor. 'It may change things.'

'You'll do no such thing. Mum's the word.' He placed one finger to his lips. 'Maybe this could be worth following up after all.'

The editor put down the phone and asked: 'Where were we?'

'Moscow,' replied Aldo.

Ten minutes later they were leaving the office and Aldo let loose his parting shot: 'Let me just check, Derek; you are giving us a free rein? I mean, no hands tied, we follow this story wherever it takes us?'

'You know the motto of this paper. *Wherever the story goes.* So beat it, the pair of you.'

'And remember next time, an appointment,' said the still cross-looking secretary outside the editor's office.

'Next time: remember coffee.' And as an afterthought Aldo added: 'Even if I have to bring the beans myself ... come on, Judith, you need to tell me more about your research. Peru, isn't it quite big?'

Roderick Ball, a trilby hat on top of a head of silver hair that he knew would be considered an inch too long in the smartest circles, enjoyed nothing more than his walk to work, especially mornings like this; a crisp bite in the air and the sun in the eyes of the taxi drivers heading into town with their early morning fares down Shaftesbury Avenue. After Leicester Square tube he went north up Charing Cross Road before cutting left into the heart of Soho.

At six foot three inches he covered the ground smartly. The walk was less than a mile and he could make it in his sleep. Rod was late but old habits die hard; he doubled back on himself at Lexington Street, putting an extra three minutes on his journey. On the corner of Frith and Old Compton Street he passed Princi's, where he sometimes stopped for a latte. He said good morning to the lad putting out the pavement sign. One morning five years ago, smart chrome chairs had materialised like aliens on the pavement, heralding the latest step upwards in Soho ambience. He missed the old atmosphere of neon lights and signs for models in doorways.

He was first in the office; time to clear his desk before last night's telexes came in – a fanciful thought – like everyone else in the parish he had a *smart phone.* He worked uninterrupted for an hour, from time to time regretting the café latte he had walked by. There was a knock at the door. 'Come in, Anthony,' he said.

No one but the new recruit from Oxford would knock on an open door.

'Good morning, sir,' said Anthony – angular, suited, shaved and even taller than me, thought Rod.

'No titles here. Rod will do just nicely.' Anthony looked uncertain in the doorway and not a day over twenty-one. Rod stood up and put on his welcoming face. 'Come in and grab a pew.' As a senior head of department he had a not inconsiderable office fittings budget that he never touched. The furniture in the office was shabby and he preferred it that way.

'I've got something I thought you should see.'

Anthony chose a threadbare beige armchair that Rod seemed to recall rescuing from a skip in Wardour Street. He was not one to stand on ceremony, another reason why he was happy to work at 27 Great Portland Street, sandwiched between Soho and theatre land, rather than the prestigious HQ overlooking the Thames. 'So how are you settling in?' asked Rod. 'I'm afraid we're very home-spun here.'

'Actually, I like it that way.' Anthony smiled. 'It reminds me of my old tutor's rooms at college.'

'Well I'm afraid there's not much of the three P's around here.'

'Three P's, Rod?'

'Pin-stripes, processes and presentations. That's what they'll teach you at HQ.'

'And what do you teach me here?' Anthony looked bashful. 'Sorry, sir, I didn't mean to sound impertinent.'

'Here,' Rod waved an arm at the tired-looking furniture. 'Here, Anthony, what we do is catch spies. That's what I do best.'

'It sounds ... what I signed up for.'

'It's hard work. To your family all you can say is you're a civil servant: that can be stressful.' For twenty-five years at home Rod had kept up the pretence that he was the salesman for an alarm company. But he chose not to share this with colleagues. People in the trade were jealous of their covers, like a favourite jacket, not lent lightly. 'Now, Anthony, you said you had something for me?'

Anthony proceeded to give him a briefing of events on case *Leuctra*. He had a notebook in his hand.

'So we had a level-two system alert yesterday?'

'That's right. The phone call came in at,' he opened the notebook, 'sixteen-zero-three hundred hours.'

'And a description of the person who took the file?'

'I didn't think to ask—'

'Don't they have to sign for the file?'

'Well he did—'

'But it could also be a she?'

'Yes, sorry, my mistake. Let me check the name.' Again he scanned through his notes. 'G. Lonsdale.'

'Someone with a sense of humour. Did you study modern history at, where was it, Cambridge?'

'Keble. Actually my history was more the ancient variety, you know, the Peloponnesian wars, Sparta—'

'*Minus solum quam solus esset*,' remembered Rod.

'Yes, I recognise that ... hold it ... Plutarch?'

'Close, Cicero. *Never less alone then when alone.*' Rod smiled. If not spycatcher, a history teacher wouldn't have been a bad second. 'Gordon Lonsdale, mastermind of the Portland Spy Ring, a friend of the Krogers – mysteriously exchanged for a third-rate spy just at the start of a twenty-five stretch. So he followed Burgess, Philby and Maclean to Russia. The Krogers did some time, and then like the ringleader they also got an exchange and went to Moscow. The Krogers always claimed there were plenty more in the woodwork.'

'I take it we're talking about the fifth man?'

'The very same. So there you have it. Not grade one material but we'll have to brief the minister. No politician wants to be playing catch-up with the tabloids. CCTV is too much to hope for.'

Anthony grimaced. 'Why didn't I think of that?' Sometimes Rod despaired. His old mentor had taught him tradecraft; it's all in the detail. Now it was all in the PR. Still, a nearly fifty-year-old case was being re-opened. Interesting. Of course it could be something and nothing. It was a standard ploy: leave a file in the public domain, bait in a lobster pot, wait to see if anyone came to take a sneaky look inside. Well someone had done more than take a sneaky look; they had walked off with the pot. Rod wrote some questions on a piece of paper: *Who? Why now?* and then *Fifth Man?* He deliberated for a moment and then drew an arrow from the word *Fifth* and wrote *Krogers*.

There was a cough from the doorway and Rod looked up.

'Will that be all, I mean, is there anything else you want?'

'No I don't think so ... except hell of a name *Leuctra*. Who came up with that?' Rod asked, although he knew the answer.

'As a matter of fact I did.' The younger man took a step back into the room. 'It's the second Peloponnesian War. Leuctra was—'

'Anthony, stop!' He had an idea. 'How long have you been with us?'

'Three months and one week.'

'Have you been out of the office yet? Fieldwork I mean?'

'No, just lunches, round the corner.'

'Lunches. Okay. First junket coming up. There's a librarian I want you to go after.'

'That sounds ... interesting, really.'

Rod still remembered the day he received his first field-visit briefing and started to sound more serious.

Sir Rufus Sinclair looked out of his seventh-storey window. As he watched across the London skyline a pigeon flew straight into the window pane, fell to the sill and then dropped out of view below. Sir Rufus stood still.

'Gosh! What was that?' asked the only other man standing in the room, next to a rosewood desk about five metres away.

'Just another reason why we have bullet-proof windows.' Without turning around Sir Rufus went on: 'We've done a deal for four hunter-class nuclear submarines that will provide jobs for the next thirty years. Tell the union they sign the agreement or we move the whole service contract to India.'

'Understood, sir.' He made a note on the electronic device in his hand. 'Anything for me?'

'Yes, actually, today there is.' Sir Rufus flicked a speck of dust from the lapel of his three-piece dark blue suit. 'Our Russian friends have decided to call in a favour. We might have some need of unit zero.' He moved towards the centre of the large room and stood across his desk from the younger man, who was looking less composed than a moment earlier. 'Who is the best person we've got there – still Kalugina?'

'Kalugina, does get very good results.' The assistant hesitated. 'But there are cheaper services available.'

Sir Rufus passed an envelope across the desk. 'You know the drill. Just let me know when it's done.'

In the middle of the forest clearing stood a man with silver hair. He walked, hoe in hand, across a well-manicured lawn. From a white-walled, low-roofed ranch house a woman, a few years younger, came towards him carrying a fully laden tray.

'Here, darling, let me give you a hand.'

'Don't be daft.'

The woman put the tray down on a small circular table. The silver tray dazzled in the sunlight. He massaged behind his right shoulder.

'Gordon, I've told you a dozen times you really should see a doctor about that—'

'It's just a sprain. Stop nagging. You know keeping the jungle at bay is a full-time job. So what cake have we got today?'

'Your favourite.' She cut him a generous slice of lemon cake. 'Such a shame that nobody from the village wants to play croquet.'

'Can't be surprised,' replied Gordon adjusting his sun hat. 'Trouble with this country, Rebecca; no tradition.'

'There's always Dimitri.'

'Dimitri,' uttered Gordon contemptuously.

'I saw a white alligator this morning. Isn't that supposed to be one of the superstitious things?' Rebecca picked up *The Times* newspaper. 'Anything interesting in the paper today?'

Gordon surveyed the scene, tasting his cake. 'Look, it's back,' he said quietly and pointed.

'What?'

'By the willow, over there.' Gordon pointed towards the willow tree on the banks of a wide, sluggish river.

'I can't see anything ... wait, on that branch, like a kingfisher.'

'With a golden tail and that amazing crest.'

'Let's check the bird book after supper. Tea?'

'Maybe it's a sign ... more visitors on the way.'

'No regrets?' She stirred the pot.

'Only all those years apart.' He smiled at her. 'Beauty is truth, truth beauty,' he murmured.

'You and your poetry.' Rebecca was pouring his tea. 'With your letters I never had a chance to be lonely,' she said, passing him his cup. 'You know it's not too late to write your own story.'

'English pubs I miss. It would be nice to take Gary down to the pub for a pint.'

'No one gets everything they wish for in life, Gordon.'

'I know.'

They leaned against each other, drank their tea and watched the parrots flit to and fro in the canopy of dense trees above the forest floor.

'Could be it has got lost,' said Gordon a few minutes later, looking to his wife who was engrossed in the paper.

'The bird book will tell us.' Her head still buried in the newspaper she asked: 'Did I see that you had a letter from Gary?'

'I'll read it to you later. You know it was twenty years ago this week we left Moscow. I've been saving a rather special bottle of Chateau Margaux for the occasion.'

'Good idea, and there's a Nielsen concert on the wireless, *The Inextinguishable* I think.'

'Radio.'

THE LONELY SPY

'We could raise a glass to Mikhail Gorbachev.'

They laughed.

'I promised to drop in and see Dimitri before supper,' said Gordon.

'You two, it's a wonder what you find in common to talk about.'

'He saved my life, remember?'

Rebecca looked up at the frail but firm-jawed and tanned figure of her husband as he stood up and marched towards the willow tree, his back slightly bent.

Rod remembered well the feeling coming back from a junket; the relief to get safely home and the desire to talk were immense – the reason operatives were not allowed to get taxis home from the airport. The de-briefing was taking place in Rod's office and Anthony was full of energy, restless in the beige armchair. He'd only been away five days searching for the missing librarian but was still warbling like a song thrush. 'So when I finally caught up with her she was on a chartered sailing boat with a nephew and niece. Aged seventy-six, can you believe it? Anyway she remembered very well the mystery borrower—'

'Ah, our lobster pot thief.' Rod felt the familiar tingle of excitement. A random strike or stealing to plan? he wondered. 'Description?'

'I'm not sure how much Miss Barton can be relied on,' said Anthony, searching through his notes. 'She identified the man from the photograph, Gordon Lonsdale, but it couldn't be.' He looked up. 'The man in the photograph must be thirty or forty and it's an old photograph. Miss Barton said the man who took the file was in his twenties.'

'A relative perhaps? Grandson?'

'Of course. Why didn't I think of that?' Anthony sounded disappointed.

'When is the file due back? Do they have a return date for these things ... you never know. Was there a copy?'

Anthony brightened up. He triumphantly produced a large manilla envelope. 'It's all here.'

'Excellent. Now tell me everything else you remember about your discussion. Leave nothing out.'

As Anthony recounted details from his copious notes Rod pictured the librarian. She had watched that one file for ten years beyond her eligible retirement date. Like a tea-clipper moored until the trade winds arrived, she had patiently waited. 'She was ordered: "Just report when the file has been borrowed and then you are free to go,"' repeated Rod.

'That's correct.'

'And she has no idea who was giving the instructions?'

'Nothing. That's it, sir.'

But it wasn't, Rod knew that. Everyone kept something back, always. All that time, on your own guarding secrets ... after a while they started to own you. He knew that better than anyone. There would still be something. 'Anthony, that's not all, is it?' Rod walked over to the window overlooking Great Portland Street. 'There's something else, isn't there, a detail you can't get off your mind. Am I right?'

'Well, as a matter of fact there was one thing. Well it was nothing really. Just that at some point she said the atmosphere changed. She used a strange phrase.' He checked his notes; '*On my own but not alone.*'

'Our friend Cicero again.'

'The same thought occurred to me.'

'So she felt she was being watched?'

'Not exactly. She mentioned that she first started to be aware of it when the phones were serviced.'

'And how long ago was that?'

'Well that was the strange thing; only a couple of weeks ago.'

'Ah-ha. So far we've assumed that if there is a fifth man, it's nothing more than just a loose end from the Cold War. The Russians would be happy to let sleeping dogs lie, unless—'

'Unless what, Rod?'

THE LONELY SPY

'Is it possible that our fifth man has found new employers? He's still active? Truth rarely takes the straightest road.' Rod had the feeling of walking on a pebble beach. 'Anthony, you've done well.'

'What do we do next?'

'We go through the files. Intelligence is like picking up stones on the beach. We just keep turning them over and one day we'll find something there that has no right to be there. Turning and asking, that's the spycatching game.'

Aldo was late getting to the airport. He expected Judith to be on time. The place was teeming, and he was fighting to get past people. 'Damn and blast, excuse me, sorry, yes, well, if you will travel with a dog. Why not take a cruise instead ... Judith! Hello, here already? Have you checked in?'

She looked relieved to see him. 'You made it. Yes, all done. But they wanted to see your passport before they allocated us seats. Nice jacket.'

'Economy class?'

'Fraid so.'

He vaguely remembered the editor saying something similar. 'You're joking. We'll soon see about that. Leave this to me.' Five minutes later Aldo was back, proudly waving two tickets above his bald head. 'First Class. Beats going to Blackpool for another election manifesto. What is it with the Lib Dems? No leadership; that's their problem ... Now we haven't much time. Let's get cracking.'

'Security?'

'Champagne in the VIP lounge. And you can brief me on your latest research. What was his name again, this spy we're after?'

'Gordon Lonsdale in Peru. It's unbelievable.'

'So you keep on saying,' said Judith who put down *A Cultural and Political History of Peru*. 'Maybe I will join you in a glass of champagne. Who knows when we'll next encounter civilisation.'

'Way to go. Leave it to me.' Aldo made a sign to the stewardess assigned to first class. 'Off the record, did I ever tell you about my night with the prime minister?'

'No, but I feel you're going to.'

'PM was flying around the world on one of those ... three stops in three continents trips ... all the rage in the eighties. We'd never heard of a carbon thumbprint then—'

'Footprint?'

'Exactly, so there we were in an RAF VC10, refuelling in the middle of the desert somewhere. So we all went off in search of a bar and some drinks – me, the PM and about half the secret service. Speaking of which ... hello, Paula.' The air hostess had arrived with a bottle of champagne. 'Lovely, thanks.' Aldo paused whilst the champagne was poured. 'Anyway, there we were in the desert and suddenly the whole group goes off on some wild goose chase and before we knew it was just the two of us left on our own. Her own security team completely forgot her. Can you imagine that? It was *unbelievable*. Me and the British prime minister alone in the middle of the night searching for a taxi—'

'I bet you were quite a head-turner in those days?'

'You bet I was, full head of hair and thin as a rake—'

'Aldo, what are we going to do when we arrive? You said you had a plan for the interview. Isn't it time you told me?'

Aldo looked serious for a moment, spreading his hands on his knees. 'For a start, Judith, you're assuming that there is going to be an interview.'

'You mean he might not want to talk to us?'

'I mean he might be dead. Think about it, if *The Times* of London knows about a supposed fifth man, who doesn't? There's lot of vested interests who don't want to see any changes to the status quo, the fifth man for starters. Beware of old cupboards, as my grandmother would say.'

'But you told the editor nobody would be interested?'

'When you've been playing the game as long as me it pays to keep the other side guessing.'

THE LONELY SPY

'Okay, and the cupboards?'

'Skeletons. Did I ever tell you about my helicopter ride with Neil Kinnock? Now there was a skeleton—'

Lima International Airport was cool and grey in the early morning. Aldo and Judith were standing by a long line of yellow taxis. 'First stop is a proper breakfast,' said Aldo. 'Do you think they do bacon sandwiches here?'

'I don't want to be the one to break up the party but do you know where we're going to stay?' Judith was starting to look through one of her guidebooks. 'We'll need a base from where to conduct the search. I've got a list of recommended hotels—'

'How do you know I haven't already got the exact address?'

'Oh yeah, like that would happen any time—' Confident like a conjurer in front of a Saturday matinee audience, Aldo finessed a crumpled-up piece of paper with GORDON LONSDALE written in block capitals and underneath a scrawled address.

'How on earth did you manage to find it?' she exclaimed. 'Why didn't you tell me?' Before Aldo had to think of an answer the cab driver was engaging them with jabbering English and helping hands. 'Judging by the size of that smile,' said Judith watching her bag being put in the boot, 'I would hazard a guess it's some drive.'

'Good. He can get some money for the dentist,' said Aldo getting in the front. 'I swear there's more gaps than teeth.' He spoke slower and louder to the driver: 'How far to go?'

'To the jungle,' the driver beamed. 'Long trip. Pay first, petrol. No plastic.'

'This could be Milton Keynes,' said Aldo as they set off in a line of cars crawling from the airport under a light falling of drizzle.

After nearly a day of driving inland the climate had changed to hot and humid. The grey skies and flat concrete jungle of Lima had given way to a landscape of low undulating hills supplemented by the occasional mountain. Aldo's water bottle had been finished some time ago. His top button was undone and he was covered with a thin layer of sweat. The car was labouring up a long climb. The driver, who hadn't stop grinning since they left Lima, was driving in the middle of the road, which had deteriorated to part tarmac, part gravel. Some miles back they had started to see more carts pulled by donkeys than cars.

Aldo, who had exhausted his knowledge of South American football some miles back, was happy to look at the scenery. All the windows were open and it was still humid and hot in the taxi. But since the last village, when they had stopped to ask directions, the driver had a new air of confidence, thought Aldo. This was backed up by the: 'Very very nearly', which he uttered at regular intervals.

As they reached the top of the mountain road, Aldo saw over the ridge a green carpet of trees below. The feeling was Spanish, old and foreign. He should listen to Rodrigo's guitar concerto again. Judith had fallen asleep an hour or two back. She wanted to be woken up at the first sight of the jungle.

The descent was slow and Aldo started to feel impatient. Finally, just when he was about to give up, he saw a hand-painted sign: Woodlands. 'There it is,' he said in a quiet voice, not wanting to wake Judith. 'Here, turn here.'

The track was cut through the jungle and after a few hundred yards curved around to show a clearing with buildings, and a river running through the garden. The car pulled up next to an American-style ranch building with white-planked walls.

'Why didn't you wake me up?' complained Judith, rubbing her eyes. 'I take it we've arrived.'

'If this is the edge of the jungle I'd like to see the middle. Listen to that noise. Sorry, I've only this second woken myself. You pay the taxi driver and make sure you get an official-looking receipt. You know what accounts are like.' Aldo slipped out of the taxi and walked to the front of the clearing. It was like stepping into a greenhouse without glass. He saw a figure ahead. As he guessed, the garden would be the place to meet the man they had travelled over five thousand miles to interview.

Gordon Lonsdale, his first controller whom he'd known since boyhood. Gordon, the prefect at school who'd become his holy trinity of instructor, mentor and protector, was advancing towards him, taking off his gardening gloves. Gordon, the talent-spotter for the KGB, who had recruited first-year undergraduate Aldo to the Portland spy ring, had hardly changed after all these years. Some lines on his face, and white hair, but the same half-reluctant smile. Gordon, who'd been caught along with the Krogers when Portland broke, but kept Aldo's name out of it, as he always had done. Gordon Lonsdale, as indelibly stamped on his being as the face of the sovereign on a coin of the realm, stood in front of him.

'Gordon. I'm here,' was all he could manage to say.

'Aldo, that was quick, I didn't expect you here before next week at the earliest.' Gordon was shaking his hand. 'You haven't changed in what ... forty years?'

'Nearer fifty. And I was never this weight before.' He patted his stomach.

'I've always read your articles. You know it's easier for us to get *The Times* here than it was in Moscow; it arrives in our weekly delivery. Did you come on your own?'

'No, I've got a young cub reporter with me. She's just paying off the taxi driver now. So you and me have never met before. That's the rubric.' Aldo took out a handkerchief to mop the sweat from his head shining in the sunlight.

'I'm glad it's you, Aldo. Have you come with a black spot?'

'No time for jokes. Gordon, I'm here to save you, not assassinate you—'

'Et tu, Brute?' They were standing on a path next to a well-kept lawn.

'We came straight from the airport. We still haven't found a hotel. Do you—'

'You'll stay here, there is nowhere else. You'll see we have plenty of room and it is a rare treat for us to get visitors. First things first, I'll lend you a sun hat.'

'Well this place is – what would the guide book say – secluded, remote? Do you get lonely?'

'Here in the jungle, there's always something new to see. I'll show you round. And drinks: you must be parched.'

'Here she comes now.'

'Gordon Lonsdale, I presume.' Judith walked across the lawn, hand outstretched, looking confident until the sound of a gunshot sent a wave of brightly coloured birds squawking in alarm into the cobalt blue skies. 'What in heck was that?' she exclaimed.

Gordon pointed to a camouflaged, combat-clothed man who was almost invisible against the backdrop of the jungle.

'So you have a security guard?' Apprehensively, Judith eyed the figure, who was slinging what looked like a rifle with telescopic sights over his shoulder and walking towards them. On closer inspection Aldo could see he carried a consortium of knives and other weapons around his belt. The military-dressed figure took up position ten metres distant, looking towards the jungle.

'Welcome to Peru,' said Gordon. 'The old conquistadores came with crosses and swords and we have semi-automatic rifles, but don't mind Dimitri – harmless as a mouse and doesn't speak a word of English. Come on, I'll show you to your rooms. Singles or double?'

'Double.'

'Single,' said Judith.

'Only kidding,' Aldo smiled. 'I'm old enough to be her brother.'

'Drinks on the lookout at six, before supper. And then you'll meet Rebecca. You'll find the day starts early at Woodlands so we don't tend to stay up late.'

Kalugina looked at the pilot, who nodded in the direction of the open door. One minute to go, final checks. The advantages of hiring one's own plane for this type of mission were obvious; you could fly under any radar, and no security pat-downs. Airport security took a dim view on weaponry, even before Al-Qaeda. The charter cost was irrelevant given the size of the fee – half paid up front. Time to go. The DZ was the open terrain before the dense jungle began. Kalugina had her customary reservations about the job but that would keep her watchful; the day she wasn't would be the time to stop. She crossed herself and jumped.

Aldo and Gordon stood, croquet mallets in hand, wearing sun hats. 'I'll say it again, wonderful place here,' praised Aldo. 'The third hoop a little close to the willow tree, mind.'

'I saw an iguana plodding across the lawn to the river last week.' Gordon was examining the lay of the land before his shot. 'You remember the croquet lawn at school?'

'How could I forget? My job was to retrieve the balls that went into the rhododendrons. And when we were playing croquet all the others were knocking twelve bells out of each other on the rugby field. What would a psychologist make of that?'

'Not to mention our devouring of the classical music LP collection in the library.'

'Agh, *Enigma Variations*.'

'Square pegs in round holes. Maybe we didn't have that feeling of belonging that others had.' Gordon struck yellow firmly and the clacking report of mahogany mallet on ball was enough to send birds flying from the forest.

'Hard luck,' said Aldo, as much to his relief yellow raced past his own ball, missing by less than an inch. This was the fifth and final day of their visit. Judith was frustrated not to be in on the interviews, which Aldo had blithely assured her were going splendidly. Their croquet duel fought under the heat of the Peruvian sun, was now at the end game. Aldo had left a five-metre shot to win the match; black to the post. He hit it hard and firm. It looked good – croquet was like riding a bicycle.

'Bravo!' applauded his playing partner, seemingly genuinely happy for his triumph.

Gordon managed to encapsulate it all; sportsman, gentleman and friend. He possessed an unswerving nobility of spirit and loyalty to friends that Aldo knew he could only ever aspire to.

'Drinks,' announced his host.

They were sitting under the willow tree where Rebecca had provided a pitcher with home-made ginger beer, laced with rum, Aldo surmised. 'Mine was a lucky shot,' he said. 'Your croquet on blue deserved to win the game.'

'Shut up and enjoy your drink,' said Gordon. 'You've deserved it.' Aldo saw in the river a large log floating by that opened one eye to admire the scenery. Gordon no longer noticed the alligators. Aldo broke the relaxed silence that hung between them like the panoramic view of a favourite photograph. He brought up the subject they had so far tacitly agreed to avoid. 'When Portland broke, it must have been bloody?'

Gordon stared at the willow tree before he replied. 'You remember Rommel's choice?'

'You were always the historian, not me.'

'Field Marshall Rommel, hero of the Third Reich, against the extermination of the Jews, the only real alternative to Hitler – he was visited by the SS and they offered him the choice: *Suicide and your family is looked after or we expose you as a traitor and execute you.*'

'I remember something,' said Aldo. 'But how's that—'

'No cyanide for me. But the choice was simple enough: tell us all you know and you walk scot-free or you go to prison for a long stretch branded a traitor. You know the rest.'

Aldo swirled the ice cubes in his glass. He'd heard it from an impeccable source that the pressure on his old friend to tell had been extreme; *just one name* – that would have been enough for him to have walked free. And yet Gordon had remained quiet, at least he supposed he had. But still Aldo checked: 'The Krogers, was that you?'

'Not guilty, Aldo. Someone else.'

'I see. Wormwood Scrubs, wasn't it?'

'Yes, I've been in nicer places but I never gave up hope. Blake escaped, so who knows what might have happened? Luckily for me the exchange came along, otherwise I would have been an old man when I was freed, if they ever let me out.'

'Moscow was hardly the Riviera?'

'No, not exactly.' Gordon spoke of his misery in Moscow; insufferable years virtually locked in his apartment, waiting for letters from Rebecca before she could join him. Then a rare invitation to an Embassy party – 'to think I nearly didn't go' – that had led to a chance meeting with Gorbachev and 'real freedom for Rebecca and me at last'.

'But you never told me about Rebecca. I don't even know how you met?'

'I'm a spy, remember,' said Gordon.

Aldo paused. He was encouraged to give a little more of his own history. 'With you in Moscow and the Krogers inside, I was all alone. I worked hard but I lived in a strange type of no-man's-land, not really living at all. I could never completely relax, I was in a state of limbo. Both my ex-wives said the same; I wasn't really there, you know ... present. Every time there was a knock on the door I thought it could be MI6. They didn't write that on the packet when they signed us up, did they?'

'You didn't try to get out?'

'How could I? Four children, school and then university to fork out for, two divorces, three homes to pay for.' Aldo took a sip from his glass. 'Someone once told me that knowing you had cancer was easier to deal with than not knowing. Sometimes I wake up in the middle of the night hoping that they do come for me. Since Anne left, number two, I get lonely. I never stopped thinking about you, Gordon. You taught me everything you know.'

Gordon placed his hand on the younger man's arm. 'Aldo, you are a natural if ever there was one. I never saw anyone with your talent for the trade; people confided in you. You were the insouciant gingerbread boy skipping through life the way you did at school – not like the rest of us.'

Over the sounds of the birds screeching in the rainforest a gong sounded from the house. 'Ten minute bell,' said Gordon. 'Rebecca's first love was the theatre, another of her sacrifices for being exiled out here.'

'They saw us as traitors, plotting the country's downfall, but we had principles, we still do. Today, the Russians are our friends. Sharing information in the war on terror is the mark of civilised countries *today*. So tell me, what did we do that was so wrong? Did we err so badly?' complained Aldo. 'We wanted to stop a war, not start one.'

'We were paid, Aldo. We'd have given away the Crown Jewels for the right price, and we're still paying. I am anyway, every day out here; same prison, different walls.'

'I'm still doing it, you know – sharing information to the highest bidder.'

'The game doesn't change – or does it?' asked Gordon.

Didn't Aldo know it. Same rules, only new players on the board; now defence contractors paid the school bills. 'But we do. The game changes us, anyway it's changed me.' He was cloaked and guarded, performing in a masquerade. He supposed there was a time when he had answered questions a millisecond quicker, without weighing his words on a scale of honesty.

'Aldo?'

'Uhm ... your man Dimitri, he's a strange one. I thought he would speak English, him being Greek?'

'Dimitri? His great-grandfather was Greek but he was born in sight of the Kremlin. After I absconded in eighty-one they sent him to assassinate me.'

'Phew!' Aldo whistled. 'What happened?'

'Well he found me, all right. He pointed his Makarov pistol at me and offered me a condemned man's last wish. I asked for a cigarette and we've been friends ever since.'

'You couldn't write that!' Aldo exclaimed. 'You're the one who can talk people into anything. I should know. Come on, let's go to entertain the ladies.'

'Yes, a certain amount of creeping up is required, from you at any rate.'

'What a shot that croquet was on blue.'

Once again the best of friends, they walked across the lawn. 'Aldo, there's one last good turn I'm going to ask you to do.' The sun was sliding behind the ranch house. 'It was why I sent you the invitation.'

'The file to the paper.' Aldo stopped. 'I knew it had to be more than a coincidence.'

'Synchronicity.'

'Who was your parcel bouncer?'

'My grandson Gary. He's keen to rehabilitate the family name, reading history at York.'

'Rebecca said he'd been out to visit.'

'When I heard he'd found a file full of photographs and press cuttings I asked him to send it to the newspaper.'

'But he doesn't know about me?'

'Good Lord, no. He just agreed to send the file to your editor. I figured that would be enough, you'd manage the rest. Don't worry, your secret is safe with me. I wanted you out here, Aldo, one last favour. Let's talk after supper, alone. I still have some secrets, even from Rebecca.'

Aldo stopped walking for a moment. He had an intense feeling of relief. 'But you're saying I'm safe, finally I'm safe. That's why I had to come, to make sure.'

'Aldo, when are any of us ever really truly safe?' They continued their walk across the lawn, which was now covered in shadow. Overhead, an echelon of pelicans was making for their evening swim at the river.

'I can see why you two like it here. What a place to retire.

Maybe I should start to visit my old school prefect a bit more often.'

'I forgot to ask, how did you find our hideout?'

'I'm a spy, remember.' For the first time since his arrival five days previously Aldo laughed openly and wholeheartedly.

Rod was early, crack o' sparrows time. He liked Wednesdays, BIG Wednesdays. It was a family joke that every day of the week was his favourite. He moved to avoid a magpie, brave on the quiet streets. 'Good morning, Mr Magpie,' he said to the bird – one of the few arcane rituals he allowed himself. He wondered if his wife suspected a covert reason for his steadfast motivation for the alarm career; maybe she considered that Soho was part of the attraction. Maybe it was.

He saw Douglas was setting up his fruit and vegetable stall on Greek street. 'Doug, say hello from me to your dad.' In acknowledgement a fresh Royal Gala sailed through the air. Rod caught it left-handed and was thankful he hadn't picked up his latte yet. A few minutes later he got to the office and noticed a light on in the second storey. It was ten minutes to seven. He walked upstairs, wondering whether he was going to meet an intruder or an early worm. He was ready for either.

'Morning, Rod.'

'Anthony. Nice surprise, if I'd known you were here I'd have got you a coffee. Looks like you need one.'

'I think we might have made a breakthrough on *Leuctra*.'

'Let's hear it then, come through.' Rod led the way and the two tall men sat down in the low-ceilinged room; a pair of daddy-long-legs hatching a plot, thought Rod with a wry smile.

Anthony began: 'We know that Gordon was swapped for one of our spies soon after his sentence began, mid-sixties. He was in Moscow until 1981 when he got himself a short-term visa to visit Cuba signed by none less than Gorbachev.'

'How do you find that out?' Rod picked up a pencil that had been lying on the desk between them.

'Well I managed to find a copy in the records. It seems we had an inside man in the Kremlin.'

'Still do, Anthony … still do. Keep going. This is getting interesting, quite like the old days. Did you find out anything else? From the university years?' Anthony detailed how he had found a copy of a KGB execution order for Lonsdale and an accompanying visa application for Peru but the mission was never signed off on the file. 'Standard practice for defectors,' said Rod. 'Does the trail stop there?' He turned the pencil between his fingers.

'You mean did the hit man succeed, sir? I'm not sure, because I found a G. Lonsdale on the flight manifest of a plane returning from Lima, Peru. But it wasn't Gordon Lonsdale, it was Gary Lonsdale, his grandson.'

'You're thinking the librarian's ID on the photo?'

'Exactly. It looks like the boy was sent by his grandfather.'

'Good beach work.' He studied Anthony's body language. 'You've saved the best bit, haven't you?'

Anthony then put the last piece into the jigsaw. In the archives he had also found a report of a KGB interrogation, translated, which made some references to *the old school*. 'I thought it might signify more than just a turn of phrase. Did it really mean the old school – which in this case was Rugby? I did a cross check, names from the school and our indexes. I didn't get anything for Lonsdale's year, 1947 or the next, but I kept looking—'

'You kept turning.'

'Right, and then I found a match from the intake of 1952, the same name on a recent flight to Lima.'

'So who was it, the match? You think it could be our man, the fifth man. Who?'

'Well it's someone you know, a household name, well in some circles anyway. He's Aldo Court, you know, *The Times*'s political correspondent.'

Between the fingers of one hand Rod snapped the pencil in

half. 'What do you know? Aldo Court indeed. I've had dinner with the man. It fits: *Off the record* is his catch phrase.' He laughed. 'Well I'll be damned. I've heard that spies are students of history, you bet your life I am. You know Guy Burgess was also a political correspondent for *The Times*?'

'Just a shame I wasn't on to it quicker. I mean he flew a week ago.'

'Well, Anthony, birds that fly the nest usually fly home sooner or later. So when he returns, we need to be ready. Meantime there's a lot to do; who's the paymaster? Do we try and turn our rooster or not? This is just the start.' Rod stood up. 'But we can't go bird-trapping on an empty stomach. Grab your jacket, I'm going to treat you to the finest breakfast in Soho.'

Five minutes later the spycatcher and his protégé walked along Brewer Street where street cleaners were finishing off for the day. '*Poor is the pupil who cannot surpass his master.* Know that one?'

'Cicero?'

'Leonardo da Vinci. Anthony, your pebble-turning skills are improving but it's your history that is starting to worry me—'

Kalugina had watched the taxi with the bald man and the girl leaving. That had left the two men from the photographs plus the wife. She had been surveying the house for three days, sleeping rough; a different hide each night, moving in ever-decreasing circles, careful not to disturb the spider's web of early warning triggers that were scattered around the house in the woods and on the hillside. Even without the photograph she would have recognised Dimitri's handiwork. Dimitri Sharanov, Colonel KGB, assassination squad. He had christened her Kalugina, after a sniper from Leningrad.

While assembling the spider's web he had made one mistake; all the trip lines led to the spider, in this case a small hut three metres square, where she was standing now, behind the door. Inside the hut was a lookout point and an old but working monitor showed a map of the forest, complete with thermal spots. Now it was a question of just waiting for the spider to come home. She had been there seven hours.

'Hello, Dimitri.'

He stopped and stared. A full second passed before he recognised her.

'You!'

'I hope you weren't expecting breakfast?' She moved from behind the door with a predator's grace; strong and supple, careful not to make a silhouette against the light.

In the time it would take for a bullet to travel four hundred metres a smile flashed across his swarthy face. His hands stayed motionless. 'I'm sorry it had to be you,' he said. 'I sensed someone was out here.'

'You should have listened. You taught me: *instinct is untaught ability*, remember?'

'What now?'

'You know the rules. I've got my orders.' Kalugina raised her Makarov pistol, with silencer.

'Any chance of a final wish for your old teacher: a last cigarette? You still smoke, Kalugina?'

In the taxi Aldo waved. Judith didn't.

'Hello, stranger.' She sounded cross.

'Oh come on,' exclaimed Aldo. 'It sounds like you've forgotten the great time we had at supper.'

'Only that you and Gordon polished off his vintage champagne before you got onto the best port. You were both—'

'Saying goodbye.' Aldo looked out of the window.

'To think as a girl I dreamed of getting a pet parrot. Four-thirty the macaws started this morning. At least we can sleep in this taxi.'

Gordon had reckoned that for the return ride they deserved higher-grade transportation than the taxi they had arrived in. Judith had agreed; the money they had saved on accommodation meant they were comfortably inside the editor's budget. Now they were riding in a fully air-conditioned limousine, complete with uniformed chauffeur. Aldo preferred the old banger and its gap-toothed driver. 'This is travelling in style, it's what we deserve. Make sure you pick up the receipt, Judith. Let's hope they recognise you in accounts, that's quite a tan you've got. All that time reading and skiving when I was busy working.'

'That has to be the longest, most boring week of my professional career. Don't for a minute think I'm not going to tell the editor how selfish—'

'Judith, let's agree I write the story and we put your name on it. At my age I'm not interested in winning any more journalistic awards.' She looked genuinely surprised. 'Okay, not exactly Pullitzer Prize,' said Aldo. 'But one award I definitely remember—'

'Cut the crap. It's a deal. Now you have to tell me everything. You two talked for hours, days even. So what is the story? I suppose you're going to tell me you know the name of the fifth man?' she sniffed.

Aldo was ready to start spinning a yarn. He still wasn't sure, in his story, would there be a *fifth* man or a *sixth* for that matter? What he could feel was the envelope in his pocket, some old Gorbachev secrets that Gordon asked him to barter in exchange for a decent pension for Rebecca. He should be able to pull it off, he was still worth something to the Russians – they had told him where to find Gordon in the first place: his old friend, diagnosed with terminal cancer, whom he would never see again.

'Come on, I'm waiting. Why all this subterfuge? Spill the beans,' demanded Judith.

'I think we'll be writing it backwards,' said Aldo, who felt an unbearable solitude enveloping him. Aldo Court: absolutely and truly perfectly alone in the world. He noticed he hadn't thought about writing for nearly a week.

'Writing backwards?'

'Good stories; it's all in the beginning. That's how it'll be with this one.' He saw the forest encroaching to the edge of the road, looking to swallow up the departing limousine like blotting powder after spilt ink.

Aldo loosened his tie: it was cool in the taxi but he wanted to get into the story-telling mood and they had a long journey in front of them. 'Once upon a time there were two boys, one five years older than the other. Both had been sent away to a school since they were aged seven. Neither of them had any friends until one day the younger boy came across the older boy in a fight with a gang of other boys. It wasn't good odds, about four to one, but the younger boy joined forces with the older boy – he had just been reading about Lancelot and the Knights of the Round Table. Of course they were both beaten up, badly. But the older boy never forgot and he started to look out for the younger one....'

Abandon Ship!

Even with all the windows open, the old tutorial rooms at Balliol were hot in the afternoon sun. It was towards the end of the Trinity term and the college was full to bursting. The sounds of students crossing the quad and the promise of impending summer were a constant distraction for those stuck in classrooms. Professor Markham threw a resigned look at the student at the back of the room who seemed more intent on his laptop than the methodology of history. 'So what did you make of E.H. Carr's standpoint, Elliot?'

'E.H. Carr, Professor?' Elliot looked up guiltily from his laptop. 'Carr maintained that the problems of the nineteen thirties were caused by a clique of evil men, dismissing Toynbee's view that we were living in an exceptionally wicked age.' There was no sign to stop from the professor and Elliot continued: 'As empirical modern historians we can analyse data and facts to see how forces shape events, but E.H. Carr failed to foresee that computers put paid to the role of chance as well as the hero in our understanding of history.'

Someone in the class groaned.

'Enough! So your premise, Elliot, is that we should all become mathematicians, master *string theory* and explain historical events empirically?'

'Well statistical inference is one of the recognised seven-step procedures for source criticism—'

'Touché, Elliot,' said the professor, moving down from the wooden dais to be among the students – who at least took this as a sure sign to straighten up. 'But so is analogy. Less empirical, more fun. So let's take one. Any suggestions, class?' Besides Elliot, who was nailed on for a first, if also rather full of himself, the class was somewhat mediocre. The professor thought for a moment. There was no rush, they still had fifteen minutes before the bell. 'Last week we saw a Swedish princess get married in the longest wedding dress for a hundred years. So why now—'

'No disrespect, but isn't that a woman's story, Professor?' interrupted Colewell, a rather short aggressive boy whose mind raced at the speed of a family saloon next to Elliot's Ferrari. Colewell as usual was about to completely miss the point. Stephanie Markham, shoulder-length wavy blonde hair and sapphire-blue eyes, was well aware that her nimbleness of foot was one of the reasons why she was the youngest full professor at Balliol.

'Okay, different story, let's make one up, something manly. How about submarines, not many women there – that suit you, Colewell?'

The class tittered.

'So we've got a submarine, nuclear powered, and we'll put it in the middle of nowhere ... say, three thousand miles from the nearest shore.'

'Nationality?' asked Elliot who was familiar with the routine; extempore was fine but parameters had to be defined.

'Fair question: we'll have her flying the White Ensign of course, what else? In international waters, how about the South Pacific?' The professor thought better as she walked and her heels made a pleasant clicking sound on the old wooden floor as she traversed between the desks.

'The officer of the watch has woken up the captain in the middle of the night. "This had better be important," says the captain. The first lieutenant explains that one of the seamen is having a mental breakdown – specifically the seaman is asking the captain for permission to take a lifeboat and abandon ship. History and facts tell the captain there is nothing wrong: safety readings all normal, they are in deep water, thousands of miles from shore, no other vessels around.' She spoke without pauses, making eye contact with the students as she passed by. 'So does the captain need to get more information before he makes a decision to put the seaman in the sickbay, anybody?'

'Well yes he does,' said Elliot.

'Why? You said yourself we can be empirical. This is a naval nuclear submarine with state-of-the-art technology costing five hundred million pounds so why does the captain need more data?'

'Because in historical analysis we have to eliminate the outlier due to anomalous causes—'

'Elliot, you're going abstract on me again. I want this concrete. This college is meant to have a reputation for pioneering. SO ... come on, let's *pioneer*!' Stephanie started to move students from their chairs, making a space in the middle of the room. 'We'll make this space the quarter deck, or am I getting mixed up with my Hornblower ... bridge, is it?' she said, overhearing one of her students who were one by one starting to stand up and gather round Stephanie directing her cast and re-arranging the furniture. 'All we need now is a crew to sail this vessel.' She made Tjebbes from Holland the first lieutenant – so he'd *have* to think on his feet. Elliot, she appointed captain *because you started it*, Colewell ordinary seaman and then, spotting one student who was still sitting down: 'I don't want to be declared sexist so let's have a female doctor on board – stand up, Dr Bright.'

A few minutes later they were ready to begin. 'Professor, I feel ridiculous. How can I be acting a seaman, I don't even have a name?' said Colewell who, she saw, clearly wasn't a leading light in the dramatics society.

Stephanie looked down to her desk and spotted Kerridge's Law of Succession book, standard reading for any historian. 'The seaman's name is Kerridge, Stephen Kerridge. Change of plan, let's leave the bridge and get over to the captain's cabin.' Stephanie re-positioned her stand-in actors. 'Right, Kerridge, what are you going to ask the captain?'

Elliot, stretching and yawning, performed a passable impression of someone who has just woken up before exclaiming: 'It's the middle of the night for Christ's sake. What's this I hear about you wanting to abandon ship? And Mr Kerridge, this had better be good. This is HMS, HMS—'

'*Electra*,' helped out the professor.

'HMS *Electra*, of course; my own boat, how could I forget? We're talking about a state-of-the-art vessel. Have you taken leave of your senses, man?'

'Well the thing is, Captain, I had a pre…premonition and I'm usually one hundred percent right with these,' said Colewell whose enthusiasm compensated somewhat for his lack of acting talent. 'So, Captain, we should man the lifeboats. And if you don't give the order I'm going to take this knife and cut the good doctor's throat.'

At this point, much to the amusement of everyone in the class, except possibly Lucy Bright, Colewell picked up a ruler and held it to Lucy's throat. 'Okay, Colewell. Drop the ruler.' The professor adopted a serious tone. 'You've made my point admirably.' Stephanie Markham looked up to the clock – this class had run its course. 'You've demonstrated the unpredictability of people. So what is history? Engels called people's spontaneous interactions an infinite series of overlapping parallelograms, the stuff of history. Everyday people like you and I interact to create a unique historical event. Alternatively, the empiricists would have us believe that history is no more difficult than the solution of a simple equation to the first degree—'

The bell rang.

'Okay, class dismissed, and you can see the new tutorial schedules on my door.' Nobody moved. 'I thought you couldn't wait for the lesson to end?'

'How about the story, Professor? How does *that* end?'

'Well I don't know, Mr Kerridge is cast adrift and plays his bagpipes so that's how he gets rescued – you work out your own ending. That's not important. The point is the methodology, the unpredictability of the ending, that's what makes it history and not string theory. Come on, I have got a home to go to even if you haven't. Class,' Stephanie snapped her heels together, 'dismiss!'

'Aye aye, sir,' said Elliot. A few others picked up the refrain.

*

Stephanie was left on her own to pick up her books and papers. A handful of lectures to go and then the long, glorious summer holiday. In the hot classroom it was easy to imagine the afternoon heat of the Tuscan hills. Three weeks with only fiction books, maybe some poetry, plenty of wine and men, well one man in particular.

The quietness in the room didn't last for much more than a minute.

'A penny for your thoughts.'

'I may not be an esteemed fellow of the college,' Stephanie tried to keep the smile out of her voice, 'but shouldn't one still knock?'

Art Strand, Professor, wasn't tall, but he had presence. His eyes, which he had a habit of rolling, were set unusually far apart and this, coupled with his flaring nostrils and full beard, gave him a striking resemblance to the bust of a young Socrates in the Bodleian; not that she would ever tell him – as a fellow of the college, confidence was one thing he wasn't short of.

'That's what's intriguing about you, Stephanie: I'm never quite sure what you're thinking. But I take it you were dreaming of siestas in Tuscany in what—' Art checked his watch, 'in thirteen days time?'

'I've still not said I'll come yet, remember. In fact I was just reflecting on the methodology of history—'

'I thought I might just catch you. Time for a quick coffee? We can get it in my rooms. And what's happened to your chairs? It looks like there's been a fight in here.'

'Just a knifing ... don't look so worried, we had a doctor on the scene pretty smartish. I'll explain later. Coffee? Good idea, but your rooms? I still have a reputation, just, to consider. I'll treat you.'

Stephanie took hold of Art's jacket and steered her visitor from the room. For a moment she enjoyed the physical proximity. Some years ago as a post-grad student she had vowed never to look twice at a married man, but the trouble with life in academia was that absolute truth was harder to find than it should be and even when you found it, disappointment often followed. Contradicting thoughts co-existing in her head had become a comfort. By comparison absolute truth had taken on a darker hue. Maybe it was time for her to revisit the classic poems of Keats and Samuel Taylor Coleridge; one summer, at the age of fourteen, she had learnt *The Rime of the Ancient Mariner* off by heart, all six hundred and twenty-eight lines of it.

Her thoughts were still divided between love and the supernatural when a few hours later Stephanie Markham sat alone in her north Oxford home drinking fourteen-year-old malt whisky and wrapped up in Mahler's tenth symphony – another of her hobbies; she had studied the original manuscript. Her last thought before falling asleep was that Deryck Cooke's elaboration of the scherzo movement possibly demanded more compositional work, but then ...

There was a knock at the door. 'Enter! This had better be important,' said the captain, who was aware that he looked like he had just woken up. In fact for the second consecutive night he hadn't slept a wink as he had lain on his bunk pondering the problem with Henrietta. He went over to the stereo, turned off the music and looked up to see his first lieutenant silhouetted in the doorway.

'You don't get depressed with that music on? Sorry, none of my business,' said Alfredo Lucca with one foot in the cabin and the other in the passageway. Even though the captain's cabin was larger than any other, boasting a writing desk, there was hardly room for two men.

The captain turned to get his jacket. He was a tall man, around six foot four. At Dartmouth his mentor had laughed when he heard he was planning a career in submarines. As time went on he noticed the continual stooping and cramped conditions more. The trouble with life on board is you live on top of one another; people start to say what they think too readily. That's why he was listening to Mahler; he was already depressed, cause and effect ... 'So, Lieutenant, what's the disaster? Have we been made to follow on?'

'Sorry, sir?' enquired Lucca.

The captain forgot that his second in command was Italian and not interested in Test cricket. 'Forget it. I'm still half asleep. So what's the crisis?'

'We've got a problem with Kerridge again. He's missing.'

'That's quite an achievement, isn't it? Well he can't get far, can he? I'll meet you on the bridge. Can someone rustle up some coffee?'

'Yes, sir,' said the lieutenant shutting the door.

The captain welcomed the opportunity to stop thinking about the email he had received a couple of days back. His best friend had written to advise him that Henrietta was 'playing away' with some teacher from college. The news punched him square in the solar plexus like it always did: last year with the driving instructor, then there had been the psychoanalyst ... wasn't that some sort of ethics question? They had only been married five years and already it was getting to be a long list. Should he leave the navy? Maybe he should email her. But first he had to find Kerridge.

'That man has been nothing but trouble since we left Portsmouth,' complained Lucca. The two of them were on the bridge. It was after three in the morning and the submarine was on automatic pilot, friendly lights blinking from control panels and far away the distant hum of the Rolls-Royce PWR2 reactors. Almost too quiet, thought the captain. Fortunately he still carried Mahler's exquisite adagio in his head. *But Kerridge is not one for swinging the lead. He's challenging, but I like him.* The captain cast his eye over the array of warning lights.

'Have we checked the security door on the torpedo bays?'

'First thing I did. Wherever he is, I don't think he can do any harm. I've sent Roberts to discreetly have a look for him.'

'And he was noticed absent from his bunk about an hour ago. What did you tell the men?'

'I said he had some repairs to do.' The captain tried to remember what navy regulations had to say about men lost on board. They both knew the problem; if they put out a general alert then the whole crew would be woken and they were suffering from sleep deprivation as it was. The submarine was one of the new Astute class and had been on alert stations for much of the last twelve days. Ongoing sea trials meant limited surface time, new equipment and drills and now one of the men had cracked under the strain.

'I'm only surprised it hasn't happened earlier,' remarked the captain. 'The men are all tired.'

'And Kerridge *has* been behaving oddly.'

The captain didn't reply. It was true Kerridge had already drawn attention to himself. He had been caught stealing cheese from stores and disciplined with extra duties. In years gone by the captain would have had draconian punishments at his disposal; now the biggest threat was reducing internet time. He had a pretty good guess that their next port of call would be Tahiti which would cheer the men up no end. But this was the navy and, for now, orders were in a sealed envelope.

The lieutenant's radio crackled into life. 'What's to report?' asked the captain anxiously. For the first time he acknowledged the feeling of unease he had hitherto tried to ignore.

'Good news, sir. Roberts has found him in the wardroom.' The captain shut his eyes for a second; he still felt terribly tired.

The wardroom resembled a small family library. Small, like everything else on the submarine, but the captain liked the cosy comfort; two red leather armchairs, incongruous against the grey bulkhead. 'Hello, Kerridge. Found you couldn't sleep? Too much cheese perhaps?' the captain added.

His attempt at levity seemed lost on Warrant Officer Kerridge, who looked distant but composed. Kerridge reminded the captain of an ageing lion with his bushy white eyebrows, a prominent forehead and straight jutting chin. 'Hello, sir. Sorry to be a nuisance but I'm requesting permission to abandon ship.'

The captain whispered in Lucca's ear: 'Better fetch the doctor.' To Kerridge he said: 'We've all been under stress, but the trials are nearly at an end.' He sat down in the armchair next to the seaman. 'A bit of shore leave will soon cheer you up—'

'Sorry, sir. I can't wait that long. It's not safe.'

'How far are we from the nearest land, Lieutenant?'

'About three thousand miles,' replied Lucca.

'You see that's the problem we have, Kerridge. Now why don't you just tell me what's up?' Kerridge pulled out an A4 notepad and started to make his case. The captain was surprised at the rating's lucidity which centred on the new Rolls-Royce engines. In a nutshell Kerridge claimed that the go-faster titanium hull in tandem with new design reactors was untested; a potentially dangerous combination. Both new technologies were meant to be secret but secrets were notoriously difficult to keep when you had ninety-eight men living in a corridor ninety-seven metres long.

'Well that's one reason why we're running sea trials,' said Lucca. The captain grimaced; not best put, he thought.

'Exactly,' said Kerridge. 'And I don't mean to be a guinea pig.'

The captain heard someone descending in the ladderwell and guessed the doctor had arrived. 'Kerridge. What's your time-in-service?'

'Fifteen years in mouse houses. Before that, carriers – ten years.'

'Phew. Maybe it's time for a change of scenery.' The captain was mindful of the doctor's presence as, bag in hand, he slowly approached. Kerridge stared straight ahead, seemingly not having noticed the new arrival. The captain knew the doctor's bag contained tranquillisers strong enough to drop a horse. He nodded to the doctor – they had been trained for just this eventuality. Only a few weeks ago a submariner had gone stir-crazy in port and shot a fellow officer. An admiralty instruction had swiftly followed: *Incapacitate not negotiate* was the dictum. 'But Kerridge, face facts, man, we've had hundreds of researchers working hundreds, thousands of hours on these issues.' He was playing for time and from the corner of his eye he saw the doctor reaching inside his black bag.

'So you agree there is an issue?' Kerridge leaned forward.

The captain noticed his intense stare. You had to admire his commitment, if not his reason. 'Kerridge, don't take this personally but what are your credentials? You're a career seaman not someone with a scientific degree from university—'

'Did Leonardo de Vinci?'

'Touché. I'm not sure he did. Lucca?'

'Search me.'

'Well you're the Italian, aren't you?' If things weren't so serious and it wasn't nearly four in the morning the captain would be laughing at the absurdity of it all. The doctor pulled out his syringe. The captain's feeling of relief lasted less than a second; the doctor's syringe was trumped by Kerridge's pistol. *Serious* had just turned *critical*.

'Not so fast, doctor. These are my demands—'

The captain patiently listened as Kerridge listed his requirements. When the seaman had finished he attempted to sound friendly and reasonable: 'I understand perfectly that you have thought about this and you are concerned. My proposal is that we say no more about it and we make directly for the nearest port where we can sensibly—'

'Captain, I can't spend another day on this boat.' Kerridge looked at his pistol. 'You have my demands.'

There was something about Kerridge's tone; more determined and final, something the captain didn't like the sound of. 'Okay,' he said. 'We'll make arrangements. Lucca, make ready the number two lifeboat.'

'You can't be serious?' said Lucca. 'This is the twenty-first century.'

'And that is a Smith and Wesson with the safety off,' replied the captain nodding at the pistol in Kerridge's hand. 'If the man wants to abandon a perfectly safe boat, I for one am not going to argue. Get the bosun to help you but try and keep it quick. Provisions for sixty days.' A couplet turned in his head: *As idle as a painted ship upon a painted ocean ... Water, water everywhere, nor any drop to drink.* 'And Lucca ... plenty of water.'

An hour later the captain and Kerridge were standing by the seaboard hatch. The submarine was on the surface and on the other side of the hatch Lieutenant Lucca and the bosun were stocking the inflatable dinghy. Kerridge had even furnished them with a list. Clearly, this wasn't a spur of the moment thing, mused the captain. It was nonetheless his duty to try to talk some sense into the seaman one last time.

'Listen, Kerridge, time in the mouse house starts to mess with your mind. You start to imagine all manner of demons that really live only in your own head. If you leave us here you'll be adrift on the open sea. One day, tomorrow or the next, you'll be a sadder and a wiser man and there'll be nothing you can do about it – you'll still be all alone.' The captain shook Kerridge by the shoulder. 'For goodness sake, think what you're doing, man!'

'Hands off me!' Kerridge was still holding his pistol. 'And I'm telling you this boat is doomed. I wish it wasn't, but it is.'

'Look, Kerridge,' said the captain. 'You've got a Very pistol in the lifeboat. We'll give you fifteen minutes to fire it. If we see the flare we'll come back for you and the authorities will never know a thing. But after fifteen minutes we're submerging and you're on your own.'

'I appreciate it, sir, you're a good skipper, but my mind is made up. I'll take my chances.'

'I'm also giving you my satellite phone. If anyone asks, I'll say you pinched it.'

'Sir, you give that to me, I'll chuck it in the drink. You know with a GPRS signal that phone is like a beacon. It could be a court-martial offence for you.' Kerridge was right, he wasn't thinking straight. He was exhausted. He'd never had training for this. He wondered if it had ever happened in naval history. Could he have handled it better?

'Okay, if that's the way you want it. Open the hatch.'

'You take the conn,' said the captain. He knew he was tired; he'd worked two shifts in a row and sleep was a distant memory.

'I have the conn,' said Lucca. From the bridge the first lieutenant and the captain watched the lifeboat through the periscope. After much discussion Kerridge had agreed to wait until dawn before abandoning ship. The captain and Lucca had used the time to attempt to make him change his mind, but to no avail and Kerridge had remained vigilant, the pistol trained on the captain until the last minute. The lifeboat was big in the periscope, about twenty metres aft. The submarine was going at funereal speed – five knots – but surprisingly quickly the lifeboat started to look smaller and smaller astern. No sign of a flare.

Damn the man thought the captain. 'Turn full a starboard,' he commanded.

'Turn full starboard.'

'No harm to circle the lifeboat at a fifty-metre radius. 'Who knows, a change in the boat's direction may get some change in Kerridge's mind.' Although the captain wasn't hopeful. As he left the submarine Kerridge had his jaw firmly stuck out; every inch the look of a man whose mind was made up. There was a sound from the hull microphone.

'What's that noise? It doesn't sound human,' said Lucca who looked anxiously at the captain.

The captain turned up the volume on the bridge speaker and soon the bridge was awash with a ghostly wailing sound. Lucca actually looked worried. When the captain realised what the sound was, he was surprised he didn't start laughing out loud.

'Bagpipes! It's bloody bagpipes, would you credit it? I don't suppose you've heard bagpipes very often?' He explained to Lucca that it was Kerridge's last wish to take his bagpipes with him. 'They wouldn't let him practise in the mess; you can hear why.'

He looked at his watch. They kept circling and the captain turned the speaker down. 'That's his fifteen minutes,' he said to Lucca, although they both knew it was more like twenty-five. 'We'll write our report in the morning. We'll do it together. I expect the admiralty may send a rescue ship.' The captain sounded like a doctor talking to a terminally sick patient, keeping it positive. 'Turn back to our nor nor-west course,' he commanded Lucca. 'And prepare to dive.' He dropped the periscope with a resigned sigh.

'Nor nor-west and preparing to dive,' replied his lieutenant. 'You should try and grab some kip. You look done in, sir.'

'I will. I'll just mark our exact location in the log. Anything to report?'

'Well there is one thing, sir. It looks like we've got a small rise in pressure in the right reactor.' Lucca was studying the flickering lights on the control panel. I should have noticed it earlier but what with what's been going on—'

'Probably something and nothing. I'll turn it off so we can have a look.' The captain went to turn off the lever that was marked *Left Reactor*. 'That's why we have two engines after all. Good to give the engineers something to do.'

'Sir, with respect you should give the order and it's *my* job to carry it out, checks and balances—'

'Lucca, you need to understand ... no, you're right. Next time I'll just give the order and yes, *you* can pull the lever, but now I'm off to bed and next time the whole crew can abandon ship before you wake me for all I care.'

The captain went for'ard. He realised that he hadn't thought about Henrietta for the last three hours. He looked at his bed, where he had spent two uncomfortable nights, with a pleasant certainty that sleep was going to come easily. Brushing his teeth he made a few resolutions; less of the Mahler and less malt whisky. He smiled at the mirror; more smiling would be another. Didn't Henrietta say that he should smile more? And then a real big decision that he should have made years ago. There had to be better ways to spend his days than circumnavigating the globe as God's super policeman, cocooned for six months at a stretch. So what if the world stops, what was the point of living on, underneath the ocean? And if there wasn't a war to end all wars what was the point of living in this water world anyway?

Part of him wished he could change places with Kerridge. God help him. But the man had a mathematical chance and he'd accepted the gift of a compass. Captain Bligh had journeyed three thousand six hundred miles in an open boat with less provisions – a feat that had earned him acclaim as one of the finest seamen of the century. Was Kerridge in that class? The captain somehow doubted it.

As his head hit the pillow he was already composing in his head the email he would start writing to Henrietta. In a few hours from now she would be just waking up at their home in a small village on the outskirts of Oxford. Maybe now they could start a family; red-haired children, that would be a first in his family. Henrietta could continue her studies and he had enough put by to stay at home for a year or two. *Dear Henrietta, the truth is I miss you so.*

A week later Stephanie was holding her end of term, one-on-one tutorials. Other universities didn't have the resources but this was Balliol College, Oxford. She had deliberately timetabled Elliot for the last slot; something to look forward to – by the same reasoning she had been keen to see Colewell early on.

'So, Elliot, if you can keep a rein on your natural exuberance and not, sometimes, forget the other point of view, I see some good work coming from you. I think the gold standard could be just the subject to get your teeth into next year; lots of number-crunching but people also. Something along the lines of: *The inevitability of a return to the gold standard at pre-war parity.* Comments?'

'Yes, Professor, you are right but I've been thinking more about the Kerridge question.'

'What? A*rt of Succession* Kerridge?' Stephanie found her eyes drawn to the book on the table.

'No, Seaman Kerridge, you know the submarine HMS ... *Electra*. Our methodology in history class. Something reminded me of it this morning. I was thinking – even if he had abandoned ship there's a chance, isn't there, that the rest of the crew would have behaved differently because of what had happened? They would have been affected.'

'That's it, Elliot. I believe you're getting it. No man is an island, back to Engels and those criss-crossing parallelograms.' Stephanie spied in the quad below the unmistakable bearded fellow of the college walking past the sundial with some student she didn't recognise. That reminded her – she had promised to deliver her answer today about the holiday ...

'Professor, is there anything else?'

'Sorry, I was miles away. I think we're done, Elliot. Have a good vacation and remember, onwards and upwards in the Michaelmas term.' She smiled as her protégé stood up to leave the room. 'By the way, Elliot, I should have asked, you said something reminded you of our submarine example this morning. What was it?'

'Something on the radio, a mention of a submarine on the *Today* programme, but I was already half out of the door on my way here. I think I heard "South Pacific" which struck me as kinda odd. Cheers, Prof, I mean Professor.' And he was gone.

Stephanie went over to her desk. She liked to have it clean and shipshape before holidays started. After putting a couple of letters in the internal post she still had five minutes before she was meeting Art for a coffee. She decided to quickly catch up on the news online.

'You're late,' said Art, 'but definitely better late than never. I like the skirt. How about a kiss?'

The Buttery was her favourite coffee place. The walls were populated with row upon row of students sitting in gowns and mortarboards in ageless graduation photographs. 'In my family we were always taught to say *you're here*. Look forwards not back,' Stephanie replied sharply, aware that she sounded like Elizabeth Bennet.

'But you're a historian, I thought you were interested in the past. Good to see you.' He leant over to kiss her and she smelt a generous sprinkling of aftershave.

'That's why I like the Buttery; history all around. Sorry, I didn't mean to sound terse.' They ordered coffee which Stephanie drank in silence.

'Is it my imagination or are you a touch preoccupied?' Art stirred his coffee. 'End of term blues?'

Stephanie wondered whether to mention what she had found out on the internet: the submarine missing, presumed lost in the South Pacific. The name of the boat was HMS *Agamemnon*, not *Electra*; but both figured in the play by Sophocles. She had dismissed it as coincidence. But the trained researcher in her wanted more information and in a matter of minutes she had been scrolling down the online manifest of the *Agamemnon*. There, she had come across a Warrant Officer Kerridge. Was it a common name, she wondered?

'Steph?'

'I was just wondering who it was I saw you with in the quad earlier?'

'I don't know, could have been anyone.'

'Tall girl, red hair, thirty-something, and very pretty. Ring any bells?'

'I do believe you're jealous, Steph.' She was folding up the paper receipt that had come with the coffee. 'That must be one of my mature students, Henrietta. She needs a bit of personal support, something of a personal crisis – husband gone missing. You know I'm allowed to socialise even with students. Of course, with a little bit more encouragement from you ... sorry, that didn't sound the way I meant.' He pulled at his beard as he spoke. 'Have you decided about Italy? I've found us the most exquisite pensione. Views to die for, that's assuming you ever let me out of the giant four-poster bed.'

Stephanie shook her head. 'You know, Art, it was a lovely invitation and I'm sorry I took so long to reply, but maybe another time. It just doesn't feel right. Sorry, I have to dash; I don't want an untidy desk when term starts again. She leant across to give Art a goodbye kiss on the cheek. 'Have a marvellous holiday. Send me a postcard.'

She left Art in the coffee place, rolling his eyes at her in bewilderment. He picked up the origami figure she'd made from the receipt – a boat.

Stephanie unlocked her bicycle from the railings and told herself to cheer up. She had the whole summer holiday in front of her and she was as free as a bird. She looked inside the coffee place and saw that Art was already busy on his smart phone – she had made the right decision on Socrates. To think at breakfast she had been planning to say *yes*. She had only nipped one love affair in the bud but still had the feeling that had been with her since Elliot left; like someone had walked across her grave.

In the South Pacific HMS *Daring*, a Royal Navy Type 45 destroyer was in thick fog. For three days they had been trawling an area approximately five hundred miles square, keeping an eye out for wayward icebergs or any other explanation for why HMS *Agamemnon* had disappeared off the radar without trace.

On the bridge the midshipman said to the lieutenant-commander: 'Sir, can you hear something over there, sounds like it might be ... could that be bagpipes, sir?' He sounded unsure. The two men listened for a second. Maybe there was some strange sound ... but then silence again.

'Bagpipes?' replied the superior officer. 'Archie, you may be Scottish but what are the chances of us hearing bagpipes three thousand miles from anywhere? I'm famished, let's get some breakfast. There's nothing out here and even if there was, the chance of locating something would be like finding a needle in a haystack.'

EXTRACT OF INVESTIGATORS' REPORT
INTO SINKING OF HMS AGAMEMNON

After an extensive search the black box of HMS Agamemnon was recovered by remote-controlled submarine at a depth of twelve thousand eight hundred feet (three thousand nine hundred metres). The exact cause of the accident remains difficult to ascertain due to the widespread distribution of debris, much of which was not recovered.

CONCLUSION:

... so that although no single cause of the sinking can be determined it looks likely that an initial minor problem in one reactor acted as a causal nexus precipitating a chain reaction of events; for example, closing down the wrong engine, losing depth, and poor communication along the chain of command. This sequence of events became terminal and irreversible after the submarine had sunk to an estimated collapse depth of nine hundred and twenty metres.

Extensive trials cannot be ruled out as a contributory factor. It is recommended that henceforth submarine sea trials should run no more than one week without a twenty-four recuperation period on surface or on shore.

THIS REPORT IS CLASSIFIED TOP SECRET AND PERMISSION FOR COPIES MUST BE PUT IN WRITING TO ADMIRALTY C.I.C.

Playing for the Queen

'Left a tad, Trev.'

'Is it clear of the frame?'

'That's it, just a smidge and you're in.'

Cordula put a hand up to shield her eyes from the sun and watch the two men pulling up the harpsichord on a series of pulleys. They were just about level with the open window sill on the first floor of the sail loft. Both men were leaning precariously out of the large aperture which they had assured her was *plenty big enough*. It could take a barge sail for repair so a six-foot harpsichord was going to be a *piece of cake*.

To start with, Cordula had been given a rope to hold but now the job was out of her reach, literally. The harpsichord was four metres off the ground and on the point of disappearing into the upper level of the cavernous two-storey building. The instrument, she knew, had been made by Jospeh Joannes Couchet of Vienna in 1679 and was insured for three hundred and sixty thousand pounds, although Cordula somehow doubted the cover was valid for barn hoists.

For a moment the harpsichord lurched a foot or so downwards. She just managed to stifle a cry as the men succeeded in getting it back on course. They clearly weren't trained for this type of operation. Trevor had one hand on the outside wall for support and the other on a harpsichord leg as he guided the precious cargo over the last critical centimetres. He was sixty, black-haired, scruffily dressed, small and sprightly with relentless energy – reminiscent of a hobbit from middle earth.

The other man, a few years younger, stronger and much larger looked like a rugby player and was giving an unrelenting mix of commentary and commands throughout the operation. 'Left exactly one cunth of an inch ... perfect! Now lower it slowly. Easy does it, Trev. Purfect!' Cordula wasn't good at accents but she guessed cockney or Kent. The harpsichord was in. She could breathe a sigh of relief.

'Great set up, John. You're right, I could pull that up with my little finger ... toughest bit was the last five inches.'

'As the nun said to the bishop.'

Cordula decided to wait for the return of the men in the small sunlit courtyard opposite the entrance to the sail loft barn. Fifty metres across an expanse of perfect lawn stood the main house, Restoration era and imposing. There was a blip from her phone as a text arrived. *See you in five* was the message. She impatiently kicked at one of the chairs with her Ferragamo leather boot. There were still plenty of arrangements to make and instructions to give before this evening's concert.

Trevor Quintell OBE, Cordula's boyfriend and world-famous harpsichordist, emerged smiling, one shirt-sleeve rolled up, from the sail loft into the sun, rings of sweat under his armpits. He put a hairy forearm around her – 'Phew! Did you see that, Cordula?' – before planting a sweaty kiss on her cheek. 'I think we deserve a drink, don't you?'

'Well you don't have much choice with John around.' She had met Trevor at a rehearsal for Bach's Brandenberg Concertos seven years previously. She'd had a lucky break when standing in for a more talented flatmate who had flu and got even luckier when Trevor, the star attraction, had fallen for her. They'd been together ever since, on tour and off. Cordula had ceased all her orchestral work and now only performed exclusive concerts with Trevor, on virtuoso pay grade, her days sharing the last violin desk by the pit exit at Sadler's Wells a distant memory.

'What a noise they're making today.' Trevor turned to watch the poplar trees behind the barn. The trees were so full of birds they looked black and swayed to and fro under the weight of swarming starlings. 'They're dreaming of flight. Do you ever dream of distant shores, Cordula?'

She was still wondering how to reply to such a question as John, owner of the Larkrise estate, emerged into the sunlight with sweat running off his wide forehead. 'What did I tell you? Piece of cake.' He spoke loudly, carrying a bottle of champagne in one of his ham-sized hands and three glasses in the other. 'Any takers for bubbly?'

'I don't think the insurers would take a bright view of your morning's work,' Cordula replied, choosing the chair that was facing the autumn sun. 'Are you sure those ropes are strong enough for a priceless instrument?'

'Nafink to worry about, pulleys and blocks, that's what built the pyramids. I grew up with knots – me dad nearly ended up on the end of one, hah hah.'

John was really not Cordula's type, but to her amazement he and Trevor got on like a house on fire. Enthusiasm was the glue that held them together – take this ridiculous escapade with Trevor's precious harpsichord. And now the two of them exuded a triumphant camaraderie. It reminded her of the early days when she and Trevor finished a concert together. Music had always been their glue.

'So waddaya reckon? Better acoustics than the Albert Hall in there I'd say. Great atmosphere upstairs, natural amphiwhat's it. But you should've seen the spiders' webs we had to clear out. Blimey, it's going to rain for yonks,' said John banging down the cut-glass champagne flutes on the table like they were throwaway picnic glasses.

Where John got his money from was a mystery to Cordula, since as far as she could make out he never did any work, just played at being lord of the manor, pottering around the estate, spending it. He was supposed to have made a fortune in property before he was fifty but John was sketchy on detail. She once voiced her fears to Trevor that John might have underworld dealings, at which Trevor had laughed.

'I thought the forecast was for a clear evening?' she asked.

'Sorry, luv. If you step on a spider, it's rain.' John fired the champagne cork across the wide expanse of green lawn, and started to fill their glasses. 'The Queen!'

John was a great royalist. Cordula, half-German, wasn't; but she stood up anyway. 'The Queen,' she repeated dutifully.

'Cheers! Glad we don't do this before every concert, right, Cordula?' said Trevor standing up with his glass. 'For a moment that was a touch—'

'Squeaky bum time,' added John.

'So what's the difference between a tad and ... what was it ... a smidgin?' Trevor asked John.

'No, Trev, a *smidge*; that's between a tad and fratch, less than a gnat's but more than a skosh.'

'And a cunth?'

'Trev, I couldn't tell you that, not with a lady—' John noticed a smartly dressed man striding confidently towards them. 'Saved by the swell,' he laughed.

'So where's my glass?' asked Hans, the new arrival. 'And where is—' Hans stopped in his tracks. 'Where's the harpsichord? And what a racket those birds are making.'

'Welcome to the country, Hans,' said Trevor. 'You know my roots are from around here.' Cordula smiled at the new arrival. He was sporting a red and black striped blazer, appearing more ready for the races than any heavy lifting work.

John put out his hand. 'Hello, I remember, it's uhm ... Frank? Hank?'

'Hans, Trevor's agent.'

'Huh ... hum,' interjected Cordula.

'And of course, Cordula's as well,' Hans added quickly. 'We've met before, John.'

'So we have. Sorry, we decided to go not fully ... Hans on.' John chortled again. 'No, seriously, it was a very difficult job and the only way we got through is we all worked together as a team. So Trev and Cordula had to do everything, just as I said. Worked a treat. I'll get you a Hackney marsh.' Their host went back into the sail loft, presumably to get another glass, guessed Cordula.

Hans looked up at the open window. 'Wow!' he said. 'I'm impressed, you really are the maestro.' Cordula had noticed this before; when it was the three of them Hans naturally seemed to accede to the smaller man's authority. She wasn't sure she liked it but the main thing was that they all got on. Trevor seemed genuinely pleased to see Hans who, around twenty years his junior, was the same generation as Cordula. Hans was an ambitious and accomplished cellist but while *waiting for his breakthrough* was also the booking agent for both Cordula and Trevor. Trevor had once confided in Cordula that he might be waiting some time.

'Good trip down?' she asked. 'Did you bring the new car?'

'I did as a matter of fact. I'll show you later – if we have time that is.'

'Don't worry, we'll find some.' Cordula was pleased to see pale and metropolitan Hans again. After two days cooped up with Trevor in his cramped and converted fisherman's loft she was ready for a change of scenery. Trevor could keep his view of the estuary – she hankered after the sights and sounds of the city. He had bought the garret, as he called it, because he loved the nature and the village that took him back to his blessed roots. He often complained that he was like a migrant bird with never time enough to see anyone other than John properly. One day when he was retired he hoped to spend more time in the village. Cordula dreaded the thought. By coincidence her own mum lived only twenty miles away. Her father had abandoned them both and returned to Munich thirty years before.

''Ere you go, son. Nothing beats a spot of bubbly straight after brekkers.' John brought out a fourth glass and mercifully not a second bottle. There was still six hours to go until the concert and she knew Trevor would want a clear head for this afternoon's rehearsal.

'And I've got something to tell you both,' said Hans with a pointed look in Trevor's direction. 'It really is urgent. It's why I'm a bit late. I already tried ringing you.'

'You know me and phones,' said Trevor. 'Did you try Cordula?' She got more phone calls from Hans than Trevor realised and was wondering whether she should have mentioned the text message earlier. 'Anyway you're here now.' Trevor patted Cordula on the arm. 'And Hans, don't worry about John; no secrets here, besides, it's his champagne. So what's so urgent for you to miss a harpsichord workout?'

'Well you're not going to believe this. It really is the most incredible news.' Hans was speaking fast and there was a glow to his freckled cheeks. 'You've been invited to play at the Palace tonight!'

'The Palace?' said Cordula, running one hand through her thick fair hair.

'Buckingham Palace. The Queen has requested the pleasure of Trevor Quintell's company for a select soirée this evening at eight in the Blue Drawing Room.'

'Blimey, Trev,' said John.

'But not a booking for two?' Cordula tried to hide her disappointment. 'Just Trevor?'

'Sorry, Cordula,' said Hans. 'Violin surplus to requirements this time.'

'Slow down and tell us from the beginning,' said Trevor, who was seemingly amazingly cool about the whole thing. So Hans told the story of how the Japanese Emperor was here on a state visit. He was a well-known aficionado of the harpsichord and Melvyn Tan was all lined up for a private performance tonight when yesterday he had crushed his hand in a car door. Trevor was the obvious replacement and London was only forty minutes' drive away. The Palace would send a car, naturally. 'And that's it?' concluded Trevor when Hans had finished.

'Anyway, the cheek of it, our Trev on the subs' bench,' said John. 'Melvyn Tan, no relation to Melvyn Bragg?'

For just a minute Cordula thought he was serious. 'Well he's one of the most famous piano players on the planet.'

'Yeah and so what about our Trev? Isn't he the cat's pyjamas too? Still, the Queen. That would be something, Trev. I could be your security—'

'Isn't there a name for that, John?' Cordula interupted. 'Like MI5?'

'But you told them we already had a booking for tonight?' said Trevor, sounding like that was the end of the matter.

'Well, it's hardly a booking, is it?' replied Cordula sharply. 'I mean it's only my mum and it's not as if we're even getting paid for it.'

'You're forgetting you asked me to put the word about,' said John. 'I've been doing the rounds. What with Trevor top of the card and a local boy done good an' all, we've got quite a few takers.'

'Oh, jolly good,' said Trevor. 'Are Ann and Pete coming?' Cordula saw at once that Trevor was thinking about who they would be playing to, whereas the right question was: how easy is it to cancel this rent-a-mob?

John started to make a roll call of the usual suspects: 'Ann 'n' Pete, they're dead certs. Pat says all right if they can get a babysitter but she's hopeful. Jane says definite but Kev wanted to know whether there would be any dancing girls, that's typical of the man, no appreciation of the arts. Tony says depends on the—'

'Stop!' said Cordula. She cast a despairing glance at Hans – he at any rate would agree with her. 'I can't believe I'm hearing this. The only reason we're doing the gig is that my mum was complaining to Trevor that she had never heard either of us play live and because she hates travelling any distance she probably never would. And then Trevor did his fine speech about mountains and prophets and we offered to come here and play in her back yard. But she would be the first to say it's ridiculous for us to put her before the Queen. I mean, get real.'

'But Cordula, I thought you and your mum were both republicans? Anyway, I don't play for fame or money; music and audiences are my reward—'

'Well that's fine when you're already loaded,' muttered Cordula. 'Why don't you speak some sense into him, Hans?'

But it was Trevor who continued: 'And I'm very pleased, John, we've got so many locals coming. How many in total would you say?'

'About twenty, not more than you could shake a stick at, but still a good turn-out.'

'It's decided,' said Trevor. 'Hans, ring the Palace, not an easy call but it's just a day in the life of an agent.'

'I still think we should reconsider. But all right, I'll make the call.' Hans sounded reluctant and trudged off into the garden.

'Anyway,' Cordula's chin was thrust in John's direction, 'I can't see why you're even interested in classical music. I bet you don't even know the difference between Bartok and Bach?' Her comment earned her a disapproving look from Trevor.

John didn't seem to notice a thing, supremely confident as always: 'If ya ooze masculinity like some of us do, you's no reason to fear classical music. But ya know I've always had a soft spot for Boccherini, wasn't it in one of those Ealing comedy films? 'Ow's about a drop more of the bubbly stuff?' He went on to top up her glass and continued: 'Now I'm retired, I'm subscribing more to the European philosophy of life, my priorities are leaning towards wine, women ... well actually, that's about it.' They heard Hans on the phone. 'Isn't that Alfie?'

'It's Hans, as you know perfectly well,' said Cordula.

'I'm impressed, John.' Trevor grinned at his friend. 'Boccherini is a most underestimated composer. The film was ... what was it? *The Ladykillers*, I believe.'

'Rings a bell. Can't tempt you to a top up?' John raised the bottle and Trevor shook his head. Cordula decided that this friendship between Trevor and John really wasn't healthy. She should have a chat with Hans about increasing the amount of long-haul bookings, some-where hot.

'Thanks, John,' said Trevor, 'but we need clear heads this afternoon. Cordula, maybe we should talk about tonight's programme. I'm interested you should mention Bach, I've got a new piece to show you.'

What did it matter what they played tonight? That was the thing with Trevor, he took every concert so seriously. 'Don't you think we've got enough Bach already?'

'Can you have too many oceans or mountains?' Trevor smoothly replied. Well the truth is, she believed, sometimes you could. She could do two or three days in the sticks but then she started to miss service and cappuccinos. Today was the first time the sun had shone since they arrived. Hans could give her a lift up to town tomorrow in his new sports car. He was walking back towards them, she could ask him now.

'Trevor. Don't get cross.' Hans sounded noticeably less confident than earlier. 'I spoke to the Palace and they put me on to some cultural events boss, anyway—'

'But you did say *no*, didn't you, Hans?'

'I tried, Trevor, really. But they were very insistent. They are sending this bigwig down to come and have a chat with you, by limousine.'

'Well it'll be a wasted journey. Come on, Cordula.' Trevor put down his glass. 'Let's go home for some lunch. Then we have some rehearsing to do.'

Trevor's garret was a good ten-minute walk away. 'Maybe Hans could give us a lift in his car?'

'Exercise will do us good.' Trevor stood up. 'John, lovely bubbly.'

'And I've got some chairs to get and I thought I'd put some flags up in the sail loft,' said John. 'Bit of a Proms-like atmosphere.'

'Anything I can do?' added Hans, looking at the three of them in turn, but mostly Cordula.

'Hans. The way I see it, your job is to keep Cordula happy,' said Trevor warmly. 'Her wish is your command.' Cordula frowned.

'Yeah there is,' said John. 'You can help me with some chairs.'

*

The rehearsal hadn't gone well. Cordula was a reasonable violinist but normally Trevor made her sound good. He had a knack of cueing up her entrance, deferring to her phrasing in a way that made her star shine like it never did at Sadler's Wells – she accompanied him, not the other way around. Maybe he knew it too but he never referred to the fact. She had once asked him what it was like to play with someone like Zukerman, and his reply had been: 'Well not as fun as playing with you.' Today he seemed more focused on his own performance which was as usual peerless. They were now descending the sail loft stairs.

'It'll be all right on the night,' comforted Trevor. 'In the last passage of the scherzo you might have a bit of unnecessary string crossing with the first finger. If you bring in the other fingers earlier and hold the first finger down you might get better support. Just an idea.'

He was only trying to help but that's what she found irritating; when he knew more about the violin – *her* instrument – than she did. 'Like our distinguished audience would notice.'

'Sorry, Cordula.'

'Yes, you're right. I'll have a look at it.'

'Anyway, I'll see you back at the garret.' Trevor turned at the foot of the stairs. 'I thought to have a quick chat with John.'

'Do you want me to come along?'

'No, you're fine. Why not spend some time with Hans, he looks a bit out of sorts recently. Have you noticed anything?'

'No, why, should I?'

'Maybe it's not fair to him to use him as our agent, you know, holding back his own career? Have a chat with him, find out what he really wants from life, will you?' He leant over to give her a peck on the cheek. 'Ciao, baby.'

Trevor went up to the main house and Cordula went in search of Hans. She found him by the large ornamental fishpond, fully fifteen metres across and well stocked with trout. John's delight was to boast of having caught breakfast with a spot of early morning fly fishing. Cordula had a sneaking suspicion he had a net concealed somewhere close.

Now she was telling Hans about Trevor's recent comments. She left out the 'What do you want from life?' as she had a pretty good idea of what the answer would be. 'He sounded odd, not like Trevor at all,' she concluded. 'And he's never said *Ciao, baby* to me before.'

'Do you think he could have found out about *us*? I mean, that was rather a peculiar comment earlier ... your wish is my desire or whatever it was.'

'Yes, it was odd. But no, I could be knocking off the entire brass section and Trevor wouldn't notice a thing. He's so naïve and wrapped up in his music, rather sweet actually. But perhaps we'd better be extra discreet for the next few days, just to be on the safe side.' Her affair with Hans had been going for about nine months. For Cordula it was certainly not serious enough to risk rocking the boat with Trevor, but she also had to look to the future.

'Why don't we come out and just tell him?' asked Hans. 'I mean, we could survive without his patronage. And who knows, maybe it would change nothing?'

'Hans. You're as gullible as he is. I've told you before: when I go it'll be on my own terms. Bail out now and we walk away with nothing more than wrapping paper. We've got plenty of time.'

'I get the feeling that John seems to spend his whole time laughing at me, that's just the half of what he says that I understand—'

'Hold on, who's that?' Cordula had stopped listening and was looking at an elegantly dressed man in a pin-striped suit with distinguished silver hair. His footsteps made small indentations on the newly cut lawn as he walked towards them.

'Good afternoon. Brian Rust, Her Majesty's Cultural Attaché, looking for Mr Trevor Quintell. I believe I'm expected.'

'Well sort of,' Cordula replied doubtfully. 'Hans, I think we'd better go and look for Trevor in the house.' The three of them trooped up to the Larkrise front door. John was not one to stand on ceremony – probably why the doorbell didn't work.

They were all sitting in what John called the library but there were so few books Cordula thought it hardly deserved the title. Trevor and John had been looking at something secretively when they arrived and quickly folded it away from view. Pornography? Cordula wondered. When it came to John nothing surprised her. People with money and no taste irritated her. John had plenty of the former and the walls of the library were covered with a collection of nude paintings – some abstract, most not.

'I feel it's one of my duties to sponsor the arts,' said John who seemed visibly impressed by the new arrival. 'I suppose in your line of work you must meet quite a lot of people like me, Mr Rust?' The attaché looked relaxed and only smiled. 'So culture wise, it's a wide area.' John, unperturbed by the silence, continued. 'I mean, for example, have you had much to do with the boxing fraternity?'

'Well the truth is the chief has never been such a boxing fan, more the gee-gees.'

'Gotcha. You mean the sport of kings?'

'Precisely.'

'Not so much boxing then?' John sometimes reminded Cordula of a bulldog with a bone.

'I do believe we might have had one of the Kray twins to a garden party once.'

'Na, ya kidding me? Ronnie or Reggie?'

'In hindsight something of a mistake,' the attaché said, looking unperturbed. 'If we could keep it between these walls.'

'Sure thing, I'll keep shtum as the grave. But that's real 'istory. Blimey, but then you look like you's been around the block a bit.'

The attaché sighed. 'Yes, I do look incredibly old, don't I? The chief doesn't want too many young faces around, you understand. Or rather one day you will. But now, I'm afraid I have something delicate to discuss with Mr Quintell.'

'Anything you care to discuss with me,' said Trevor, 'I'm keen for my friends to hear.'

There was a sound as chairs moved closer towards Brian Rust, the Queen's Cultural Attaché. His speech lasted around five minutes and he slowed as he neared the end, choosing his words carefully, like a modern composer dishing out melody. Cordula could see he was used to making speeches. He concluded: 'So it's not what you can do for your Queen, Mr Quintell, it's what your Queen can do for you, sir.' There was an unmistakable emphasis on the *sir*. If anybody was in any doubt, there had been an earlier reference to Paul McCartney's private concert for a prince, before he became Sir Paul.

So a knighthood on the table for Trevor. Cordula wondered if being married to Sir Trevor Quintell would make her a lady something? The ways of the English aristocracy had never been her strong point. She nodded to Trevor as if to say: *that's decided then, you've got to take it now!*

Trevor smiled. Hans sat open-mouthed and John clapped; a real serious well-meant spontaneous putting together of hands. 'I'll give you a few minutes to discuss. I'll be waiting in the limousine,' said the attaché. 'Shall we say ten minutes? John, It's been a privilege to see your lovely house and your interesting art collection, as well as your fine friends.'

'Our privilege to be sure, Brian. Here, let me escort you. By the way, strictly speaking it's Jonathan—' The two of then left the room together.

Cordula was left with Trevor and Hans, the three of them together again. Was this her destiny? 'Of course, one idea is I perform alone tonight or,' she added with real enthusiasm, 'we could just cancel.'

'I hate to let people down, especially your mum.' Trevor added tenderly: 'You really love me, don't you?'

'Of course, why wouldn't I? You know I love you more than

anything in the world.' She pressed his hands and was satisfied to feel a reciprocal squeeze. 'To be honest, Klara really won't be disappointed to miss you. It's me she wants to hear.'

'I don't suppose, Hans, you brought your cello with you?'

'Doesn't fit in the new car,' replied Hans to Trevor. 'It's a TR6,' which was like saying *diminishing chords* to a five-year-old.

'So you'd be happy to do the concert on your own, Cordula? You'd do that for me?'

She didn't know she'd ever heard Trevor sounding so touched. She wondered if she'd overdone it. 'Of course. You'd do the same for me.'

'Yes I do believe I would,' Trevor replied. 'Well I guess it's time we got moving. *The great affair is to move:* Robert Louis Stevenson, I think. I've got a few things to pack.'

Cordula and John waved Trevor off in the limousine, which drove off slowly down the Larkrise drive. 'They'd better get a leg on,' said John. 'At that rate he'd miss his own funeral.'

The starlings were continuing their infernal racket and Cordula wondered where Hans had disappeared to. 'What was with the *Jonathan* to the attaché?'

'Garden Party invites, don't wanna miss the boat, many a slip and all that—'

'John, do you really think that attaché was for a minute taken in by your fawning?' Cordula opened her Gucci handbag to look for her sunglasses.

'No worries, Cordula, or should I call you Cinders? So you got a ticket to the dance?'

'Dance?' What are you talking about?'

'Redundant, surplus to needs at the Palace. So, doll, it's you and me for tonight's show. I reckon—'

'John, two points: first, don't ever call me doll again and second, there will be no show.'

'But we promised Trev, your mum.'

'Do you really think that if I needed advice I would turn to some low pond-life who can't even speak English?' She put on her sunglasses.

'We come from different worlds you and me, Cordula. In mine there ain't no time for bright lights and 'ockey sticks. The only game we played was to survive or go to the wall. If ya didn't win ya just didn't finish. You probably don't understand that, ya cupid stunt. So tell everyone the concert's off and I'll serve drinks anyway. Why, if I was Trevor I'd 'ave you 'cross me knee—'

'Well thank God you're not. Why do you think he was so keen to get to the Palace? To meet people from our own class. You know he only pretends to like you.' She tossed her hair back. Cordula didn't stick around long enough to try to understand John or give him the satisfaction of having the last word. She started to walk towards the sail loft.

John shouted after her: 'You're *wrong* about that Cordula. *R O N G* wrong. I know a good bloke when I see one and Trevor is a diamond geezer.' She'd pricked that veneer of self-confidence at last. There was still a couple of hours before guests were due to arrive and she was conscious that she had overlooked Hans. She was slightly miffed that he hadn't intervened to get her to the Palace – he was meant to be her agent as well. She would go and find him. It was five o'clock and the concert wasn't due to start until seven.

Hans and Cordula were together in the sail loft. 'You're sure it's all right for us to be here?' Hans asked after they had shut and bolted the old wooden door.

'Sure, John said to treat the place like home. He's finished whatever he was doing upstairs. Now let's see how much you've missed me, really.' Cordula started to unbutton his shirt. Hans was like a small boy with a big drum when he could have her to himself. The sail loft had a comfortable enough sofa and a fridge with white wine and a relaxing hour went all too quickly. 'I'll have to tell the guests the concert's cancelled,' said Cordula.

'I wouldn't put it past some of them to ask for their money back.'

'But it was a free—'

'Exactly. See you later. You'd better disappear before John comes snooping around.'

'Okay Cordula. Kiss you soon.'

'That's nice. Where did you get that from?'

'Dunno.'

Cordula decided to wait outside the sail loft to inform the guests of the cancellation. She took up position at half-past six. She had contemplated cancelling her mother on the phone but this way she could still count this evening's meeting with her as a visit. She waited, wine glass in hand, for the first guest.

John came down from the house in black tie, which she considered totally inappropriate for this occasion. 'Hi, Cordula,' he said, walking past her. 'How's tricks?' So, they were still on speaking terms, just. She did think that John would start to become a problem. She toyed with the idea of inventing some inappropriate advance she could report to Trevor. The only problem was that Trevor had never shown any signs of jealousy – not yet anyway.

She wasn't at all nervous about having to explain Trevor's summons to the Queen. These villagers weren't her friends, and were hardly on more than nodding terms with her and Trevor. In spite of what Trevor liked to think, they were the *outsiders*. Cordula's thoughts were interrupted by the sight of the first guest walking up the driveway. Something familiar about this small man with a white bow-tie. Had John delivered a dress code? Then to her astonishment she recognised Trevor, wearing a cloak she'd not seen before. 'What are you doing there ... but I saw you getting into the limousine?'

'Only for a lift down to the garret. And I wanted to sort out a few things. I wasn't going to miss this concert for the world.' Trevor gave her a kiss on the cheek. 'And Cordula, I know that you didn't mean a word of what you said about your mum and me – you were just doing what you thought was best for me, I understand that.'

For a minute Cordula panicked but then she realised that besides Hans and John nobody knew of the plan to cancel and by good luck her cocktail party frock was here in the sail loft. 'Oh, is that the time already? I was just about to change. Oh hello, John,' and she turned to smile at him sweetly. 'John was being my rock of support, weren't you, John? Of course, now you're here, Trevor, I'm feeling fine. Just need some time to dress. John, would you be a darling and fetch my shoes – I think I left them up at the house?'

'Church pews, righteo.'

Cordula would have preferred her customary entrance to the stage than this uncomfortable feeling sitting in front of John's barmy army. Trevor, in his best concert tails, was now introducing the programme like they really would be at court: '... and my good friend John who has made tonight possible. Sorry, John, no Boccherini tonight—' Cue guffaws of laughter from John. In her designer cocktail party dress, Cordula felt like first prize at the village fête. No wonder – John had been as good as his word; English flags were draped everywhere.

'... finally, I'd like to dedicate this performance to Cordula's mum, to *Klara*. Ladies and gentleman, this evening, this spectacular setting, it's like I would be playing for the Queen.'

Her mum smiled – she had no idea. To think, mused Cordula, that a virtuoso at the pinnacle of his career, who could choose to play before emperors and royalty, would instead prefer these peasants. Didn't the English have a phrase for that – pearls before swine? Centre row sat her mum with a beaming smile and looking every one of her sixty-seven years. There was a more than polite round of applause led by John – who else? And then the opening chords of the Bruch from the harpsichord. Cordula picked up her bow in readiness.

*

The concert had gone marginally better than the rehearsal, not that any of this audience would have noticed, but Trevor nodded at her appreciatively at the end. Afterwards John had arranged a reception party downstairs in the sail loft where villagers were falling over themselves to get at the free drink. To Cordula it looked feudal and typically English. 'Not much has changed in two hundred years, has it John?'

'Yeah, just watch them fill their boots,' he replied proudly. She overheard Trevor saying goodbye to her mum Klara, as if she really was the Queen. He even kissed her hand when she left, and then came over.

'I think she enjoyed it, don't you?' Trevor was always like this; up after a concert, however small the audience. And whatever John claimed, tonight's had been small.

'I heard someone saying afterwards they were disappointed I didn't sing,' replied Cordula. 'Then it really would have been the Beggar's Opera. Don't they realise that if they wanted to book us for a private concert they wouldn't get much change out of ten grand?' She spoke in clipped tones. 'Anyway I could see you enjoyed it.'

'I certainly did. But how do *you* feel, Cordula?'

'How am I supposed to feel?'

'Things will look different in the morning, I promise. John was talking about getting the harpsichord down tonight. Maybe I'll have a quick chat with him. I think he's upstairs. Look after yourself, kiddo.' He touched her sleeve as he spoke – as if she would come into danger downstairs in the sail loft where villagers crowded around the bar like pub regulars at the bell for last orders. She was about to follow him but was a fraction too slow to avoid two women who came bearing down on her.

'Hello, dear. Now we were admiring your dress. We were wondering, could we be so bold as to ask—?' It wasn't Cordula's idea of fun to be explaining to John's cronies the difference between Bach and the Beatles. She concurred the latter had the advantage of carrying a tune and also being British.

'You wouldn't Adam 'n' Eve it how much they enjoyed the show.' For once she was pleased to see John who arrived at her side with a full jug of beer. 'And talk about *Ladykillers*, Cordula, you was smashing, gal, the dog's bollocks, make no mistake. I thought we'd get the ol' Joanna down tonight—'

'What?'

'Ol' Joanna, you know piana.'

'Ah ... the harpsichord, I think you are referring to?'

'Yeah, right, while we've still got all hands on deck. Speaking of which, where is he?'

'If you mean Hans, he's here. What about Trevor, wasn't he with you?'

''Ello, 'ello, have we got ourselves a gatecrasher?' Both looked up to see a young man entering the sail loft. He was about thirty, not a familiar face to Cordula and too smartly dressed to be an agent. 'Sorry, mate, you're late. Show's over.' John went to steer the guest from the sail loft.

The man stood his ground. 'I'm looking for Cordula Schmidt. I tried up at the house but I was told to come down here.'

'That's me.'

He turned to face her. 'Miss Schmidt, I'm here from Girlings and Sons, under instruction from Mr Trevor Quintell.'

'Trevor sent you?' Cordula felt she needed to sit. 'You're a lawyer?'

'May I?' The young man sat down in one of the chairs that scattered the downstairs area of the sail loft. 'Mr Quintell was hoping to avoid an unpleasant scene.'

'But I've got nothing to be ashamed of—'

'Quite so, quite so.' The lawyer opened his case. 'But Mr Quintell knows about your affair with Hans and is hoping to make a clean break—'

'Hold on, just a minute,' said Cordula. 'Should you be talking about this in front of all these people?'

'As I said, I've been given my instructions ... but if you would like this discussion in private?' Cordula checked the room. In fact only John and Hans were listening, everyone else was too busy drinking.

'Anyway, it's hardly what you'd call an affair, maybe once—'

'This afternoon, right here under this roof ... that would be—' The lawyer spoke in a matter-of-fact way without even looking up from his notes.

'He's sent you to do his dirty work. Well before I talk with you I can get my own lawyer—'

She was interrupted again. She had an uneasy sensation that the lawyer was anticipating all her responses. 'Cordula, of course, that is your prerogative but it is also just the sort of publicity and mental anguish that my client was hoping to avoid. And he wants to ensure that you don't feel abandoned. For that reason he has instructed me to convey to you an offer, a one-off, take-it-or-leave-it opportunity. I think you're going to find it a most interesting proposition.'

'Better 'ear this one out. I've seen theatre worse than this,' enthused John.

'Hans, you stay, but John – *out*.'

'Suits me. I've got things to do.'

Cordula waited until John had walked off, leaving her alone with the lawyer and Hans. The lawyer went on to play down her chances of a big settlement; they weren't married, Mr Quintell would claim that he had already materially helped Cordula's career with bookings.

'Well that's true,' said Hans. 'I can vouch for that.'

'Shut up, Hans. Whose side are you on anyway? So what's on the table then?'

'The harpsichord. That's what Mr Quintell is prepared to offer as a one-off gift, letting him walk away from the relationship with no commitment or claims.'

Cordula needed time to think. 'You mean this harpsichord? The one upstairs ... the Couchet?'

Again the lawyer checked his notes: 'Evaluated at three hundred and seventy-five thousand pounds.'

Hans whistled.

'What's the catch?' she asked. She couldn't believe it. This was very generous of Trevor: his precious instrument, much more than she had reckoned on. And she knew for a fact that the harpsichord insurance evaluation was on the conservative side. 'Is it really worth that much?' she asked.

'As I said, my client wants a clean break, so in return he is asking for you to sign this agreement stating that you agree to take the harpsichord as settlement in full. It transfers to your property with immediate effect – from the minute you sign, that is.'

'And this is a legally biding contract? He can't change his mind?'

'That's it, madam. Watertight. Mr Quintell was very particular about that. But of course, as I advised Mr Quintell, this is highly unorthodox and I should similarly advise you that of course you can instruct your own lawyers and we can start due diligence as early as next week—'

'Yes, I'm sure you lawyers would be more than happy to take your cut. Give me the pen!' she commanded.

'As I said, a highly unorthodox offer that you should consider most carefully—'

'Life has taught me, what's the phrase – *don't look a gift-horse in the mouth*? I don't need nurse-maiding. Sign here?' Cordula signed with a flourish, watched by the lawyer and Hans. She looked up at Hans, triumphant. Out of the corner of her eye she imagined she saw a face at the small corner window with bars across. But then she looked again and the face, if there ever was one, had vanished.

Outside the sail loft Trevor gazed up to the first floor where John stood with the harpsichord at the ready for its descent. Trevor put both his thumbs high up in the air.

'S'long, Trev, I'll miss you.' John leaned out of the large opening and responded by raising his hand in salute. In his other hand he held a rope holding the harpsichord suspended in mid-air. 'Send us a postcard from Rio.'

'Goodbye, John. See you at the next Palace garden party.'

'Na, not if I see ya first. Now hop it, some of us 'as work to do.'

Trevor waved, picked up his bag and disappeared into the lengthening shadows.

Now that Cordula owned the harpsichord she had a sudden desire to feel the gilded gold rails under her fingers; *Just think, nearly half a million*, she whispered to herself. 'Come on, Hans,' she said. 'Let's inspect our winnings.' She went outside the sail loft but then remembered the harpsichord was still upstairs. She looked up to see John manoeuvring some pulley. 'Careful with that, John. Hans will come up and give you a hand ... Hans.' Cordula motioned with her hand for him to go up and Hans went inside.

'So what's made you Florence Nightingale all of a sudden?'

'I told you be careful. You have—'

'Talkin' to me or chewing a brick? Wadda ye say?' John was leaning out.

'Never mind. It'll wait.' He was leaning out more. And he seemed to be having some trouble. Was it right that the instrument was swaying like that?

'Cordula?' John sounded anxious.

'I said it'll wait.'

'Bugger! Cordula, the knot's slipping. I can't hold it.'

She peered up into the gloom.

'*Run!*' roared John.

After that everything seemed to happen in slow motion. Cordula saw the harpsichord rushing towards her. The instrument had flipped through one hundred and eighty degrees and the lid was open to one side making it resemble a giant, one-winged bat. She managed to take a step back and was still close enough to feel the down force of air as the harpsichord smashed to the ground beside her. For a millisecond there was silence and then an almighty crashing noise. The sound of splintering wood mixed up with Top E's and F's and bass notes created a discordant harmony, like some unpublished composition from Stravinsky.

'You all right, doll?' shouted John. 'I'm coming down.'

'No thanks to you. That could have killed me.' And then Cordula remembered that was the least of her problems. It wasn't Trevor's harpsichord any more. It was hers. Her reward for seven years stuck with a lover twenty years her senior. Hans rushed out of the sail loft. John soon emerged from the shadows like a murderer in the final act of an opera. Onlookers crowded around the doorway. 'Damn you, John. I'll make sure you pay for this.'

'Slice of Friar Tuck ... luck ... missing you I mean.'

'You're hopeless ... why, if you were the last man and I was the last woman,' Cordula felt the rage rise within her, 'it would be the end of the human race.'

John was implacable: 'The thing about you, Cordula, no offence intended, but you haven't got enough of the superficial things that really matter.'

'Hans, did you hear that? Hans, I want you to defend my honour right now, this minute.' Hans didn't move. Of the lawyer there was no sign. He'd made a quick getaway, suspiciously quick. Surrounded by pieces of broken wood and twisted metal Cordula had the feeling that the whole thing was a set-up. A light drizzle started to fall. Something was missing. 'Has anyone seen Trevor?' she shouted and raced around the corner of the sail loft, just in time to see the tail lights of a car leave the drive – that must be the lawyer. 'Where's Trevor? Has anyone seen Trevor?' But there was no one to answer her. She was on her own in the driveway.

Something else was missing; the incessant sound of the starlings from the poplar trees had gone. Even in the fading light the trees looked green, motionless and empty.

'Bastard,' she whispered. 'You bastard!'

*

Little more than a hundred metres away Trevor was setting out on the footpath across the orchards with a curious gait that comprised a mixture of skips and hops. As the diminutive figure sauntered along, he sang a song to himself.

In the half-light of dusk and shadows the cloaked creature resembled more than ever a character from a different age and a different earth. He was still singing some time later as he climbed the wooden stile over the boundary fence of the village.

> *'Playing for the Queen,*
> *Oh what a scene!*
> *Shame about the toff,*
> *Music filled the loft.*
> *Palaces come 'n' go*
> *Dreaming Ri-o!'*

Black Christ

In a world that was disintegrating glance by glance, the blue walls of the medical centre stood imposing and safe, a reassuring reminder that some people still needed him. Ricardo rested his head against the side window. The joy of the new car smell, so important weeks ago, now seemed absurd. He would gladly exchange it for the moped he had as a medical student if he could have his lover back. *The magic has gone* ... The words running around in his head like a playground taunt. And the revelations were addictive. He wanted to punish his lover by enacting every last excruciating detail of the betrayal, but the more he heard, the more he suffered. They had talked and cried and argued until finally the sun loomed over the mountain and shone onto their balcony. Any other morning they would have embraced, lucky to share such a magnificent view and each other. Leaving for work this morning, it was as much as they could do to look at one another.

On the drive to his office he saw people out dressing the boulevards in purple. Tonight the Lord of Miracles carnival would begin. The streets of Lima would be brimming with people celebrating the twenty-four hour procession from Las Nazarenas church in downtown Lima to where the Black Christ picture was painted. Normally he would be looking forward to the evening. They would plan the best place to be and bars to visit – but tonight his lover would rather be with someone else.

Work. When he started out as a medical doctor he had high hopes of helping slum children who divided their time between streets by day and shacks by night. But then, to pay for his condo and fancy furniture, he had taken some private medical patients, part time. Soon afterwards the men came from behind their smart blue walls with their offer of a permanent contract at St

Lukes, the most prestigious private medical clinic in Lima. Now his main concern for the kids on the street was that they would scratch the paintwork on his limousine. He parked under the shade of an olive tree.

There was a *squack* of the central-locking system. *The magic has gone...* The words resonated to his heavy tread on the gravel path. Even on this cool morning sprinklers on expensive green lawns sprang into action. When he walked back this way in the afternoon nothing would have changed. His lover would still love another.

'Good morning, Doctor. Newly registered patient. Ten minutes.'

Ricardo smiled at Fabiola, devoted to him and her job.

He sat down and looked at the computer-generated internet booking. Man, thirty-eight years old, symptoms left blank: not much to go on.

He stared into space.

'Lorenzo Alvarez,' announced Fabiola.

When the patient walked in Ricardo had a feeling in the first five seconds and knew for certain within forty-five. He couldn't explain it to other people; gay people just spotted each other. It was a secret language of looks and gestures they had, most of them learnt since second or third grade.

Lorenzo Alvarez looked like a young Cary Grant but taller and darker, with short hair and strong features. He carried himself with the easy confidence of an athlete, muscles rippling under a tight-fitting white shirt. Some patients walked into his consulting room fearing the worst. Lorenzo looked like he'd walked in the wrong door. Attractive and desirable yes, but nothing compared to Augusto.

Augusto, five years younger than Ricardo with the body of a young god – love at first sight for him, but he was worried it would be a hopeless one-sided attraction. Ricardo didn't believe in God but in desperation he had struck a bargain: if Augusto became his lover he would go to Mass. For two years he went to Mass every Sunday.

Normally he liked a bit of small talk with the patient to break the ice, but this new patient sat down and got quickly to the point. There was a mole on his back he wanted to have checked out. 'Okay, let's have your shirt off,' said Ricardo, 'and I'll take a look at it.' Lorenzo was tanned, with a sculpted musculature that had taken hours of work; Ricardo guessed either the gym or, judging by the tan, more likely the swimming pool. The mole looked normal and regular, perfectly healthy. 'Any itching or change in size or colour?'

'Nope. Not a thing.'

'How often do you go swimming?' asked the doctor, going over to his desk to fetch a magnifying glass. Lorenzo looked surprised. Ricardo never got tired of seeing his hunches pay off. It was easier than it looked.

'Well, every day, I suppose. Just chilling out with a few drinks after work. I've just moved to a new condo with a pretty decent pool.'

'Yes, I notice you weren't registered here. So is it this side of town?'

'It's the new development, Reservoir Falls ... ouch!'

Ricardo had pressed a little too hard. Before he had been content to feel the soft, warm skin under his fingers; now he wanted to puncture it. 'Oh, I didn't know they were ready yet.'

'I've only just moved in, one of the first tenants. Got the pool to myself. But what do you think of the mole, anything to worry about?'

'You can put your shirt back on now,' commanded the doctor. Ricardo watched Lorenzo pulling the white shirt back over his smooth skin. He pictured 'Men at the Sea' by Edvard Munch that hung over their bed with purple sheets. Would Augusto want to take the print with him?

'So?' A turning of the Rodinesque shoulders. 'The suspense is killing me.'

'It's quite large but there's no sign of discolouration and the colour is light. You can always get it removed if you like, but then probably every person in Peru should get one done.'

'Just as I expected,' said the patient with quiet satisfaction.

Lorenzo went to sit down. 'What made you worried in the first place?'

'One friend just said I should get it checked out. Calls me angel, thinks I'm too good to be true,' boasted his patient.

And Ricardo knew who the friend was. After the first deal with God had succeeded so well he had lived in fear of losing the affections of his young lover who had never committed to another man before. Never even shared a flat. His second deal was that if Augusto moved in he would take the sacrament at Mass. Augusto moved in and he tasted the blood of Christ without fail every Sunday. He remembered how Augusto used to worry about him, at the start. When was it exactly that Augusto had stopped calling *him* angel? 'I don't suppose your friend recommended which medical practice?'

'No. I just chose the most expensive – private health insurance. Nice to get a clean bill of health before the party tonight. I hear it's quite a happening. I might try to get some tickets for the bull fight. I've never been. Plaza del Acho, isn't it?'

Every year Augusto had clamoured like a small boy, desperate to see the bull fight. With a sickening feeling in the pit of his stomach Ricardo realised that his lover hadn't even mentioned it this spring. He had already found his new partner; his new angel. 'How long ago did you say you moved here?'

'I didn't. But it was about ten weeks ago. End of July.' Lorenzo was gathering his jacket and sunglasses, looking like a patient who'd got the answer he was looking for. As far as he was concerned the consultation was over.

Augusto had said last night, or was it this morning: 'someone from the new Reservoir Falls development'. *End of July.* Just before he had started to notice things getting more complicated at home. *The magic has gone*... And it had started to go at the start of spring – Augusto's late nights in the office when he was a creature of pleasure, not of work. Ricardo should have seen the signs.

Ricardo had a new tune resonating in his head: *Is it destiny? Is it destiny?* He believed in fate and now, on the Lord of Miracles day, the prisoner had been delivered to his citadel. For a moment the doctor pictured the procession as it would be tonight: barefooted dancers moving along in a quick-step to Latin American music. Fate had delivered Augusto's lover to him and what he chose to do with the cuckold was up to him. But he needed to be quick and light on his feet. 'Is there anything else you would like whilst you're here... tests?' They both knew that the doctor was referring to HIV tests. Most gay men he knew measured their peace of mind from the time of their last test or last encounter, whichever was more recent.

'No, I'm fine and I'm careful.' Lorenzo looked at the doctor and smiled, full and sensuous lips. Is that why Augusto had preferred the young Lorenzo?

'Good, always best policy. But whilst you're here let's take your blood pressure. If you could roll up your sleeve for me.' Ordinarily Ricardo might have done it himself but he didn't want any distractions. He still liked to use the traditional mercury blood pressure gauge.

The first reading was high, one hundred and ninety over one hundred and twenty; maybe the young Lorenzo was feeling some attraction for him after all, he mused. The second was higher still, two hundred over one hundred and twenty-two. Hypertension, often no initial symptoms, the so-called silent killer. Good luck that he had come to see the doctor. 'Your blood pressure is a *little* on the high side,' he lied. 'Is there any family history of heart problems?'

'Well, yes, my father, but he was overweight.'

Looking at Lorenzo, obviously fit, the doctor guessed poor diet, too much drinking and a genetic predisposition. The sensible step would be an ACE inhibitor immediately and some straight discussion about lifestyle and diet, no delay. But still he paused.

'I see you smoke. How many a day?'

'Just social smoking, what three or four? Would that cause high blood pressure?'

'Not directly, but it can complicate things.'

His patient had lost the cloak of invincibility. Ricardo remembered Augusto desperate to explain: *I told him I wasn't cruising but he just laughed ... laid eyes all over me.* Ricardo saw anxiety written behind those same wide come-to-bed eyes. Lorenzo wasn't invincible. He could be beaten. 'Look, I think you really should get some medicine right away, just to be on the safe side. It's a public holiday starting and it may be difficult to find a chemist. I've got some starter packs. The pharmaceutical companies are always giving them out.'

'Thanks Doc. I appreciate it.'

Ricardo went over to the medicine cabinet and unlocked it. On the top shelf the ACE inhibitor medication for the treatment of high blood pressure; on the shelf below Midodrine, a treatment for hypotension. The small oval-shaped white tablets had a sustained impact on the heart rate, producing an elevation of blood pressure.

Looking at the rows of medicines Ricardo offered up to God another deal: if Augusto came back he would take the sacrament *and* he would go to confession. Was he inviting the ridicule of the Black Christ?

After Lorenzo had left he put the new patient registration form through the shredder. There was nothing to connect his patient with the clinic.

In contrast to the morning the almost summer heat of the afternoon promised a pleasant evening for the carnival and the scrunch of his leather shoes on the freshly raked gravel felt lighter; something had changed – hope. He squinted up at the olive tree where the cicadas were buzzing. Within seconds of turning the key in the ignition the car had acclimatised to twenty-two degrees but still he was sweating profusely. Ricardo treated himself to his first cigarette of the day and selected the music for the drive. He chose *Forza del destino*, one of his favourite operas. Turning out of the clinic grounds, he contemplated for a minute going home via the gym but it might be closing early for the holiday; diversion and street closed signs were starting to go up in the road.

He thought about Lorenzo Alvarez; any sudden shock could kill him. Augusto would be hurt but he was also young: he would recover, with the right support. The sellers were on the street selling homemade sweets. He saw an advert for the traditional bull fight: a matador with a swirling cape risking his life in front of a charging bull.

The Battle for San Vincente del Cerrito

Little Ofelia saw it first. 'Look! A giant orange!' she shouted.

When the *arribos* first made their appearance everyone was at work in the cocoa field. The children put down their watering cans and the fathers put down their machetes to stare at the large, silent, moving sphere, which had come from out of nowhere, brilliant orange against the blue Bolivian sky. It could have been a painting by Salvador Dali.

I wondered if any of them had ever seen a hot air balloon. I'd only ever seen them from a distance and this one looked like it was about to land. Soon it was enormous, blocking out the cliffs that bordered the sides of the cocoa field. The eerie silence was broken by a sound that I would then always associate with that miraculous arrival which was to change our lives forever. It had the villagers stepping back from the approaching novelty in alarm and me smiling at a memory; the unmistakable melody of bagpipes.

'Kerridge. Permission to dock, sir?' He was the first to jump out of the basket, with the bagpipes still under his arm. There was another four to follow. It was difficult to tell whether they were men or women, young or old, since they all had shaved heads and wore white cotton smocks. They smiled and went about their tasks without a word. One pair started the job of tying up their ship which was sifting on the breeze, docile like an elephant tired after a long journey. The other pair were bringing some bundle from the basket. But the villagers saw Kerridge first, the one with the magic pipes. They assumed he was the leader.

'Welcome to San Vincente del Cerrito,' I said.

'You're English,' Kerridge replied in surprise. He was the oldest of the group, perhaps fifty-five, bushy white eyebrows and a weatherbeaten face, someone who had spent a lot of time outdoors.

'Yes, that's what all the villagers call me. Not very imaginative but I like it. We don't have much to offer you, it's hardly a top spot for tourists.'

'Well, English. Don't apologise, this is the first civilisation we've met in a year.' That really surprised me. If he thought *this* was civilisation, where had they been? 'Look, we've got an injured man here. Have you got something that we could use as a stretcher?'

I realised that the bundle was a man, wrapped in a red and white sheet. Villagers were instantly hurrying to assist, entwining together to make a cradle of arms and helping hands. As the impromptu procession came closer I saw it wasn't a coloured sheet, just a white smock like the rest of them. He was *really* injured.

'What I need is a high table, water and a fire. Can you help? I'm Cam by the way.' A second man from the group introduced himself to me with a firm handshake. I was just about to show the way to the communal room or *celeiro* when the king arrived.

King Yanomami III dragged his left foot; his left eye was permanently half-closed. He didn't know in what year he was born but he remembered the first great war with Paraguay which, according to my *History of Bolivia* book, made him at least eighty. His kingdom stretched from the top of the valley in the north to the gorge in the south, about ten square kilometres. His subjects were the ninety or so villagers, if you counted the children and, for the time being, me. The king raised his wooden staff. 'Messengers from the gods delivered to save us,' he pronounced. Maybe he really thought it was that simple. I wasn't sure if he'd seen the bundle or not with his one good eye. He looked in my direction.

The villagers of San Vincente del Cerrito spoke Guyara – close enough to Spanish for me to get the gist of. I had questions queuing up like commuter trains at a mainline station but one thing I had learned in my nine months out here was patience. On the other hand we had a wounded man in our village square who looked like he was bleeding to death. Still, it doesn't do to upset a king. I translated: 'The king has declared a royal welcome to our honoured guests.'

The youngest of the group, about my age – I later found out she was Sofie and exactly my age, twenty-four – looked at me intently. 'That's great. Do thank the king and I wonder, could he help get things moving with the fire?' She had a lovely smile and a quizzical expression *plus* the most amazing green eyes.

In a surprisingly short time the one called Cam had supervised the construction of an emergency operating theatre in the *celeiro*. Bowls of steaming water were standing on a bench next to the long trestle table where the wounded man was lying. From his black bag he had produced a selection of surgical instruments, syringes and glass phials. All were laid out in a pattern of orderliness. Cam stood with a stethoscope around his neck. 'Some of these drugs are past their use-by date but I don't see Trevor complaining.' He was rolling up his sleeves as he spoke. 'All set?' He nodded to Sofie, who appeared to be his assistant. If he wasn't a doctor he must have been an actor. Sofie nodded back and Cam picked up a scalpel.

'Here, let me give you a hand with that. I'm Barraquer by the way.' My job was to keep the boiling water coming and the man who offered to help was about the same age and height as Cam, but there the similarity ended. Barraquer had a Latin American complexion compared to Cam's fair skin and freckles. I thought I was fit but Barraquer moved quickly and lightly on his feet, carrying pails of boiling water in the afternoon sun, as if he would never get tired. Throughout the afternoon we heard a few moans from the *celeiro*; the patient was still alive at least.

Word quickly spread: the gods had sent them to save us from Calvera and work for the day soon stopped. I saw boys going to gather yumanasa berries and mangos from the rainforest. A little while later we all heard the sounds of squealing pig.

The operation lasted about two hours. Villagers gathered around the *celeiro* and gossiped in groups. This was the sort of drama they enjoyed. Cam emerged into the sunlight. He had blood up to his elbows and a triumphant smile on his face. 'Was it a success?' I asked. 'Anything else you need?'

'A pint of best bitter?'

'Does he need a transfusion?'

'It wouldn't harm but judging by the pulse I'd say it's still a Class III haemorrhage – that means two or so litres of blood,' said Cam. 'Best of all the pulse has stabalised and we've stopped the bleeding. He'll need a new days to recuperate and lots of liquids. But I'd say he should pull through, just.' Kalugina, a muscular woman who was had been collapsing the balloon with the help of some villagers, came over. Cam nodded and she gave him a kiss.

The arrivals or *arribos* were given a room in the annexe next to the *celeiro*. With the exception of the small black bag that Cam carried and Kerridge's bagpipes they came empty-handed. What sort or people travel without luggage I wondered? I was keen to talk to them but they had other priorities.

Kalugina went to the patient and the others spread the balloon out on the ground behind the *celeiro* and started to inspect some large tears in the canvas. I was intrigued to see how they worked together. I saw exchanged looks and hand signals. I assumed (wrongly as it turned out) that this was a secret language developed by balloonists to make conversation unnecessary. I asked Sofie about the tears in the balloon canvas.

'We had a run-in with some pretty high overstorey trees. It's called an envelope, by the way,' she added with a smile.

'So you must be quite an experienced ballooning team, to end up here?'

'Our first flight actually. But you're right about the team bit.' She looked up at me. 'We've seen things you wouldn't believe.'

And that was as far as we got with that discussion as we were interrupted by the sound of the village gong. The feast had begun. Sofie looked at me and touched the sleeve of my jacket as if to say: *we'll talk more later.* Looking backwards on our brief time together I think I fell in love with her from this point. I thought what a sensitive person she was. I felt she needed my protection. Boy, did I miss the point!

You had to hand it to King Yanomami III, he knew just how to lift the spirits of his subjects. It was difficult to imagine anything was less than idyllic in that little cocoa grove of ours. The villagers had hung garlands of flowers around the *espacio* – the equivalent of our village green although more dried earth than grass. Food was laid out on tables and three pigs turned on spits above an open fire. There was music, dancing and some of our limited home-brewed beer. I made sure Cam got the first glass – it looked like he deserved it.

The villagers were taking turns working as sentries, at the perimeter of the valley. Calvera and his men could return at any time, we knew that. There wasn't much we could do when they did, but we'd learnt to get women and children into the caves, out of harm's way.

It seemed quite natural that I would be with the *arribos* and we sat at the same table. The children sat in an excited huddle on the ground, watching us intently. The bravest of them, little Ofelia, came forward to ask a question which I translated: 'Mister, is it true you have seen the dragons from the high plains?'

'Of course it is,' said Barraquer. 'Where do you think we got the hot air for our ship?' which got everyone laughing, except Ofelia whose eyes were wide in wonder.

'She's asking if you can draw the dragon' I translated. Barraquer got down to one knee and started to draw Ofelia a picture with a stick in the dirt.

I spoke with Cam to find out more about the operation. He told me had to remove a flint arrowhead from the stomach; a fraction to one side and it would have pierced an artery. 'Well,

English, I can see you're curious to find out about us. Ask me a question, anything you like.'

'Are you ... are you members of a religious group?'

He laughed. 'Quite the opposite I would say, fact is—'

'So, English, how long have you been around and why here?' Sofie decided to join in our conversation. She had the innate alertness and nimbleness of a monkey from the forest, avoiding attention and missing nothing.

'Nine months.' I told of my dream to write and my father's challenge. 'He didn't want me sitting around at home and told me: "If you are a real writer you can write even in the middle of nowhere." We had some trouble finding *nowhere* until one of his business contacts remembered buying cocoa from King Yanomami III.'

'Nine months in the middle of the rainforest with nothing,' said Sofie. 'Impressive.' Honesty compelled me to point out that I had a satellite phone and my PC. Internet was possible, although the solar-powered battery had its limitations. 'Still, internet connection ... might come in useful,' she said to no one in particular.

I was about to ask some questions of my own but she was ahead of me. 'So why don't you just tell us what's going on. It's obvious you're expecting some bad company sometime soon. And there's a definite feeling in the air that we are part of the solution but we need to know what the problem is.'

Kerridge surprised me next: 'You've got four guards on two-hour shifts.' He spoke without taking an eye off the dancing.

'You don't miss much.'

'Done me fair share of watches, English. I was hoping not any more, matey.' It was time for me to tell them about Calvera, our black cloud whose only silver lining was his own pocket. Every three months he turned up to take his share of the new cocoa crop. He sold it on to the Colombians who ground and refined it for their cocaine. The last two visits Calvera had raised his demands to fifty per cent. The whole village was almost starving and we didn't even have money for basic supplies. His next visit was already overdue.

'Why don't you change the crop?' asked Cam. 'Bananas, coffee or something?' I explained that cocoa was ideal for the village because it required minimal investment in infrastructure – it could be stored for months.

'But you could just say *no*,' said Barraquer, shaping his hand into a fist, 'to this thief, Calvera?'

'The last time they chopped down some of the mature trees – the shade protection for the crop ... also one of the girls, only thirteen, was raped – a lesson to us, they said. And they are armed. They come in truckloads.'

'Raped?' said Kalugina.

'They?' asked Cam.

'The *companeros* – bandits, devoted to Calvera.'

'How many *companeros* are we talking about?' asked Barraquer.

'Well I haven't counted but it's usually two trucks, forty at least.'

'Weapons?' asked Kalugina.

'Yeah, they all carry rifles and pistols,' I replied. 'They look like real bandits.'

'I meant do *you* have any weapons?' said Kalugina.

'Machetes aren't much of a match for automatic guns. We're farmers, remember.'

'But no real weapons?'

'Nothing, unless you count an abandoned machine gun.'

'Ammunition?'

'It's being rusting in the jungle since the last Paraguayan war. Anyway, we're all farmers here. Even if it did work who, would fire it?' Cam and Barraquer looked at Kalugina. The absence of hair accentuated a large face with strong features: a Roman nose and wide mouth. If Sofie was a monkey, Kalugina was the panther of the forest, strong and supple, she slunk around with a big animal's grace. I learnt later that upset Sofie and you might fear her quick tongue. Upset Kalugina? Well, you wouldn't want to.

After supper Kalugina asked to see the old machine gun. We found it rusting in the back of the storage shed amongst the broken farming implements. 'PPSh-41, Chinese Type 50,' she pronounced under her breath. She examined the mechanism and seemed not displeased. 'Straight barrel; that's good.' There was a box of cartridges but they were ruined, no gunpowder. She thought for a minute. 'Do you have any fertiliser?'

That was the one thing we still had good supplies of. 'Yes, but—'

'And oil?'

We were joined by Barraquer. He stopped in his tracks when he saw the machine gun and said nothing. His amazingly white teeth contrasted strongly with his dark, olive skin. He and Kalugina paused to smoke a cigarette. They were delighted when I had given them a packet earlier but enjoyed them sparingly. I still knew virtually nothing about the *arribos* but it looked like a strong will was mandatory. These two had a connection that was more than just tobacco. Time for me to return to the party.

I was woken by the sound of boys shouting. Calvera's convoy had been seen at the head of the valley, two trucks. The road down to the village was in poor condition. We had ten, maybe fifteen minutes if we were lucky. Women and children ran for the caves. There was only one road into the village and ten minutes later I was standing beside it. Sofie, Cam and Kerridge waited with me and the remaining villagers looked at them expectantly. But what could they do unarmed against trucks full of mercenaries? Of Kalugina and Barraquer there was no sign. When I look back on the Battle for San Vincente del Cerrito, this was one of my favourite memories. We weren't armed, we didn't have a plan and we didn't have a chance. Wrong on all counts.

*

The first string of machine-gun fire had the macaws rising into the forest in fright and a rain of dust exploding in front of the oncoming trucks. I realised later it was just a warning shot. Kalugina didn't miss, much. A number of Calvera's *companeros* jumped down from the trucks and started to fire indiscriminately into the forest. We were all running for cover amongst the trees. I had no idea where the machine gun was and neither did Calvera's men. The second wave of fire came in shorter bursts and was accompanied by men's screams. Parrots were flying squawking into the air and the monkeys started to throw coconuts down from the trees.

The *companeros* panicked. I suppose real resistance, machine-gun fire, was a new occurrence. Soon they stopped shooting and concentrated on picking up their wounded, whose cries were adding to the jungle cacophony. The trucks did U-turns before driving off at the highest speed the road would allow, leaving behind a cloud of dust like angry words left hanging in the air after an argument.

The villagers emerged from the sides of the forest, brandishing machetes above their heads and shouting. Kalugina and Barraquer climbed down from a makeshift platform which afforded them a birdseye view of the approach road. They must have been up all night.

The whole village was gathered in the *espacio*. Their gods, the *arribos*, had delivered their promise just as they had said they would. It was six hours after the rout of Calvera and the *arribos* were being treated to good food and a party atmosphere.

'Kerr-idge ... Kerr-idge,' the villagers were chanting. He had become their talisman. The *arribos* sat on low benches with bowls of roasted pork, looking somewhat bemused.

'Charcoal and fertiliser make good gunpowder,' said Kalugina, 'but I aimed low. What was the king telling them?' I explained that the villagers were clamouring for another holiday but the king had put his foot down.

THE BATTLE FOR SAN VINCENTE DEL CERRITO

'Good to see a royal family with a work ethic. By the way, I saw a couple of the children with swellings on their eyes,' remarked Cam. 'It looks like Chagas disease, nothing serious, but it should be treated before it becomes chronic and life-threatening.'

'Yep, they know all about it,' I said. '*Vinchuca,* they call it.'

'I don't understand,' said Cam. 'The antiparasitic treatment should be readily available and not expensive.'

'You're right. We used to have regular stocks. But you see, since Calvera started to take more of the cocoa harvest ... we ran out of money. So do we buy medicine or food?'

'I didn't realise things were so bad,' said Kerridge, who stopped eating from his bowl. 'I mean, what about the feast yesterday?' I told them it was the first time in months we had eaten pig and every week we had been making hard choices on what we spent our few coins on. We were running low on everything.

Kerridge handed his bowl to one of the villagers. 'From now on I eat what the cocoa farmers eat,' he said. 'And we've got plenty of coffee, right? I could settle here. Did you know that the king has three wives?'

'Kerridge, you amaze me,' said Sofie. 'A man with your looks and charm, why on earth would you settle for just *three*?'

'Got to leave someone for Trevor.' What I noticed about the *arribos* was that the higher the stakes, the more they larked about. This crew could handle pressure like I still had no idea.

'And how is Trevor?' I asked. I knew that once Trevor was fully recovered there would be no reason for the *arribos* to stay. I already dreaded seeing Trevor fit and well and I didn't like myself for thinking so.

'Trevor is like Lazarus,' said Cam. 'The colour is coming back to his cheeks. A few more days.'

More time for me to get to know Sofie and the others. I still knew hardly anything about them. 'So why don't you tell me your story?'

'Great coffee,' said Kerridge appreciatively, looking at the others.

'English, you don't think our story is over yet?' Kalugina asked me. 'Do you?'

'Now this is not the end, it's not even the beginning of the end,' declared Cam. 'Perhaps if we're lucky the end of the beginning.'

'Stirring stuff,' said Kerridge. 'Sounds good.'

'Not me. Churchill.'

Sofie smiled.

'But Calvera will think twice about coming here again,' I said.

'People like Calvera don't give up that easily,' said Kalugina.

'The best games often go to extra time,' added Cam before looking serious again.

'Yes, I see that now,' I said reluctantly. 'The odds haven't really changed. I mean there's only five of you.' I realised this sounded lame. 'Naturally, I'm in too.'

'And don't forget Trevor.' For the first time Barraquer spoke. 'My old boss would have loved it: 'Now we are seven.'

'Against truck loads of *companeros*,' I said. 'It's still not good odds.'

'We like the odds,' replied Cam, matter of factly.

'I thought you said you were with us, English?' Kalugina stared at me straight between the eyes.

I wondered: did I irritate Kalugina? 'Of course,' I replied. 'But still I don't get it, why do you want to stick around? Where are you going to anyway?'

'Because, English, what we've been through. *Stories have been told.*' Kalugina emphasising each word.

'About Calvera?' I was surprised.

'No, she means our own stories. Remember we've been together a long time,' said Sofie quietly. 'Running away isn't on the list of things we believe in.'

I wanted to kiss her, not because of any fine ideals but because she was feminine and pretty. The king was listening intently. I did a quick translation although I was starting to suspect he understood English better than he let on. I put it to him that a prolonged battle brought its own risks. What did he think?

He replied and I translated: 'At my age a little excitement is welcome. We lost the war against Paraguay because it had no meaning for us but this kingdom is my life's work.'

The king was with us.

'I've put my life on the line for worse causes than this.' Kalugina clenched her fist and nodded her head in support of the king. 'I say this is something worth fighting for.'

The group turned towards Sofie. 'I agree,' she said. 'And we must find a way to annul an enemy with superior firepower. We must think.'

Sofie's Odysseus to Kalugina's Achilles.

We talked about the possibilities to defend the valley. The trouble was that even if we blocked the road to the south, the north, with its network of tracks, was more difficult to protect. 'We can slow down the *companeros*. We can get in their way, be a nuisance even,' said Kerridge. 'But can we stop them?'

'What we need is a cure for the disease,' said Cam, 'not just a palliative.'

'You're right: an *in*. Okay let's talk about something else.' Sofie had fingers pressed to each side of her forehead. 'What do we know about Calvera? He is their effective strength.' She wanted to know details and I was keen to please. I described him. Sofie was interested he wore gloves. 'And he never takes them off? That's curious.' It encouraged me to mention something else – I noticed that on one of his visits Calvera had checked the seal on his bottled water before opening it.

We returned to the plans to best defend the village. 'Of course, it'd be a lot easier if we lived in a place like Calvera's,' I pointed out.

'What do you mean?' asked Sofie. So I described Calvera's mountain top hideaway – a natural fortress surrounded by rocks and accessible only by a single track from the gorge below. We shared the same river but there the similarity ended. Our river ran through a wide valley, upstream at Calvera's the sides became a steep gorge, sheer cliffs and impossible to climb. It made the *castillo* easy to defend.

'That's right,' chipped in Kerridge, 'we saw the gorge from the balloon.'

'At the *castillo* they can see anyone on the approach road miles away, a surprise attack is impossible,' I reiterated. 'Just the sort of natural defence we don't possess.' After more discussion going round and round, the meeting broke up. As far as I could see we still hadn't got any closer to the *in* that Sofie was after.

One decision we did make was to double the guards at both ends of the valley. Some of the villagers were keen to build a roadblock until it was discovered that Kalugina only had cartridges enough for a few rounds of machine gun fire. The villagers lost motivation after that and returned to work in the fields but much of the time they looked anxiously over their shoulders. The next day one of our sentries spotted one of Calvera's men. It looked like the enemy were getting a feel for our strength – or lack of it. They wouldn't be ambushed a second time. There were mutterings in the *espacio*. Some villagers were saying that the *arribos* only made things worse with Calvera: 'They will turn the village into a graveyard.'

The night after the attack Kalugina announced a council of war. There were six of us; Trevor was still recuperating in bed. 'I think I've found us an *in*,' said Sofie. 'Barraquer, today you were showing Ofelia how to use the spinning top.' She picked it up and spun and dropped it to the ground. It made a few revolutions and then spiralled ever slower before dying on its feet.

'You're as bad as Ofelia,' said Barraquer. 'That's the wrong way up.' I'd complimented Barraquer earlier on the hand-carved wooden top. I remembered his somewhat cryptic reply: 'You can master anything with enough time.'

'Like Ofelia, we've been looking at this from the wrong way up,' she continued. 'All the time we've been thinking how to best defend and you bet Calvera is thinking how to best attack.' Sofie turned the top and with minimum effort sent it spinning. 'We need to turn the thing on its head. We're sitting on a secret weapon.'

'But they know about the machine gun,' I said.

'Wooden tops. Wooden horses.' Sofie stood up. Hands on hips. 'Calvera is in for a surprise. ...'

The top was still spinning and Cam was laughing. 'I've got it, wooden horse. Element of surprise,' he said. 'Of course, it depends a lot on the wind direction.'

Sofie tossed a blade of grass into the air. 'Where did you say that Calvera's retreat was?' I pointed up the valley in roughly the same direction as the grass had blown to the ground.

'Nor-nor-west,' added Kerridge, never without his compass.

'It just might work,' said Cam, 'If anyone can pull it off, you can.'

'Perceptual geography,' said Sofie. 'Take him out in his own backyard and we'll break the spell. Calvera is master from one end of the valley to the other. When we own Calvera, we own the valley.' I didn't know what either of them was talking about. But they looked plucky and confident.

After ten minutes the rest of us were starting to share the enthusiasm. 'Still, an awful lot could go wrong,' I said.

'Let's roll the dice,' Sofie picked another blade of grass, 'and feel the fear in our enemy's eyes.'

'Churchill?' asked Kerridge.

'Coldplay. English, couple of things,' said Sofie. 'Can I borrow your laptop and your satellite phone?'

'Sure, I can show you how it works.'

'Also we should try to get our hands on some corrugated iron.'

'There's always the storage shed roof.'

The next morning I saw Sofie's fingers moving like a concert pianist's across the keyboard of my laptop. She looked up at me and smiled. 'Smart piece of kit, English. They've got even faster since we've been away.'

'Anything I can do to help?' I asked after a while, pretty sure there wouldn't be.

'Yes, you could get me the GPRS co-ordinates for the clearing next to the bridge, the one with the big rock in the middle.'

'You mean the Egg. But how?' Sofie showed me how to make a GPRS positional mark with the phone and I set off to walk up the side of the river the five kilometres or so to the Egg, in a state of frustration. It was baking hot and I was sweating after the first hundred yards. I was twenty-four years old. I'd dreamt of sleeping with hundreds of women and so far made love to three of them. The chances of Sofie joining this select club seemed slim.

I was still thinking of this roughly eighteen hours later standing in a wicker basket at two thousand feet looking down on the forest, intermittently shrouded with wraith-like ribbons of mist. Sofie had declared the early morning wind ideal: north-west. It meant air currents were calm and predictable and the direction was almost directly up the line of the gorge. Besides me in the balloon were Sofie and Kalugina, Cam, Kerridge and Barraquer. I wondered how many of us would climb out. At around five in the morning the forest was already starting to wake up. A flight of pelicans on morning patrol passed just below the basket. Nobody spoke.

My first trip in a balloon. What struck me was how big everything was. The basket was about three metres square and the envelope billowed above us – big as a house. We travelled in a cocoon of silence interrupted only by the intermittent burst of sound from the hot air burner that Sofie controlled – she was the pilot and Kerridge the lookout. Our primary target was the *castillo* itself on the mountain top. If that failed we would have to think of a plan B.

I had always thought that balloons just went with the wind.

Earlier Sofie had explained that she could change direction up to ninety degrees with the different wind currents at different altitudes but no amount of skill or luck could get the balloon to sail upwind. So after the *castillo* we would make a second landing; downwind, where hopefully six villagers handpicked by the king and me, our support crew, would be waiting.

'Tricky stuff to steer,' I said to Kerridge.

'I wasn't sure about Sofie to start with either,' he replied. 'But that was before she landed our plane on a lake. She saved all our lives that day.'

'Did you say ... lake?'

Kalugina looked to us and frowned. We were on a mission and up here sound travelled far. Silence again, only interrupted by the occasional burst of the gas burner.

The first deviation from our plan was movement under some blankets in a corner of the basket. We found a wide-eyed and frightened Ofelia. 'I didn't want you ... want you to leave without me,' she said between tears.

The evening before, the villagers had stood and watched in silence as we had inflated the balloon in the late sunlight. No doubt some were happy to see the back of us but the rest of them watched in silence before walking away with a collective dejected sloping of shoulders. The bulk of the village, like Ofelia, had no way of knowing we were planning on a return. Ofelia was five years old but looked younger, and had quickly become a favourite of the *arribos*, especially Barraquer.

'This is no place for a small girl,' said Barraquer. 'We should turn back.' He was overruled.

We sailed on. Nobody spoke until Kerridge pointed to a smudge on the horizon where the gorge kinked to the right. For a minute I thought it was a low-hanging cloud. 'Look, there it is.'

Sofie fired the burner. 'The higher you go, the more the current veers to the right,' she explained. Sure enough a few hundred feet higher I saw the change in direction. We were flying straight for the mountain top. Kalugina had a knife tucked into a belt at her waist. Back at the village I had asked about the guards. 'Leave that to me,' had been her reply.

I'm still amazed the way that Sofie mastered the balloon. Just when it looked like we were veering off course she had an uncanny instinct to drop or gain height to choose the right current from the invisible myriad of wind layers. I'd heard of three-dimensional chess. This was three-dimensional sailing. She allowed herself a smile of satisfaction as we reached a position directly above the *castillo*. High walls of grey stone made a seamless line between rock and battlements. Inside the walls was a large plateau where we planned to land: the DZ.

The last twenty metres were the worst. I saw Kalugina cross herself as we approached the top of the old fortress.

'All set, everybody?' said Sofie quietly.

'Remember, when I say *Run!*' whispered Kalugina. Kerridge made hand signs that now seemed appropriate. Not for the first time I wondered: *were the arribos military?* Kerridge pointed out two armed guards, looking out over the valley. But just as the balloon had surprised us in the cocoa fields our noiseless arrival caught them unawares.

Kalugina must have leapt from the basket before we even touched the ground. I saw her advancing on the plateau just as we landed. One guard started to walk hesitantly towards her, pulling a rifle down from his shoulder. Kalugina was a phenomenon. Empty-handed, she eschewed walking or running and instead cartwheeled across the plateau. The guard, bemused, stopped to watch this perfectly co-ordinated sphere of arms and legs spinning towards him out of the shimmering light. The distance from the balloon to the sentry was about ten metres and Kalugina covered the ground in two or three seconds. She knocked him out with an outstretched foot to the throat. Senseless with one blow.

'Where did you learn to move like that?' I asked her later. 'Moscow State Ballet,' she told me. 'Hated it – and the boys there, ugh!'

The other guard raised his rifle. Kerridge marched straight up to him and, ignoring the pointed weapon, punched him straight on the chin. He collapsed like a falling building. Then from out of the shadows a third guard, one we hadn't seen before, started to flee from the mountain top. Just when I was starting to think this could ruin everything there was a whisper of wind and he fell to the floor without a cry. Kalugina's knife rested between his shoulder blades.

'On *me!*' she hissed. As moths go after light we followed Kalugina towards the enemy, regardless of what lay ahead.

The *castillo* was built on many levels. The top, with the wide plateau, and a few rooms built into the sides of the *castillo* walls were the safest. This is where we expected to find Calvera's quarters. The first room was the guards' room, empty. In the next we found Calvera, asleep. It was my job to identify Calvera which I duly did. His distinctive moustache and fox-like features made him unmissable. He was alone. Morning light was just seeping in through the stone windows that overlooked the valley.

'Now!' said Sofie.

'Cam had the syringe at the ready and quickly inserted it into Calvera's arm. Calvera struggled, blaspheming in Spanish, but Barraquer and I kept him down and before you could count four *wood-peck-ers* the anaesthetic had taken its hold. Barraquer picked up the drugged bandit like a sack of potatoes and carried him to the balloon.

'Quick!' whispered Kalugina. 'We don't know how much time we've got. There may be more sentries.' Amazingly we had got away with it. The whole operation had taken less than five minutes.

'Where's Ofelia?' asked Barraquer, back at the balloon. 'I told her to stay in the basket.'

'I didn't see anything,' said Kerridge, who had stayed with the basket. 'She must have crept out of the back, followed you.'

'Give me two minutes,' said Barraquer.

'Just find her,' said Sofie. 'We'll wait as long as we can.' Now I was nervous. It was getting lighter by the minute and the balloon, pulling at its tethering rope, looked how I felt; ready to go. We heard shots.

'Prepare to let go of the rope,' said Sofie.

Barraquer came racing from Calvera's quarters towards the balloon. He was carrying something in his arms – Ofelia. Half a dozen *companeros* shouting in Spanish were running about thirty metres behind. Another shot rang out and he fell. Almost before I had realised it had happened Cam and Kerridge leapt as one out of the balloon and raced over to pick up Barraquer. He still held Ofelia in his arms. They moved towards us like a wounded crab. Arriving at the basket the men reached up and heaved Barraquer and the girl over the side. Something dropped.

'Cast off!' shouted Kerridge.

The balloon lurched upwards and I jumped out of the basket. My instinct was right. At the last moment Ofelia had slipped between the men and the basket. I picked her up. She was light like a rag doll. I think it was Kerridge leaning out of the balloon who leaned down as I reached up to hand the young girl to safety. Within a second the balloon basket was a couple of metres from the ground, tantalisingly close but out of reach. Was it also instinct that made me keep running downwind of the balloon as it rose in the air behind me?

I kept going a further twenty yards, glancing over my shoulder. I saw the guards were getting nearer. When I heard their breathing I stopped and turned around.

Alone, I faced my execution squad. Five men in a line. They were roughly dressed, moustached and none of them looked in negotiating mood. All carried rifles. The shouting had ceased. There was nowhere for me to run to and they had no reason to hurry. I prepared to die. I remember thinking it was a beautiful morning and this was my last sunrise. Only a minute ago I had been with the others. I thought I'd never kiss Sofie ... I'd never write a book ... I'd never ...

Then I realised it wasn't the sun, it was the balloon coming

THE BATTLE FOR SAN VINCENTE DEL CERRITO

back. The basket was bearing down on the *companeros* but too far to the right. I saw Kalugina waving wildly and I understood. For the balloon to hit the *companeros* I had to get them into its line of travel – much easier for me to manoeuvre than the balloon. I started walking briskly towards the northern end of the plateau. There was no escape, just a sheer cliff falling five hundred feet to the gorge below and step by step the guards followed. One of the *companeros* shouted out '*Parada!*' I risked a further two paces to the north. So did they. Now we had them just where we wanted. They raised their rifles. A couple of them were grinning, enjoying the situation. I figured either way I had seconds left. The balloon was returning from the blind side in a straight line towards the row of men and they had no idea of what was about to hit them. I thought of a giant ball in a bowling alley. The *companeros* took aim. Now only four feet off the ground, the basket traversed across the plateau.

The heavy basket spread the companeros like scattered skittles.

'*English!* Grab the rope man!' commanded Kerridge.

I looked up, bewildered. The balloon was already moving fast away from me.

'English. RUN!'

That's what got me going; that shout from Kalugina. I sprinted after their outstretched arms. Before I knew it strong hands were pulling me up and depositing me in a heap on the floor of the basket. 'English, you did good,' said Kalugina before attending to Barraquer.

Now I appreciated the corrugated iron sheets that Sofie had laid on the floor. They reverberated and jumped to the bullets from receding rifle fire.

Watching Barraquer die in the balloon was the hardest thing I ever saw. Cam did the best he could but his worried look told us Barraquer's fate from the start. 'Not good news I'm afraid,' was all that Cam managed to say.

Before Barraquer died he spoke in a low voice to Kalugina. We wanted to give them privacy but in the confined space there was none. 'Remember hunting the Chisgo, you have to find the Chisgo and ... Kalugina ... great times, wouldn't have missed—' Then he sighed his last breath.

Kalugina watched him for a minute before she shut his eyes. I'm sure she'd seen death before. For the return flight she stood with an arm around Ofelia looking over the jungle.

The silence was heartbreaking.

'We've still got a job to finish,' said Sofie.

At the second DZ our support crew had been waiting with some of the village canoes. We paddled the dugouts downstream past the rainforest and cocoa fields to San Vincente del Cerrito, keeping a watchful eye for any *companeros* lurking on the river bank, but the only company we heard was the *cribbits* of tree frogs. During the journey Calvera had shown signs of waking but Cam had delivered him another shot. We needed him unconscious.

Arriving at the village the feeling of relief in the air was palpable. The villagers could see that the *arribos* had come back and what's more we'd returned with their arch enemy. I explained to them that celebrating had to wait.

It was time for phase two of the plan and Cam had work to do.

'You left the note?' Kerridge asked me for the second time – he was feeling the pressure too. I confirmed that I had left the letter – in which we informed the *companeros* in Spanish that if they wanted their chief back he would be ready for collection at the Egg at noon. It was already ten o'clock, and hot. There was a lot to do and we were all conscious that the unpleasant task of burying Barraquer still lay in front.

Calvera started to wake up on our journey to the Egg. I think when he realised he was still alive he was surprised. He held his side, lying in the back of the only vehicle of San Vincente del Cerrito, an open lorry that smelt of cocoa that bounced and jolted along the rutted jungle track. The Egg was about five kilometres away. We had to be there before noon. Sofie had made me be very specific about this point in my note. The king had insisted on accompanying us.

'They're on time, good,' said Sofie checking her watch as we arrived at the meeting point. The *companeros* had parked their two lorries in front of the enormous piece of black granite rock, a landmark for miles around. Sofie instructed us to park our own lorry a few hundred yards away under some palm trees. We were to walk the last metres to the rendezvous.

Calvera understood it to be good news when he saw his well-armed personal army had come to collect him. On the nod from Sofie I explained the terms of our truce: Calvera returned to his men on the condition that the people of San Vincente del Cerrito and their cocoa harvest were left in peace.

'Thiz is easy. This next day when I be feelin' a little stronger—' Calvera put his hand to his stomach. 'Mebe then we, how do you say, we av ourselfes another parlez. Ow you say ... *negociar*, negotiate more. We iz seeing again. Mebez you bring some nice young girls, like the last time. No?' And he turned to wave an outstretched arm to his heavily armed supporters, chuckling.

So Calvera could speak English. Sofie decided it was time to play her ace. 'Kerridge, would you be so good as to lift Mr Calvera's shirt?' There was a gasp as Calvera saw for the first time the six-inch scar that ran to one side of his stomach. It was swollen and the bandage was dark red in dried blood. 'You see, Calvera, you really should take it easy you know; you've had a little operation, for *our* own good you might say. Our doctor,' she pointed at Cam, 'has inserted a container of deadly poison into your stomach that is inactive as long as the villagers stay safe. It's completely harmless unless someone operates this radar remote control.' She held up my old MP3 player. 'One press of this button and the poison is released. How quickly would you say it works, doctor?'

'Two to three minutes,' said Cam. 'Time to say your prayers.'

'So you see, Mr Calvera. We have an insurance policy. And we have two controls. The king has his own and I have one. One nod or phone call or word from the king or his son and I press this button. Am I clear?'

When Sofie had heard Calvera was a hypochondriac she and Cam had cooked up this plan. Of course there was no poison, just like there was no remote control in my MP3 player, but there is nothing as powerful as an idea that has taken root, *a continuous itch*, said Sofie.

Calvera had turned a shade of white. She was clear. She checked her watch again. 'Oh, one last thing. Your men have just under one minute to leave those trucks.' Calvera looked blankly at her. Sofie looked back and checked her watch. 'Forty-five seconds.' Sofie looked to the sky and Calvera's eyes followed hers.

'*Fuera rápida! Rápida!*' he commanded. The men, many of whom had followed this conversation, ran for the jungle. Calvera had better eyesight than me. I saw them a split second later: two American Typhoon fighters that came coursing across the valley, each flying one side of the Egg. Some last remaining *companeros* leapt out of the lorries. The jets peeled away, each in its own large arc and the sound of thunder rolled across the tree tops towards us. They reunited to return side by side, blazing back down towards us like a rush of blood to the head. This time there was a twin flash of light and smoke coming from underneath the planes. Two rockets. Two lorries. I was pleased we were standing well back. By now I had my hands over my ears. I had a feeling of *déjà vu*; *companeros* running for the forest.

'The King of San Vincente del Cerrito has friends in high places,' said Sofie to an open-mouthed Calvera. The fighters screamed away, banking over the jungle canopy, leaving behind two burning lorries and a lot of scared men. Calvera returned to his *companeros*, visibly shaken. The king was smiling from ear to ear.

'Pretty impressive, Sofie,' said Kerridge. 'How on earth did you do that?' It seemed that no one knew that Sofie had a second ace up her sleeve. I guess that the GPRS co-ordinates of the day before and my PC had something to do with it.

'One day, Sofie,' said Cam, 'you are going to have to stop surprising me like this.'

'You know there is a new theory in the Pentagon that drug money is used to fan the flames of terrorism,' Sofie continued matter-of-factly. 'Once you've hacked inside the CIA computer system pretty much anything is possible ... as long as you're a patriot.'

'You're not kidding,' said Cam.

'And it helps that Americans also still love the word *cavalry*.' We stood there in the scorching heat of the middle of the day. It was only noon and I felt I'd been awake for a week.

'Come on,' said Sofie. 'We may have won a war but we still have to pick up the balloon.'

'And honour the dead,' said Kalugina.

'Zadok the Priest,' said Trevor. 'If we were making a film I think that's the music we should have for the descent to the *castillo*.' It was two days later and Trevor, looking quite fit, started to play a familiar tune on the marimba, a large xylophone-type instrument, played with wooden mallets.

'You sound really good,' I said. 'I'm sure you could earn money playing like that.'

'Why thank you, English. I'll be certain to remember that.' I had enjoyed getting to know Trevor especially, since he was the one who was happy to tell me everything about the *arribos*. He explained how they had been on a small charter flight with a dozen passengers from La Paz in Bolivia to Rio de Janeiro when the captain had a heart attack. Sofie had landed the tiny plane on a lake on the Altiplano.

'Lucky for us she was on board. As soon as she got into the cockpit you could see that she'd flown before.'

'But you said there were thirteen survivors. Where are the others?' Trevor explained they had been rescued from the lake by some monks. 'They took us back to a walled monastery and that's when our real troubles with the Owslafa began,' he told me.

'The what?'

'Religious fanatics, from Holland originally. To start with they said we just needed to build up our strength for the long trek, but then it became clear there was never any intention of a departure.'

'You were prisoners?'

'The Owslafa. I wonder how the others are coping?'

'You didn't try to escape?' I asked.

'In the beginning we talked of nothing else. Julia was the only one who seemed genuinely happy to be there; she liked the silence and the stillness. But then things changed. Stockholm syndrome it's called, I believe.'

'That's when you end up liking your kidnappers?'

'Right. After a while we were splitting into two camps, *us* you know, and the others who just lost interest in getting away. In the monastery there was no violence and occasional acts of kindness, so long as we kept to the rules.'

'Rules?'

'They forbade us to speak between sunrise and sunset. "Meditation is good for the soul," they told us. They shaved our heads – and the clothes. We waited for the evenings – we told each other stories.'

So that explained the secret language of hand movements and gestures. 'What about during the days? What did you do?'

'What could we do? Barraquer learnt woodcarving. Julia and Perkins played their own invention of fantasy Test match cricket. Erik invented this crazy game, *Déjà vu*, which I never got the hang of. We wrote down our stories – somehow that seemed more positive than writing last letters home – we spent a lot of time on that. Trevor showed me a thick pile of single pages tied together with rough home-made string that I hadn't seen before. 'But most of all we dreamed of escape – those who still wanted it.

I've been reminding myself of them. The ones we left behind: John, Yvonne, Erik – what a character – Julia, Tom and Perkins, he kept our spirits up. Some wonderful people—' Trevor paused, his hand resting on the pages.

'So what happened? How did you escape?'

'The Owslafa knew we were planning something, so they took Michael. They put him in solitary confinement.'

'What happened?'

'English, I'd love to know. But he must have been brave because he never told them about the balloon. By then we'd already found it. Poor Michael, in the end we decided not to wait for him. I still don't know if that was right.'

'It seems we weren't the first prisoners, nor the last either. I'm lucky to be alive. You don't know how that feels.'

'You mean when you were wounded?'

'Don't forget the crash landing.' My own thoughts returned to the bowling alley on the plateau.

'Maybe that's the biggest surprise in life, English. When I turned fifty I thought that's it, life can't be as much fun any more. But life is wonderful. It just keeps on getting better and better.' As I left Trevor was hammering out 'What a Wonderful World' on the wooden bars. And he was right; on the third evening after the battle for San Vincente del Cerrito was won, Sofie took me to bed.

'Normally you'd have to wait much longer,' she told me, 'but a year locked up with religious fanatics does wonders for the sex drive.'

She wasn't joking.

For a week the wind blew warm and steady from the south. We were invaded by butterflies, some of them as big as your outstretched hand, and the most amazing bright colours: blues, greens and yellows. I had never been happier. I suppose, like every lover since Adam, I wanted to know when Sofie first felt something for me.

'When you went back for Ofelia. I thought that took real guts. I saw you differently after that.'

'Nothing compared to you. I was scared as hell,' I said.

'Bravery is when you conquer fear. One per cent of people don't feel fear. I think Kalugina may be in that category, but for the rest of us, for you and me, conquering our fears is one of the meanings of life.'

For you and me – how often I would repeat that mantra to myself in the weeks, months and years ahead.

'So what about landing the plane on a lake. Were you scared then?'

'Mad not to be. Cam was with the captain, heart attack. Someone had to have a go. I'd never flown before—'

'But Trevor said—'

'Listen, English, can you keep a secret?' Sofie looked at me. Her hair had started to grow a thick dark brown, and in tangles that gave a suspicion of curly hair to come. I nodded. 'Truth is, I learnt to fly on my brother Paul's PlayStation. He had a game called "Night Fighter" which I got pretty good at. But you must promise not to tell the others.'

I promised. 'I suppose you've never had a lover before either?'

'Not like you I haven't!'

If I didn't know it already, those hot sultry nights with the incessant chorus of cicadas and sounds of the jungle confirmed to me that Sofie was spontaneous, complicated and the most incredible person I had ever met.

Then one morning I woke up and the breeze felt refreshing and cool on the skin. It was coming from the north and we both knew what that meant.

The liquid gas containers had been refilled in readiness and the villagers had stocked the basket with fresh fruit and water. The whole village assembled to say goodbye to the *arribos*.

Kerridge, who had each arm draped around a village woman,

half his age, said he wasn't going. 'Enough long journeys on my watch. I think I'll stick around here a while.'

We waited for Kalugina who had gone to pay her last respects to Barraquer's grave. 'He's not dead, just living in my head,' she had told me once, which I thought a strange way of looking at it. Kalugina remained a mystery to me.

I was nervous saying goodbye to Sofie. 'Rio de Janeiro is about one thousand four hundred miles as the crow flies,' she had earlier told me. I would ask Sofie her telephone number if she had had one, and she wasn't the sort of person to be tied to a landline 'But Sofie, how can I ... I mean if you wanted to, how can I—'

'English, what's your real name?' she asked me for the first time.

'It's Andy.'

'Okay, Andy. You said you wanted to be a writer and you came out here to get some ideas. Well – catch.'

She threw me the parcel of papers tied up in homemade string.

'Write the book and leave me a clue somewhere in the pages. I'll find it and I'll find you. And that's a promise.' The others were climbing into the basket. Kerridge was giving them hugs and to Sofie he gave his precious brass compass.

'You really want us to make Rio, don't you?' She appreciated the gesture and took the compass, then added for my benefit: 'And don't let Kerridge persuade you into writing any exaggerations about any of us. We're none of us gods, you know. So long, Andy.' Sofie winked at me. 'It's been fun.'

'Preparing to cast off,' said Kerridge who had untied the tethering ropes from the stake in the ground. 'After this I really am retired, shipmates.'

'Are you sure you won't change you mind, Kerridge?' said Cam. 'When we get to Rio I'm going to treat all the others to an ice-cold beer. I know just the bar, with aluminium bar stools. A real piano for Trevor. And the best beer in Latin America.'

Kalugina joined in: 'Come on, we can't stand all day watching you two lovebirds. I've got unfinished business after Rio. Some of us have got connecting flights.'

The villagers of San Vincente del Cerrito waved and cheered as the *arribos* rose into the air. I was hoping that this was the beginning of my story with Sofie but watching the balloon rising orange and majestic into the blue Bolivian sky, it felt like ... the end.

Epilogue

'A man who has been through bitter experiences and travelled far enjoys even his sufferings after a time.'

Homer, *The Odyssey*

For days and weeks afterwards I cursed myself for not getting into the balloon with Sofie. I suppose the point is that she never asked me to. That's what ate me up. But after a while thinking about it I realised that Sofie had probably been doing just that; thinking about it. I needed more time to grow up.

It's been two years since that goodbye and we've not exchanged a word since but I feel she's getting closer. I remind myself that Odysseus took ten years to return from Troy.

And it's not like I've been just sitting around, I've been busy working with the stories. The publisher was all for getting a team of ghostwriters and copy-editors on the manuscripts, 'finding a voice' Miles called it, but where possible I wanted to keep the original voices. The way I see it, it's not my book, it's theirs. So you are reading mostly first-hand accounts. A lot of the stories I've hardly touched. Of course, with some like Black Christ and Wheel of Fortune, I had more work to do – more of that in a minute.

The news of the forthcoming book created ripples like a stone thrown into a pond. Anyone who had a friend or relative missing in South America wanted to know if I could give any answers. Letters were forwarded from the publishers every day. I was starting to dread the arrival of the postman. Then one day I received a postcard from Erik in America, a Buick on the front, and he had written: *After the getaway the balloon really went up – oh boy! Perkins and I planned our own escape from the Bastille but the Owls did for Perkins – who were those dudes?!*

Please pass my mailbox no. to the others. I enclose Michael's Bible. RIP. PS Tell 'em I'm terrified of heights – ONLY reason I couldn't go – period.

With the letter came a worn copy of a Bible. Only later, by complete chance, the secretary that Miles kindly lent me to help with all the correspondence came across the Bible and worked out that the pencil markings weren't random. Wheel of Fortune must have taken days and days to write. I know because it took me nearly a week, and all the way to the Book of Job, to get it down. I did want to do something for the memory of Michael – without his defiance of the Owslafa, Sofie and the others might never have escaped – so I wrote Tunnel.

Erik had a mailbox and I wrote twice but received no reply. More encouragingly I had a letter from a doctor's secretary working in Lima, Peru. She told me that her boss had committed suicide when he had heard of flight CF 861 from La Paz to Bogota, missing and presumed lost. She enclosed a copy of his suicide note – the doctor wrote that if he had known the patient was a pilot he would never have written the prescription. But that letter became the basis for Black Christ.

Finding the truth about the pilot encouraged me to dig further into the other stories. What surprised me was how difficult it was to get even basic information on flight CF 861. There was no passenger list – apparently not uncommon for small charter flights in Latin America. What did get column inches in the quality newspapers back home was Trevor Quintell missing, presumed lost, but that was before I had left for Bolivia and I had no reason to pick it up.

Some things were easy to verify; Dermot Young is still competing and winning on the seniors' tour – I've changed his name of course but anyone who follows golf may have a pretty good idea of his real identity. The Hick-Boo, I discovered, was an invisible goblin in a fairy story written just after the war, who lived in a cupboard and helped his tailor creator to make a fortune. I never contacted Dermot for obvious reasons; he wasn't going to corroborate the magic putter! I'm assuming the only person who could is still in the monastery.

Did they ever get to Rio?

I was starting to think I would never get an answer to that question but then I had a couple of lucky breaks that convinced me they did.

First off, Trevor Quintell's residential address in England was a matter of public record and from there the inimitable John and splendid Larkrise were easy to find. John was very pleased to see me, a great host, but when I raised the subject of Trevor or Trev, he clammed up. Just before leaving I was in the kitchen for a glass of water and I saw a postcard from Rio on the fridge door. Coincidence? Maybe, but ringing him to thank for the hospitality a few days later I was informed John had gone on a long holiday – why hadn't he told me that when I was there?

I also tracked down Cordula, playing second violin at Sadler's Wells. She was keen to get back in touch with Trevor and was (I think) slightly interested in me until she discovered I was nothing but an unpublished author.

Because of Barraquer's last words to Kalugina I was particularly motivated to find out about the Chisgo. Then came my first real break. Following the trail of his pop star wife brought me to Guildford Police Station. Chaz, or Chisgo, had died about six months after the balloon set sail for Rio and an open verdict had been recorded. I could tell the police sergeant wasn't telling me everything and we arranged a drink at a local pub.

She was called Julie, freckled and she had something of Sofie about her – the green eyes and the quick mind – but there was no real comparison. After a couple of drinks she did admit that the pop star husband death was being treated as suspicious: there had been signs of *torture*. What really got me interested was hearing that the police were drawing similarities between this and Sir Rufus Sinclair's sudden death a few weeks later. She was convinced that someone high up was *trying to keep the lid on it* –

her emphasis. But then I must have looked too curious. She accused me of working for the newspapers. So that was the end of that. But if Kalugina followed up a dying man's last wish they must have made it.

Some other stories I never got anywhere with. I couldn't find any news reports about a bank worker walking off with millions. I did interview a bank security expert who assured me there was no such thing as a weevil program. Another dead end was Forgotten Present. The only clue I got there was a Lionel Train from 1974 sold at auction for six hundred and seventy thousand pounds to an anonymous bidder and Sotheby's refused to give any information, even about the seller.

But the judge definitely existed. I know it because he got married to Miss Lantern (name also changed). On a whim I asked to speak to the clerk of the court and was informed Perkins had never returned from a winter holiday to watch cricket in the Caribbean.

Kalugina's story was probably the one I had to do the most work on. I used some artistic licence on the MI5 details although Gary Lonsdale knew quite a lot of his father's secret service background. The journalist is still writing – again you know him by another name. Gordon Lonsdale was cremated and his ashes scattered on the croquet lawn at Woodlands in Peru – where Gary enjoyed a game with Dimitri, who evidently survived the Russian stand-off with Kalugina.

I wasn't able to find anything about a monastery in the Altiplano – high plains in Spanish – also described as *otherworldly*. The mountain range covers seventy thousand square miles from Northern Argentina across Bolivia into the flatlands of Peru – so plenty of space to hide a monastery. Anybody who escaped the monks still had the Andes at their wildest, tough terrain, vast lakes and extinct volcanoes to navigate. There is anecdotal evidence of forgotten tribes and missing people but none of whom were taken prisoner and survived to tell the tale – besides that postcard from Erik.

Intriguingly, I did find one report of a Dutch ballooning expedition that disappeared ten years previously. I contacted the Dutch Balloon Club and they informed me they didn't have many details but they could confirm that the envelope was orange in colour.

I did some research on Stockholm syndrome. It seems kindness serves as the cornerstone of Stockholm Syndrome. Also the intensity of the emotional experience has an impact. I guess that it doesn't get more intense than surviving a plane crash. The average percentage of captive who end up siding with their kidnappers is around thirty per cent. This, and escape in an untried balloon with a novice pilot – even if she has successfully crash-landed your plane – probably explains why only six out of thirteen (seven, if you count Michael) wanted to take their chances.

I couldn't find a doctor called Cam with a description that fitted the Cam I knew and had just about given up when I came across a Mr Iain Cameron – a pancreatic and liver surgeon, one of the best, who had gone on a lecture tour to Latin America never to return.

So why didn't he come back?

I started to be pessimistic again until someone sent me a leaflet advertising a new training seminar for surgeons in Peru. Who sent that and why? Sofie's hand at work? There have been a few lucky breaks along the way, which make me think I'm not completely alone on the project – for example, the report into HMS *Agamemnon* was anonymously delivered to me. Who else besides Sofie could get hold of something as top secret? So you can see why I think I'm getting closer.

The king is still ruling the village at San Vincente del Cerrito. I know because Kerridge has sent me two Christmas cards (one took four months to arrive). In the last he mentioned he was trying to get the king interested in growing marijuana. I'm assuming this is a joke. If Kerridge was to come home the media storm would be sensational. He could make a fortune, but I get the feeling that's not what he wants. He also wrote that Ofelia has learnt English and she waters the flowers on Barraquer's grave every day.

I've read Glass and Water the most. Now I understand Sofie better. By the way I did get to play the 'Night Fighter' PlayStation game and the best I ever managed on the crash landing programme level three was twenty per cent, so it was a good job that it wasn't me in the cockpit that day!

The select club still stands at four. I've dropped in the clue and Sofie is going to pick it up. I'm confident.

A.L.
Collioure, 2012

Acknowledgements

The second story in this book I told to Tom Fenoughty and Ken Austin over twenty years ago. 'You should write that,' they told me. I'm sorry The Magic Putter (as it was then) took so long. Along the way there have been many other people to thank for motivating me and helping to make this book possible.

The readers of my early drafts, Lauri Lipasti, Arto Strandberg, Robin Lloyd-Jones and Sarah Waiton who encouraged me to write more.

On the editing side: Fiona from Choir Press who raised the bar with such style at the finish, Laurence Jones, David Blyth and Marius Gabrielsen were, combined, a truly formidable unit. Miles Bailey and the team at Choir Press I would like to thank for doing such an all-round professional job and the ever-amazing Julia Dvoriankina for her first-class cover design.

For specific stories I would like to thank Erik Torseke – he gave me the idea for The Neighbour. Playing for the Queen was inspired by Trevor Pinnock who really did a recital for his mother in my parents' sail loft, although I should add that his girlfriend was lovely and nothing like Cordula.

There was a whole host of people for whom I was writing (with or without their knowledge). They include: Simon Rust, Rod, Sarah, Vic and Maureen Ball, Harry Jenkins, Steve and Stefanie Kerridge, Elina Strandberg, Lauri Törhönen, Hannu and Salli Hakala, Jukka Isotalo, Timo Pesonen, Juha Airaksinen, Chiara Lombardini, Olli Riipinen, Kai Aholainen, Mike Young, Kaarina Kaikkonen, Stuart Arbuckle, John Kearney, Tomi and Päivi Yli-Kyyny, Päivi Takala, Jeremy Gold, Matti, Bronwen and all the Great Scotts, Ann and Pete Jones, my sister Claire, Ljuba Langdon, Aunt Julia and Jeremy Tjebbes.

On a personal note I would also like to thank (again) Mr Iain Cameron for the nine-hour operation that did so much to save my life and his anaesthetist Andy (name changed to Luke in Cup Final Day). In Finland I want to thank my doctors, Maija Tarkkanen and surgeon Arno Nordin, who finished the job.

I also could not have written this book without the ongoing support from my children: Jim, Alfie, Max and Joe. These stories wouldn't have been half as good without my brother Steve who was my go-to critic and never stopped inspiring me to reach for the skies.

Finally, I would like to thank my co-author, Sari Langdon, who wrote one of the stories in *Connecting Flights*.